PRAY FOR
THE DEAD

RICHARDS

PRAY FOR
THE DEAD

PINNACLE BOOKS
Kensington Publishing Corp.
www.kensingtonbooks.com

PINNACLE BOOKS are published by

Kensington Publishing Corp.
119 West 40th Street
New York, NY 10018

All Kensington titles, imprints, and distributed lines are available at special quantity discounts for bulk purchases for sales promotions, premiums, fund-raising, educational, or institutional use. Special book excerpts or customized printings can also be created to fit specific needs. For details, write or phone the office of the Kensington sales manager: Kensington Publishing Corp., 119 West 40th Street, New York, NY 10018, attn: Sales Department; phone 1-800-221-2647.

PINNACLE BOOKS and the Pinnacle logo are Reg. U.S. Pat. & TM Off.

ISBN-13: 978-0-7860-3665-3
ISBN-10: 0-7860-3665-6

First printing: March 2016

10 9 8 7 6 5 4 3 2 1

Printed in the United States of America

First electronic edition: March 2016

ISBN-13: 978-0-7860-3666-0
ISBN-10: 0-7860-3666-4

CHAPTER 1

The moon stood full in the northern Arizona sky and cast deep shadows from the nearby trees. Chet Byrnes wore his warm clothes against the cool night, riding single file with his crew through the towering, sweet-smelling Ponderosa pines. The occasional creak of saddle leather, a deep grunt or snort from one of the mounts, the clack of iron horseshoes on an exposed rock in the path underfoot, this was all that marked their passage.

Chet Byrnes would have liked to be back in his own warm bed at the ranch house instead of out on the rim country after five horse thieves. Behind him in the line, his wife, Elizabeth, rode a smooth-gaited strawberry roan. Never a complaining word spilled from her lips. Unlike most women he'd ever known, she simply enjoyed being along on trips like these. She'd become a regular partner in his travels during the first year of their marriage, helping run down criminals, find lost herds, and check in on their half a dozen ranches. Life as a rancher had been busy enough, but it was nothing compared to wearing the badge of a Deputy United States Marshal.

* * *

Chet had learned a lot since he'd moved here from Texas. Arizona's sheriff/tax collector system left large holes in the ability to enforce the law. The federal judges sitting on the territorial court benches had used the marshals to shut down much of the widespread crime in the area, holding publicity down while keeping violence to a minimum. His task force operated in southern Arizona, chasing outlaws coming across the Mexican border on horse-stealing raids. This early morning mission was aimed at doing just that.

The so-called Barrett Gang had been stealing horses and reselling them in mining camps and to passers-by on the Marcy Road that led to California farther north. The Good Lord knew in his book where they'd sold the rest. But Chet and his men had trailed the gang back to their hideout after their latest theft, and now it was time for a raid of their own.

Two of his men, Cole Emerson and Jesus Martinez, were especially skillful at this business. Cole, in his mid-twenties, came from Texas and had worked as a ranch hand on Chet's outfit before he became one of his guardsmen. Jesus was twenty-one and came from Mexico. He, too, had worked on the ranch, and his proficiency with Spanish and skills at tracking made him vital to the team. They were Chet's backups. If anyone saw him, they saw at least one of those men with him, too.

Chet twisted in the saddle and whispered, "We're getting closer."

No answer. None was required. They soon rode out in the edge of a great open meadow. A log house and corrals sat on the far end of the meadow bathed in moonlight, just as his paid informant had described. His source had also said to expect all four of the gang to be camped there.

"Liz, you stay here and tend to the horses. Keep low, though. And keep your gun handy. This crew might not want to rot in some county jail. Most of them are ex-convicts."

"God be with you, *hombre*." She crossed herself.

"Amen." Dismounted, he kissed her on her cool forehead.

They hobbled the horses, drew their rifles from their scabbards. Chet and his two men took off on foot along the edge of the timber.

Every team member knew their place to be in these raids like these. Cole was to control the back door to stop anyone from escaping that way. Chet and Jesus covered the front door. A couple of dogs went to barking. Someone inside the house, in a hoarse, sleepy voice shouted, "Damn you, shut up."

But the dogs didn't hush and Chet could only hope Cole would soon be in his location behind the building. He and Jesus took positions in the corral with a good view of the front door. A few loose horses in the pen were spooked by their invasion in the first pink light of dawn.

Chet fired his pistol in the air, holstered it, and took up his rifle. "U.S. Marshals out here. Throw up your hands and come out unarmed or die. You're surrounded."

"Like hell," someone shouted. A shot from out back told him that Cole was around there taking care of things.

"How many are there?" someone else called from inside.

"Damned if I know! But they've got both doors covered."

"Alright, listen to me," Chet yelled. "You have any women or children in there send them out. No tricks."

Wrapped in blankets, two women came out shouting, "Don't shoot. Don't shoot."

"Sit on the ground past the well," Chet said. Crying and moaning, they did what they were told, and the dogs joined them there. They even stopped barking, too.

"Now we've not got all day. You've only got a minute before I torch that cabin and cook you all. You come out with a gun in your hand, my sharpshooters'll gun you down. Surrender or die."

"How did you find us?" a voice asked from inside.

"That you, Barrett?"

"Hell, yes. Who are you?"

"My name's Chet Byrnes."

Someone else said, "He's that big rancher from Camp Verde."

"What in the hell is he doing up here?"

"You can talk all day, you're either going to surrender or die." He raised his voice. "Cole, you got the coal oil ready?"

"Got plenty enough to burn that fire trap, Chet."

Someone in the house swore, "Son of a bitch, what're we going to do?"

"Give up," Chet shouted at them.

"Live or die. I ain't going to no jail ever again—"

The fool ran out the back door firing his revolver. The single report of Cole's louder rifle silenced it.

"He won't go to jail," Cole shouted with a laugh. "Only feet first."

A glass window broke and Chet said to Jesus, "Get down, they want to fight."

He squinted down his sites at possible targets, then opened fire from between the corral rails, levering in a fresh load each time he squeezed the trigger. His bullets splintered the log wall, the wooden door, and broke more glass. He set down the rifle to go for his Colt.

Out of the twilight, a man with a six-gun in his hand staggered from the doorway. Jesus put his last rifle bullet in him, the slug striking the man's chest with a dull slap. The felon's knees buckled, and he tumbled off the porch.

Blinking burning eyes from the acrid gun smoke, Chet covered the doorway with his reloaded rifle while Jesus, still on his knees, shoved more cartridges in his own.

"Cole, you alright?" he shouted.

"I'm fine. How many more want to die are in there?"

"Just me—I give up—can't walk. Toad's dead, maybe."

Jesus leaned his rifle on the corral. He said, "You be careful; sometimes even dead rattlers can strike you."

"I'll go see."

He was over the corral fence with his six-gun in his fist. Chet kept his rifle up and at the ready, aimed at the door. The spooked horses in the pen behind him had kicked up lots of dust during the shooting and were still blowing devils out their noses. Both women seated on the ground were crying louder than the morning ravens cawing.

Damn fools made their own decision to fight—not him.

Jesus, in the doorway, had holstered his gun. Things must be alright in there. Chet took both their rifles and went out the gate, joining his men inside the cramped house. Toad—or whatever his name was—had died. The last man was shot in the leg. Cole cut up a blanket to make a tourniquet to stop the bleeding.

"Big mess, huh, boss?" Cole said, binding the wound.

"They made it one." Three dead. One wounded. Two women left outside. One of them was moaning over the dead one in the yard, on her knees pleading with God. The other now sat on the porch bench, stone-faced and rocking where there was no rocker.

Jesus and Cole carried out the first corpse from inside and laid him out in the dirt beside the one already there. After that they went for the third one out back. One more to bring out—the wounded one. Maybe just leave him there for now. He can't run.

Chet heard a rider and horses coming up the meadow in a lope. It was Elizabeth, the string of horses trailing her. She slipped from the saddle and looked around. With a frown at the sight of the dead men on the ground she asked, "You alright?"

"Not a scratch," he said. "Gather these women and get them to making some food. We have plenty if they don't."

Liz went to work, spurring the two girls to action and unpacking pans from the packhorse. Food, at least, was in good hands.

Jesus and Cole brought the last dead one from in the house. Chet went back inside and found the wounded one on the bed.

"What's your name?" he asked the pale-faced outlaw.

"Willy Cameron."

"Who owned this place?"

"Barrett said he owned it."

Chet scoffed at the notion. "I doubt he owned much of anything."

"He said so anyway. Told us it was six hundred forty acres."

"That's probably a lie, too. Most of these homesteads are half that many acres or less. I know. I buy them all the time."

"All I know is he said it was his section of land, mister."

"How many horses are up here?"

"Close to thirty, I'd guess." The man winced and exhaled through clenched teeth.

Chet could see that wounded leg was hurting him, but he needed more information on their operation. "Who did he sell them to?"

"He had several buyers; I didn't know them all."

Chet got out his small notebook and pencil to write them down. "I want names."

"Cecil Brown up by Saint Johns. His ranch is the Circle Y. Jim Davis lives over by Hackberry took some."

His nephew Reg could find him. His ranch was near Hackberry, and his wife, Lucy, was raised in that country. She'd know this man Davis if anyone would. "Who else?"

"A guy named Lupine down by Tombstone. And Devore in Silver City."

Chet nodded, writing it all down. "What's Lupine's first name?"

"I'm not sure."

"I'm going to have one of these here lad͟ies give you some painkiller. Think hard. I need every name."

"Oh, thank God. It's killing me." He gripped his leg and looked sick ov͟er it

Everyone was setting up the cooking part, starting cooking fires in the yard.

"Someone give that wounded one some laudanum. Two tablespoons of it."

"I can do that, señor," one of the women said. Chet noticed for the first time that she was Mexican.

"Do that, Lupe," Liz said. She obviously had things firmly in hand out here.

"Oh, *sí*."

"We're getting there," she said to Chet about the food business.

"No rush. I'll unsaddle the horses and hobble them. They should be grazing."

"The men can help you."

"I can do it. Tell them to find some shovels and start on a common grave."

"Oh, yes. We have that to do, too."

"The horses are easy. That digging'll be tedious and hurt my shoulder."

Then he heard a gunshot. His hand went to his holster. On a dead run he sped back toward the house. There in the gun smoke stood the pale-faced Mexican girl, spoon in one hand, medicine bottle in another. The rustler was on the bed, his blood sprayed across the wall. Suicide.

Chet holstered his gun and walked over to hug her shoulder. "What did he say?"

"I—have—my own medicine."

"Is everyone alright?" Cole asked, coming through the open back door.

"He must have had a gun. Cole, take her out of here."

"She only brought him medicine to help him," Liz said from his side.

"Not her fault. She was ready to give it to him. He couldn't face a future in jail and crippled." Chet's stomach soured. What a waste.

What started out to be a simple arrest and gathering of stolen horses they had on hand had turned into a tragedy. *God help us*.

CHAPTER 2

Some black and white camp robbers boldly flew in to share their breakfast in the yard. Fried pork strips, biscuits, and gravy with German-fried potatoes made up the morning meal. The white woman was thirtyish, pock-faced, and hard looking. Her name was Ellen May Raines. Unlike Lupe, she didn't have much to say except to ask if they were going to leave the two of them there.

"Not my plans. We will take you out of here."

She nodded and thanked him.

After breakfast the corpses' pockets were gone through for money and any valuables.

His notes read like this—

*Elrod Barrett, age 34. Six foot tall, lean built.
    Blue eyes, scar above his right one.*
*Willy Cameron, age 20-something. Freckles, red
    hair, green eyes.*
*Toad Franklin, age 20–30. Short 5-6. Black hair.
    Missing a thumb on his right hand old roping
    wound. Buck teeth.*

Layman Collette, age late twenties. 5-10. Wavy
*   black hair, fancy dresser. Thin mustache. One*
*   gold tooth.*
Jesus removed it with a hammer.

The total money in their pockets was close to two hundred dollars. Four jackknifes, two large bladed ones. Two pocket watches with other men's names engraved in them. Cameron had a plain gold wedding ring wrapped in a handkerchief—no answer for that one. Neither of the women knew why he had it. They had an assortment of cap and ball firearms, and two Winchester repeating rifles. Their saddles, bridles, and spurs were not the shiny kind.

It took most of the day to dig the common grave, but by late afternoon they lowered the bodies down into it.

Chet asked for their silence.

"Father, we send these men to you, and do so for their mothers and fathers that raised them and hoped they'd do better than die in their boots and be buried in a common unmarked grave. Lord, may those parents find peace in their lives. Their children have been sent to you. Amen."

Chet nodded and turned away. The covering began, shovel by shovel.

"Tomorrow we'll ride over to the Windmill Ranch. You ladies can come along and in a few days we'll be back in Preskitt. I can buy you a stage ticket to the south if you so desire. Or I can pay you twenty-five dollars and give you a horse to ride out on here and now."

"How will we prove it's not stolen?" Ellen May asked, suspicion written in her dark eyes.

"I can give you a paper says you were awarded the animal by a U.S. Marshal."

"That ought to be good enough. I'll ride out in the morning then."

"Lupe? What about you?"

"If I may, señor, I would use your stage pass to go south."

"That'll be fine, but we'll have business to do on the way."

"That is no problem. I can work and help Ms. Elizabeth."

"She's a good worker," Liz put in. "So is Ellen May. Maybe we can find a place for her to fit in?"

"Oh, I will find a place, miss," Ellen May said. "Probably in some house of ill repute. I ain't no stranger to them."

"I will pray you do better than that," Liz said, looking very seriously at her.

Chet never laughed, but he would have had his wife not sounded so serious about Ellen May's choice of workplaces. No doubt that's where the dead men had found her, and she had few skills or good looks to expect much more than to return to such a life. The world around them was a tough, dangerous place to live. One day you were alive, the next your toes were turned up, with no one to mourn your passage. He silently hoped the girl found a better life, too.

After supper, they turned in at sundown. He promised the men they'd round up all the loose horses they could find the next day and head for the Windmill Ranch. Then, followed by his wife, Chet took his bedroll and they went off by themselves to find a place to sleep and have a few private words.

He found a level spot out beyond the house place. He

scraped rocks and limbs out of the way with the side of his boot, and they rolled out the bedrolls on their hands and knees.

She looked over at him. "It has been a long day."

"Very long. I'll be glad to be back home."

"Yes, we have a wedding coming."

"Rhea and Victor's."

"Yes. I'm glad they will be in the big house on the Verde Ranch."

"So am I. And Adam will be close enough so we can drop in on them. It won't be like having him right with us, but we can go down there and stay if we miss him too much."

She undressed under the blankets. "You aren't upset that your wife didn't say, 'Oh I will take care of him'?"

He shed his boots, socks, and pants, laying them close by before joining her. "No, we've talked. You gave up a lot to be with me. Rhea is a good nanny, so she can raise my son. I am sure she would have him, anyway, if my first wife had lived."

"I didn't mean to bring up bad and sad things in your life. I love you, *hombre.* I love every day we ride together. I just don't want you disappointed in me."

"No chance of that happening." He rolled over and kissed her. At least on this hard ground he had her with him to cuddle and love.

Morning came too fast, but the three women were up in the pre-dawn making coffee and cooking breakfast. Cole and Jesus gathered the loose horses close by while they prepared the food. Chet was drinking his first cup when they ran them into the corrals. He stood up to look them over. They looked slick—fine ranch horses, most of them. Obviously these thieves had only taken the best.

Cole dismounted to shut the gate. "There may be a few more. We can get them and hit the road after breakfast. Sound okay, boss man?"

Chet nodded. "We'll ride that way after we eat."

Cole spoke out, "Wait. I want a word with you."

"Sure."

Cole came close, talking to him in a quiet tone. "My mother-in-law, Jenn Allen, always needs help at the café in Preskitt where Valerie works. That Ellen May could fit in as a waitress and Lupe would be great kitchen help."

"That sounds like an answer to Liz's prayers."

Cole smiled at his words. "Maybe Jenn's, too."

"Thanks. I never thought of them doing that, but they might."

The younger man clapped him on the shoulder. "Get 'er done."

Chet walked over to the cooking fire. "Ladies, Cole has an idea. His wife works in a busy café in Preskitt. I found most of all my help there when I came to Arizona. The owner's name is Jenn. She's a real lady, but she needs help. We could find you two a small house to help get you started. Might not be a mansion, but it'll be dry and warm this winter."

"What if she don't like us?"

"Ellen May, you put on a smile and work as hard as you two have here, she will hire you."

"But I've got to smile?"

"Ain't any worse than working in a red light house. You have to smile at them coming and leaving, right?"

Everyone laughed.

"You're right, Mr. Byrnes. Lupe, you going to check it out with me?"

"Oh, *si*, I think so. Sounds better to me, no?"

"Yes. I think we can try it."

Lupe smiled. "We supported each other here? We can try there."

Ellen May quickly said, "Yes. You guys and Ms. Elizabeth were better than any of my kinfolk ever was to me."

Chet squeezed his wife's shoulders and said softly, "Prayers do help."

"I know. How do you think I got you, *hombre*?"

His plate piled high in biscuits, gravy, fried potatoes, and crisp bacon, the saliva filled his mouth as he headed for his place at the makeshift table.

Thank you, Lord, one more time.

Mid-morning, they took the dim wagon track northwest. Liz led a bay mare at the head of the line of loose stock. The horses were trail broke and had an established pecking order, so there was little fighting in the ranks moving out. The two women led the packhorses while his men kept the stock in the herd. The day passed with little incident.

It was late evening when they arrived at the Windmill. The commotion from all the horses brought everyone out.

"Chet, what do you have?" Susie asked, carrying her hem off the ground. She was the wife of the Windmill's owner, Sarge. She was also Chet's sister. Sarge was on the trail with the cattle herd they shipped every month for the Navajos in New Mexico and surrounding lands. "Oh, you're doing law work now?"

Chet laughed, dismounted, and hugged her. Susie and

him had been real close before they moved out there from Texas. She still held a warm place in his heart.

"We had a shoot-out with four men and buried them all. These two ladies were with 'em. Now they're going to look for work in Preskitt."

Liz came running and the two women hugged.

"How is your boy, Erwin?" Liz asked.

"Growing too fast. I guess Adam is growing up, too."

"You wouldn't believe it. He's ready for Rhea to move to the Verde Ranch. He walks and babbles."

"Come on in the house. You ladies come, too. We'll fix up some supper."

The two women joined them and went inside. Chet broke off and spoke to the man Sarge had left in charge, Johnny Hart. "They got off alright I guess?" he asked.

"Yes, sir. Gathering those cattle up ahead of time solves lots of that road-fighting on the way."

"Well, you men make it work. Lots of folks would like to have our contract, but bringing them good cattle on time helps us keep that job."

"We all understand how important that is."

Chet grunted. "Railroad ever comes, we'll have more competition for it, but that's still years away."

"Will they ever get it built?"

"Oh, they will some day. Keep the faith."

"I sure appreciate you and Sarge letting me try for Victor's spot," Hart said.

"You earned it."

"Only thing, I can't play a guitar like he can. Victor's very good at that. He said he was with you and your first wife when you bought that ranch out west on the high country."

"He was the camp cook on our honeymoon."

"He's going to be your farm man at Camp Verde?"

"My foreman over there, Tom, has enough to do. I think Victor will do good at it."

"He's a smart guy. He showed us a picture of Rhea holding your son."

"That's Adam. They'll have him down there. It's a big house."

"Oh, a grand house, I've been there for several events."

"I bet the girls have coffee made." Chet sniffed the air. "Come on up and we can visit more."

"I'll be there later," Hart said. "I have a few things to check on and then I'll be along. Thanks for the invite."

"Good talking to you, Johnny."

They parted. Chet knew Johnny had been under lots of pressure talking to the big boss by himself, but Sarge said the man was quick on his feet and understood the ranch and its needs. And Chet felt in time the man would be more at ease with him.

"Those girls work," Susie said, her boy in a high chair and her feeding him.

Chet agreed. "They've done well since the start."

"And I love your wife. I am so glad you found her."

He laughed. "Oh, yes, she's a grand wife. We share a lot and she can be a tornado, but she tempers down well."

"You have any big plans coming up?"

"None that I can think about today. But I am certain there will be something, though. I'm going to have Bo look into the place where we found the outlaws. It was supposed to belong to the leader, but I doubt that. It's a section of land that has a great hay meadow on one end that could be fenced. Has water and looked like it could be a bargain."

Susie smiled. "We've bought lots of those places but I agree in time they may be invaluable. And they don't cost much today because nobody wants them."

"The reason no one wants them is because there's no way to make a living on one. The railroad will change that."

"You're right about that. I will miss Victor. So will the whole crew. He's such a talented musician besides being a nice guy. You saw that in him years ago, didn't you?"

He nodded. "I need a job like that for Cole. He's a great backup but he needs a place to run. He's really made a great hand."

"He and Valerie aren't expecting a baby yet?"

"No, or he'd'a told me. But she does good working for Jenn at the café. Keeps her occupied. But he needs a ranch foreman job. I'll find him one."

"What about Jesus?"

"In time. In time."

"I figured that. How are JD and Bonnie doing?"

"Wonderful. They have a new boy, Samuel. That ranch is really growing. The artesian water will make it grow, too."

"I knew about the baby. That matchup is a miracle. JD was so lost."

"Bonnie was, too. But they've both grown up."

She shook her head. "Man. In Texas we were simple ranchers."

"No, Susie, we had Mexicans growing crops for us and were doing good. Out here there have been more opportunities to expand. We got here soon enough. Cattle drives to Kansas made Texas ranchers rich and they bought up their neighbors. You recall we had a safe full of money and not much worth anything was for sale around us."

"Oh, this was the place to come to and we have done well here," Susie agreed. "The women about have supper ready, so I am going to put my boy down. Chet, I want to tell you. I am as happy as I have ever been in my life. Sarge is a great husband and I couldn't be more pleased than I am today."

"That's good. I knew it was a tough transition for you."

She kissed him on the forehead and left him alone in the living room. He set his tight, sore shoulder back against the leather chair and stretched. There was plenty to do, but he could take a few moments to relax.

Liz brought him a cup of coffee. "You in here thinking about more things to get into?" She took a seat on the chair arm and looked at him expectantly.

"Oh, you know me, Liz. I'm always thinking about something."

"You do recall we have a wedding in two weeks for Victor and Rhea?" Chet nodded. "Lots of things that I need to get done before then. She has a room upstairs for us tonight. I know now how close you two were in Texas. She's a grand person. Losing a husband and finding another in a pregnancy. She made it work and working really well."

"Exactly," Chet said. "But Sarge was determined to have her if he ever got the chance. When she became a widow, he stepped in resolved to have her and he won."

"She told me most of it. But she is as organized as you are."

"That's where I learned it all."

They both laughed.

"What is so funny?" Susie asked, coming back from the bedroom.

"You," Chet said, and his wife shook her head to try to stop him.

"How me?"

"You made me organized."

"Well, you did a wonderful job on your own," she replied. "Liz, when we were just kids he ran that ranch in Texas and made money. I was amazed how hard he worked. And after the cattle drives to Kansas we had lots of money."

"He's a good man, we both agree." Liz hugged his head and kissed him. "Time to eat, though. Where are your boys at?"

"I'll ring the triangle and they'll come in," Susie said.

Cole and Jesus arrived and they all sat down to eat.

"After supper," Susie said, "you women can take baths. My man is heating water now for the three of you."

Ellen May and Lupe thanked her.

"We must smell," Liz teased. Everyone chuckled. "Thanks, Susie. You are a great hostess."

"No problem. I have clothes or robes for all of you to wear."

He and Liz left early the next morning to make the Verde Ranch and arrange some things. Free of the slow-moving herd of horses, the two of them reached the Verde Ranch before lunchtime. Lea, the Hispanic woman in charge of the big house, fixed a nice meal for them and talked about all that was happening. Tom, his foreman, came by the big house for a talk as well.

"I think we're in good shape for winter. We have some late calves need branded, but we can catch them later. The crew is building the west holding fence on the property line, so that will save a line rider having to stay out there to turn the cattle back."

"How long is it?"

"Three miles on the property lines. I had it surveyed and the line's well marked."

"The start of things, huh?" Chet asked, considering more fencing needs in the future. "I bet someday we have it all fenced."

"We may have to. What else?"

He shook his head. "Nothing. If you don't have anything, I'll go back to the Preskitt place after we eat and see how things are there."

"Cattle are looking good. Been a good year for ranching."

"I know. Tell Millie hi."

"Oh, I will."

Liz came to get him for lunch. "Everything okay?"

"Yes, going well. After we eat we'll ride home, huh?"

"My plans now."

"Good, we'll go there. Lots I need to do yet."

"I understand." They went in and ate.

It was late in the evening when they arrived at the Preskitt Valley Ranch house. There was a buckboard and some tired horses parked in the yard under the moonlight. Someone sat up in the back and threw back the covers in the starlight.

Chet's hand went for his gun.

"Mr. Byrnes, that you?"

Cautious, Chet was slow to answer. "Yes. What can I do for you?"

"My name's Able Thornton. I came to ask you for some help?"

"What's wrong?"

"Well, to start with my son's in jail for a crime he never done. I ain't got the money for no high-priced lawyer and I figured you could get him out."

"Have you talked to my housekeeper?"

"No sir. It was dark when I got here. I didn't intend to wake anyone. Some *Messican* come by and asked why I was here and I told him my story and situation and he left. Guess he figured I wouldn't hurt nothing. He kept saying, 'But Mr. Byrnes is not here.'"

"I have a cot in the barn for tonight, sir."

"I reckon you're tired, coming in this late. I'll be alright here. My horses are tuckered out but I'll water them again in the morning. They'll be fine."

Liz started to take his horse, but Chet said to her, "I will get them put up. Go on to the house, I'm coming."

"Good evening," she said to the man.

"You can unhitch them," Chet offered.

"No, I'll just sleep out here. I don't want to bother anyone. It's my boy I'm worried about."

A stable boy arrived then. "Señor Byrnes, I will take your horses. I was not expecting you."

"It's okay, Manuel. I'll let you take them."

"This man said he must talk to you."

"Oh, yes. I will talk more to him tomorrow. Good night, sir."

"Thank you, Mr. Byrnes."

He extended his hand. "The name's Chet. Able, I'll see you then."

"I won't forget it, sir. I mean . . . Chet."

"Who is he?" Liz asked quietly going upstairs.

"Able Thornton, and I don't know one thing more but that his son is in jail for a crime he says he didn't commit and wants my help."

"Wonder how long he's been waiting for you?"

"Liz, I have no idea."

"I was only teasing you."

His arm over her shoulder and he hugged her to him. "We'll learn his business after we get a night's sleep. Love you."

The next morning, Able Thornton was drinking coffee from a saucer seated at the kitchen table. Monica had the kitchen fireplace crackling. Must be a cold morning outside.

"Morning, Able. Don't get up. You get any sleep last night?"

"Plenty for me, mister. Ah, I mean, Chet. This lady is a *mouey granday* cook."

"Yes, she feeds us all well. Now tell me more about your son?"

"Ratchet—that's his name—is eighteen. He's a good boy and works hard for folks. Does day work for ranchers. Gets along good with most of them, but Beacher Plane was a hard man to get along with and I cautioned him about doing work for him. Beacher hit him up to cut a few of his cull cows out and pen them up so he could send them to the butcher. Ratchet knew the cattle, one was blind in one eye, the other two were mossy horned ones probably come from Texas years before. Beacher'd been thrown off a horse and was on crutches, but he had a chance to sell them to some Mexicans to make jerky.

"Ratchet said he gathered some other cows to help herd them three into the ranch. Said Beacher rode up and had a fit before he could explain about the reason for the extra cows. Ratchet finally had enough and told him to herd his own cows and he left for home. Told me the whole story when he came in that afternoon and I said fair enough. Next thing we knew the sheriff deputy came, arrested him for shooting Beacher to death. Said they got in an argument and the boy shot him."

Chet shook his head. "Where was the man shot?"

"Once in the chest, coming and going, they said."

"They have the bullets?"

"Chet, I'm not certain. They said his gun was recently fired and that backed their idea about his guilt. That boy shot a coyote the day before and hung him on a fence post to scare off the others."

"Beacher have any family?"

"Got him a wild young wife. They ain't been married a year. She's twenty years younger. Name's Emma Lou, and she'll spend all his money now he's dead and sell that ranch in no time. She ain't a ranch wife, I kin tell you that. More like a"—he lowered his voice—"whore."

Chet nodded. "Where do you live?"

"East of Mesa out by Fort McDowell."

"That's in Maricopa County?" Chet had to be certain.

"That's where they've got him in jail. Ratchet ain't no liar. He said he only had words with Beacher."

"Who found Beacher's body?"

"A guy named Ash Carnes."

"Who's he?"

"A gambler sort of guy that trades horses. He said when Beacher didn't come home that night, Emma Lou came over to his place and asked him to go look, fearing something had happened to him. Told him she ain't a rancher's wife or she'd looked for him herself." Able shook his head. "Carnes found him and brought his body into Phoenix. Chet, Ratchet didn't kill him and whoever did is getting off with it."

"You go home. I've been gone running down horse

thieves, need to catch up some ranch business, and then me and my boys will come down there to look at the entire deal. In three, four days maybe. I can't promise you anything but we will investigate. Don't say a word to anyone about our coming—I don't want any cover-ups."

"Thank God. I won't say a word to anyone."

"Able, all we can do is go look at the facts and if they aren't right, change them."

"You were the only hope I had. Thank you so much."

"We haven't done much so far."

They laughed.

"I better get home. Maw and the kids are there alone. Thank you, it was sure good food."

Monica smiled. "I will burn candles for your boy's release at my church."

"Well, God bless you, too, ma'am."

Chet followed him to the door. The old man smelled bad and it would be a long while till spring bath time. Maybe some cinnamon sprinkled on him might have helped. When Able was on his buckboard seat, he waved and Chet hoped those spindly horses would make it back, too. He closed the door.

"Don't close that door all the way," Monica said to him, shaking her head in disgust. "It still stinks in here."

"Sorry. He was a man needed some help and came to find it."

"I'm surprised we don't get more stray dogs and cats that folks left off out here for you to feed."

"Oh, Monica, it is good to be home for a few days."

Rhea came packing the boy and she wrinkled her nose. Adam's nanny was a nice-looking girl in her late teens, and fixing to be the bride of his farm foreman on the Verde Ranch. He took the boy and went to talking to him about riding a bronc before breakfast. Then he bounced him on his leg and Adam laughed. "Paw Paw, ride."

"That's all Paw Paw gets to do is ride horses somewhere and back."

"Was Victor alright?" Rhea asked.

"He was with the herd of cattle going to New Mexico. His last cattle drive. Susie said he was fine. He won't miss your wedding." They both laughed.

"Oh, Chet I know that. I miss him when he's gone and I know he needs to work."

"Rhea, the Verde Ranch job will make a foreman out of him. He's getting lots of experience about what makes a ranch tick."

"And I can keep Adam and we will live in the big house. I'm very pleased. I will have the best of the best."

"You deserve it," Liz said, and came to scoop up Adam from his father. "Where did your man go, Chet?"

"The smelly one? He has gone home, thank God," Monica put in. "I feel sorry about his son. Maybe you can find a way to prove him innocent, but I don't want him back."

"Aw, a little cinnamon sprinkled on him and he'd been fine."

The women had heard all about his cinnamon story on the day he met his present wife and his smelling it—they chuckled.

"I am going down to Phoenix in a few days and see what it all entails."

"Taking your boys along?" Liz asked.

"Yep. Them too."

"Am I invited?"

"Yes, ma'am. You sure are." She might learn more than he could.

"What is on your agenda for today?" she asked.

"See my land man, Bo, and learn about that outlaw land ownership. We may buy that if he owned it. I need to check the wanted list at the sheriff's office. There may be rewards for my men on them."

"Just what you need is another ranch," Monica said, delivering him his breakfast.

"We're paying all our bills and we have money in the bank. Some good ranches, too. Why not buy one more?"

"You were just saying how busy you are."

"That was then, this is now. It could be a good ranch."

"Is it way over there?" Monica asked.

"Yes, why?"

"Maybe you can get smelly Pete to run it over there."

"I give up. That poor man will take a bath."

Monica frowned. "When?"

"Next spring when it gets warm enough."

"Oh, Lord, he will really stink by then."

Chet's foreman, Raphael, came by and spoke to him. There were no problems except a mountain lion had killed two calves. His men ran him down after the second kill and shot him.

"He was an old tom. His teeth were worn down and he could not catch a deer anymore. So he is gone now." Raphael paused. "That man who was here? He asked for your help about his son, no?"

"Yes. We're going to see about it."

"I am glad you came to this country. You help lots of people from the time you went after those killers who shot my boss and his number one man. And you cleared the border business. We sure needed you, *hombre*."

"Raphael, it's people like you making this territory entitled to be a state. I only help."

"We have more than enough *frijoles* for all the ranch people to eat for over a year."

"That bean-growing project worked real well, and I appreciate all the women that helped you, too."

"I wondered if we could give my church some of them for the poor?"

"Good idea." Chet slapped the table. "You handle it."

"*Gracias*. We will do that." The thickset Mexican left the house smiling under his broad mustache.

Monica came by and said, "He is becoming a good foreman, no?"

"Oh, he always has been a great one. Now he is even better."

She was watching Raphael head for the barn. "The world could use many more men like him."

Chet agreed. He had some reading to catch up on. The *Miner* newspapers were laid out for him to look through. Liz and Rhea were playing with the toddler, who went waddling from one to the other laughing. His men would be there with the stolen horses sometime in the afternoon, along with the two women they'd "hired" for Jenn's café. And he still needed to check with Bo on the rustler's ranch ownership, too.

Liz's lady-in-waiting Anita had gone back to Mexico to check on her mother, who was sick. She'd left before they went to run down the rustlers. He wondered if she had written Liz a letter about how things were going. Jesus would also ask when they got up there if she'd sent him one.

"Anita wrote me her mother is some better but she will stay another week. I am going to answer her," Liz said. "Oh, and there are three letters for Jesus here. I only got one."

He put down the paper. "You can tell who is important to her."

"Of course. Are you going to town today?"

"After lunch. That bunch is coming up here today."

CHAPTER 3

Chet hustled around. They would probably be all day driving the loose horses up there. "I think we better go to town. It will be some time before they get up here today. I can ask Jenn about her help needs and then they will know more, too."

"I'll be ready after I brush my hair," his wife said, seated at the dressing cabinet before the big oval mirror and brushing hard.

"I'm not rushing you."

"Yes, you are. You always act like, 'Well maybe I'll go,' then you jump out of the chair and say, 'Daylight's burning. Let's go, Liz.'"

He kissed her on the forehead, laughing. "Darling, things run in streaks."

"I'll be there. Go harness the team. While we're in town, I must make an appointment for Rhea to get her dress measured."

"I'll remind you."

"Go. I am coming."

"That stable boy has them hitched already."

"Bless his heart, I will slow him down after this."

They told Monica good-bye and left with the team in a trot. Liz hugged his arm. "If we weren't so busy all the time, what would we do?"

He about laughed. "Play checkers?"

"I doubt you could sit down that long."

"Is all this business getting to you?"

"No, but few men fly around and get things done like you do. I really love being a part of it and being with you. I just tried to imagine what you'd be like if you ever slowed down."

"I imagine I'd fall asleep."

"Probably. Who comes first?"

"Jenn will be over the morning rush and we can ask about the two women working there."

"Fine. She'd do anything for you."

"I know. But this is business."

"Of course, but who else goes out to arrest outlaws and comes back to find work for their women?"

"I feel I have a responsibility to help them."

"Cole has been with you so long, he thinks the same."

They both laughed.

Jenn and Cole's wife, Valerie, both hugged him at the café and spoke to Liz.

Valerie was excited because she knew with him home her husband was not far behind. "Everyone alright?"

"Everyone's fine. They're bringing the stolen horses to Frey's Livery and will be here today or tomorrow."

He quickly explained about the pair of women, and Jenn said she could use them. They had a cup of coffee and Liz told them about the shoot-out and recovering the horses. Then they left for Bo's office.

The tall real estate man stood up behind the desk when they walked in. "What's up with you two?"

"The usual," Chet said to him. "Let's look at a map. A rustler I caught said a man owned a section." He walked over to search for the property on the wall map, found the section he wanted. It was marked as private land. "Maybe he did own it after all." He pointed. "Is that a full section?"

"It's section number six." He took down the range and township line and gave it to his assistant. "We'll find out who owns it," he told Chet.

"I doubt the rustlers holed up there owned it."

"Where are they?" Bo asked.

"All dead. So I figure we need to own it."

Bo's assistant looked up from his dusty play book. "Tom Sturgis, Bellville, Texas, is the last owner listed."

"See if you can buy it. It looked worth the money."

"We can do that. What else do you need?"

"I need to rent a house for two women," Chet said. "Nothing fancy."

"I have one empty on Dell Street."

"Is it a mess?"

"Probably not bad."

"Consider it rented."

"Oh, and there was a man in here two days ago. He wanted you to partner with him on some citrus acreage down in the Valley."

Chet shook his head. "We're doing that down at Diablo. But there's no chance of being close enough to a train to ship them out of anywhere but around Tucson. Not enough market for one yet."

"I told him we'd consider it."

"I have."

Bo smiled. "You've sure found markets for cattle,

anyway. And that guy at Oak Creek can raise more fruit and vegetables than ten men."

"That was a good buy, and finding Leroy and his wife to run it was my good fortune."

"You got him back from kidnappers in Utah before that."

"As well as Ben Ivor's wife."

"She's had a baby. He's going to have a big second family."

Chet shook his head. "He doesn't complain."

Bo laughed. "No. He speaks highly about her." The broker turned to Liz. "Mrs. Byrnes, you still riding all over with him?"

"Oh, I am, but my friends call me Elizabeth."

"I'm sorry. We don't know each other well enough. He used to have lots of get-togethers and I knew everyone, but he's gone so much now it saves him the money he spent on them."

Chet laughed. "We have been busy. Liz and I have to go. Tell your lady friend Shelly we said hi. Thanks, Bo."

"You never said what you'd give for that place?"

"That's why you handle those deals. Cheap as you can buy it." They went out the door.

"Are you turning that list of those dead men over to the sheriff to check for rewards?" she asked.

"No, we have a better chance of collecting if I mail the list to the U.S. Marshal's office in Tucson."

Amused, she shook her head. "I won't go into it with you and the local sheriff's business."

He helped her on the buckboard. "That's fine. I'm in a good mood."

"Where do we go next?" she asked when he took his place on the spring seat and clucked to the team.

"Dress shop, huh?"

"Oh, yes. I need an appointment for Rhea."

"I'm keeping up then."

"Maybe I should stay here instead of going to Phoenix and do more about their wedding?"

"We can handle the deal down there, but I have no idea how long it will take us to get back."

"We need to have a special event for those two."

He stopped and she dismounted the buckboard.

"I will talk to Dorothy in here about when I can bring Rhea in for the fitting and we can decide later today if I should go. I'll be right back."

He sat the seat and watched the traffic. The folks he knew on the sidewalk waved. Friendly place. Folks in Arizona came from lots of places. He'd found them a mixed bunch of nervy folks that had the spirit to leave their homelands and come west to a new land. Oh, they weren't all good citizens, but most of the arrivals were real great Americans.

Liz came out of the dress shop door smiling and he pulled her up on the spring seat. "Are we through for today?"

"All set. I'm as excited about this wedding as I was about ours." She hugged his arm. "It's lots of fun being your wife."

"Since Bo has a small house for the two women, you can oversee that for me if you stay. When my bunch is through with bringing in the horses, I intend to take a stage to Phoenix and see what I can do for that boy."

They were halfway home when they met the horse herders. Raphael's men were driving them so Cole and Jesus stopped to talk.

Cole said, "We left those two women at the ranch. Did you ask Jenn about them?"

"Yes. She wants them to come to work and Bo has found a house for them. We've got another job in the meantime, though. A boy in jail down in Maricopa County needs our help. He's been accused of a murder his father said he didn't do. I think Liz has about decided to stay here and keep up with the wedding plans for Rhea, plus handle the women's settling down in Preskitt."

The men nodded.

"Jesus, you better go back to the ranch. You and I need to leave tonight. Cole, check those horses in at Frey's Livery, file a found claim, and Thursday night load your saddle and bedrolls on the stage unless we send word not to. That gives you a little wife time."

"Thanks a lot. I'll be right down there on Friday morning."

Chet agreed and shook his head. "Sorry but this matter needs to be straightened out. His father is convinced he's being framed."

They trotted the team home with Jesus along on his horse. Liz told Chet about the plans for her tasks and how she'd get it all done. They left Jesus with the stable boy to arrange for a buckboard to meet the stage that evening, then to come on up to the house.

Jesus quickly told the stable boy what he needed, then rejoined them headed for the house. Liz teased Jesus about the letters. He shook his head. "She writes better than I do. But I will answer her today."

"I will mail it. Come and write it. I have nice stationery."

"That is very kind. I will."

"Did you have lunch?" Chet asked, walking up the drive to the house with them.

"No, it was too early."

"Monica will have lunch. Eat with us."

"I am very dusty."

"Come anyway."

"I will."

Liz hugged his arm. "You two be careful down there when you get to Maricopa."

"We know how."

"I would miss all of you if anything went wrong."

Monica stood on the porch. "Fast trip. I have beef roast, *frijoles,* and fresh biscuits."

"Sounds great," Chet said loud enough for her to hear.

The meal went smoothly. Jesus wrote Anita a letter. Liz fixed Chet a war bag to take along in case their time was extended. They even found time to take a *siesta* together.

His wife rode with them to meet the stage at midnight and kissed him good-bye. He wore a denim shell jacket against the cool night air. Their saddles and bags loaded in the backspace, they strapped in and left for Hayden's Mill and Ferry.

The sun was well up when they got off at the ferry. They ate lunch and took a stagecoach to Phoenix. With rooms at the Vista Hotel, they went out and ate supper at a Mexican restaurant with loud *mariachi* music and dancing girls clacking castanets. They smiled at all the activities, and the food was good.

"In the morning you will speak to the sheriff?" Jesus asked, wiping his mouth with a napkin.

"And the prosecutor," Chet replied. "I told you all I knew about the case on the ride down last night."

"It sounds like a tough one. But you are good at figuring things out. They know you are coming?"

"No. I asked his father not to tell anyone."

His partner smiled. "Good. Maybe we will shock them."

"We need to get at the truth, and if he's innocent get him out of jail."

"That's our job."

The next morning they ate an early breakfast and went to the county courthouse. The offices were housed in several adobe buildings near where the new stone structure was being raised.

Chet spoke to the desk man and asked if the sheriff was in.

"No, señor. He is doing tax work today."

"Is his man in charge here?"

"No, señor. What can I do for you?"

"I'm Deputy U.S. Marshal Chet Byrnes. I'm here to see about the charges against Ratchet Thornton."

"Oh, he's guilty. He was messing around with Beacher Plane's wife. Plane caught them together and Thornton shot him."

"Is that what you know about the matter?" Chet asked the desk deputy.

"Oh, everyone agrees that's the case."

"You have a report on that here?"

"I can't show it to you without asking Sheriff Limon's permission."

"When he returns tell him I want to see his report."

"You have a court order for that?"

Chet held his impatience in check and shook his head. "You won't want me to get one."

"I'll tell the sheriff what you said," the man said stiffly.

"Do that. He doesn't want a federal grand jury poking around."

Chet turned and motioned to Jesus to follow. Outside, he headed for the next building, where the prosecuting attorney's office was located.

Jesus kicked at a rock in the dirt. "That isn't Able's story, is it?"

"No. We need to check some more."

"That sheriff going to stop you?" his partner asked as they waited for a wagon to pass to cross the street traffic.

"He better not try. We'll get to the bottom of this."

They learned that the prosecuting attorney was one Robert Hardin. His secretary, a little mouse of a man called Elder, went in to announce that he was there with his deputy. Hardin agreed to see him and they were shown into a plain, undecorated office.

Hardin rose and stood at his desk to shake their hands. "Have a seat. I've heard about your work in law enforcement. What can I do for you?"

"We're here to investigate the case of Ratchet Thornton."

Hardin leaned back in his creaking chair. "Oh, that." He waved dismissively. "Open-and-shut case. That boy got friendly with the wife of the man he was working for. The deceased came home, caught them making love. They fought, and Thornton shot him twice."

"You have testimony to prove that?"

"Certainly."

"May I read it?"

Hardin stopped. "You think I don't know my business?"

"A young man faces murder charges, Hardin. I'm here to investigate the case."

"Who hired you?"

"No one hired me. As I said, I'm here to investigate

the case, and if you don't show me those papers, I can get a judge to get them for me."

Hardin leveled a hard look at Chet. "Listen, Byrnes, you need to go back to Preskitt and mind your own business."

"If you're refusing me access to those charges and evidence, I'll get a court order."

"You aren't threatening me." Hardin jumped to his feet, red faced.

"I'm not threatening anyone. Either I see those charges and your report, or I'm going to get a judge to tell you to deliver them to me."

"Well just you try."

"Jesus, this man isn't going to help us. Maybe he'll talk to a judge nicer than to us."

"Go ahead and try."

Chet looked him in the eye. "Hardin, we'll see about this and you may regret it."

The attorney spat. "Get out of here and don't come back."

"Oh, we will be back."

Out in the hot desert's blazing sunshine, Jesus shook his head. "What now?"

"We find the judge, explain our concern, and get the order."

Judge Walter Buckus was in his office at the makeshift courthouse. His secretary introduced them to him.

"Well at last I meet the man who's taming Arizona." The gray-headed man look congenial enough.

"I spend lots of my time at that," Chet agreed with a chuckle. "But I have a small problem. Prosecutor Hardin refuses to show me his evidence or any part of the Ratchet Thornton murder case he has."

"You need to investigate it?" He gestured them to the chairs before his desk. "Please, sit down."

"Ratchet's father drove clear up to my ranch at Preskitt to get my help. I came down here to look at the circumstances."

"That's reasonable."

"I need an order from you for them to cooperate with me."

He spoke to Jesus. "Get my man in here. We can handle that right now."

"Garman," he said when his secretary appeared. "Prepare an order from the court for the prosecutor and sheriff to cooperate fully with Marshal Byrnes on the Plane murder case and let me sign it."

"Yes, sir."

"That should handle it." The judge leaned back in his chair. "I understand you have several ranches. I need to buy a few Scottish bulls. Can you recommend a breeder?"

"My foreman, Tom Flowers, knows all about them, sir. I'll have him write you the names of good breeders he knows."

"That would be fine. I wish you luck straightening this matter out. I can't see why either office acted so upset toward you."

"It sure smells to me, too. It's a simple enough arrest if he's the murderer, but he claims he quit the job and left the man alive. There's an issue, the deputy said, that he made a pass at the dead man's wife and was discovered."

The judge shook his head. "I hadn't heard that. I understood when Beacher didn't return to the house, a neighbor rode out and found him dead."

"Now it's an altercation over his wife according to the prosecutor and the deputy at the jail."

"I see your concern."

"Who would the coroner be?" Chet asked.

"Justice of the peace Aaron Stutters handled it, I think."

"Would he be a witness about the death?"

"Probably."

"No medical person involved?"

"I don't know that, but you have a point."

"I want to find him."

"He lives on a farm south of here."

"I'll find him."

"Garman will have that order shortly. You get any more resistance, I will fine them."

Chet shook his hand. Garman brought the order in to be signed. The judge used his ink well and signed it with a straight pen. He blew it dry before he handed it over.

"You have a great reputation at bringing law and order to this territory. I know you get small repayment for your efforts. Thank you."

"We just try to do it right."

Chet and Jesus went to find the JP after lunch. He was busy putting up sweet-smelling alfalfa hay in a field near his house and cattle pens when they located him. The JP stopped pitching the hay on the wagon and let his Mexican help continue on.

He pushed a straw hat back on his head. "Gentlemen, what can I do for you?"

Chet introduced himself and Jesus. The JP nodded, said he appreciated their law work and knew about the force and its efforts.

"What did you find out about the death of Mr. Beacher Plane?"

"I held a hearing, as requested. Mr. Clements from the

Green Fields Funeral Home gave me the information that Plane had been shot twice. Once in the shoulder, then in the back, and he had two .45 caliber bullets from the body he brought with him. The one that struck him in the shoulder was from the front, and then he thought the man had turned and ran when he was struck in the back that went straight through to his heart and he died."

"You know they were .45 caliber bullets?"

"He showed me those lead bullets he swore were from the body wounds. They were .45 bullets."

"At that time was Ratchet Thornton mentioned as a possible killer?" Chet asked.

"No sir. My report says by party or parties unknown."

"Did you think both bullets came from the same gun?"

"I'm not a bullet expert. I thought the second one might have been shot from a newer gun than the first bullet in the shoulder wound. It had more marks from the barrel's grooves."

"Is that in your report?"

"No sir. I am neither a doctor nor an ammo expert. I merely took the evidence I had and passed it on to the sheriff."

"Who swore out the warrant for the boy's arrest?"

"I'm not sure. Usually a grand jury does that."

"Mr. Stutter, there are some people concerned that the boy is being falsely accused."

"Not in my justice of the peace court, sir," the JP said solemnly. "Someone swore out a warrant for his arrest. I had no part of that."

"Did the prosecutor order it?"

"I have no idea, but it wasn't from me."

"I'm sorry, but you sound to me like you're avoiding my question."

"Chet Byrnes, you must not fear the devil himself, but I, sir, have to live here. I have a good wife and children I love, and I don't want any part of this business. I avoided it in my court and I won't talk about it with you or anyone else. I have hay to stack. Good day, sir."

They watched the man walk off.

"There is something going on here," Jesus said quietly.

"There damn well is," Chet agreed. "And I think he spelled it out and wants nothing to do with it."

"Is the judge's order any good?"

"We'll know in the morning. Cole should be here by then, too. We'll start with interviewing Ratchet at the jail. Then we'll meet the sheriff and find out who swore out the warrant for his arrest. There's something not right here, and we've got to figure out what it is. I'd say we've taken a big bite of it already. Stutters doesn't look like a man easy shaken, but this business has him shook."

Jesus agreed. They unhitched their horses and mounted up. Chet viewed the man and crew helping pitch off the hay on a stack. This whole case against the boy looked more serious than he'd ever imagined—Able had had good reason to drive up there to get his assistance. At the moment he felt unsure about what to do next, though.

He sighed. "We better find supper and get some sleep."

Jesus looked back hard. "This business may be harder to settle than that big lost herd business in Texas."

Chet couldn't help but agree. "*Mi amigo*, we are going to be seriously challenged before this is all over."

They set their rented horses to a trot. Near sundown they found a restaurant and ate supper, after which they retired to the rooms in the hotel. Chet used a night lamp to write Liz about their findings and tell her how he missed her. How he hoped she was getting lots done on the wedding and that he would try to be home shortly.

Then he lay on the bed in the hot room and wished for sleep to find him.

CHAPTER 4

Morning came in a pink seam on the far-off Superstitions and the Four Peaks Mountain. Chet could not see them, but could see the eastern sky had lightened with the coming dawn.

Jesus woke and threw his legs off the bed. "Still hot here, huh?"

"Like Mexico?"

"Oh, I don't live there anymore. My home is at Preskitt." He laughed while pulling on his shirt. "Your wife was smart to stay home."

"Amen. Let's meet the stage and take Cole to breakfast."

"Fine." He buckled on his gun belt and put on his hat to follow Chet out of the room.

The stage stop was a block away, and they saw the coach arrive in a cloud of dust. Cole was beating the road dust off his clothes with his felt hat and looked up with a smile as they approached.

"Valerie alright?" Chet asked.

"Fine. Those women start work today. Your wife got

them set up at the house and helped them a lot. She's a real leader. House, food, dishes, and a stove to cook on—she has it all done. They're in the house and have all they need. Both of them were crying over how good she's been to them."

"Jesus and I haven't gotten much done here. Maybe you can help us do more. Jesus suggested we go back to the hotel and try and cool off yesterday."

They put Cole's saddle and war bag with the stage agent so they could go to breakfast. In the Mexican café, Chet told him all about what they'd found the day before over breakfast and some real good coffee.

"No answers so far?"

"Right. You catch some sleep. We're going to interrogate the boy if they let us in the jailhouse today."

"Forget sleep. You have the judge's order, right?"

"Yes, I do. Let's go do it."

Jesus smiled about Cole's not wanting to miss a thing and looked at Chet. "I knew exactly how he'd take this—do it."

Chet agreed, smiling. "He's our backup." He paid their bill and they went the two blocks to the county jail. Phoenix was waking up around them. In the streets there were trains of burros loaded with sticks for firewood and water, and goats for milk stripped into pails provided by the woman buying it.

They arrived at the jail to find a man in his forties wearing a suit standing beside the desk officer. He appeared to be waiting for them. "Marshal Byrnes?"

"Yes. You must be the sheriff." Nothing cordial in the man's manner or his voice.

"I am the legal officer in charge of this facility and I ask you to vacate these premises."

Chet snorted. "No, sir. My badge gives me the authority to be here on any business concerning the law and law enforcement in this territory. I also have a judge's order for you to show me the information on the circumstances surrounding the arrest of the young man, Ratchet Thornton."

"I won't give you a damn thing."

"I can and will arrest you for not obeying a federal judge's orders."

"You wouldn't dare," the man snarled.

"Sheriff, I've arrested border bandits and thugs all over the West and Mexico. I won't hesitate to arrest you."

"Can he do that?" the pale-faced deputy asked his boss, facing the three of them spread out with their hands on their gun butts.

"Shut up."

"Deputy, I can and will put both of you in a cell if you refuse to obey this order."

The sheriff sighed and bit his lip. "Get that prisoner up here and in my office," he told the deputy.

"Cole, go with him," Chet ordered. "I don't want that boy hurt in any way. And Sheriff Limon, don't even think about going for that gun in any way. Remove it with two fingers and put it in that desk drawer."

"I don't know what you intend to prove. That boy will hang for killing Beacher Plane in cold blood."

"You want to tell me your case on this matter?"

"Hell no. I'm the law here."

"Jesus, watch this desk. Limon, step in your office and get me that report."

"I don't—"

He raised his voice slightly. "You will be locked in a cell if you don't, and I'll find the report myself."

"It's over there in a file."

"Stand right there. I'm going to open that file. You better not have a gun in there."

"There's no gun in there."

Chet opened it and parted the paper folder. He saw no gun. "Go ahead."

Limon took a large folder out and put it on the desktop. "There."

Chet did not move. "Is that all of it?"

"That's the case."

"Who swore out the warrant for his arrest?"

"Read it yourself," Limon said imperiously. "We have the killer. It's the boy your man just went to get. Shut and closed."

"Go sit in a chair. I want to read this after I talk to the boy."

"You won't change one damn thing."

Chet backed up to the desk. "Then what the hell do you have to hide?"

"You may be the big hero lawman, but I live and work here and keep the peace. It isn't an exactly headline-grabbing job, and I have got to be elected."

"But you can't break the law, enforcing your ideas on it."

"I ain't breaking no laws," Limon shot back.

"That's not for me to define, but maybe a grand jury'll decide if you are or aren't. Right now I'd tell them you were operating illegally in this office."

"Chet," Jesus said at the doorway with the prisoner.

"The deputy says there's a key in his desk for this ball and chain on his leg."

"This your work, Limon?" Chet asked, going for a key.

"He's being held for murder. I'm doing what I have to, to hold him for trial."

The haggard-looking young man cracked a smile. "Mister, I don't know who you are but God answered my prayers just now. I owe you my life, sir."

"It isn't over yet, Ratchet. But you'll get clean clothes, a shave, a haircut, and a bath."

"Why waste taxpayers' money?" The sheriff sneered. "He's going to hang anyway."

Chet had had enough. "Take Limon back and put him in his cell," he growled at Cole. "Maybe he doesn't understand that a man is innocent under the law until a jury says he's guilty."

"You can't—"

"The hell I can't. Sheriff, I've found enough violations to have you removed from office. Don't tell me what I can and cannot do. I feel for your own safety you need to be detained. Now, Cole, put him in that cell. Deputy, go back out front and act like nothing is wrong. The sheriff will be back in a few hours. Do you understand me?"

"Yes, sir."

"Jesus, get this young man some water and some real coffee."

The youth was seated in a chair, rubbing his leg where the clamp had been locked on it.

"Your man Jesus said you were Chet Byrnes, the big rancher and U.S. Marshal."

"That's me." Chet nodded. "Now tell me about that day you had the quarrel with Plane."

"It was no quarrel. He hired me to collect three cows

he'd sold to some Mexicans for jerky. I knew those old culls, but when I tried twice to drive them in they'd break back. So I got a handful of cows, got them in that group, and started the drive for his place. He rode out there and started raising holy hell why I had so many cows when he only wanted three.

"I'd worked my ass off to get those cows up there and I was so damn mad, I told him to stick them in his ass and quit. I rode off to him hollering and cussing me."

"Where did you meet him?"

"There's an old wrecked wagon in the dry wash where I aimed to cross, half buried in the sand. I rode due west from there and hit the Stone Road to our place."

"Next day you shot a coyote and hung him on a fence post to scare off his kin folks?"

"I did, sir."

"What caliber is that handgun?"

"An old .44 Navy."

"Do they have your gun here?"

"I suppose so. Why, sir?"

Chet put his finger to his lip. "Cole, start looking in these drawers for it."

"Why?"

"The JP report said he was shot twice with a .45."

"There are four bullets in my gun. I never have one under the hammer."

"Most folks do that. Wait, here it is in this drawer. Tag says Ratchet Thornton's revolver."

"That's my six-gun, Marshall."

"When Cole goes back and brings Limon in, don't you say a word."

"What do you need now?" Cole asked.

"Get Jesus in here."

"Sure." The younger man went to the outside door to call Jesus in.

Jesus came in and shut the door.

"Jesus," Chet said, "what did the JP say about the bullets in Plane's body?"

"He thought they came from two different guns. Both .45s."

"Then Ratchet didn't shoot him," Cole said.

"This is getting better all the time," the boy said. "I may not hang after all."

"You aren't going to hang for this one, partner, that's for damn sure."

The youth collapsed back in the chair, tears in his eyes. "Oh, thank God."

Jesus took the keys and laughed. "We may be back in the pines sooner than I thought last night."

When Cole brought Limon in from the cell in the back he looked none the worse for his short stay. "What do you want from me now?" he demanded.

Chet lifted the revolver, held it in his palm. "Identify this pistol."

"That's the gun killed Beacher Plane."

"Where's the JP death report? You read it?"

"Hell, yes, I read it. Plane had two bullets in him. One coming, one going. Obviously the boy shot him in the shoulder first, then in the heart from the back with the second shot. They came from that gun."

"And what caliber is this gun?"

"It's a .45."

Chet shook his head. "Wrong, Sheriff. This revolver is a .44, and no way did that boy shoot Beacher Plane with .45 lead carrying this gun."

"How in the damn hell did you find that out?"

"I asked the JP presiding on the coroner's report. He said it was a .45 and so did the undertaker who removed them. Go get your prosecuting attorney. Cole, you go with him. I want this man processed out of here in thirty minutes."

Limon paled, stopped dead in the doorway. "Then who in the hell killed him?"

"That's your job to prove," Chet replied. "I'm a U.S. Marshal and my job is to see that the law is done right."

When Cole returned with the prosecutor, he was red faced. "Your man said that we have the wrong man and wrong gun?"

Limon told the prosecutor to get off his high horse. That they owed them and Ratchet an apology. Chet could tell by then the sheriff wanted it swept under the rug at any expense.

The youth's release paper was soon filled out and handed to him. The sheriff said he could have a horse he had captured and was unclaimed at the livery, since Ratchet's father took his horse back to the ranch.

At the livery, Chet rented horses and they rode out to the family ranch together. It was a two-bit outfit, to be sure. Riding up to the house, Ratchet's mother and sisters came out, saw Ratchet, and started crying that he was home. They never figured he'd see the light of day again.

Able, seeing his son, cried some, too, thanking Chet and his men for everything. Before they could leave, Ratchet asked Chet if he could ride with them, that his family was doing fine now that he was free and they really had no work for him on the ranch.

"What do you two think?" he asked his partners.

"I think we can use him," Cole said. He winked. "With a shave and haircut."

"I think so, too," Jesus said with a laugh.

Chet looked at Ratchet. "We're catching the morning stage north. Thank you all."

"God bless you, Chet Byrnes. And your men." Ratchet's mother hugged his arm and followed him to his horse. "I know you will take care of my boy. Able said you had a beautiful wife that he met up there. Thank her for me, and for letting you come do this wonderful thing for the whole family."

They rode back to Phoenix. Chet knew one thing— they'd be back in the cool pines in twenty-four hours.

CHAPTER 5

A reunion was always nice for him and her. Liz ran from the house to meet him when the buckboards returned him, Jesus, and Ratchet from the stage stop. Cole was already with his wife at their house in town.

"Oh, I should have gone in to get you with the buckboards. I'm so sorry." She hugged him tight like she couldn't get enough and after they kissed, he held her tight.

"No problem. This, Liz, is Ratchet Thornton."

"Oh, I am sorry. I am such a bad hostess, all I worry about is this *hombre*. So you're free now?"

Hat off for her, his freckled face beaming, he said, "You don't need to worry none about me, ma'am. I'm so glad to be free and with your man I can't do or say enough to both of you. My mother said to tell you thanks for letting him come to help me."

"He's a great *hombre*. Now, the three of you come on in the house. Monica has food and fresh coffee made for all of you. Is Cole alright, too?"

"Valerie took him and ran," Chet said, laughing.

"I don't blame her. Jesus, you come, too. You have more mail." She hugged Jesus's shoulder.

"Jesus's girlfriend Anita is in Mexico seeing about her sick mother," Chet said to the youth.

"Yes, sir, he told me about her on the stagecoach."

"Well, Liz, how's the wedding coming along?"

"Oh, fine. Rhea will have a beautiful dress. Her relatives are coming from Mexico and Tucson."

"And all the ranch hands, as well." Chet hugged her again. "Sounds like we're going to have fun."

"Oh, on Saturday we are going to have fun. I've planned a party for everyone to come here and welcome you all home."

"Is Bo invited?"

She nodded her head at the back steps. "I heard him say he had been left out from them. Yes, he is coming."

"No problems?"

"None they told me about, anyway."

He hugged Monica in the kitchen and after washing up they all took places at her table.

"This must be the young man you saved?" Monica asked.

"Yes, he is, and he's going to join us. His name is Ratchet, and you met his father Able."

"How he ever drove that poor team clear up here, I will never know. But I am sure you were pleased when these men showed up."

"Miss Monica, I surely was. Please excuse the swear word, but I was damn glad they came."

"We are proud of him, too. I hope you enjoy working here. We all try hard to make this place work."

"Thank you, ma'am."

"Chet, please say the grace." His wife waited for his nod.

"Our dear heavenly father, please bless this food and be in all our hearts here at the ranch. Protect the cowboys herding cattle to the Navajos and all the rest of our families on our far spread ranches. In his name we pray amen."

Monica crossed herself. "I went to Mass while you were gone. I lit a few candles. Thank you for the grace, we have so many blessings and now we have Ratchet to help us."

Chet noted Ratchet blushed at her words.

"Anita is alright?" Chet asked Jesus.

"Her mother is better. She plans to come back soon."

"That's good news. Hot as it was down in Phoenix, I bet she's ready to get out of Mexico."

"Mexico is hotter than that."

They all laughed.

That week, life on the upper ranch went back to normal for Chet. They'd set up two large tents that his nephew Reg had bought from some people passing through on their way to California. Raphael's men raised them Saturday morning for the party. Jesus and Ratchet lent a hand, and then everyone on the ranch helped move in the tables and benches stored in an outbuilding.

Tom and his wife Millie came early from the Verde Ranch and the two men talked business while their wives ran the show. Things happened quickly when the entire ranch crew got involved. The *vaqueros*, their wives, and even the children helped. Chet had no doubt it would be organized by afternoon and ready under Liz's expert supervision.

His new employee Ratchet Thornton told him he could not believe how everyone jumped in and did things. Riding with the *vaqueros,* he learned more about the ranch operation each day, but the way everyone pitched in amazed him.

"This was my first wife's father's ranch," Chet told him. "He gave it to us, but when I first came back from Texas, there was a tragedy. His foreman and his number two man trailed some horse thieves off south toward Bloody Basin. They were ambushed down there and killed. Raphael and I were on their trail, but I had to send him back to take care of the dead men. I caught those outlaws far over at Rye. They aren't among the living anymore. When I came back, the ranch needed a new foreman. None of my other ranches have all Mexican cowboys, but this system worked here. So I wanted to keep it that way, and the pressure was on me to make Raphael foreman. I've never looked back. You'll meet my other foremen, but Raphael handles things quietly and does a great job. These people have so much more here than they ever could have in Mexico. They really appreciate it and I think they work double hard to keep those jobs."

Ratchet nodded. "I saw that riding with them this week, but it's things like this party they are so smooth at."

"Raphael got the idea a year ago for them to raise *frijoles*. Raised about twelve acres, and we have beans this year for all the ranches—a big food item that only cost us the price of the seed. He's even feeding the poor at his church with some."

"It is part of why you have such a big empire?"

Chet laughed and slapped the younger man on the arm. "You'll see tonight why I have to have one."

"I'm anxious to meet all these people," Ratchet said. "I keep thinking only a week ago I was sitting in jail worried about my hanging. Have you ever figured who murdered him? Planes?"

"I think two people did it."

"Why that?"

"The JP told me the bullets came from two different guns."

"How could he know that?"

"He said one bullet was damn near smooth, and the other one came from a new pistol with sharp marks of the rifling."

"Is that in the evidence?"

Chet shook his head. "No. But the sheriff will figure it out. Someday."

The kid was silent for a moment. "What if he doesn't?"

"I went down there because your father came here and asked for my help. I had no official authority as a marshal to investigate that murder. I used what power I have to find out the facts, but any citizen could do that. The sheriff didn't want my help."

"Well, I am sure grateful you did it. I wish you could've solved it—I mean who murdered him. I never loved Beacher, but I also didn't want him shot down, either."

"Better to let the locals deal with it."

"If they can, huh?"

"If they can. Maybe you should move next to the Verde Ranch. Learn things on that ranch. You need anything? Clothes or anything?"

"Maybe a winter coat. The men I rode with said it would soon be cold up here."

"Take Jesus to town and buy one. And some long john underwear. He'll help you."

"That's mighty nice. Thanks, sir."

"Glad to have you. We always need new blood."

"I'll try to live up to that."

The fires cooking the meat were going strong. The weather wasn't real cool, but shawls covered most of the ranch women's shoulders as they were busy doing final things for the evening festivities. By mid-day folks began to arrive.

Hampt and May arrived via buckboard. Chet's two nephews and their sister rode small horses along behind. The baby Miles was having a big time crawling all over his mother when Hampt helped her down. Chet kissed her forehead and welcomed them both. Then he spoke to the boys, "How are the cowboys and sis?"

"Ready for snow."

"I hope it doesn't do that tonight."

Ty looked at the clear sky. "Won't come till your party's over."

Chet laughed and went off with Hampt to talk ranch business. Liz took May and the baby to the house. The two men took a bench on the south side of the big barn in the sunshine.

"Things went alright down there?" Hampt asked about his last situation.

"Yes. That young man is up here working for us. After Verde Valley, he'll be yours for a few weeks to show him the ropes."

"We can handle that. I need to tell you May's family's in a big turmoil back in Texas. Her parents died and left the estate to both girls. May was shocked. She thought they'd disowned her when she married your brother. Now her sister is suing for all of it, saying May abandoned the family moving to Arizona and remarrying me."

"That's a big estate."

"Yes it is. She doesn't care, but her children are entitled to their part. Do you remember a good lawyer in that area?"

"They'll be in San Antonio. I know one can handle it."

Hampt agreed. "We can talk more later. You know about these things. I'm more a farmer and cowhand than a law clerk."

"We'll get her some good help. If they left her half I think she should have it, regardless."

"You know May," Hampt said. "She's too damn nice at times, even to me. You out of problems to run down?"

"Yes, unless one springs up, it looks real quiet right now."

"You can stand the rest. Hey, May and I are going to have another baby next spring. I can't believe it, but those things happen."

They laughed. "You two still having fun?"

"Lordy, yes. Chet Byrnes, a few years ago I was thinking I'd never get another job. Thought I would never have a wife or family, and now I'm starting a tribe."

"Ranch working?"

"We'll rebuild that Ralston place you bought. Now we've cut back on the number of cattle like we said, and with a few more good seasons, that new place will be back in grass. I can see it coming."

"Good."

"That Navajo cattle deal still working?"

"Yep. That's what saves us. Sarge takes good care of his business with them. That agency hasn't forgotten the skinny cattle they were supplied before we took it over."

"We work on supplying good stuff."

"We all work at it." Chet nodded.

"I can tell you, the other ranching families appreciate you sharing that market with them."

"All I can say is until the railroad comes to northern

Arizona, our success will depend at the whims of having that market to operate the ranches."

"I knew it was important. We have probably two years' supply of hay at my place. I know we may need it, but I'm right proud of our operation."

"So am I, Hampt," he said. "So am I. I know Tom and them get lots of praise. You don't have a second seat to him."

"I know. You think Victor will do good down there?"

"I do, but he will listen to you. Help him, I think he will be good at it."

"I promise I will do all I can for him."

"I better move. Liz may have work for me." Chet stood up.

Hampt rose to his full six-four frame. "She's happy here, isn't she?"

"She's a very happy person. You saw all that going to look for the lost herd."

"I worried she'd miss Mexico. She was almost a queen down there, wasn't she?"

Chet laughed. "She was. She came in a white coach to my camp."

"I know how happy she is after I rode with you on that trip, but I still marveled about it."

"I thank God a lot for her."

They parted, and Chet met Liz sampling cooked meat with Roseanna. She fed him some mesquite smoke-flavored beef from her fingers.

"Very good."

"I talked to May." Liz told him. "She has a problem."

"I talked to Hampt about their deal. I can wire an attorney in San Antonio and get it handled. I'll do it tomorrow. Who has Adam?"

"He and two of the ranch boys his age are playing in the living room with Rita—you know, Rodney's wife?"

"Good. How's the bride-to-be?"

"She's helping the other women and getting a chance to socialize. Her dress is very pretty. And she is excited with only two weeks until the big event. Can we leave the tents up?"

"I don't see why not. I'll tell Raphael to do that."

She hugged his arm as they walked around the activity. "Chet Byrnes, I am still so glad I found you. My life tingles with neat things happening, and better yet that I am a part of it and I have you."

"No one else in those years as a widow ever tempted you?"

"They were all like paper dolls cut out of a newspaper and holding each other's hands."

"I can't believe one guy didn't come by and turn your head a little."

"He did. He was standing there at a camp below Tubac on the river."

He laughed and hugged her.

"What is funny, señor?" Raphael asked.

"Oh, there was this very pretty lady stopped at the Morales Ranch in a fancy coach and asked to buy some of my yellow horses."

A big smile crossed his face and he shook his head. "Jesus said you both were struck by lightning in that instant."

Liz laughed and hugged her husband tighter. "He told you the truth."

"Ah, *sí,* I agreed when I saw you two together the first time. You were meant to be together."

"I had such a short time, too, to convince him."

Chet shook his head. "Those hours we spent on the river that day and night were years long."

She drew a deep breath. "They were."

"The wedding is only two weeks away," he told Raphael. "We can leave the tents up, can't we?"

"Oh, *si*. That would save some work. We will keep the ropes tight. That will save my men lots of work. *Vaqueros* aren't like those carnival men who came to set up your wedding tent. They have to think a lot about doing it."

Everyone agreed and Chet took Liz to the house. Things were going fine.

They found the small children playing on the floor with the young woman in charge sitting with them. She stood up, a little embarrassed.

"Rita, you don't have to get up for us," Liz said.

"Oh, señora, they are having much fun."

"We can see that." Liz reached down and picked up Adam.

He talked real quick about his playmates in his jibber. "Oh, yes, Adam. You have lots of friends."

Put down, he returned to his playmates. They went to the kitchen to talk to Monica, who was getting the noon meal ready.

"No one has come for your help in four days," she said, stirring a boiling pot of stew.

Chet, amused, shook his head. "This makes five?"

"Exactly. Sit down. We have beef stew and corn bread."

"Sounds good." He put the chair under his wife at the table.

"Things are going very smoothly," Liz said. "As usual."

"The ranch people could please a president setting up a party." Chet chuckled.

Raphael knocked at the back door. "Chet, a boy is here with a wire for you."

Monica shook her head with a hard stare. "Day five just went to Hades."

Liz laughed.

Chet waved the boy to come in and took the telegram.

DEPUTY US MARSHAL CHET BYRNES
A GANG OF OUTLAWS ARE APPARENTLY
ROBBING AND MURDERING TRAVELERS
COMING OUT OF UTAH HEADED FOR THE
LEE'S FERRY. REPORTS FROM U.S. DEPUTY
MARSHAL KENT HAYES SAY AT LEAST
SEVEN PEOPLE HAVE BEEN REPORTED
MISSING TRAVELING THIS REGION GOING
FROM ST GEORGE TO THE FERRY NEVER
ARRIVING THERE. NOR IS THERE ANY
SIGN OF THEM ON THE ROAD. SOME
PROPERTY OF THESE PEOPLE HAS BEEN
OFFERED FOR SALE TO PASSERSBY. IF
YOU CAN HELP SETTLE THIS I WOULD
APPRECIATE YOUR GIVING ATTENTION TO
THIS MATTER.MORE INFORMATION WITH
NAMES AND WHATEVER ELSE I HAVE
WILL FOLLOW IN A LETTER.
ACTING US MARSHAL HOWARD JESSUP.

"What is it?" Liz asked.

"Trouble on the north rim of the Grand Canyon."

"Serious?"

"Sounds so. Several people have disappeared in the region and they think they were murdered and robbed."

"Who will go with you?"

"Cole and Jesus. I doubt we can be back in time for the wedding. You better handle that. I have a letter coming from Marshal Jessup. When it arrives, we'll go see what we can do."

"Monica wasn't far from wrong."

"No, she wasn't." He turned to the youth. "Sit down and eat. I'll write an answer to this message."

"I am—"

"You are perfectly fine. Take off your hat and coat, wash your hands, and sit right here. I have plenty of stew." Monica took his coat and hat to hang on pegs and he went to wash his hands.

"No one goes hungry around here," Raphael said, and waved good-bye to leave. "I better go back and check on things."

Liz made a face at Chet. "That is some journey you have to make, isn't it?"

"I'm just glad it won't be as cold as the last trip we made up there to get Leroy Sipes free. It was bad."

"Better take some jackets. It is getting to be fall already."

"We will. I hate to tell the guys, but they're always ready to go."

"When will you leave?"

"Probably next Tuesday. I want to wait for his letter with the names of the missing people and anything else he has. There are not many people on that side of the Grand Canyon, but that sliver of land belongs to Arizona but should have been a part of Utah."

"The surveyors got lost?" Monica asked.

"No, it was intentional, probably to show federal authority to the Mormons. But not the best move for people who live up there." Chet shook his head. "Nor lawmen, neither."

Liz made a face at him. "What do you call this, then?"

"There were people in the government who, at the time, disliked Utah. They wanted the line not in respect to where it had to be, but where it should be not to give the Mormons an inch more."

"No matter. You need to go examine the problem and solve it."

This drew a smile. "Yes, ma'am."

"Can I ask Raphael to give the bride away?"

"I think he should do that, since her father can't be found."

"We tried very hard to find him. He hasn't lived with her mother in years. But I really wanted you to give her away."

"Raphael will be a great one. He's my major here to handle things. The stew was good, as usual, Monica, but now I need to write that young man a message to take back. Excuse me."

His wire to the marshal explained when he and his men would leave for the north rim, and to please inform his Utah counterpart he would be in St. George in a week or so. Chet signed on the bottom of the page.

When he gave the young man the message, he also paid him a half dollar that made him smile. "Thank you."

"Ride careful. It will be dark soon."

"I will, sir. And, ma'am, thank you. I really liked your stew and corn bread."

"God bless you," Monica said, and the messenger left for town.

"Folks are arriving already."

"Liz and I are going down to meet them, right?"

Bo helped Shelly get down, and a *vaquero* took the reins to park his buggy.

"Well, darling, this is Liz," Bo said. "And you've met ol' Chet."

"I was at the wedding. I met you then, too." They shook hands and Liz told her they should go to the house until more arrived. She agreed and they were off, leaving the men to talk privately.

"You have plans?" Bo asked.

"I have to leave for Utah and the north rim country. There've been some crimes on travelers unsolved up there."

"If Arizona has a rectum, that north rim is it."

"Oh, it isn't that bad."

"Yes, it is. They can never build a railroad in there. No river you can reach. It's down in the canyon, and it will always be the back woods of this territory."

"I'm not buying any land up there."

"Good."

"Talking of buying land, is it too early to know if that owner will sell his ranch over east where the rustlers were denned up at?"

"Yes, but I am certain whoever is in charge will sell it."

"Good."

"You ever thought any more about buying the railroad sections on opposite sides of the track?"

"Is the price down any?"

"Not really."

"Bo, they are still crossing Kansas. That leaves New Mexico to cross before they get close."

Bo laughed. "I'm not selling you any of that."

"Not here anyway."

"Oh, I tried."

"Bo, you have done wonderful buying me homesteads and ranches."

"And I am sober."

"That is better than anything," Chet agreed.

"Yes, it is."

"Our business holds and we should be fine come the end of the year. The Verde Ranch is going to contribute a large herd of market-ready steers that we have not had before."

"What will you raise on this new ranch?" Bo wanted to know.

"Cattle, if we get it."

"No horse ranch?"

"These Arizona ranchers don't have enough money to buy good horses," Chet replied. "You couldn't sell a horse in Texas until those ranchers sold cattle in Kansas and had money in their pockets."

"These folks depend on our Navajo business and small sales to butchers to make a living. It's a tough job. You have lots figured out about this ranching business."

"I've been running a ranch since I was fifteen. And I've still not learned it all. My nephew is running a bunch of Mexican steers. They have little to eat down there below the border on most ranges except for the big *haciendas*. At three years old, they are full frame and I think I can get them fat on our gamma grass."

"How could you move them up here?"

"Water wagons and wooden troughs to fill in. You can water them from Tucson out to the Gila River. We can find irrigation water after that to get by Hayden's Ferry and the Salt River, and then we'd have to water them up Black Canyon. Hassayampa has water in it most of the time. It would take some organization and some hard-working hands, but I could gather those men from my ranches and we could get them up here."

"You've made that trip so many times. I bet you have the *saguaros* beside the road named by now."

"I've been down there a lot," Chet said.

"How many would you drive up here?" Bo asked.

"Two thousand."

The broker whistled.

"A hundred head isn't worth anything." He shrugged. "I also have an advantage I could get them up here early and hay them until the grass comes."

"When you going to do that?"

"I want to do it next spring. If we get that ranch on the rim. I may use it for that."

"Who will run it?"

Chet thought for a moment before answering. "I'm thinking hard on Cole. But I don't know if his wife would like the wilderness."

"Cole's pretty solid?"

"Oh, he is every bit solid. But we don't have that ranch yet."

"I'll work harder," Bo promised. "You never stop figuring how to make money, do you?"

"That's what they have me for. I don't do much manual work."

His partner laughed. "I can't get it, I will find another."

"I bet you do."

"I see Hampt coming. I better go greet him."

"They have lemonade up there," Chet told him.

"I'm not drinking. She'd kill me."

"Good for her."

"Chet, you know through it all that you saved my life, as bad as it was."

"I knew you were worth saving." Chet clapped him on the shoulder and went to kiss May and shake the big man's hand.

"How are you feeling?" he asked his onetime sister-in-law.

"Big," she said simply.

"Boy or girl?"

"Oh, I don't know or care. He will love it regardless. That's all that matters anyway."

"Hampt told me about your sister and I already wrote a lawyer I know in San Antonio," Chet told her. "I told him to represent you. He'll get it straight."

"But what does he cost?"

"The ranch can pay it. This is your place, too."

"Oh, Chet, I don't want to be a burden."

"May, you've never been a burden to me."

She hugged him and smiled. "Thanks."

"You're going to sing, aren't you?"

She bobbed her head. "You know I'd do anything for you, Chet Byrnes. You're my family."

"Part of it. The store man Ben and his wife Kathrin are here."

May nodded and smiled a little. "I'm not the only one here with a child to be am I?"

"No."

"She never had any children when you found her, did she?"

"No. I think that was why her ex-husband married two sisters and she left him over it."

"I recall that story. Then she only could find an outlaw for a mate."

"That's right." He nodded.

"But she and Ben are happy."

"I'm sure they are. Ben's first wife left him to go back east."

"I bet she regretted that."

"No, May, she was not generous. She was very self-centered and had no passion for anyone else. Or she'd never left Ben."

May nodded. "I always am amazed how you can see people and draw a picture about them."

"Liz is coming. She's jealous of your condition, but she means well."

"I know she does. Maybe someday, huh?"

Chet smiled. "We try."

May shook her head with a smile, then she lifted her skirt in hand and went to join his wife.

Hampt came from the corral area and joined him. "Jesus said you're going to Utah."

"I got a wire this morning from the Chief Marshal in Tucson. He asked me to go check on some disappearances of folks on that Mormon Honeymoon Trail."

"They call that road that?"

"Brigham Young sent many young couples to places like Mesa, Lehigh, and Saint David to farm. They took that route on their honeymoon. Still do."

"I never knew that. Jesus calls it the Frozen Road."

"You remember when we went up there and got those killers and the outlaws?"

"And rescued the orchard man Leroy Sipes? That was

the best one you ever found, Chet. Man, he brought all of us apples a week ago. He is a hand at the place."

"And his wife Betty, too."

"Oh, yes. She came to Marge and asked for your help getting him released from those kidnappers?"

"They did lots up there at their place. What's new at yours?"

"We fixed a little fence some damn rogue longhorn bull tore up."

"Whose bull was he?"

"I never looked. We turned him into jerky. I damn sure didn't want a calf out of him."

Chet could hardly keep from laughing. "Sounds like ranching got real western."

"Just an everyday deal." Hampt shrugged. "You ever thought about who might be the outlaws up there causing that ruckus?"

"I don't know a soul except the folks at Joseph Lake who have the store there. But we'll find them."

"Be careful. There's lots of desperate men up there. That's about the last holdout for wanted men in the West now."

"I'll heed your advice."

As they started over to greet others coming in, Hampt said to him, "You know that's the outlaw trail that comes clear down there from Montana. You recall that lady I checked on a few years ago out west of the ranch?"

"Yes."

"She told me they came by her place and they used that road and the ferry. But they never stopped if they thought a man was there."

"Hampt, I remember that. Let's talk more later. My

banker is here." They walked over to greet him. "Hey, glad you could make it."

"Why, Chet, good to be here. I love your parties. There are always laughs, music, and great food. How is your lovely wife?"

"Fine, Tanner. She'll be glad to see you. She and May are around here."

"And everything alright in your ranching business?"

"Fine, thanks. You know Hampt, my east ranch fore-man?"

"Yes, I do. He and his wife have an account with me. Good to see you, Hampt." They shook hands. "How is May?"

"Big. But she's fine and will be glad to see you."

"Yes, you better see May since she could soon be a bigger depositor. They're trying to settle her parents' estate back in Texas," Chet told him.

"Oh, I will. All your banking is going fine?"

"Liz says we're good."

"I always like to check. You have an amazing amount of business."

"And a large payroll."

"But I appreciate you buying cattle from the small ranchers. That's helped me immensely in my business. And them as well."

Chet nodded, and left to meet another couple driving up.

The evening was soon in full swing as he was talking to old Frey, who owned the livery in town.

"The time is about up on those horses I'm holding. What should I do?"

"I will ask my men, but I'd say sell them, deduct the bill, and split the money between Cole and Jesus."

"Let me know what they want. There are several good horses in that lot."

Chet agreed. "If I was stealing horses, I'd damn sure steal good ones."

Cole and his wife arrived. She ran over and kissed his cheek. "Those two women are hard workers, Chet. Jenn said she couldn't come in because her legs are bothering her, but to thank you. Cole already heard you were heading out Tuesday."

"Tell her it wasn't important that she came for this if she felt bad."

"No, no. Anything you do is important to her, and to me, too. We're your biggest fans. Our new workers are so good. Thanks from both of us."

There were lots of guests, and the music flowed. His *vaqueros* and their wives took great pride in these events, serving and dancing. They made polite hosts and hostesses. At last, Chet joined his wife. She was very excited—much more than normal for her.

"Good thing I am staying home," she said with a sly grin. "I may be carrying your baby."

"Really?"

She nodded very quickly and blushed. "But—"

"If it doesn't work out, Liz, we still have each other," he told her quietly. "We'll always have each other."

She squeezed his leg under the table. "I have you and I know that. I'll be brave with what ever happens. But good things do happen."

"Yes, they do. Use your faith, too."

"I will. I could not have found a better man to share my life with. I didn't know what to expect from you as my husband when I decided to join you. But you showed traits like patience with me that made you so dear. I will be here no matter what."

"Great. I'll go to Utah to settle that trouble and then ride home to my lovely wife."

"Oh, Chet, I'll be here," Liz said with quiet passion.

"I am counting on you."

The evening swept on, and at last those going home called for their conveyance and the *vaqueros* delivered them under the lamps hung to light the way. Chet shook many hands and wished them all a safe ride home. Hugging Liz's shoulder, they sent the company leaving, home. Hampt and his bunch, along with Tom and Millie, spent the night.

The ranch was quiet at last and the two sat on the porch swing to discuss the event. Temperatures were growing cooler as fall advanced. Liz wore a shawl on her shoulders.

"I plan to stop riding until we know something."

He agreed. "It might not be a bad idea. But I don't want to restrict you from being yourself."

"I know that," she said. "At times you are too good to me, you know."

"No. I want you to share the rest of my life."

"I will, I promise."

He hugged and kissed her. Those issues were his main ones. And being away from her on this next chase made him feel guilty. Damn, what would he do without her? No way did he want to consider it.

CHAPTER 6

The letter from Marshal Jessup arrived, and Tuesday morning in the pre-dawn temperature close to frost, the four loaded packhorses moved about nervously, anxious to be on the road. Chet kissed his wife good-bye. They exchanged a few private words before he gathered the reins and stepped into the stirrup of the big gray horse Diablo, from the ranch by the same name. Raphael's best horseman had ridden him a lot and agreed this one had lots of bottom.

Chet swung into the saddle. Ready for any foolishness, he held the gray's head up, but he still danced on his toes with the short leash, prancing around and making Liz laugh. "He looks ready to ride to Canada."

"Or buck all the way," Cole said with a smile.

They waved good-bye and rode out under the overhead rail at the front gate. Diablo was still skipping along sideways, but Chet had not given up on the notion he would buck for the entire way to the main north-south road they'd take off the mountain.

By the time they swung around north, the gray had settled a lot.

"Can we make the timber mill on the rim today?" Cole asked him.

"I doubt it. But we do need to stop and see Robert tomorrow. Him, his wife, and that crew make lots of money skidding logs for our operation. I never thought it would make money, but we surely needed the lumber they cut. Robert is a very good manager, and our teams do all the skidding and log delivery to that sawmill."

"Yes, and she learned how to make coffee after he married her." Jesus laughed.

"She's a Mormon and still is. But her girlfriends and family members told her not to marry him or she would regret it, him not being one of them."

"Pretty lady, too," Cole said. "I bet she hasn't regretted one day with him."

Chet agreed as they descended the narrow road carved out of the mountainside. "We won't stop at the Verde Ranch today, but push on to the military road that goes to the rim. We should camp over there at the base tonight."

His men agreed and when they reached the bottom, they pushed into Red Rock country.

Wednesday mid-day they rode up to Robert's house. A very pregnant Betty came out of the cabin and greeted them. "Robert will be mad that he missed you."

"When will he be back?" Chet asked, dismounting. Cole took his reins.

"Probably be dark."

"We'll spend the rest of the day here with you, then."

"Good. How's your wife? I didn't feel in top condition to go to your last party."

He hugged her. "She's fine, just busy with the wedding for Rhea and Victor."

"Where are you going? Out to Reg's place?"

"Maybe we should, but up in the strip country they've reported several unsolved murder-robberies and wanted us to go check on the situation."

"I am so glad you stopped here. Robert stays so busy keeping the horses sound and solving problems."

"We sure appreciate him. How are you making it up here?"

"Fine. I have church now up here and he takes me. Can I make you and the boys some coffee?"

"We'd drink some. You don't sound like you regretted marrying him much."

"Those silly friends and relatives were all wrong. He and I have a wonderful life, and as scarce as money is, we don't have a problem thanks to you. I know several sisters who have real hard trouble making ends meet. No, I will never regret marrying him."

He sat down at the table and she hurried to make coffee. Cole and Jesus came to the house with the horses put up and spoke friendly to her.

"Our Mormon hostess is making coffee for us," Chet explained.

She took her seat, with the coffeepot put on her wood range to heat. "You may laugh, but several of my church friends don't have a range to make coffee on if they wanted to. They use a fireplace to cook in. I'm very proud of this house, the things I have, and his job working for the ranch."

"We all are," Cole said, taking a seat. "The Byrnes family has become our family, and we're all grateful for things it does for us."

"How is Val?" she asked.

Cole smiled at her question. "Fine, but we aren't waiting for any additions to our family."

Betty about blushed. "Well to tell you the truth I'll be glad when this first one gets here."

"I bet so."

She told them about things happening at the mill and how busy it was sawing lumber for people. Before long, Robert must have gotten the word and rode over to greet them.

"How are things going?" Chet asked after they shook hands.

"Oh, busy is about all I can say. We keep the mill in logs and they seldom complain, but it takes some real effort. Tom sent me six new teams of draft horses. They're big and stout. Personally, I like the horses, but good big mules are so hard to find. Besides being obstinate, they're tougher than horses. I myself like driving horses, but I have a few mule skinners that get a lot done in a day."

"Tom and I talked about that. The big mules have to come from Missouri. Those folks raise them back there, but we're at such a distance, they can sell them short of here."

Cole laughed. "Wait for the railroad. Then we'll get them."

"If it ever can come here," Jesus said. "All my time in Arizona they've said it was coming. But I've never heard a train whistle up here yet."

"You're right," Chet said. "And when it finally comes, we'll have more troubles."

"What is that?" Betty asked, up to pour the coffee.

"The riffraff that comes with the new settlers will mean more crime."

"I bet that's true."

They rode out the next day after a fun evening with

Robert and his wife and an overnight in a real bed. Chet was glad he'd found Robert. The man had been young when he took the job, but his sincerity showed right off. The logging operation had funded many of the ranch projects, and Robert handled the problems that came up all the time very well. Chet knew that he'd never know all the things his man simply settled and never asked for any help with. At times he worried he was overlooking Robert because he was such a good manager.

The men rode past the already snow-capped San Francisco Peaks, and around into the sagebrush desert country of the Navajos. The trading post provided a ferry over the Little Colorado and was a gathering point for many less desirable characters. Cole noticed a one-eared man in the population and quietly told Chet that he'd seen a reward poster for such a man.

"What'd he do?"

"Oh, it wasn't a high crime."

"We don't have time to fool with him. Closest jail is at Preskitt and we don't have time to take him back there."

Both of his men smiled and agreed while they ate in the only place in the settlement that wasn't a joint.

"That's kind of tough." Cole made his point with his fork. "You find a felon and have no way to arrest him."

"Things will get tougher ahead," Jesus promised him. "I'll never forget when we went after the men who held Leroy for ransom and came back with those murderers. It was so damn cold, it froze your breath coming out your mouth."

Chet laughed. "That's as cold as Jesus ever had it."

"I sure hope we get back home before it does it again."

They spent the night in the country beyond the trading post since no one was too interested in staying there. Chet bought grain to supplement the horses' diet since the forage was short along the road for them, and they fed it in nosebags. The pungent smell of the sage filled the air. Off to the left was the deep chasm of the Grand Canyon, red bluffs rising parallel to their wagon track road. They met a few teamsters coming from the north for lumber plus several newlyweds from Utah going to settle land down near St. David.

They rode north. Cole commented about an attractive blond bride who, with her shorter husband, had stopped to ask them about the road ahead.

"That girl was sure pretty, but I swear she'd married the dumbest boy in Utah."

"He wasn't so dumb," Jesus said as they rode on.

"Why, he couldn't do anything I could figure out. She had to drive the horses. She said he was inept at that, even."

"What does inept mean?" Jesus asked.

"Can't do it." Cole shook his head.

Jesus laughed. "He must've done something right, he got her."

Cole and Chet shook their heads and they rode on. But Jesus was right, Chet laughed to himself. The tall, attractive blonde with her braids piled on her head would have made any red-blooded man stop and consider her. He wasn't interested, of course. He had Liz. He watched some buzzards drift by on the updraft, checking on any available meal. How was his wife doing? he wondered. But he would have to wait until he returned home to find out. Somewhere north of there were some unnamed killers he needed to find and stop.

A teenage boy and Mrs. Emma Lee, the ferry owner's

wife, came across and greeted them. Obviously from England, her accent amused Chet and his men.

"Me husband John is gone at this time, or perhaps he could help answer your questions about crimes committed on the trail. For my part, I don't know a thing. A marshal came down here a few weeks ago and asked him lots of questions. But we run the ferry and don't know of any outlaws in the area."

"Thanks," Chet told her. She didn't want more than four horses on the ferry at any crossing, so it required two trips. She remembered them from the time they had all the outlaws to take back.

"There was a lady with you then?"

"Yes, ma'am," Cole said. "She's married now to a man in Preskitt who has a store and is expecting another child soon."

"May I fix you and your men supper?"

"Indeed you may. We're tired of our own cooking," Chet told her with a laugh.

They were mounted and on their way again by dawn. They were still two days' ride across House Rock Valley to Joseph Lake on the Kaibab Mountains west of there. Then they'd need to push farther on into the vast, dry country of Utah if they could learn little at that settlement. Their job ahead had lots of problems to solve, and a needle in a haystack might be easier to find.

That evening, two men on horseback with a pack mule stopped at their camp. Both wore business suits, and looked like just the kind of travelers stopped by the outlaws they were seeking.

"Evening," the man with the snowy mustache said, tipping his hat. He was big and bluff, and sat astride his bay horse with the slouch of an expert rider. "Pardon us. We smelled your smoke. Kind of a lonesome country."

Chet rose from his rock and agreed. "Come on and join us. We're from Preskitt."

"We're from Montana. I'm Jack Hopkins, and this is my brother-in-law, Wayne Dotson."

Chet gestured to his partners. "This is Cole Emerson and Jesus Martinez. I'm Chet Byrnes."

"You fellows look like ranchers to me."

"Quarter Circle Z brand."

"That sounds familiar," Hopkins said. "I'm looking for a copper mine."

"I wouldn't know anything about that. You been on this road long?"

"We came down from Salt Lake City. Why?"

"We were warned there were highwaymen working this road," Chet said.

The older man shook his head. "We've not seen any."

"That would be all we'd need," Dotson pitched in. "My horse coliced and died two days ago and we had to buy this horse from some cowboy or walk."

"That's interesting. Did he say where your horse came from?"

"No. Why's that?"

He shrugged. "He's a well-bred horse."

"We thought so, too," Hopkins agreed. "He asked us a hundred dollars for him."

Dotson shook his head. "And wouldn't take a dime less."

"Chet," Cole said quietly. "You thinking what I'm thinking?"

"Yep. Most cowboys ride mustangs. Especially up here."

Chet and Cole walked around the horse, making a visual inspection.

"He's not branded, either," Chet noted. He turned back to Dotson. "Tell us about this cowboy."

"I have the sale papers on him. He was in his late twenties, called himself Lars Olsen. Sandy-colored hair, blue eyes. Rode a dun horse that day. Said he lived in Salt Canyon."

"He give you a brand?"

"I take it you're lawmen?" Hopkins asked.

Chet held up his badge. "Deputy U.S. Marshals. Several people have disappeared on this road. Highwaymen robbed, then killed them."

"What makes you suspect this horse?"

"What Cole said. He's a well-bred horse. He wasn't caught running around up here."

"We never saw any bandits," Hopkins explained. "We were wondering what to do when Wayne's horse died. Then he rode up and talked to us. Said he had a good horse at his place he'd sell us."

"You don't think he was trailing you?"

"Could have been, I guess. He simply showed up, then went back for the horse when we agreed to pay him a hundred dollars—if it was as good a horse as he said it was. And it was, so he wrote us a bill of sale. We were so glad to have met him, we never suspected any foul play."

"There may be nothing to this, but we have to be suspicious of anything we can find . . . He have any scars you noticed?"

"No, sandy headed when he took his hat off. Handsome guy."

"Thanks, fellows. Be careful and keep your guns

close. We don't know who or if there is any truth to the robberies. Just be careful."

"You think he was stolen?" Hopkins asked.

"I have no way to know. You may never hear about it again."

"I certainly hope so. Thanks for the warning. We won't be so openly friendly," Dotson said.

In the morning, Chet and his crew had the Kaibab Mountains ahead of them. They took the steep mountain road that wound its way skyward and into the pines, arriving in the small settlement at Joseph Lake close to sundown. Since his last trip, there was a new man who owned the store, a sprawl of buildings, and corrals. In his white apron, he met Chet and shook his hand.

"Deputy U.S. Marshal Chet Byrnes."

"Arthur Sherwin. You were the man arrested all those outlaws up here I heard about."

"Yes, sir. My men and I had quite a roundup that time."

"Come back for more?"

Chet shook his head. "We heard about some highwaymen working the road."

Sherwin looked around to be certain they were alone. "Some travelers have disappeared."

"Any idea who they were?"

"I can think of four parties. One or two people who never showed up at Lee's Ferry after they left here. There aren't many places to get off that road without coming back here or jumping off in the canyon, huh?"

"Right. How do you know that?"

"I spoke to Emma Lee from the ferry when she came up here for supplies. She never saw any of them. Two of the families of the missing parties hired a private detective to come down here and ask about them. They searched the road to the ferry and found nothing."

"You know these detectives?"

"I have a card from one of them."

"I may send him a letter and see what he found out."

"He said he found nothing," Sherwin said again.

Chet nodded. "We talked to two businessmen earlier today from Montana. Hopkins and Dotson on the road. One of their horses coliced and died."

"Oh, how sad. They stayed here one night."

"A cowboy who called himself Lars Olsen came by and offered to sell them a big, stout bay horse. This was no common range pony. They bought him and started back on the road when we met them."

"I never heard that name before."

"Sandy-headed man in his twenties, rode a dun horse."

"Sounds to me like Curt Malone. He works for the Cassidy brothers. Don't mention my name, though. I have to live and do business here."

"Where are they at?"

"Buckskin Mountains. There's a road about two miles east of here, goes north back up in the Buckskins. It is on the left side. Their place is about five miles up. Bar CB is their ranch brand."

"Thank you kindly. We need to put our horses up and board our packhorses while we ride the country."

"My wife Norm will feed you supper at the house and you can sleep in the bunkhouse."

"We may sleep outside. The weather isn't cold yet."

"I understand. My man Aaron will help you unsaddle, feed your animals, and show you where to store your panniers. I am so glad that you came to look into this.

This is a lonely country, and things like this upset all the God-fearing people here."

"I know."

"I'll warn you, though. Those Cassidy brothers are tough bullies. I made them leave my store at the point of a shotgun when two of 'em came in drunk and spoke obscenities to my wife. Harold, the oldest, came back and apologized, but only because he needs my store here or has to ride fifty miles one way for supplies. He wasn't sorry, he simply wanted to use the store."

Chet shook his head. "Well, I sure thank you for the information. And don't worry, your name won't be mentioned. I better go help my boys. We'll wash up and be back for supper. Thank you, sir. And we will pay you for all this."

"No rush. I'll go tell her you three are coming."

Washed up, Chet and his men filed into the well-kept house and Sherwin showed them seats and introduced his wife. She was a charming woman in her early twenties who said she was glad they were there.

"Our pleasure, ma'am," Chet said, silently wondering at the match with the forty-some-year-old husband.

When she went in the kitchen, Sherwin said, "Norm and I have been married a short time. I lost my first wife, Scarlet, last year. Norm was chosen by her elders in Utah to be my bride. She's a very good cook and an excellent wife."

"You are very fortunate. I have a very fine wife myself, Elizabeth. You're ever down to the Preskitt area, you and Norm should stop by and be our guests."

"Oh, how nice. But I'm always so busy here, I doubt we could make such a trip."

Norm proved to be a polite hostess and a very good

cook. Over dinner, she told them she was acclimating slowly to her new surroundings. Raised in Salt Lake, she found the country around the store beautiful, but she missed life in the city.

The three slept out under the stars, and were already up and saddling their horses to leave when Sherwin invited them to breakfast. Before long, they were off again, headed north from the main road on the road he'd told them about, a little-used ranch track through the pines and open meadows. They topped a rise and saw a cluster of corrals and log buildings.

Chet stopped them. Not a soul was in sight, but he felt uneasy. "I don't know what to expect," he told Cole and Jesus. "Be ready for anything. They may meet us with guns if they feel we're a threat."

"We'll be ready," Cole said with quiet confidence, checking his pistol's loads.

Jesus shook his head. "I have not seen anyone."

"They may be gone somewhere, too. Just be ready for anything. Jesus, you ride out to the left, angle in from that smokehouse. Cole, you're with me."

They spread out across the open ground between them and the buildings. A dozen different possibilities of what could happen next ran through Chet's head like a runaway horse. Would they fight? Would they run?

A woman appeared with a water pail. Seeing them, she screamed and ran back to the house. "They're coming!"

They booted their horses up. A half-dressed man with a pistol in his hand came out on the porch. Jesus reined up and jerked out his rifle. Chet shouted for the man to drop the gun.

When the man didn't obey, Jesus's Winchester

cracked. The hot lead spun the man around and dropped him to the wooden planking of the porch.

"Put down your guns! We're federal lawmen," Chet yelled. He pushed his mount toward the house, angered by the sudden turn of events.

The woman came out again, waving her arms. "Don't shoot. I have no gun."

He slid his horse to a halt. Cole rode around the structure, checking out things around there. Jesus joined Chet near the porch.

"Who else is here?" he asked the thin, panicked woman standing before him.

"No-no one," she stammered.

"Where is everyone?"

She turned her hands up and shook her head.

Chet holstered his pistol and walked toward the house, aware that another threat might appear at any second.

"Who's that?" He motioned toward the still man on the ground.

"Thad Cooper."

"Where are the others?"

"They rode out yesterday. They never tell me a damn thing."

"How soon do you expect them back?"

"Days, a week. Hell, I don't know anything." She shrugged.

"How many members are there?"

"No more."

Cole came out through the front door and checked on the downed man. "He's dead, boss."

"He did it to himself," Jesus grumbled.

"She says the gang's gone and she has no idea where they went or when they'll be back."

"They didn't use the road we rode here to ride out on," Jesus said. "No fresh tracks on it but ours."

"Which way did they go?" Chet asked her.

She turned her open hands out.

"She doesn't know anything. Look around maybe we can find where they went."

"We'll find out." Jesus left on the run.

"Give me a hand," Cole said to Chet. They lugged the outlaw's body farther out from the porch and left it there.

"Better find a blanket," Chet said. "Those buzzards circling may be hungry." Cole nodded and headed for his horse.

"Wait!" The trembling woman waved her hands. "I better tell you something."

"What's that?"

"I had nothing to do with it," she cried. "Nothing. They threatened to kill me if I even talked to her."

"Who's that?" Chet demanded.

"That squaw that they got chained in the shed over there."

Chet jerked his head at Cole who had returned with the blanket. "Check it out."

"They have her chained in a shed?" Cole asked under his breath. He shook his head in troubled disbelief. "Which way?"

She pointed, off to the right at a rude little shed off past one of the corrals. Cole headed that way and stopped at the door.

"It's padlocked," he called back. "I'd shoot it off but I don't want her hurt."

Chet rounded on the woman. "Who's got the key?"

"M-maybe Cooper," she stuttered, nodding at the dead man. "He fed her."

Chet walked over and searched the body, found a key strung around the bandit's bloody neck. He used his jack-knife to cut the rawhide cord and then straightened.

He held it up in front of her. "This it?"

A jerky nod. "Y-yes, sir."

"I believe this may be the worst crime we've ever been on." He tossed the key over to Cole, who unlocked the lock and opened the door. In the far corner of the little room cowered a terrified young woman, naked but for a few loose rags hanging from her shoulders. She held her hands up to shield her face from the light and screamed.

Chet knelt down. She looked Indian. "You savvy English?" he asked.

"Yes."

"We're here to rescue you. I'm a Deputy U.S. Marshal." He fished his badge out of his vest and at the sight of it, she nodded woodenly.

"Cole, you think that key will fit the locks on her leg chains?"

"Doubt it, boss. Different kind of lock."

"Bring another blanket so we can cover her. We'll find a file and cut them off her." Chet turned back to the girl. "How long have you been here?" he asked her in a soft voice.

"I d-don't k-know—" Tears and sobs cut her voice off.

"Don't worry about that." She was terrified about her captivity and had no idea whether or not they were any better than her kidnappers. What kind of hell had she been through? How long had she been their slave? No telling.

She would sure need a bath, though. And some clothes—a doctor? Hell only knew how far away one of them was located. Chet's stomach soured simply thinking about caring for her. *Bastards!*

Cole returned with the blanket and put it over her shoulders. She nodded her gratitude and wrapped herself in it. A Navajo woman knew how to use a trade blanket to hide herself in even with her ankles locked in chains.

"We need to find a file," he said, standing.

"There might be one in the barn. I bet Jesus has one with him, but he's gone to find the direction they went."

"You and I need to get her loose."

"They must have an ax around here. I can chop that chain in two and she'll be loose anyway."

"Let's do it."

Cole nodded, walked out to find an ax.

Chet knelt down again. "We're going to cut the chains until we can get the padlocks off. Are you hungry?"

"No, no. I am grateful to you," she whispered. "I thought I would die here."

"We're not going to let that happen," Chet said angrily. "That's a promise."

"Thank you." She shook beneath the blanket. "I'm so cold."

"We'll heat some water so you can bathe and warm up. What's your name?"

"Deloris."

"I'm Chet."

"Will you help me stand? I've been here so long my legs are weak."

He had to hug her to get her slender form up and on her bare feet. For stability she used her hand on his chest and thanked him again. He stayed close so as to catch her if she fell, and led her outside.

Cole had an ax and wood block ready. Chet held the

chain taut and turned his face away. It took three hard blows to separate the first link, and three more for the other one. Deloris sagged, let out a long breath.

"It's over."

"Damn right," Cole agreed. "You're free now."

"Cole, let's arrange for her to somehow take a bath."

"Got it, boss man."

Jesus rode back in and dropped off his horse to hitch him to the corral.

"What did you learn?" Chet asked.

"They left on a trail headed west," the tracker replied. He nodded to the Indian girl. "Who's this?"

"Name's Deloris. They had her in chains in that shed as their prisoner. We need a file to get those shackles off her legs. Cole chopped the chains, but they need to come all the way off."

"I have a file. I'll do it."

"Good. Cole is arranging bathwater for her."

Deloris sat on a crate in the warm sun. He walked back over and touched her gently on the arm. "Jesus will file off these shackles. It'll take some time, but he's a good man."

"How will I ever repay you?"

"That's not necessary. Where are your people?"

"Over across the Colorado River on the Navajo reservation."

"You have a husband?"

She shook her head. "No."

"Who did you live with?"

"My grandmother and my younger sister."

"My ranch sends cattle each month to that reservation."

A nod. "I have never seen you there, but a man whose

name is Sargent who rides straight-backed like a soldier is the man who brings them to the trading post."

Chet chuckled. "He's my brother-in-law. Married to my sister."

"The people talk good about him. He always comes on the day he is supposed to. We had bad suppliers before he came. I never saw you there."

"I only came the first time we set it up."

"How come? Are you a lawman, too?"

"To stop people like the ones kidnapped you."

"Today I am glad you have time for that."

Jesus approached with the file and introduced himself.

"Nice to meet you. How come you have the white man's name for their God?"

Jesus blushed. "My mother loved him so much, she wanted me to be like him. In Mexico many boys have his name."

Cole came and told her the water was hot enough to pour in the bathtub set up inside. He had soap and a towel for her, as well. Deloris thanked him and she turned to Jesus. "I want them off, but I'll smell better for you to work on me if I take a bath."

He smiled. "That will be fine."

"Where did the other lady go?" Chet asked.

Cole nodded to the house. "She's sleeping on a bed inside the shack."

"Good place for her. We better bury that dead man and make a report."

"She had no idea when they'd be riding back?" Jesus asked.

Chet lowered his voice and turned away from Deloris. "She's tetched in the head for my part. Not all here in her mind. She's a slave here, too, I bet."

"I wondered about her from the start," Jesus said. "She makes me feel uneasy simply being around her."

"I know what you mean," Cole muttered.

"Well we're waiting to welcome them back, and hell only knows when that will be," Chet said. "We'll have a list of their names by then, I hope. After Deloris bathes, we need to search that house. I'd bet there are some things in there would point to some murders and robberies."

"Let's find a shovel and a pick, Jesus. This'll be some afternoon's work."

"I can tell you right now, he don't need a real deep grave."

Cole agreed with his partner. "Can't argue with that."

Deloris came out soon after, looking much refreshed after her bath. Chet told her the boys were burying the dead man, and then they would file off the locks.

"Thank you again. The bath was very fine."

"I'm going inside to search for anything that might give us an idea of who we're dealing with."

The other girl was sprawled facedown, snoring heavily in her skimpy wash-worn dress. Chet searched the crate cabinets and found several cheap watches, rings, and a few Masonic pins the killers sure never earned in any lodge. Some whorehouse tokens and Mexican coins. Nothing really worth having.

Were these not the right people, after all?

That's when he half-tripped on a throw rug in the back parlor, revealing a crude trap door underneath. He dropped to his hands and knees, and soon had the hinged door open and laid back.

Lighting a candle lamp from a nearby table, Chet eased down into the hole by way of a rickety wooden ladder. In the feeble, dusty light at the bottom, he found new expensive saddles, bridles, spurs, men's boots, clothing, and several women's dresses stacked in neat piles. There were several panniers full of trade items, and even some patented medicine in one. One large lard can with a lid contained real railroad and gold watches, diamond rings, and tiepins.

He'd hit the mother lode. These *were* the men they were after. They must have been robbing and killing people passing by on the Honeymoon Trail for months to collect all this, and had gotten away with it until now.

How could he inform the families of the victims what had happened to their people? It would be a big chore, but they'd have to try.

Chet climbed up the rickety ladder into the sunlit room.

"You ain't supposed to go down there," a woman's voice said from behind him. "Earl Carson whips people's asses they even look under that lid."

Chet turned and found the lady in the blue dress staring at him from the bunk she'd been sleeping on. "I won't tell him. What's your name?"

"Candy."

"Just Candy? No last name?"

She shrugged. "Why have one if'n I ain't married? You could marry me and I'd use your name."

"I have a wife, thanks. Don't need another."

"You ain't a Mormon, huh? They have several wives. I ain't one, either."

"Were there other women here?"

"I don't remember. Maybe so, maybe not. There's some nice dresses down there. You know she wanted it?"

"Who wanted it?"

"That woman he brought up here. They argued and he said no. He made everyone go outside and we all did what he said—I guess she left after that 'cause I never seed her again."

"Did he kill her, do you think?"

"Maybe, maybe not. I don't know. But them guys took a shovel and were gone all next morning. I asked him where she went and he backhanded me so hard my mouth bled all day. I ain't never going to ask him nothing again."

"Hey, guys," he called out the front door to Cole and Jesus. "Come look what I found."

The boys climbed out of the grave, dusting themselves off.

"Is this deep enough?" Jesus asked.

"For him, yes," Cole said.

They mounted the porch and walked through the front door. Chet pointed to the yawning hole in the floor and handed Cole the candle. Jesus followed him down.

"Boy, they have plenty of loot, huh?" The younger man laughed, playing the light around.

"They've been operating a long while, I'd say. Longer than we thought. Bring up one of those dresses, though, Jesus. It might fit Deloris."

"I can do that. But why have they hidden it and not sold it?" Jesus asked, coming out with a dress on his shoulder.

"Money has no identity. Those things are personal items and anyone who knows the owner's family would report them if they saw something they recognized. They probably planned to haul them far away and sell them later."

"These guys are real killers, aren't they?" Cole followed his partner up the ladder, shaking his head in disgust.

Chet agreed. "Worst I've ever heard about, especially if all those people were murdered."

They all walked back outside. Chet helped Cole dump the body in the grave while Jesus took Deloris her new dress, which she promised to wear as soon as he had the leg irons off her.

He laughed. "That'll take some time, señorita. But I can get them into two pieces."

"Oh, I will sure appreciate that."

Jesus took his file from his saddlebag and went to work on the shackles. Meanwhile, Chet and Cole were covering the dead outlaw, shovel by shovel, with dry gravel and rocks.

"We going to set up and wait for these guys to come back, boss?" Cole asked.

"As much as I hate sitting around doing nothing, yes. We don't know where they went or what they are doing, but we do know they'll be coming back. And we have to be ready for them when they do."

"This is the strangest case we've ever had."

"I'm going to make a list of them from Candy tonight. Deloris can help, too."

"Who's Candy?"

"The woman inside."

Cole grunted. "Well, the guy they left got planted."

"The rest might be tougher," Chet warned. "Let's not underestimate them."

"Amen. She—Candy?—said the boss killed a woman for arguing with him?"

"I think that's what she said. She's kind of suspended out there at times."

"She isn't lying is she?"

"I don't think so. But she is a little light-minded." He straightened; his left shoulder was aching some from the old bullet wound.

"Hey, I can finish this, boss," Cole said, the concern in his voice evident.

"I'll let you. My shoulder's complaining some."

Stretching and rolling his arms, Chet strolled over to squat beside Jesus and the Navajo woman. Jesus nodded, busy filing away.

"The first one's about cut through, Chet."

"Good. I bet she's proud of you. Tell me something. When you scouted on up the trail, did you see a place up on a mountain where we can set up watch for when they come back through?"

"Yes, sir."

"Good, we'll take turns. But if they don't come soon, one of us may need to go to Joseph Lake and pick up one of the packhorses. The food stocks here aren't much."

One of the rusty shackles broke and clanged to the ground. "There you are," Jesus said.

Deloris rubbed the skin on her leg where the chain had been. "Oh, thank you so much. I feared I'd go to my grave wearing them."

"I bet that does feel better." Jesus nodded and started on her other ankle's lock. "How long have you been a prisoner?" he asked.

"Over a month."

"Have they gone away like this before?"

"I guess I was so desperate to escape I never noticed what they did."

Jesus frowned and continued to file. In another hour, he was done and when the chain fell, she jumped up and kissed him. "Thank you so much! I may walk home now."

Chet shook his head. "When we're through here we will take you home."

She dropped her chin. "Then I'll owe you even more."

"No, no. You're fine. This is what we do."

"I'll still find a way to repay you."

"I would like to know something, though," he said. "Why don't you have a man?"

"That is a long story," Deloris said. "See, many young men in my tribe drink whiskey. I know what whiskey does to them. They go home and beat their wives or run around with other women. I won't consider a man who drinks." She shrugged her shoulders under the too-big dress.

"That's a good cause to keep. You'll find someone. A good man."

"I've regretted it many times while I was here. Even a drunk would have come looking for me."

"You'll be fine," Chet said, patting her on the shoulder.

"I can shoot a gun," she said. "When they come can I have one?"

He chuckled. "I don't see why not. If you won't lose your mind shooting at them."

"Not likely." Deloris frowned. "Not after what they did to me."

"Cole, find her one of the dead man's guns and holster. We have a new marshal."

Everyone laughed.

Two days went by with no sign of the gang's return. But in the afternoon of the third day, Jesus had just relieved Cole on guard duty up on the mountain when he spotted the dust of approaching riders—a whole mess of them.

"Madre de dios!"

Without another look, he jumped into the saddle and spurred his horse back down the mountain.

"How many?" Chet demanded as Jesus rode back into the yard, spraying them all with dust and gravel.

"Hard to make out." Jesus panted, breathless. "But at least six. Maybe more."

Chet's mind raced, going over the list he'd made of the gang's members:

Harold Cassidy

Nick Cassidy

Curt Malone (perhaps the horse seller)

Farrell Stein

Cutter Cline

A breed Indian

That would be more than enough for them to handle even with a crossfire trap set up. If there were more, though—things could get ugly real quick.

Thinking fast, he spurred his people into action. He put Deloris in the house with Cole, guns at the ready out the front door and window. Candy he made sit on the floor, warning her not to scream. She was to bury her head and not say a word. If she disobeyed, he told her, making his point clear, he would deal with her personally.

He placed Jesus in the shed across the yard, then took up his own position behind a woodpile nearby. He checked his Winchester and levered in a round.

It was not long before the band of men rode in. They were unkempt and casual, completely off their guard . . . like they weren't expecting anything.

A big man on a large horse said harshly, "Where's that dumb Candy at?"

Chet poked his head up from behind the woodpile, rifle at the ready. "U.S. Marshals! Raise your hands or die. You are all under arrest."

One man on horseback in the rear went for his gun. A single rifle shot from Jesus's Winchester knocked him off his horse and he toppled over into the dirt.

"Who else wants to die?" Chet shouted.

The outlaws all checked their horses and reined up— all except the Indian. Long, black hair streaming out behind him, he drove his horse into the narrow alley between the house and shed. Cole shot the mount out from under him, but the breed shook loose of the stirrups before the horse's face struck the dust. His moccasins hit the ground running, but not fast enough to outstrip Jesus's .44/.40 lead. The slug caught him in the back. With a strangled scream, he threw his arms up into the air and collapsed facedown in the grass.

"Who else wants to die?" Chet asked again.

A long moment came and went—then, their hands held high, they surrendered.

One by one Chet made them dismount as Deloris and the boys covered them. Then he disarmed them and shoved them toward the hitch rail.

"Who the hell are you?" the big man demanded, minding Chet's threat well.

"Deputy U.S. Marshal Chet Byrnes. You must be Harold Cassidy."

"How long you been here?"

"Four days. Your guard was dumber than you are, outlaw. We buried him."

"Good thing. He knew I'd've killed him if you hadn't."

"Oh, you're one tough *hombre*, aren't you?" Chet shoved him forward in disgust. "Well, Cassidy, your killing days are over. Get over there and stand by the hitch rail."

"How do you want them?" Deloris asked. She still held the dead man's gun in her hand.

"Don't shoot him, Deloris. The law will settle with him."

"I won't," she said, her voice hard. "But I damn sure could."

"I don't doubt that. But don't even think about it." He nodded to the hitch rail. "Cuff him on one side of it and another guy on the other side facing opposite directions."

Deloris lowered the gun and locked Cassidy's right wrist in a pair of handcuffs. She ducked under the rail and faced his brother the other way and cuffed him. Then, with one swift and savage move, she kneed Nick Cassidy in the crotch with every ounce of strength she had. He gasped, bent over coughing, then went to his knees.

Deloris grabbed him by the hair and spit in his face. "That's for raping me."

Cole just shook his head and laughed. "I think that about says it all. No doubt about her toughness, huh, boss?"

"Not here there ain't," Chet agreed.

With the bandits shackled and under control, Chet and Deloris set about collecting and hitching horses.

"Looks like they brought food, at least." He motioned to a trio of the loaded packhorses.

"No more oatmeal and beans?" she asked hopefully.

"I bet there isn't any corn-fed beef there, but there is food."

Jesus returned from the side yard. "That breed isn't breathing, boss."

"They can dig the grave for both of them. Pick out a couple of grave diggers and put them in leg irons so we don't have to run them down."

"With pleasure," the younger man said with relish.

"Deloris, go find Candy and get her started making us a meal."

"I'd rather do it myself."

He shook his head. "Put her to work."

She nodded. "I savvy."

"Good. Cole, let's search them for any more contraband before they go to digging that grave."

They found little money on the two dead men, but the Cassidy brothers' pockets yielded a bloody gold ring Chet figured had been cut off a dead man's finger. The two brothers they left cuffed, while the other two were placed in leg irons and issued a shovel and pick.

"You can't prove a damn thing on us," the head Cassidy bragged.

"Oh, yes we can, *hombre*," Chet replied. "Deloris is charging you with rape and kidnapping."

"What jury would believe that Injun whore?"

Chet ignored his comment. "There's also that wagonload of stolen goods down in the cellar. Got an explanation for that?" No response. Chet laughed. "I didn't think so. You and your gang are going to hang for it all."

He left them standing across from each other and went to see what the women were working on. He found Candy stirring a pot on the sheet iron range and singing "Sweet Bessie from Pike." Beside her, Deloris was busy slicing and frying bacon in a large skillet.

"We're getting there," she told him. "I have biscuits in the oven."

"No rush."

"What are your plans?"

He leaned back against the counter. "Rent a wagon

and team and take you home, then haul all these stolen goods home with us as evidence to the court in Preskitt."

"I can ride a horse home by myself," Deloris said.

"I know. But you're our ward now. Your safety is our job."

She agreed with a nod. "Chet Byrnes, I am envious of your wife."

Chet smiled at the mention of Liz. "Why's that?"

"If you weren't so content with her, I'd steal you."

A laugh. "I'm flattered, but one wife is all I need. She's a handful, too."

"Does she ever go with you?"

"Usually she'd be here now. But one of my boys from the ranch who sends the Navajo cattle is marrying my son's nanny. His name's Victor, and hers is Rhea. Liz—that's my wife—is busy arranging that wedding while we're gone."

"I see why she is not with you." She dried her hands on a towel. "All this business has changed my life and way of thinking—I am changing my life. I don't know exactly how, but I will no longer be Deloris the goat herder."

"That's a good thing."

"Tell them to come eat." She brought the large pan of biscuits out of the oven and nodded at him. "It's a lot better to be here, doing something, than chained in that damn shed being abused by those men."

"Deloris," Chet said. "I'm just sorry I didn't come quicker."

"Chet Byrnes, I'm just grateful you even came at all."

He hugged her shoulder, then went to get the boys. What a world they lived in.

Liz, I won't be long getting home now, he silently promised her.

After lunch, Jesus was dispatched back to Joseph Lake to hire a wagon to haul the loot down to Preskitt. While he was gone, Chet and Cole rounded up the gang's horses and got them ready to travel. By sundown, the two dead outlaws had been shipped to hell and preparations to leave completed. Jesus returned in the twilight, followed by a pair of empty wagons hauled by two local men, packed for the long trip and told to expect a goodly payment for their trouble. The evidence was loaded by midnight, and they all rode out together at dawn.

Jesus reported that he had told the storekeeper and his wife about the capture and the evidence. He passed on their good wishes, and the happiness of the other folks in the region at their having rounded up the gang.

By the second day out, they'd reached Lee's Ferry. On the other side of the Colorado River, each of the lawmen hugged Deloris and said good-bye. She had a good horse from the outlaws' bunch, and two packhorses that they'd set up for her. Tears streaked her tan cheeks when she told each of them how much she appreciated all they'd done for her. Then she hugged Candy, climbed on her horse, and headed off for her own people.

Two long days later, they crossed the Little Colorado at a trading post five days from the Verde Ranch—five cold days that threatened on and off to spit snow and ice upon them at any moment. Jesus reminded Chet more than once how cold it had been the last time they passed that way in winter.

They came off the north rim into the Verde Valley near dark, but went to the bottom before they stopped to set up camp. Leaving the others at the camp, Chet took a sound horse and rode on for the house alone. It was well past midnight when one of his *vaqueros* challenged him at the gate.

"Brazos, that you?" he asked, recognizing the voice.

"Ah, *sí*. It is you, Señor Chet. Are you alright?"

"I'm fine this time. And damn glad to be home." He dismounted and hugged the man.

"You must have known. The wedding is tomorrow. Victor and Rhea will be happy to hear of your return. It's a good omen."

"I don't know about that, *hombre*," Chet said, and laughed. "But the Lord works in mysterious ways."

"Give me your horse. There is light on up there, someone may still be awake."

"No problem. I can find my way."

"It is always good to have you back," the *vaquero* said. "Did you find those bad ones?"

"Oh, yeah. Four of them. The boys should be back in with them tomorrow or the next day."

"You do good work, *hombre. Vaya con dios*."

Chet circled the house and entered through the back door. All was quiet, but a single light still burned in the front parlor. Putting his hat and gun belt on the hook, he froze when a familiar voice broke the silence.

"Is that you?" his wife asked.

"It must be, darling," he replied. "Why are you still awake at this hour?"

"Oh, I couldn't sleep. I knew something was going to happen."

He had her by the waist, kissed her, then swung her around. "The rest are at the Verde tonight, but I had to come home. Oh, baby. I have missed you so much."

"No more than I've missed you, *hombre*. Did you get those outlaws?"

"It's a long story and I can tell you all about it in the morning. I'm tired, dirty—"

"I would take you anyway, you know that. Tomorrow we can clean you up. Oh, Chet Byrnes, I am so glad to have you back in one piece. The others alright, too?"

"Not a scratch. But that gang needed to be stopped."

"I'm so happy you are here."

"No more than I am to be here. Let's get some sleep."

And they did just that.

CHAPTER 7

The next morning with the boiler running, Chet had a bath, a shave, and clean, fresh clothes. In the kitchen, full of the smells of home cooking, he hugged Monica as she tried not to cry.

Rhea brought Adam down and hugged him fiercely. "I am so glad you came back in time for the wedding."

He kissed her on the forehead. "I lost track of the time but I made it. Man, he's grown some more, hasn't he?" He grabbed the boy and raised him over his head.

"The doctor said some day he would be as big as you."

"Maybe bigger." He laughed.

"*Sí*, maybe that, too."

"Better eat breakfast or we'll get scolded."

He sat down still holding the boy. Hard to believe how much he'd grown. Well, life went on whether he was there or not. The night before his wife told him there was no baby coming for them. There had been many tears. That cut his heart, too, not for him but for her. He understood her expectations—simply the hand they had drawn. But they were still young enough. Time would tell, just so it didn't destroy any part of their lives and the great relationship they'd built with one another.

"No trouble while I was gone?"

"It may be a world record, but no one came by asking for help," Monica announced.

"You do have some mail, though," Liz added.

"I'll get to it this morning. Are Reg and Lucy coming down for the wedding?"

"No, we got word a few days ago. Reg is healing from a horse wreck. Not many details, but the wagon ride would have exhausted him, Lucy said. They send their best to Victor and Rhea, though."

"Glad he's okay." He must have gotten on a stemwinder, Chet decided. Reg was damn hard to be thrown.

"We expect JD and Bonnie today. The crew from the Verde and Suzie and Sarge are coming, too. They spent the night with Hampt and May last night," Liz continued. "I guess May and Susie were real close before May got married."

"Like sisters," Chet nodded.

"That lawyer in San Antonio has straightened out May's problem. She'll be getting her share of the family estate after all. She told me about it earlier. Were her parents rich?"

"Oh, yes. And they never approved of anything May did, while her sister could do no wrong. When she married my brother, they turned their backs on her. Told her she was disowned."

"That's terrible," Liz said.

Chet agreed. "I can tell you it broke her heart, but she survived. My brother married her because he had three children to care for when his wife died. One was a baby."

He didn't mention the oldest boy, Heck. Stage robbers

had kidnapped and murdered him when they had started back home to Texas after buying the Verde Ranch. That still stabbed his heart.

"Folks are arriving," Monica said, looking out the window.

"I'll go welcome them," Chet said, finishing off his coffee.

"Rhea, I get Adam today," Liz announced.

"I can—"

"No, no. He's mine. One of the *vaquero*'s daughters will be here soon to help me. You go be the leisurely bride today and next week."

"I never expected you to do so much for him and me," Rhea said with tears in her eyes. "This wedding and the rest . . . my dress . . . You're spoiling me. It means so much."

Liz put a hand to her wet cheek. "You know I never had a daughter, so you are mine to spoil."

In the back hall, Chet put on his gun belt, jumper, and hat, waved to the breakfast party, and went out to greet the first comers. The cool mountain air swept along his clean-shaven face, and the turpentine smell of the pines filled his nose. Back home at last. Everything looked perfect. The large tent set up with the small triangle flags on the posts looked important, festive. The well-dressed *vaqueros* in their black pants and ruffled white shirts greeted folks at the road and showed them to their places. That, no doubt, Liz's influence, and the boys sure did look spiffy in their new clothes. She'd dressed the black cowboys in Texas, so this arrangement was no challenge to her. Besides, he could see they were proud of their appearance. No one but Elizabeth would have made that decision. He was lucky he'd found her—or rather, that she'd found him.

The first arrivals that morning were another ranch family from south of town, Morgan Strokes and his wife Earnestine, and their two teenage boys. A *vaquero* was there to take the team and wagon, and asked if they would like them unhitched and watered.

Morgan acted a little uneasy answering. Chet moved in to hug Earnestine, and assured the fellow rancher that his men would take good care of his team.

"Thank you, Chet."

"And thank you for inviting us," Earnestine gushed. "We're so glad to be here today."

"You go in the back door. My Liz and that bunch are inside waiting for you. Morgan, if you and those boys want to see some of those yellow horses we talked about a while back, there's a boy up there can show them. Nice to have you."

He could see the two boys were excited about that and they headed off as more wagons arrived.

It was good to be home among friends and family. Things were breaking loose and half the population of the county would probably be there before it started.

Good enough, Victor and Rhea sure deserved a real wedding.

My, how my Arizona family has grown.

When they'd arrived, it had been he, his sister Susie, and May, with a small crew to mind the wagons from the end of the railroad tracks in the panhandle to the Verde Ranch. The Texas boys all got homesick before long and had left. Men like Jesus and Cole took their places, and had become his guardsmen to ease the worries of his late wife, Marge. More good boys had joined, and some of the more dependable ones, like Roamer, Shawn, and the Morales brothers, had been sent to handle his Force in the south, holding down banditry on the border.

The Force was something else that he needed to check on in the nearby future. But he was going to take the next few weeks and go over the financial condition of the ranching operations. Liz helped him keep the books, but he still needed to know all about what was going on and what they'd need to do in the future.

He moved about greeting the arriving guests. The day had begun to warm up and the sky was clear and blue for the occasion. Hampt and a very pregnant May arrived with their two boys and one girl on smaller horses.

"Hey, look here the boss man's back. How are you, fellow?" He bear-hugged Chet after he climbed down.

"Great. Good to see you two. My sister stay with you last night?"

Both men moved to help May off the wagon. With her feet on the ground, she glanced back down the road. "They're coming—somewhere. You alright?"

"Doing great. We got back to the Verde last night. I rode on up here by myself."

"Wonder why he did that?" Hampt teased.

"Hampt." May frowned at him. "Oh, thanks so much, Chet. That lawyer you got for us? He's really straightened out that bunch at Mason on my inheritance."

"I knew he was good. I'm glad he got it taken care of."

"How is everyone?" she asked.

"Not got a list but everyone here seems good. I guess Reg had a wreck."

"Lucy wrote me. He broke his leg in two places and is bedridden."

"I bet he's a wonderful patient, too," Chet deadpanned.

May suppressed her laughter. "I bet he is. About like you or Hampt would be. I'd leave home on either one of you. How was that rim country you went to check on?"

"Hey, we rounded up the bandits and have lots of evidence. They should be up here shortly. I left the gang at the Verde late last night."

"Don't ever send a boy when you need a man," Hampt said, and got a small shove from his wife. They laughed.

"There's your bunch coming now, I think," May said. "Speak of the devils."

"What do you know?" Chet squinted, caught sight of the caravan coming down the lane. "I better go see them."

"I'll join you," Hampt said.

"Good morning," Chet said to Cole when they reached the lead horse. "Any problems?"

"Not except for their bitching. I am tired of that. I thought maybe Valerie was already here. This the wedding day?"

"You bet it is. Get those guys in the jail and come on back. It'll be middle of the afternoon if I got it right."

"You have a big start already on people," Jesus said, looking around.

"They won't be married in the church?" Cole asked.

"No, the priest Father O'Brian said God was everywhere and there wasn't enough room for all of us in his small church. Here was fine."

Cole shrugged. "I recall it was sure crowded when you married Liz."

"It was that. Get them in jail and get on back here. That paper I wrote will get them locked up and we can talk to the assistant federal prosecutor about them later."

Cole nodded, then waved at Liz as she came down the road to greet them.

"Thanks for taking such good care of him," she said, clutching Chet's arm possessively. "I owe you another one."

"It was a tough job, but we managed." Cole smiled and tipped his hat. "We'll be back before things really get started."

"We'll have another couple of guests, it sounds like," Chet told his wife.

"Oh, who's that?"

"That second woman from the gang's hideout, Candy. Cole dropped her with Millie, and Millie's found her a dress and bringing her along."

"Two women?"

"I guess I forgot. I told you about that Navajo woman they had chained up in a shed, right? Well, Candy was there, too. She isn't all there, though. Talks to herself. I think she's had some bad experiences and now ignores life."

"No, you didn't mention them."

"Well, you know me," he said. "I feel sorry for folks like that."

"That makes four women like that in a short while."

"I'm not keeping score. I can't stand for a woman to be mistreated. She won't hurt anyone. And she damn sure does not appeal to me."

"I've not said a word—"

"But you sound like you're thinking it," he pointed out.

"I'm thinking I'm so glad you do the things you do for everyone. As for the women, I'm not worried. I won't ever let them have you." She hugged his arm.

Chet laughed. "Good. Don't ask me what I'll do with her, though. I have no idea."

"Millie and I will solve that for you when she gets here."

He turned, kissed her forehead, and said, "Good. That's what I've got you for. Keep me out of scrapes."

They headed for the cooks and helpers, with Hampt trailing with them.

"You two beat it all." Hampt laughed. "I thought I had a bad case on May. But after I came home from that lost herd episode I told May, I never knew a man and woman as close as you two are who could smooth the waters in a stormy ocean in three sentences."

"That one took four," Chet corrected.

"And you know what?" Liz said to Hampt.

"What's that?"

"I never expected to find anyone like him in this world."

"He's a rare breed," Hampt agreed. "Came here from Texas, told me just how things would be, and they turned out exactly like he said. I was doing day work. Ryan had run me off the Quarter Circle Z for arguing with him, put the word out not to hire me. No one but some small ranchers needed day help would hire me because they all feared Ryan so much. Then here came this soft-talking Texan. Jenn introduced us and he told me I had a job soon as he got control of the ranch. I thought, 'Yeah and hell's going to freeze over.' But he got it away from them—bad guys.

"Liz, he turned my life around. Me, Tom, Sarge, and a bunch of other hands on the ranches were all out of work and banned from any jobs. He saved our lives. Amen."

"I know he saved mine, too," Liz said. "I wouldn't trade my spot in his life, either."

"Aw, you two would have made it anywhere you went," Chet replied.

Liz shook her head. "You heard him. You heard me. So suffer, *hombre*."

"Dadgum right."

In Spanish, she addressed the busy cooking crew. "How is it going today?"

"We are ready, señora."

"*Gracias, mi amigos,*" she said in return. She turned back to Chet. "We don't have one thing to worry about here."

He hugged her. "I never worry about our people. They all work hard as you and Hampt do. It's the people that make these ranches work. I've been lucky as all get out to find you. We had a nice ranch and setup in Texas, but it would have been hard to expand like this there. The cattle drives to Kansas led the economy. But I'd never had this much land or opportunities back there. I loved it until the feud threatened to kill off my family. But I never looked back. Arizona is the new frontier."

"Well, Hampt and I are glad to be along. More folks are coming. I'm going to change clothes, dear. You'll want to welcome them. I'll see you later."

"Thanks," Chet said after her.

"I better go find my wife and be sure she has what she needs," Hampt said. "We're going to have a real ranch out my way. And my family is growing. That oldest boy Ty is talking about going on to school. I'm encouraging him."

"You need any money for that boy's education, just let me know."

"Thanks. I'll tell May that, too."

"I better get to shaking hands. More folks are coming in."

For the next hour, Chet worked the crowd. Millie and Candy arrived with Millie's kids in a buckboard. Tom and his oldest, they said, were checking on a few things and would be there later. Several of the ranch hands were there. Susie, Sarge, and their baby arrived, with three of the Windmill Ranch hands trailing behind.

Bo Evans and his intended, Shelly, drove in. Tanner from the bank arrived in his light buggy. The Freys came with all their offspring, then Ben Ivor and his wife with their baby, Kathrin looking ready to deliver another. She'd told him once, privately—"My first husband and I never had any children. Now I can't get far from my first baby. But I'm happy, and I feel very lucky thanks to you."

"I'm simply pleased that you have him and are happy," he'd replied.

"You ever need me, just holler."

"Kathrin, you've helped me lots in this life. You owe me nothing."

"Chet Byrnes, you took a big chance bringing me down here considering my state of affairs at the time. You saved my life for much better things. I won't ever forget that."

Now, helping Kathrin down off the rig, Chet gave her a hug and shook his head at her swollen belly.

"What will you call this one?"

"If it is a girl, Mira. That's for the miracle part."

"And a boy?"

"That's up to him."

"I better get going. Good luck to both of you."

"Tell Liz hi. I love her, you know. She's as smart a woman as I've ever met."

"Me too, Kathrin," he said with a nod of his head. "Me too."

More folks arrived and they gathered for lunch in the tent. Chet said a short blessing, then stopped and apologized when he realized the priest was already there, too.

"The Lord was pleased to hear it from you, Chet."

"Thank you, *padre*."

Chet smiled sheepishly and sat beside his wife. "How many are coming?" he asked in a whisper. "Did you invite the whole county?"

"You feed them too well."

"I'll cut back next time."

Liz stifled a laugh. "No you won't."

"Have you seen Jenn and Valerie yet? Have I missed them?" he asked.

"They're at the house and will be here shortly. Said they passed the boys and the prisoners on the road."

"Cole and Jesus should be back by the start of the wedding."

"I am sure they will," she said. "Your aunt and her husband came, too, did you see?"

"I need to hug that man."

Liz made a face at him. "Why's that?"

"In Texas she was the biggest pain in the backside I had. Nothing I did ever pleased her."

"Oh, she speaks so highly of you now. What happened?"

"Some outlaws kidnapped her thinking she was Susie and I rescued her."

She snorted. "Sounds just like you. But she really is

happy in her new life. Maybe that was part of the problem in Texas."

He stopped eating. "Maybe. She is happier, though. My father's brother was her first husband and father of those two boys—JD and Reg. He was killed in the war— the very last days, we think. Records weren't kept all that well back then. I always thought he might have survived and would turn up someday, but I think now after all these years he really did die."

"I'd never heard that story."

"I guess someday I should write it all down, make a record of our family history."

"When would you have time to do that?"

He laughed. "Good question."

"Did you learn anything about those brothers you arrested in Utah?"

"Not much. They complained all the time and would have killed any and all of us if they'd gotten half the chance. They couldn't believe how we'd found them."

"I guess they thought they were real smart?"

"Or too tough to be caught."

"Can they be hung?" she asked.

"I've no doubt they will be tried, found guilty, and executed."

"I'm simply glad you made it back."

Chet hugged her close. "So am I."

"You have any plans?"

"Maybe go check on the Force down south, and JD's operation at Diablo soon. But that can wait until the newlyweds get back, since you and that girl will have Adam until they come home."

"Good. Maybe we can slip down to the *hacienda* in

Mexico while we're down south? See how things are going down there?"

"Sounds good to me."

After lunch, Rhea arrived in her spectacular white dress, and Victor waited up at the large horse barn for the hour hand on his watch to get close to two. More folks arrived, and Jesus and Cole came back from town to report the prisoners in jail and the evidence under lock and key.

"Good. No more plans today. When Rhea comes back after the honeymoon, we may go to Mexico to Liz's place, check on the Force, and see JD and his operation."

Cole's wife shook her head and smiled. "Always busy," she said.

"No rest for the wicked," Chet affirmed. He led the way off toward the tent to prepare for the service. Halfway there, Valerie left Cole's side and hurried forward to speak with him.

"I didn't make a face at you back there, Chet," she said. "I know Cole is proud to be with you. I am, too. We've all benefited. I'm just a wife who misses him."

"No problem, Valerie. I understand."

"Valerie, I make the same faces. Don't worry about it." Liz hugged her.

They went inside to find seats. Raphael was already there in his new suit, the slender Rhea at his elbow, ready to take her to the altar and give her away.

It was a great day on his ranches—another wedding. A wedding between a wonderful girl who cared for his son like her own, and a very talented young man who'd proved his worth over and over. A great day in spite of crimes committed by greedy people like the Cassidy brothers and others all across the frontier. These were the days that made it all worth it, and they were twice as fine as their discovery of the bloody evidence under the floor of that house, and the knowledge that people's lives had been cut short by the greed of a few cutthroat outlaws.

"You look awful serious for such an occasion," Liz whispered.

"Just thinking about the good and evil in this world." Chet nodded, tight-lipped. "This is the good part."

"I agree."

The wedding march began, Raphael marching down the aisle, taking Victor to his bride. A glorious event in the ranch's history, as neat as his own wedding to Liz had been. New book, new chapters to fill. Chet had never even dreamed things like this could happen here on his own ranch. Surrounded by so many he called family, he listened to the priest's blessing, watched the couple share communion and their vows. Finally, they were pronounced husband and wife.

Let the *fandango* begin.

After the ceremony, Chet kissed the bride on the forehead and shook Victor's hand. Then he led them to the decorated buckboard, all loaded and ready for their trip to Oak Creek. Rita held Adam up for Rhea to kiss one last time, and then they were gone among shouts and cheers.

He hugged Liz close to him. "Best thing that's happened since I got back and hugged you."

"Hugged me?" She shook her head.

They both laughed and turned to go back to the party.

CHAPTER 8

After the wedding, it was time to get back to the business of ranching. A horse wreck had occurred earlier in the week while sorting cattle, sending a *vaquero* to the doctor's office with a broken arm. Raphael reported the man's arm was set and that they'd be bringing him home in two days. Horse fine, cowboy fine in a few weeks. That was the nature of the thing, and they were all thankful it hadn't been worse.

Chet also spent some time with Adam. Monica had everything up on higher shelves to save them from the boy's ever-growing explorations. His staggering trips around the house to new places entertained his father all afternoon. They rolled a ball at each other, chased each other around the house, laughed and laughed while wrestling on the living room floor. But Adam's attention span always quickly shifted to something else, leaving Chet to watch the diapered backside disappear down the hall. Nonetheless, they had some rare private time to share some manly things.

The short rest came to an end late in the week. Jesus had gone and gotten the mail, and came back with a letter

for Chet. He handed it over. Opening the envelope with
a bone-handled letter opener, Chet unfolded the notepa-
per and read the neat handwriting.

Dear Marshal Byrnes
 *I have heard much about what you do for
people and their problems with outlaws. I am
a widow. My husband of ten years, a sober
Christian man named Arnold Hayes, was shot
six months ago by an outlaw named Burt Clayton
for no obvious reason. Three witnesses testified at
the JP hearing that Clayton became irate over
something Arnold had nothing to do with: a horse
he had bought for a stallion but was infertile.*
 *The JP ordered Clayton arrested for his
murder, but no one has arrested him nor even
tried that I know about. I spoke to the justice of
the peace, a Mr. Franks, and he says he gave the
arrest warrant to the Yavapai County deputy
Reagan, who says his constables don't have time
to go arrest him. Heavens, Clayton is in town
several times a week.*
 *Would there be any way you could help bring
justice to this legal oversight?*
 *I think Clayton is a rich man who has bought
off the Sheriff's deputy and the rest of the law. My
ranch is due south of St. Johns. Your drovers drive
cattle by my place all the time but I can never
catch them. If you could see justice was done,
I would appreciate it. I can tell you right now I
have no money to pay you.*

                         Sincerely Yours
                         Lilac Hayes

Liz came in the living room packing his son. "Somebody needing help?"

"Widow woman. Someone shot her husband. A warrant was issued but the killer was never arrested. Deputy said he was too busy to serve it even though the man who did it is in town several times a week."

"So you're going to arrest him?"

"I will if there's a properly issued warrant by a justice of the peace to arrest him."

"Will the sheriff here honor it?" she asked.

"If it's a real warrant he has to," Chet said. "Then a grand jury will have to decide his fate to be tried or not."

"I see."

"We'll ride up there, drop you off to visit my sister, collect this man Clayton, and bring him back to jail."

She took a seat on the arm of his chair. "You make it sound so easy. He may not let you just arrest him quietly. He may run off or fight. A lot of them have."

"But in the end, we always bring them back," he replied.

"True. I just worry is all." Liz sighed. "But fine, let's do it. Then we go up and see Lucy and Reg, right?"

"And the Force down at that end of the world. That still good?"

"It's fine, you just make these trips sound so short and pleasant—like we go and then come right back. They always end up taking so much longer. I don't mind, I'm just telling you it'll take longer than you think."

"I'm an optimist," Chet said.

His wife laughed. "You're something, alright."

"We'll wait to go until Rhea and Victor get back."

"You know anything about this lady?"

"Only that she's God-fearing and has no money to pay me."

"Well, don't you go expecting to be paid then, Marshal Byrnes."

"Here, let me carry big boy." He scooped Adam up and spun him around through the air. "I smell supper."

"Rita will be back from town soon. He's had a big day playing with you."

"Curious Adam. Can't keep him in one place for nothing."

"There's no one here to tell us how you acted at that age. I bet they couldn't hold you in one place, either," Liz teased him.

"That is pure speculation."

"But probably a pretty accurate one." She laughed. Taking the boy back, she hoisted him up on her hip and winked.

The honeymooners came back Friday night, and Adam was overjoyed to see Rhea. Chet and Liz attended church on Sunday, then ate dinner at the Palace Saloon. The wind was out of the north driving home, not too sharp but still jacket weather.

"What will the weather do next?" Liz asked him as they dismounted back at the ranch.

"Oh, maybe snow a little. Looks like it might."

"We still going north in the morning?"

"Most likely. You and Susie can stay in by the fireplace after we get you up there, though."

"I worry more about you than I do myself."

Chet waved the idea away. "I will be fine. Snow is simply another nuisance that goes with the job."

"Alright. I'll be ready to go in the morning. But I'll ride a horse off the mountain, no buckboard."

He saluted. "Yes, ma'am."

She hugged his arm going into the house. "There are

lots of great folks up here. They accept me like family. I worried some that they would think bad of me."

"Why would they do that?"

"Stealing you, of course. And being Mexican and all."

"They aren't worried about that," he assured her. "Oh, some folks may harbor a grudge, but most are simply happy people scratching for a living, looking for a good time every so often, like the parties we have here. Lots of good food and dancing is fine entertainment to most of them."

"I guess so. I'm just happy to be here."

"And I you, my dear."

The next morning dawned cold and white as the sky spit snow down upon the foursome, Chet, Liz and his usual shadows Jesus and Cole. They rode out with their packhorses, headed for the Verde Ranch, the sawmill, and then on to Windmill.

When Susie left the day before, she'd told them to leave Liz at her house for her company when they got to her place. Liz had replied that she was going with Chet. She loved being with Susie but wanted to stay with Chet. Susie had wrinkled her nose but accepted it.

Cole's horse was giving him some troubles that morning, bobbing and rearing until the young man could finally get him settled down.

"How did I get this one?" he asked, his breath misting in the cold air.

"Want me to spell you on him?" Chet grinned playfully. That was Cole's usual line to him about a sour horse.

"Lord no. But it's funny. Jesus never gets a wild one."

"Are you trying to tell me you want a raise for this kind of duty now?"

"I sure might. Did Liz tell you that we may be parents soon?"

"No, she didn't. That sounds wonderful."

"I thought the same thing. Cross your fingers."

"I'll cross my heart for you two," Chet said solemnly.

"I did, too, you just must have been picking the fuzz out of your ears," Liz piped up from behind them. They all laughed. "Where did Val come from originally, Cole?"

"Kansas," Cole replied. "Her folks came out here to get away from the war. But when they left for California, she and JD's wife, Bonnie, ran off for Tombstone and what they thought was going to be a brighter life. She got sick of it fast, though. Ended up as a waitress. We found her there, put her on the stage to come back and work for Jenn. She told us where Bonnie was working, too, but by the time we got there, she'd been kidnapped. We followed the trail down to Mexico. Chet told you that story about his horses and the trade he made to get her back, right?"

Liz said, "Oh, yes, and had he not done that, I'd never have met him."

Chet chuckled. "Lots of things tied to those horses. We sold enough to freight the outfit to west Texas. Saved us lots of wagon miles. But my best trade in the deal was meeting you."

"Mine too. I was so self-sufficient, I sure didn't need a man. I feared the man I had lost could never be replaced. That all evaporated when I met you. The Morales Ranch wasn't a bad place, but it was not what I expected as being headquarters for the famous American lawmen chasing down the border bandits."

"We never worried about comfort down there, and

were gone most of the time, anyway. The Morales boys' wives guarded our things, fed our extra horses, and cooked wonderful meals."

"They did a great job for us when I was there," Cole put in.

"Yes, but I had seen a picture of your national capital. I could not believe such a powerful police force lived in such a small, run-down place."

Chet shook his head. "It's not always a big deal. Why, the county courthouse at Phoenix is a cluster of adobe buildings right now. The big stone one still isn't finished."

"It'll be something when they finish it," Jesus said.

Chet agreed. "They should have built a State capitol courthouse here in Preskitt. That way we wouldn't be moving back and forth between here and Tucson after every legislative session."

"Why didn't they?" Liz asked as they pushed off the steep mountain grade.

"Tucson had more votes. They think Preskitt is too isolated in the mountains to ever get a train. And some folks hated Lincoln and his idea to get away from the rebels in southern Arizona and have the capital up here. That's how things go when you ask for a vote."

They reached Robert's house long after dark. A heavier snow had begun to fall in the afternoon, and they all were nearly frozen through. Liz went and knocked on the door while the men put up their horses.

"Hey, what are you doing here so late?" Betty demanded. "We expected you hours ago. Get in this house right now. You look like a snowman, Liz."

"They're still up." Liz shouted back to the men.

Chet and the boys soon were in the warm house holding their hands out to the wood stove. The heat felt good and it was a relief to be out of the saddle. It had been a long day and they were all sore.

"Where to this time?" Robert asked him.

"Saint John," Chet said. "There's a killer up there no one can arrest."

"You sure get the good jobs." Robert shook his head in amusement. "I sent word to the men to come in when it began to snow this morning. You never know if the snow is going to be deep or pass over, but I don't take chances with men or horses and bring them in."

"Sounds good to me. It's been snowing since we started to climb the north rim."

The snow tapered off during the night. They rode on north the next day through knee-high drifts, and were east of the Sacred Mountains when they camped that night. They set up a tent, cut down some dead pines, and had a fire. They all slept in the tent and were up breathing vapors of steam before dawn.

Jesus helped Liz fix breakfast and coffee while Chet and Cole fed the horses. Despite his heavy coat and clothes, Chet felt the deep cold that preceded the snowfall in his bones. But his wife never complained and later when he asked her if she was alright in the low temperatures, she replied with a smile. "I'm with you, that's enough to keep me warm."

They rode on, arriving in St. John at dusk, where they found a hotel, stabled their horses, and ate a meal in the local café. Chet told them that the next day, he planned on finding the justice of the peace named in the letter and checking on the arrest warrant and that Cole and Jesus would come along.

Alone in their hotel room later, Liz was curious.

"Chet, what do you think is happening up here?"

"I have no idea. It's a long ways from Preskitt, but that's no excuse. This Clayton may be a powerful man, but it's no way to handle a crime in a democracy."

"Can you buy your way out of prosecution up here?" she asked.

"You're not supposed to be able to, but he may be trying to. We'll know more in a few days."

"Good. Cold or whatever, I'm proud to be here with you." She hugged him tight and rocked him.

"So am I. So am I."

CHAPTER 9

The next morning, after breakfast, they mushed through the snow piled in the streets to the office of Mr. Franks, the JP. They found him in a cold office, trying to build a fire in a potbellied stove.

"Good morning, sir," Chet introduced himself and his deputies, and gave a quick sketch of what they were after.

"Yes, I did, indeed, issue an arrest warrant for Mr. Clayton," the JP told him. "The deputy in charge, Joe Reagan, told me he was too busy counting cattle for tax purposes to serve it."

"Who else could serve it?"

"Any other lawman. Do you want to serve it, Marshal?"

Chet nodded. "Is this Clayton some bad outlaw or powerful man?"

Franks pushed himself up to his feet and clanged the stove door shut. "Don't ask me, but they say even tough folks ride around him."

"You don't?" Chet asked.

"I've not had the pleasure of riding around him so far."

"Do you know where he frequents when in town?"

"Oh, that's easy. The Silver Spur Saloon."

Chet had seen the business when they rode in the evening before. "He bring his crew with him?"

Franks nodded, looking grave. "Some of them."

"May I have a copy of the warrant?"

"Sure. I'll make you one like I gave Reagan."

"Thank you kindly. You have any advice for us going into this?"

"I've heard about you and your men before, Marshal. I'd say he has no idea what he's going to be up against."

Franks's stove was beginning to generate heat. When he finished the document, they shook hands and headed back to a café. He sent Cole to check on the saloon, but not let anyone know his purpose. He was back by the time they'd finished their second cup of hot coffee.

"Ordinary saloon," the young man said with a shrug. "It's empty for all purposes right now. Too early. Long bar is on the west side of the room. Poker table in the back, and tables with a stage on the right."

"We need a description of him and his men," Chet said. "And some idea of a count."

"I bet the guys at the livery could do that," Jesus said. "I'll take care of that."

"Good. Meet us back here at lunch."

"I'll go do some more checking, too," Cole said. "I don't like the feel of this place."

Chet found Liz and went down to the hotel lobby, which was heated and comfortable despite the cold outside. They took a pair of stuffed chairs near the windows and read the local newspaper, sharing some words here and there. Chet always hated these times where he had to wait around, but knew they were sometimes necessary. He couldn't always go charging off into the middle of things, after all. Some matters required patience and subtlety.

If their man didn't come to town, they'd bring the law to him wherever he was. This was the best place to arrest him, though, if he really frequented the village like people said. No fortress, no means of escape. Time would tell.

They weren't to be disappointed. Cole came in and reported their man was already at the saloon. Chet sent him to lasso Jesus and come back there.

"You stay here," he said to Liz.

"I planned to," she replied. "But is there anything I can do?"

"Being here is good enough."

Out the front window, he saw Jesus and Cole coming across the street. Out of habit he shifted his six-gun on his hip and kissed her on the cheek. "I'll be back."

In his heavy coat, he crossed the slushy lane between passing traffic and joined his men. They'd cleared off some of the boardwalks, but his boots squished farther into the mud and muck with every step.

"He's a big man," Jesus told him. "Full mustache, sandy hair, some freckles."

Stone-faced, Chet nodded his understanding. They marched through the stiff right-hand double door, the usual batwings tied back for the winter. The air inside was close, sour-smelling, overheated. Across the sawdust-littered floor, several men stood around a card game at a table. They all turned casually to look at who entered, then turned back to the game.

Chet moved that way. Nearing the table, he drew his pistol slowly from its holster and leveled it on the group.

"Don't anyone move fast," he called. "I'm a Deputy U.S. Marshal and I have two more deputies ready to back me. I'm here to arrest Burt Clayton. Don't anybody be foolish, now. You get foolish, you won't leave this room alive."

"Bartender!" Cole growled, his own six-gun drawn. "Put your hands on the bar."

The big man at the card table pushed the chair back and rose to his feet. "What's the charge?" he demanded with a sneer.

"Murder. Death of Arnold Hayes."

"That was settled by my lawyers," the man said, waving it away.

"No. But it'll be settled by your arrest and trial in Preskitt."

"You don't know who I am."

Chet narrowed his eyes. "I know you were found responsible for Hayes's death by a justice of the peace, and that's enough for me. I'm here to take you to Preskitt for trial."

"You have no authority."

"I'm a federal officer and representative of the courts," Chet declared. "And you, sir, are under arrest. Jesus, put the handcuffs on him."

"When I get through—"

Chet shook his head. "I don't want to hear it. We're parking you in the jail and tomorrow we go to Preskitt. Tell your friends and employees not to try anything if they want to live."

"Just who the hell are you?" Clayton demanded.

"Chet Byrnes." He fished out his star and thrust it in the big man's face. "And this badge tells you I'm big enough to haul you, or anyone else who gets in the way, to jail."

"You—you—I'm not through with you."

Chet jerked his head at Jesus. "Let's get him out of here. Put his coat over his shoulders. Do you have a horse to ride?"

"No."

"Okay." He smiled. "I'll just buy a mule for you to ride—bareback."

"Where do you want his horses and saddle?" a shorter man asked. Chet held back a chuckle. He'd known the threat would make a horse and tack available.

"At the livery. Ready to go first thing in the morning."

The man nodded. "He'll have one. You want anything else?" he asked the big man.

Clayton shook his head.

"Let's go." They left by the front door, marching down the boardwalk for the jail. Jesus held the handcuffed prisoner by the elbow, with Cole out ahead and Chet covering up rear.

The guard at the jail jumped out of his seat as they came through the door. "Y-you can't—"

"Just watch me," Chet told him. "This man is a prisoner of mine. Stand down and go open a cell to put him in."

Reluctantly, the jailer picked up the keys on the desk and placed Clayton in a cell. Chet removed the handcuffs and told the man that he'd be back bright and early in the morning.

"I could take to disliking you real quick," Clayton said with a sneer.

"Clayton, you can hate me all you want, but headfirst or belly-down over a saddle, you're going to Preskitt and stand trial."

"We'll see about that."

"In the morning. You better be here. I don't mess around with escapees."

"Is that a threat?"

"No, it's a promise."

He stepped out of the cell and locked it behind him. Standing in the outer room, he considered Clayton's threat. Would he be there in the morning? He had better be there. At the moment he had little use for anyone so uppity.

Chet told the jailer that he would be held personally responsible, and face charges of obstructing the law, if Clayton wasn't still there in the morning. The man nodded his head in fear, and Chet knew he had his bluff in on him, too.

Satisfied that his orders would be followed, he led the way out to get Liz and have supper. A red-faced man in a canvas coat caught up with them sometime later in the hotel restaurant.

"Listen here, whoever the hell you are. I'm Deputy Joe Reagan, and you can't put an innocent citizen in my jail."

"I have an arrest warrant and I'm a Deputy U.S. Marshal. My authority trumps yours. A JP ordered him arrested for murder and you did nothing. Now I think that perhaps a grand jury should look into that—maybe you're his kin? I demand he stay in that jail and be ready to be transported to Preskitt in the morning."

"I ain't his kin," Reagan shot back angrily. "Mr. Clayton is a law-abiding citizen and pillar in this community."

"Then he shouldn't have shot Arnold Hayes."

"That was self-defense."

"Mr. Hayes didn't have a gun."

"He simply got in the way."

"Shooting an unarmed man is criminal. He goes to trial."

"You . . ." The deputy's face had started to turn from red to almost purple.

"Listen carefully," Chet said in a low voice, on his feet now and pointing his fork at the man's chest. "If he isn't in that cell at dawn, you and that jailer will both face obstructing justice charges and I will see you get the maximum sentences allowed by law. You get me?"

"I'm wiring the sheriff."

"Wire whoever you want. But I will prevail."

"You won't get ten feet out of this town."

"Then when the shooting starts, Clayton goes first. Remember that. Now get out of here, I'm tired of your mouth."

Reagan stomped out, muttering under his breath.

"He's gone," Liz said sweetly. "You can sit down now."

"Yes, ma'am," Chet said, replacing his napkin in his lap. "Boy's got a big mouth."

Cole and Jesus grunted in agreement.

"What will he do next?" Liz asked.

"I have no damn idea."

Everyone laughed except Chet. What *would* he do? They'd know in the morning.

CHAPTER 10

Chet and his group headed out of the hotel in the cold, blue light of pre-dawn. Frozen snow crunched under their boot soles. Jesus and Liz went on to saddle the horses. He and Cole went to the jail and woke the sleeping guard.

Chet picked the keys up off the desk and walked over to the cell. "Get up, Clayton. Put on your coat and come toward me with your hands held out. One wrong move and you'll ride with them behind you. Savvy?"

Unshaven and haggard, Clayton only nodded. The jailer never said a word and Chet felt the man watching them for a long time before he closed the jailhouse door against the winter weather. With Clayton's wrists cuffed, Chet pushed the prisoner ahead of him on the walk to the livery, Cole pacing them not far behind.

With the help of the stable boys, everyone was soon loaded and ready. Clayton had a big, stout dun horse they put on a lead rope that would be held by Jesus. Cole had the packhorses, and Liz was free to ride as close to Chet whenever she could. With Chet in the lead, they rode southwest for the Marcy Road. It would be a long ways to the Windmill Ranch, and the snow on the ground would slow them.

The biting north wind needed to stop, but Chet had no idea when or if it would even quit. Liz fed them cold bean burritos for lunch in the saddle, and they stopped for just long enough to pee and get back up on their mounts. Clayton sulked most of the day. For his part, though, Chet didn't miss his lack of words as they pushed on.

Few settlements or places to stop dotted the high open range country as they headed back, and it was well past midnight when they reached the Windmill. They would have had no choice but to make camp, anyway. Their horses were spent, and so was Chet's shoulder and back. Hurt as he did, though, he worried more about Liz's condition from the long ride than his own, but she told him she was fine, just tired.

Susie was up in no time, and Sarge brought a lamp down to the corral to help them unload. The women made food, and the prisoner sat on the floor, sulking in his handcuffs. Chet had no worries about him. The boys took turns guarding him through the night. They woke him for breakfast. At least partially rested, they loaded up the horses and rode for the Verde River place. Thankfully, the snow melted away and it became almost hot as the day wore on. They arrived before sundown, much to everyone's relief.

Tom provided guards and they all got to sleep that

night. Chet played with his son before turning in, and then slept upstairs in his own bed with his wife. It was a wonderful event for them both.

"You're still a great honeymooner," Liz whispered in his ear before they fell asleep.

CHAPTER 11

Chet was up early the following morning after arriving at the upper ranch. Raphael visited with him in the kitchen over Monica's coffee while Chet ate breakfast. His foreman had always already eaten before he came up to the big house. Raphael was in his mid-fifties, and never wanted to be any sort of a beggar or show up like one. The fact had become a point about him that Chet understood, though few others did. But he still always drank coffee with his boss and freely informed him about the operation.

Raphael's workers were all Hispanic—*vaqueros*—and their families. This group took care of things handily. They operated a guard shift to protect the ranch head-quarters twenty-four hours a day. They also acted like one large, extended family. This was why he was so disturbed when he had to deliver the news that one of his men's wives, a girl named Darling, had been to the doctor and told she had cancer.

"Is there anything we can do for her?" Chet asked.

Raphael opened his calloused hands before him.

"Pray. Make sure she is comfortable. It is a very bad disease and little is known about treatment."

"I'll ask Liz about what she thinks."

"Darling's always a big help at our *fiestas*. I know it would make her feel better if your wife would talk to her."

"She'll be happy to do that."

There was silence for a moment. Then Raphael asked, "Was this *hombre* you arrested hard to get?"

Chet shook his head, cradling the warm cup in both hands before sipping it. "No. We arrested him in a saloon among his men. He had a fit and so did some of the others, but we locked him up for the night and brought him here for trial. Thought for a while that his men might try to free him, but they didn't. I got damned tired of his threats and talk about suing me, though."

Raphael laughed. "Big men like being caught the least."

"True enough." He sipped his coffee. "How's the rest of the outfit doing?"

"Good," the foreman said. "We've shipped seven hundred fifty head of big steers and cull heifers to the Windmill this fall."

"That'll damn sure help. Good job."

That meant they'd made a profit on this operation. Chet had the figures in his head about the cost of the *vaqueros*, Raphael, and the food they ate. Of course, the ranch stood the cost of the *fiestas* and other things like the house and Monica's pay, but it was on the profit side of the ledger because of the Navajo beef contract sales.

Which proved the value of the agreement with the agency.

Things looked brighter for all his operations. The

Verde River Ranch had its largest sale of big steers, cull heifers, and cows that year. It took two to three years to get cattle fat enough for sale, and the previous manager had sold the calves off the cows, so there were not any sale animals for that period from the big operation. Tom had sold that many or perhaps a few more. In the future they'd be in good shape. Up on the rim, the ranch that Reg and Lucy ran had the least overhead, but had still sent two hundred fifty head. Hampt's East Verde Ranch had sold four hundred head and nearly broke even. Of course, Diablo Ranch, down on the border, was still building and carried lots of expenses. But he felt JD was doing a good job controlling those during the building phase.

Robert's timber-hauling business made money every year, along with the beef-supplying contract to the Navajo that Sarge ran from the Windmill Ranch. His spreadsheet would be good when he got it out for the year. He stood up and hugged his wife when she joined them.

"Raphael told us this morning that Darling went to the doctor and that she has cancer. He asked that you comfort her."

"Oh, my, that is so sad. Yes, of course," Liz said, taking her seat at the table. "I'll go down there and see her."

"Tough job. Give her my concern, too."

"I will. What else?"

"These ranches have pulled us along this year. Things look very good. We've sold lots of cattle thanks to the Navajo contract."

"Not to count all the people around here you sold cattle for," Monica said. "You have helped lots of people, too. Every time I am out among them, they say you saved them buying their cattle."

"The project has worked well," Chet replied. "But not a day goes by that someone else tries to under-bid it. As long as we can deliver on time and have good cattle, we can hang on."

His wife clamped her hand on top of his. "We do that, don't we?"

"Oh, we try our best. I plan to round up our business here and head south about mid-week. I promised you that. How does that suit you?"

"Fine."

"We can drop down and see about your *hacienda* as well."

She smiled. "I'd like that very much."

"Then we can be back here for Christmas."

"Monica, that may leave lots of work for you to get ready for the holidays," Liz called across the kitchen.

"Raphael and I can get it all done, señora."

Liz stretched her neck. "I must have slept hard. My neck is stiff this morning."

"No wonder. That was a fast trip."

"Did Sheriff Simms have anything to say about it?" Monica asked.

Chet shook his head. He had done his best not to get in a war with the elected sheriff this time.

"You ever want to be sheriff, I can get you lots of votes," Monica said.

He shook his head and laughed. "No, thanks."

"He doesn't need that job," Liz added.

"But people want him to be the sheriff."

"Monica, there's already plenty for me to do."

Monica poured him more coffee. "You're still their choice."

"And I bet the prisoners would like you to be the jailhouse cook, too."

Everyone laughed.

"No, thanks," Monica said, her words firm.

"Same here."

Chet and Liz went to town and checked on things. They stopped by Jenn's café first. She was in the pre-lunch slump and had time to talk to them.

"You two look rested."

"Oh, we're getting that way," Liz said.

"Of course I let Valerie off today when her husband came home. They're still newlyweds."

"But that's better than some relationships."

"Oh, Liz, I love it. But those two were meant for each other."

"Your new help still here?"

"Oh, they're doing great. I found you help on the start and you've paid me back."

They left for Bo's and found him behind a desk piled high in paper documents.

"What's happening?"

"Oh!" Bo stood up and smiled. "I have lots of business. You two are back, I understand, from arresting a murderer."

"He's up in the hoosegow."

"I learned that this morning. What next?"

"We go south to check on things. Oh, Christmas Eve we'll have a party at the ranch. You and the lady are invited."

"We may be married by then."

"Oh, how nice!" Liz said. "When?"

"Shortly."

Chet frowned.

Bo lowered his voice and looked away. "There may well be three of us soon."

Just as he'd suspected. Chet nodded. "You want a witness for the wedding? Liz and I will stand in."

Bo put his hand on Chet's shoulder. "I'm so scared. I lost one wife trying to have a baby. Shelly is twenty-eight and never had a child."

"She's healthy and active. I think she'll be fine," Liz assured him. "You two are so lucky."

"Oh, I hope so. Six p.m. tonight at the Methodist church. Please don't tell anyone. You two will be my witnesses."

"We'll be there," Chet said. "And best of everything to you."

They left Bo to his business, papers, and worries.

"You saved a good man," Liz said, climbing in the buckboard.

"Yes, I did. I wondered why they hadn't married before now. She's a widow."

"Who knows how widows think? I was settled with being one until you popped up."

"Thank God."

"Which reminds me. Go by the church; I'll pray for Darling and light some candles."

First thing's first. He still had the saddle shop and the bank to check in with, but he wheeled the horses off the hill in the direction of the Catholic church. There wouldn't be time to go back to the ranch to change clothes for the wedding. He just hoped Bo and Shelly wouldn't mind if they weren't real dressed up.

After prayer, she stopped to talk to Father O'Brian

about Darling's health problem. Once on the seat, Liz asked him to drive over to Shelly's house. He'd never been to Bo's bride-to-be's place, but knew where it was at. They drove through the black iron gate, up the drive, and found themselves before a large, two-story brick house.

"Impressive place," he said, helping her down.

"A very nice place."

A maid answered the door and told them her mistress wasn't expecting company.

"Excuse me. She'll see me." Liz went by her and the maid let him come in the hallway.

Chet grinned, a tad embarrassed. "My wife knows her," he said with a shrug.

The young woman shook her head. "I'm only doing what she told me."

Liz reappeared. "She wants you to fix us some tea. Chet, come on in. I told her you were here, too."

Sitting on the couch, Shelly saw him and struggled to rise as she saw him enter the parlor. He waved her back down. "Don't get up. I'm fine."

She shook her head. It was obvious she'd been crying.

"I told your wife, but I am so embarrassed. I love Bo, but I never expected we'd conceive a baby. I was married for four years and nothing ever happened like this."

"It's no problem. It happens. Shelly, I was my first wife's third husband and she'd never birthed a baby, either. I feel very lucky to have Adam." He handed her his handkerchief.

"Oh, Chet. I knew about that and I felt so sorry for you."

"So there," Liz told her. "Start celebrating your own good fortune."

She wiped her wet eyes and nodded. "You're so kind.

Thank you so much for stopping by. I'm feeling much better already."

"Bo invited us to witness your wedding tonight. I hope you don't mind?" Liz asked.

"Mind?" Shelly chuckled dryly. "Of course not. You may have given me the backbone to actually go through with this."

Liz smiled. "Shelly, I had the same feeling after I lost my first husband. That I didn't need anyone. Then I met Chet and lost my mind. Get up and let's go look at the dress you plan to wear. We can fix your hair." She turned to her husband. "Chet, go see the banker and stop by the saddle shop like you planned. I can handle things here."

Marching orders in hand, Chet told the maid he could find his own way out. The three women left the room together, all talking at once. He almost laughed when, going out the front door, he heard the maid say to his wife, "I told her that twice. At least she's listening to you."

Everyone had to listen to Liz, he mused, clucking at the horses to go.

At the bank, he found out that Tanner was out on business, so he drove up to the saddle shop and found four of his *vaqueros*'s sons stitching saddles. McCully was busy showing one of them the trick to wrapping a saddle horn properly.

"I see they're working out right nicely," he said to the crippled man, who crossed the room on his crutches to shake Chet's hand.

"Oh, these boys are great saddle makers," McCully said. "I'm glad you stopped by. I need to speak to you. They can do this now; let's go talk in the office."

Once inside, he closed the door. He looked pale. "You know my daughter you went and rescued?"

"Of course I do," Chet said. "Petal."

"That's right. Well, we got her back too late—I am afraid he got her with child."

"Oh, God, man. I am so sorry."

"One of the boys from your ranch wants to marry her, but I didn't want you to be mad at me for letting her do that."

"He knows about the baby?"

"*Sí*. She told him."

"What's his name?"

"Vincente Dais."

"Pablo Dais's son, right?"

McCully nodded. "He is good worker and is learning fast. And he speaks well of you."

"I'll talk to him. Then we'll get the *padre* and bring his parents into town for the wedding. But let me talk to him alone first."

"Thank you, Chet," McCully said. "I knew you could get all this straight. I'll just go get the boy."

The boy came in. He was about eighteen, dark, handsome, and quite serious. He bowed politely and called Chet '*Patron*.'

"Chet is who I am, son. So you and Petal want to get married?"

He perked up. "*Sí,* Señor Chet. Will you help me?"

"Only if she agrees. But you do know that she carries another man's child?"

"*Sí*. She told me she did wrong, but that you saved her and brought her home."

"I simply brought her back here and helped her father start this business."

Vincente bowed again. "And I am grateful to you, señor. I am so pleased in becoming a saddle maker."

"When she is your wife, you must honor her, take this child as your own, and provide for her," Chet continued seriously. "If you ever beat her or harm her in any way, I will harm you in return, no matter where you are. You must be business-like and make a place for yourself in this business."

"I will, señor—I mean, I will, Chet." The boy smiled. "I am so happy I could cry."

"Will she tell me the same thing?"

"I hope so."

"Go to the store today. Buy a new pair of pants, a white shirt, and a tie. I'll pay for them, but wait until tomorrow to wear them. I'll bring your family into town so you two can get married. You can have your honeymoon down on Oak Creek. I have a cabin there. Do you know the place?"

"*Si, señor*. I took a wagonload of wood up there once."

"You'll need supplies for one week on my bill. I'll loan you a buckboard so you can make the trip."

"I think I am going to faint. Mother of God!"

Chet wondered if he would, the boy looked so pale. "Well, don't do that, there's too much to do now. But first, go get your girl and bring her in here to talk to me."

"*Si!* I mean, yes, señor—Chet—" Still stammering, he hurried off out into the shop. Soon he returned with an obvious pregnant Petal in tow.

She looked in a daze. "He said—" Her eyes rolled up into her head and she stopped talking.

Chet caught her before she hit the floor. "She's fainted," he told the boy.

They sat her in a chair. She looked very much out of it.

"Can you hear me?" Chet asked, squatting down beside her.

"Hmmm?" Her eyelids fluttered open.

"Listen to me now, Petal. Is this your man?"

"Oh, yes. I love him . . ."

"He says he loves you."

Vincente had a hand on her shoulder. She reached up to clasp it. "We love each other."

"That's good. You must never forget that. I'll bring his family into town tomorrow and have the priest marry you. Then you can go for a week to Oak Creek. You have to get revived enough to follow my orders. You need to go buy a decent dress. They'll have some on the rack at the dress store. Make a list of groceries you'll need for a week away at the cabin. Leave it to be ready at the store to pick up on your way out of town. Do you hear me now, Petal?"

Vincente hoisted her to her feet and held her tenderly. She was nodding the entire time. Chet couldn't help but laugh. All she could do was nod. He hoped she'd heard him.

"Take your father's buggy and go get all that. I have charge accounts at the stores, and I'll write you permission to get what you need. Tomorrow I'll have a fresh team and another buckboard to take to Oak Creek."

"You will bring his family?" she asked in a cracked voice.

He nodded. "That's right."

"Oh, Chet, that is so nice. I don't deserve all this."

"Listen. I saved you once, once more won't hurt me. But if you two don't love each other for as long as you live, I'll whip the hell out of both of you." Chet looked at Vincente. "Do any of you boys have a horse here to ride out to the ranch?"

"*Sí*. We keep two."

Chet picked up a pen and a receipt for leather and started scribbling on the back.

"Go get the smartest boy in there and bring him to me. He needs to take a note to Monica and Raphael about our plans."

Monica,

 Tell Raphael that Vincente is marrying Petal McCully tomorrow morning at the Catholic church. Time not set yet, but say 10 a.m. Raphael can explain it to Vincente's parents, tell them I approve. Everyone can come. The honeymooners will need a buckboard, team, and camping cooking gear for a week at Oak Creek. They will get their own food in town.

Chet

Vincente brought one of the other boys in as he licked the envelope shut. "Saddle a horse and take my note to Monica at the ranch. Vincente is marrying Petal tomorrow. You're the messenger."

"I can do that, *patron*."

"Tell them Liz and I will be there."

He wrote out the permission slips for the stores and told Vincente and Petal to get busy. They fled.

McCully hobbled in on his crutches. "I heard most of that. God bless you, Chet Byrnes. I owed you my life before. Today I owe you my soul."

"I didn't do a damn thing but work it out." Chet laughed, hugging the crying man.

"Thank God you did."

"I better go join my wife or I'll be dead meat myself."

With that, he walked back out to the buckboard and headed back to Shelly's place.

"Where have you been?" Liz asked with a smile.

He hugged and kissed her. "Arranging another wedding. Too long a story to tell right now. I lost track of the time."

"Shelly's to meet Bo at the church after five o'clock."

He checked his pocket watch. "Get her. We won't be late. My horses are ready."

Liz disappeared to get the bride and her maid. He put the three of them on the spring seat and stood up behind to drive the team to the church, keeping them entertained with details about the next wedding he'd set up. He jogged the horses all the way, and they were there by five thirty.

Bo walked out of the church to claim his bride. He kissed her like they'd been apart for a long time, and thanked them one and all. The maid—Cary—blushed to see the display. Chet winked.

She smiled and whispered, "He acts like he missed her since yesterday."

"Good for him," Liz said, and the three laughed.

They took seats in the second row of pews. The organ was playing "How Fine Thou Arte," and the minister stood before them. The winter sun had set, so candles sparkled on the polished wooden walls and the cross above the altar. Bo and Shelly looked happy and prosperous in their fine attire, waiting for the ceremony to begin. It was short and sweet, but no less moving for it. The couple kissed, and Chet, Liz, and Cary joined them in the aisle to congratulate them.

"Cary has supper in the oven at home," Shelly gushed. "Please join us. You can spend the night so you don't have to go home."

"Yes," Bo agreed. "Please be our guests on this great evening."

Liz looked at Chet and smiled. "I think we can do that."

They thanked the minister and went back to Shelly's house for supper and the night. After dinner, the newly-weds were excused and the Byrneses went in the living room, where Cary soon brought them coffee and cake.

"Can you play the guitar?" she asked. "Most people from Mexico can play it."

Liz sat up and smiled. "I once could. Do you have one?"

"Yes. Ms. Shelly's first husband played. I'll go get it."

"Thank you." She left the room in a hurry.

"I didn't know you could play the guitar," Chet said, sipping coffee.

"Shocked? I'm sorry. I never felt like I was very good at it."

"Not shocked. But I am ashamed I never asked you."

"Why is that?" she asked.

"May was in my family for years and we never knew she could sing and play the piano. Not even my sister knew and they were closer than anything. When she married Hampt, he found out. You ever heard her sing?"

"She is operatic. I'm a smoky *cantina* singer." Liz laughed as Cary returned holding a gleaming guitar. "My, that is a beautiful instrument, Cary. Thank you."

Liz's fingers flew, adjusting and strumming the instrument until she felt familiar with it, then she began a tune that sounded like the wind and rain.

Then she began to sing about a horse no one could catch. He recognized the song—Victor sang it, but he was a tenor, his voice nowhere near as high and strong as Chet's wife's, nowhere near as moving. Chills ran down Chet's spine as she bent over the instrument, the Spanish words clear over the strumming of the strings. He and Cary sat as though tied to their chairs by the chords, listening intently to the pictures Liz painted with her words and voice, amazed. As the last note faded, both shook their heads as though coming out of a trance.

"Why, Mrs. Byrnes," the maid gushed. "That was as pretty a song as I've ever heard."

"Thank you, Cary—"

"Play some more. Please! I'm intoxicated by your talent."

"Alright," Liz said, blushing. "But it gets worse from there."

She played and sang some more, soft songs of love and heartbreak in her native Mexico, followed by a lively tune of adventure and fun. Finally, she asked Cary for some water and lay the instrument aside.

"That's enough. You two are a fine audience." She took a sip from the glass the maid handed her and looked at Chet. "Surprised?"

He shook his head. "All I can say, after the wedding tomorrow, I'm buying you a guitar."

"Oh, no, you're not," said a voice from behind them. They turned to see Shelly and Bo gazing down upon them from the stairs. "She's taking that one. Bo and I heard her in the bedroom and have been listening from here. Elizabeth, you are so talented."

"I can't accept that, Shelly. You're too kind."

"But I'll never play it, and you will," the other woman said. "Beautifully."

"After tonight, I fear so. What have I done?"

"Made a very important evening in my life wonderful. Hasn't she, Bo?"

"Liz, you are a wonderful singer and I was struck by your playing and voice. I hated that you quit."

"Thank you. You've all made me blush. I've not sung— well, since my first husband was shot in my house."

Chet pulled her into his arms. "We didn't mean to bring back any bad memories."

She leaned her head on his shoulder. "I know. And it felt good to sing here tonight, just a little . . . bittersweet. I'm glad Cary asked me."

The girl beamed. "I didn't know, but most people from Mexico can play and sing."

"It was a great moment for all of us," Bo said.

"Do you dance, Cary?" Chet asked.

"I can, sir."

"Come to the ranch with Bo and Shelly for Christmas. I have several hardworking men out there that would be proud to dance with you."

It was her turn to blush. "Oh, I couldn't do that—"

"She's bashful, Chet," Shelly said with a laugh. "We'll bring her, though."

"Good. It's been an interesting evening."

Liz beat on his arm. "A very interesting one, *hombre.*"

Bo stopped them, waving a finger. "I've been to your parties, and there's a tradition your sister made you do once. I want you to put a blessing on Shelly and me, on Cary, and on the couple getting married tomorrow. In fact on your entire family."

How could he deny such a request? Chet nodded, took a deep breath, and bowed his head.

Lord give me the strength, the words, and wisdom for this prayer.

"Most Heavenly Father, we are gathered here tonight to celebrate Bo and Shelly's holy union. May they have a great life together, raise a family, and live out their lives together in peace and happiness. Fortunes are made and lost, but may they walk through their lives in good stead with your Book and find the joys, the pleasure, you have promised them. May they be blessed by Your Hand. Please take this lovely woman who works for them, Cary, and help her find her place in this world, a man who worships her, and a family of children to tend to her and bring her great pleasure in her life here on this earth.

"Lord, we ask that you be with Elizabeth. She yearns for a child. Please help us conceive one so she can become the mother she longs to be. Be with my extended family on the ranches and the Force, keep them in the palm of your hand away from harm and ones with evil in their hearts. Please be in all our hearts, as we ride through this trail we call life together. Amen."

Amen.

CHAPTER 12

Back at the ranch, and two days later, the snow was gone and Clayton, in town, awaited the grand jury's decision. Chet sat on the porch, drumming his fingers, impatiently awaiting the outcome while he made plans for the upcoming trip south.

Liz came out the front door under a shawl. It was just cool enough to need one.

"Can we leave Friday instead?" he asked her.

"Well, I am not with child and my time has come. It would be more convenient to leave then."

"No problem. I'll have Jesus tell Cole he can stay two days longer. Nothing is that pressing."

"I'm so disappointed I can't have children. Others do it so easily and—" she sighed, dashing tears from her eyes. "Oh, I don't want to dwell on the subject."

"We had two shotgun weddings this week and I know you are feeling sad that you still aren't that way, but it does not matter to me." He swept her in his arms and kissed her hard. "I still love you, and I always will. Is breakfast ready?"

"Yes. Monica sent me to get you."
"Let's eat."

Luggage and saddles loaded and secured, Chet and Elizabeth, followed by Cole and Jesus, climbed on the Black Canyon Stage for Hayden's Mill and Ferry. It was just after midnight Friday morning, and so cold that they had to wrap themselves in blankets to keep from freezing. In two days they would be in Tucson, and then on to the Force headquarters at Tubac.

His law enforcement business on the border had trickled down over the past few months. His man Shawn, though, had been keeping the records and filing all the necessary reports to continue their funding. Chet was pleased with the young man's efforts. He was a damn fine deputy, a steady man who, with his buddy Roamer, had helped Chet back when he'd had to fight to get the Verde Ranch away from the crooked foreman.

By dawn the air had heated enough down in the *saguaro* desert, they didn't need the blankets anymore. By noon, they'd stopped to switch coaches at Papago Wells for the final leg into Tucson. They caught a quick lunch and climbed on board for the southbound trip. The stage driver delivered them at the Morales Ranch gate south of Tubac after midnight.

Bronc's wife, Consuela, was still awake, and rushed out the door to hug Liz. She welcomed them and reported that the men of the Force were all gone running down some bandits near Tombstone. She showed them to the hammocks that had been strung behind the house for them, and they were soon asleep, exhausted from the trip.

Sunup came early and they awoke to the delicious

aroma of Consuela making coffee and breakfast. Her sister-in-law, Ricky, was helping.

"They left two days ago to check on some reports of armed robberies on the border," she told him, stirring some gravy. "I don't expect them back for some time. It has been very quiet down here lately."

"I know," Chet replied, gnawing on a biscuit. "That's why we're here."

"*Sí.* And we appreciate how you have helped us. We're really growing as ranchers. We sold several steers and replaced them with cows so we could grow more. Your operation made it all possible."

"We may ride over to Diablo tomorrow, then."

"I could go with you," she offered.

"Nah." He waved her off. "We know the way."

"Tell everyone hello and how much we miss them."

After the meal, they saddled their horses to head over the mountain to visit JD, Bonnie, and the rest. They rode out with the sun and crossed the steep grades to descend into the wide-open desert beyond after mid-day. With a few hours left to ride they gnawed on some jerky for their noon repast.

When the ranch finally came into sight, Liz looked at him and smiled.

"I was so happy to sleep at that ranch last night. There are so many good memories for me back there."

"Maybe I should have washed your feet."

She laughed. "You may joke about it, but you doing that made me think about Jesus doing that to his apostles."

"I'm so glad you did. I just wanted to impress you. I had the same fear that our time was too short and I didn't want to lose you if I could prevent it."

"My boldness embarrassed me. But somehow I needed

to impress you or my life would never have been settled. I knew that. No man had ever turned my head until that day. Then I fell like a ton of adobe bricks and lost my senses."

Cole reined in next to them. "Both of us were as impressed, that day, by you as the boss was."

Jesus laughed. "Maybe more. I thought you were a princess."

"Well, it sure turned my life upside down."

Chet nodded in deep thought. "No, you make my days much easier. You going along with us looking for that lost herd. To arrest criminals. My whole life changed."

"I agree. We have a wonderful life together, and nothing will take it away."

He reached out to hold her hand. "Nothing."

When they reined up at Diablo, Bonnie came running from the ranch house. "You finally made it! Maria, go ring the bell. JD'll bust his buttons to get here."

All the workers' wives and children hurried to see what the fuss was about.

"The *patron* is here! The *patron*!"

Dismounting, Chet shook his head at the girl's excitement. "We just came by to see all of you."

She hooked his arm. "Come see our showers." She led him over and from outside the slotted floor she pulled the rope, watching the water cascade from above. "We have several of them. And wait until you see the alfalfa and the orchards we've planted. These people have worked so hard." She hugged him tight. "There's a new one in my belly, too. I am so happy down here, I can hardly tell you. I dreaded coming down here at first, but we've had no time to feel sorry for ourselves. These people are so friendly. They're my family now. The first baby walks, and now another one is on the way. I still remember thinking my life was over when they started to take me to Mexico City—you gave them your horses for me." At that point she fell in his arms crying. "I hope I can repay you someday. I'm so lucky to be alive and here."

He nodded and patted her. If there was one member of the entire crew that ever concerned him—Bonnie had been the one.

"Don't cry, sweetie. We're here with you. I am so pleased you and JD have such a great life here."

She almost swooned. "I am truly in heaven. Truly."

Liz came up beside them and took Bonnie's hands. "I know what you feel. I have that same feeling. I know from your confession how much you appreciate him. But if he hadn't given those horses to that man, I'd have never met him. I met him to buy some of them at the Morales Ranch on my way back to Mexico."

"I know. And you still ride with him, don't you?"

Liz smiled. "I do."

Bonnie wiped her eyes. "I'm making a fool out of myself. Chet, the men will put up your horses. All of you come to the *casa*—I mean house, and get rested."

The two women were lost in their conversation as Chet and the boys followed them inside. He smiled after them, and looked out across the acreage. Three windmills were whirling in the warm breezes out of Mexico, and they had plenty of water stored in tanks, as well. Obviously, they were watering the short orchard plants like citrus and grapes. The place was impressive.

What would all those doubters about JD's ability think if they saw this place and all that these people had done? It was a miracle in the desert.

They were brought much food and many cool drinks.

The baby was the center of attention and they passed him back and forth. Cole and Jesus excused themselves to walk the ranch, see all the developments themselves. While they did that, Chet looked over the ranch books. Development was not cheap, but he knew what they were spending now would come back to them in the near future.

JD and Ortega arrived that afternoon, to many hugs and much talk. It was good to see both men. They looked slimmer than he recalled them the last time, but no doubt they had been working hard.

"Chet, wait till you see those Mexican steers we bought six months ago."

Ortega added, "They sure are pretty. They've done real good on the ranch."

"Now where can we sell them?" Chet asked.

JD looked over at his partner. "We can sell some in Tucson. We checked on some markets that want some good meat. Old man Clanton's still been bringing them some sorry beef."

"How many can you sell a month?"

"Fifty."

"That isn't enough. Where else can we sell them?"

"Clanton has the army and reservation contracts tied up."

Chet drew a deep breath. "I know that. But if we're going to make money, we need markets."

"Well, we'll try to find more places that need beef. You got any ideas?"

"There's lots of mining going on up at Globe and that area," he suggested. "They may need beef."

"One of us will ride up there and see what we can learn."

"Fellas, I am not down on you. We just need something

like the Navajo contract we've got for the Verde Ranch until the railroad rolls in."

JD hung his head. "We're trying, boss."

"I know you are. There's market out there. Finding it'll be tough because you have lots of beef producers competing with you. Clanton buys local cattle at a great discount when he can't steal them in Mexico."

Bonnie came and whispered in his ear. "Can we have a party?"

"Hey, any time you want one."

"We started, but I decided since you were here, I'd better get your approval."

He turned back. "They want a party. I said hell, yes."

They laughed.

"We'll find a market," JD promised. "The Tucson supply should take more than fifty when people learn we have fleshy cattle."

"That's six hundred a year."

"Yeah, Chet, but my pencil says we need three times that to make a profit."

Chet nodded. "I like your pencil."

Ortega's Maria came by with some *soapayas* and honey. "I have a treat."

"Wonderful," Chet said. "How are things going over here?"

"Oh, much better since I am home. Was it alright over at Tubac?"

"Oh, yes, but we missed you."

She blushed. "I am where I belong. But I worried those girls would not do all of it right."

"No worry, they treated us like royalty."

"Your wife is still the prettiest woman I know."

"Thank you. She still recalls the day she came there and I washed her feet."

Maria laughed. "That was some day."

"Very good. This is great," he said, his mouth full.

Everyone toasted her as she left. She looked pleased to be with her husband at last and helping Bonnie. In his mind she was a special woman with all she did for the Force. He'd always appreciated her.

He and JD spent a day by themselves checking on things from the saddle. They left out early and saw lots—range conditions, water development. The alfalfa field at the artesian well was spectacular, and fenced with stake and wire fencing.

"Bonnie did the figuring, but it amounts to fifty-two acres."

Chet smiled. "Hampt tell you how?"

"May did," JD replied with a sly grin of his own. "In a letter. He told her what to write. Really worked, too."

"May's about to have another baby."

"She's real happy. She never hardly said anything back in Texas. Those stepsons had her treed. You had to scold them."

"I recall that well. I think Ty's about to go off to college."

JD shook his head. "That would be something. An educated Byrnes, huh?"

"Wouldn't hurt none."

That bright green patch of alfalfa impressed Chet. It showed what they could do out here, and how much of an effort JD had made to make the place work. They rode on talking about things.

"These people appreciate all we've done. No one's raping their wives and they get paid regular. We expanded their houses. Bonnie and Marie teach school to the children three days a week. They treasure the orchards and gardens they keep now. Only one thing bothers me . . ."

Chet reined up his horse. "What's that?"

"Well, Ortega and I caught three men and a boy herding a dozen cattle for Mexico. They were rustlers. We caught them close to the border, then rode ten miles, I bet, to find a tree big enough to hang them from. I remember when the three of us hung those horse thieves up near the Red River. They were the same stamp as them. That boy would have grown up to be one, too. But—" he shook his head. "I see him in my dreams, Chet."

Chet nodded. "Being judge, jury, and executioner is a tough job. When those guys killed Marge's foreman and his right-hand man, then raped a nice lady, I ran them down over at Rye and hung 'em. Some onlooker wrote it down in a newspaper. Didn't have my name on it but might as well. Everyone knew it was me.

"Cole said he came looking for work with the man who done that. But lots of folks hated me for it. You simply have to believe it was necessary."

"You ever think if we hadn't hung those boys, it would have prevented the feud at home in Texas?"

"No. That fight was inevitable. We were progressing. Living beside us, they couldn't stand that."

"You mean if we hadn't done it, we'd still have had a war?"

Chet nodded. "I believe that. I do. A conscience is a good thing, JD. But sometimes it's also a burden we must bear."

"I'm learning that. Don't get me wrong. Bonnie and I get on our knees before we go to bed every night and pray to God. We were both headed for a bad wreck, but our faith let us get beyond it . . ." JD held his arms out wide. "And made all this happen."

Chet thought he might cry. He rode a good distance before he dared talk again.

"Chet, I didn't mean to upset you. I wanted to tell you how far the two of us have come—thanks to you."

"It shows the power of God. I'm just so glad you told me all this. You and Bonnie have found a special power. Keep your faith and her, too. I can see you have used all your mental and physical ability to not only make your lives better, but this ranch stronger."

Thanks, Lord . . .

CHAPTER 13

JD and Bonnie insisted they take two ranchmen with them to Mexico. Paulo and Cisco Salinas were brothers, and JD considered them two of his best men.

Chet learned Paulo, the older of the two, had a wife and family on the ranch. Cisco, on the other hand, was a bachelor in his early twenties. Both men were pleased to be chosen to ride along and help protect the *patron*.

"They're very polite," Liz commented when they were alone.

Chet agreed. "It won't hurt to have them. They know the lay of the land."

Two days later, they left the Diablo Ranch for Mexico and Liz's own *hacienda*. The visit left Chet with a good feeling in his heart. His nephew had grown up, and his life with Bonnie looked like a very mature situation—something that had bothered him in the past now appeared settled. Their project was growing, and they would find a beef market soon, he was certain. Orchards took a long time to flourish, but when they finally reached maturity, they produced for years. He'd sleep easier in the future about the desert place. They'd conquered a big part of it.

The sky was a deep, clear blue as the six of them and their pack train rode out for Mexico. Chet knew his wife was excited to be going home. She gave up a lot to become his wife. While she never complained, he realized this trip had been long overdue. He'd spent more time chasing down outlaws and kidnappers below the border than he had in social events. But for his part, this trip was purely social. Elizabeth wanted to show him off.

The first night out south of the border, they stayed with a ranch family Elizabeth knew from her time here. The Valdez family was very warm and friendly, and excited to at last meet the man she'd married. With playful grins, they accused her of hiding him to keep him all to herself. Liz blushed and took him by the arm into the dining room to eat. Over dinner, the eldest daughter, Crystal, asked about the blond-headed cowboy riding with them.

Chet told her that was Cole, but he was married. She wrinkled her nose but thanked him for the information.

"But, Crystal, there are two single men out there. Jesus and Cisco. I can introduce them to you, if you like."

She shook her head and everyone laughed at her expense.

"No, thank you, señor. But he is a very nice-looking man."

Chet and Elizabeth traded a knowing glance. "He is that," Liz agreed.

"Have they been with you long, señor?" the mother, Elaina, asked. "Your men?"

"Oh, yes. For several years now. Jesus Martinez came first. He's a good tracker and a very dependable young man. Cole came a few years later. He has a quick mind and is a great bodyguard as well. Both men will be foremen for me someday. The other two work for my nephew on the big ranch we have south of Tucson. He wanted us to be safe while we're in Mexico."

"It is a good idea these days. We are so glad you stopped. We had heard about you before, and knew that Elizabeth had married you."

"Elaina, that was the best thing I have ever done, too," Liz said.

"My dear, I could tell when I saw your face in the yard. You're happier than I've ever seen you."

"If you knew all the places he's taken me, you would be amazed. As a girl I read about the Spanish explorers like Cortez who explored the lower United States. In the past two years, I have seen those places he called a great sea of grass. They're wondrous, too. We even have a ranch near the Grand Canyon. He's made me a road tramp and I love it."

"You have no fears, then, of running off the edge of the earth?" the woman teased her.

"That would be at the Grand Canyon. It's so deep you cannot believe it."

"You always were adventurous. Did you know when you first met him you would go to such places together?"

"That I would go to those places?" Liz shook her head. "No. But I saw right off he had patience for me. He has more patience than any man I ever met."

"Do you grow weary of the travel?"

"Never. We live a very exciting life. You know in the United States he is a lawman. Only a few weeks ago we went and arrested a powerful man who killed someone, and no one would arrest him."

"Are there shootings?"

"Sometimes. They make me stay back and hold the horses. But I don't miss much of it."

Elaina acted like she could not believe that. "Most women want to live at home and be pampered."

"But, Mother, think of the excitement she has," Crystal said. "I envy her."

"My dear, she told you what to look for—a man with patience for you."

"How long will you stay at your home in Mexico?" the father asked.

"Better ask him. He plans these trips," Liz said with a smile.

Chet took the safe way out. "As long as she feels she needs to stay."

"There, Alejandro," Elaina said. "See why they have so much fun?"

"My dear, he must have good help. My help would ruin this place if I was gone very long."

"Alejandro, he has a good foreman," Liz said. "A great Mexican man who runs his wife's home place, the ranch where we live. The help there is all Hispanic. They have been since her father built the place. I can't tell you how good they are at watching out for our safety, and the safety of the ranch. They consider it and the family their responsibility."

"Raphael is a very intelligent man," Chet agreed. "He doesn't have a great education, but he knows people and how to manage them. We can do the paperwork. Last year, he figured out how to irrigate maybe ten acres, and grew enough *frijoles* for all my ranches and the church's efforts to feed the poor."

"Maybe you can help me," Alejandro said. "I have to tell them every day what to do."

"You find a man, give him the authority to ramrod the place, tell him what you want done and when. Then give him the authority to have some *fiestas,* too. You have the right man and he will build your force. The wrong man, you lose."

Alejandro nodded. "I am going to try your system."

His family applauded.

"Be sure you don't let little things they do wrong become elephants in your garden, though."

Alejandro laughed. "I saw one of those in Mexico City. I think I know what you mean."

They turned in early so as to be ready to leave at dawn. In bed that night, Liz told him, "I think you put him onto a way for him to have more free time."

"Only if he uses it right."

In the luxury of the great feather bed, they made love. Before he shut his eyes, Chet promised himself they'd have a bed like this one at both the Preskitt and the Verde Ranch to sleep in from now on.

Two more days they rode, with no more delay than waiting for a herd of sheep to pass or getting a firewood-laden pack train of burros aside enough to go by. Finally, in the afternoon of the second day, they reached the old *hacienda.*

Elizabeth's brother-in-law, Manuel Carmel, and his bride Rickola were waiting for them, having received a letter she'd sent before they left the Verde house.

Rickola was a sparkling, dark-eyed girl he'd met before, but had somehow forgotten how lovely she was. Maybe marriage had brought it out of her. Liz had looked better to him after they married than she had before.

His mind went back to Bonnie, another woman who had blossomed in marriage. Marge had done the same thing—

That brought him up short. He'd not thought about Marge in ages. Flying over those high jumps—such a shame—her death came so quick.

But the good Lord had found him Liz, and she'd filled the vacancy in his heart very well.

He thought now, too, of Adam. How was he doing at the lower ranch? He'd bet Rhea and Victor both were spoiling him rotten. By this time in their marriage, Marge had been pregnant with him. That weighed on poor Liz, and on him, too. More than he wanted to admit, actually.

With these thoughts still flowing through his head, Chet followed their hosts into the house to eat. The *hacienda* crew put up the horses and later brought their luggage in.

As they prepared to eat, Manuel filled Elizabeth in on the family wine business and how good it was going. They had the recent crop well on its way to becoming wine already. Liz listened intently, and thanked him for the business reports he mailed her.

Rickola stood at the meal with a glass of wine to announce that in the summer, she and Manuel would have a child. Everyone cheered.

Chet knew the news would be like a knife in the gut to his wife, especially if her thoughts were going anywhere like his just then. There was nothing he could do, though. Somehow he had to get her over it—but that would be difficult . . . unless he could convince her that not being able to have a baby meant nothing to their relationship or how much he loved her.

Tough business in his life—their life. He'd work harder on her about dismissing it.

After the meal, Manuel took him on a tour of the *hacienda* from horseback so they could talk, man-to-man.

"Is there any way you can talk her into selling me this place?" he asked as they rode through the well-kept vineyards and orchards.

Chet scratched his chin, thinking. "Have you asked her if she would?"

"No. I have no claim on this place. My brother built it before he found her. I was going to college and being, shall we say, a playboy at his expense. Things that Fernando never got to do because he was too busy building this *hacienda*. He finally had the money to do anything he wanted. So he went and found her. Really he kidnapped her, then took her home, married her on the way, and consummated the whole thing that night."

Chet smiled tightly. "I heard that story from her side. He must've been a powerful man."

Manuel nodded. "That is what got him killed at the door, I believe. He had no fear, and they knew that. They shot him down when he opened the door. But they thought this pampered, rich man's wife would be easy prey. She wasn't. And so she gunned *them* down. It was a bloody mess. It took me three days to get up here. There was still blood all over. The people who worked for my brother were so shocked—like God had died on them.

"But Elizabeth soon had them back to working. I helped her. I never thought she would find another man, though. Some sorry ones came by. And some rich, powerful ones, as well. They wanted her, but she shook her head at them and sent them packing." He smiled. "Next thing I knew, she came home babbling about golden horses and the man who washed her feet in sparkling sunlight on the banks of the Santa Cruz. I had seen the golden horses at the *hacienda* she spoke of. But she talked about this *hombre* who stood ten foot tall and was *so nice*. I knew then unless you didn't want her, she was yours."

Chet reined up his horse in the shade of some great gnarled cottonwoods. "She wanted to go riding. I had no palomino horses there. It was just a ranch we used for headquarters for my men on the Force down there."

"She said that disappointed her," Manuel agreed. "All that talk about such a powerful force, and you had hammocks and canvas tents for offices."

"We were chasing bandits," Chet said simply. "All we needed was a base to work out of. Anyway, we went riding. There were some wonderful reflections filtering down through those big trees and she asked to go wading. I was pleased to sit and watch this beautiful woman who fascinated me kick water up. I had a million questions I wanted to ask her but didn't dare to for fear I might spook her. I knew she was a widow, and I could tell how special she was. When she finally had enough wading, I got a towel out of my saddlebags and dried her feet just to touch her. Nothing was on my mind about Jesus or the apostles when I did it. I knew the story, but it never entered my mind until she told me later."

They both laughed.

"She came home and told me her story. I didn't know, but I suspected she must have sampled you. That worried her. She confided in me that you might think she was a loose woman." Manuel shook his head. "But when your letters came, she immediately began making plans for me to run the *hacienda*. I knew then I had to shape up and learn it all. Her mind, her body, and all the rest of her would soon belong to this big *hombre* in Arizona. She really was upset about joining you at Tubac, though. She was too proud. If she had not been a widow for so long, it might have been easier for her to think I will go to him."

"I was shocked," Chet admitted. "But I agree. She had convinced herself to be the martyred widow."

Manuel disagreed. "Those suitors came to run her *hacienda*. They told her a woman could not possibly do so. That made her mad as hell. 'Oh, I can run this place much more efficient than you are, marry me.' Not a one came and courted her like a man would have. It was you who did that. You never even asked about her business down here. You wanted her as a person and a wife."

"When she climbed out of that stage, I was in a fairy tale I once read. We fit so well as a man and woman. I never considered her consent as any more than a gift she gave to me alone." Chet got choked up, remembering. "I helped her bathe that day. She wanted me to see her and what she really looked like. My heart has to be strong, or it would have busted then and there. We made love that night in a haystack. I'm never around the smell of hay anymore that I don't think about that night with her. She did that on purpose. And she wears cinnamon, too. She denies doing it, but I know better."

He agreed. "Help me if you can, please, Chet. I would like to own this place for my children. If she ever has a child, you have plenty to provide them."

"Yes, I do, thank the Good Lord."

"I love your story. I met my wife at a festival. Her aunts

chaperoned her. Of course, I do not have my brother's force, and I did not attempt to steal her. But she and I had fun playing the proper way and she is mine now. She is not Elizabeth, but she is a good, dedicated woman, and all I could ask."

"Beautiful lady. But she's not a snob. That's one of Liz's best traits, too. She can talk to anyone and they accept her open heart."

"I have been blessed. Running this *hacienda* has been a challenge, but now I feel I am doing the right things and making it work. Remember, before you took her I was just the playboy who had few responsibilities. After his funeral, I began to learn the business and settle down. That was good for me. But I knew when she went to meet you that I had lost my boss and I was the one in charge—she wasn't coming back."

"Only to see you and wish you and your wife a good life."

He and Liz talked that night in bed. She agreed he needed something for his family to inherit and would consider selling.

"I want you to know something," he whispered. "You're not having a child is not stressing me. I love our life and I love you. Don't you worry one more minute about that."

"I won't. I love you, big *hombre*. And I always will."

He was finding a goose down bed when they got home for sure.

CHAPTER 14

Mexico was a quiet time for them. They rode back to Nogales in three days without a single incident. The morning they boarded the stage, he shocked Paulo and Cisco by paying the brothers twenty dollars apiece for their services. They shook hands in parting and headed back for Rancho Diablo with the ranch horses they'd borrowed for the trip south. He sent a thank-you note to JD and Bonnie with them, as well.

His Force had come back in while they were in Mexico and went out again to look for stage robbers. He left them a note, too, telling them to wire him if they had any trouble.

A sharp wind whipped up the desert dirt, and it was a sharp cold day for that far south as the stage clattered across the dusty landscape. There was no letup in the chill at Hayden's Mill and Ferry, when they changed back over to the Black Canyon Stage for Preskitt.

"It'll be good to get home," Liz said, wrapped in her blanket.

"I may become a bear and hibernate till spring," Chet told her. She laughed.

"Cold as it is here, it won't be any warmer up the hill," Cole put in.

"I know! That's why I wanted to be a bear," Chet said with a chuckle.

The trip went through the night and on into the cold pre-dawn. Two ranch buckboards met them at the stage stop east of town—one to take Cole to his house in Preskitt, the other to take Jesus, Liz, and Chet to the ranch in the valley. By the time they got home it was spitting snow, and Monica welcomed them to the house with food and coffee.

"Any problems arrive while I was gone?" Chet asked. Sure as the wind howled, she handed over a stack of letters. Opening them one at a time with his jackknife, he read them under the lamp over the table. Every time he looked up from a letter, the snow outside had increased. The wind began to batter the house in waves.

> *Dear Chet Byrnes,*
>
> *I am sad to announce that my mother Kathren died a few weeks ago. The doctor said she had pneumonia. We were all shocked because she was always so strong. I was recently married to Tom Acuff, and I still have my grandmother to care for. But I know you would never know and she would not ever write and tell you, but my mother conceived a son with you before you left for Arizona. We all know, but she swore us to secrecy. He is now going on four. Tom and I would gladly*

*keep him and raise him as our son, but I felt since
he is your progeny, you might want to raise him.*

*Please let me know your desires. I know this is
a big shock to you. I also know why Mother never
told you. She knew you had a life to live out there
and this boy was her memory of the love you two
shared. He can grow up in our house or yours.
I wanted to offer your son to you if you feel you
want him. Now I won't say I won't cry if you
claim him. May God be with you, sir.*

Cady Hines Acuff

"You look upset," Liz said, seeing his face. "What's
that letter about?"

"Oh, my." Chet struggled to find words. "I'm thinking
how to start to tell you the entire story. There . . ." he
sighed. "There was a woman in Texas I was very close to
before I came out here. Her name was Kathren. When I
had to move the family, her father had a heart condition
that she felt he couldn't stand the trip. I even warned
Marge that if she'd come out here, I was obligated to
her. Kathren had a teenage daughter then named Cady.
She wrote this letter. Her mother had a son by me after
we left Texas that she's kept secret all this time. But
Kathren died of pneumonia, and Cady has offered me my
other son."

"What's his name?" Liz asked.

"I'm sorry, she just says a four-year-old boy that's
mine."

"Can we go get him?"

"We can do anything we need to do. I can tell by this

letter it'll break her heart if I take him, but yes." Chet nodded, tears in his eyes. "I want him."

"Oh, Chet, I want him, too. I know he might make me stay at home, but he's your son."

"Oh, I don't doubt that and knowing her—" he swiped at his eyes. "She knew before I left he was inside her. Like her daughter said, it was her piece of me and she held on to him."

She was up and hugged his neck. "I am so sorry, Chet. This must tear your heart out. But just think! You have two sons now."

"You're right, though. Let me think on it. I want him here. If his mother was alive I would leave him be there with her. She was a great lady. And even greater than I imagined keeping that secret from me."

"She loved you," Liz said quietly.

"Yes, she did, despite our stormy times. Big story to tell you when I am not so challenged by this new fact and what to do about it."

He kissed her and she went back and sat down. With shaking hands, he opened the second letter.

Dear Chet Byrnes,

My name is Albert Hannagen. I am trying to establish a stage line on the Marcy Road from Gallup to a stop on the Colorado River. There is a stage line from that point to the coast in operation, but none beyond. However, due to outlaws and other problems, I am having trouble establishing stage stops, feed, and the rest to go with this development. I have been told you own property all over Arizona territory and enforce the law, as well.

When and where could we meet? There are some lucrative mail contracts available for this operation. I am prepared to offer you a share if we can get this operation under way in nine months.

Sincerely yours,
Albert Hannagen

"Who's that one from?" Monica asked, refilling his coffee.

"I guess my new partner."

"Doing what?" Liz asked.

"Building a stage line from Gallup to the Colorado River on the Marcy Road."

"Well, if the railroad won't come it would be a good idea," Monica said.

"What are you thinking about now?" Liz asked.

"Who'll head up that operation for me. But first I need to send him on another project."

The two women traded confused glances. "What are you talking about?" Liz asked.

"When this snow lets up, I'm going to send Cole and his wife to get my boy. When they get back, I may be a partner in the stage line business, and if so, Cole will be my point man."

"I think it's a much better idea to send those two after him."

He stood up and studied the blizzard swirling outside the window. His wife joined him.

"Cole comes from Texas, but no one back there knows he works for me. He can go in there, get the boy quietly, and come right back. He's the best man to do that for me.

Plus, his wife will get to see some country she's never seen and help him care for the boy."

"Who will raise him?"

"That we'll have to see about. But you, my lady, as long as you're not housebound by a child, ride with me."

"I would raise him, but you're right, I love traveling with you and want to continue doing so."

What in God's name would he do without her? He hoped he would never have to do that.

CHAPTER 15

The snow piled up deep before it quit, and the drifts were tall. All Chet could think about was the water going into the good earth, the snow melting from beneath because the ground was still warm. As soon as the road was passable again, he would send Jesus with a buckboard to go get Cole and the mail. Monica wrote out a long list of things she wanted as well, and warned Jesus not to return until he had it all.

While he waited, Chet wrote a letter to Cady that he was coming or sending a responsible party to bring his son out to Arizona. He thanked her sincerely for her honesty and goodwill, and told her how anxious he was to see his son.

After sealing that letter, he wrote another. This one was for Mr. Hannagen, the stage tycoon. Chet gave his compliments and offered to meet the man at the Windmill Ranch when things cleared up some and he could spare the time. Hannagen could wire Chet at Preskitt when he was on his way.

Then he wrote one more letter, to Susie, about his new

son. She and Kathren had been close when they were in Texas, but he doubted she knew about the boy, either.

He put all three envelopes into the ranch mailbag. That steep mountain road was not open yet, so the mail would have to wait to go out. He'd bet the snowfall from this storm had beaten all the past weather records by a mile.

Later that day, Raphael reported that the road to town was open. Instead of sending Jesus, Chet and Liz decided to go themselves. The next day they drove into town huddled together against the cold. They found Cole at the café, and his man looked shocked to see the two of them in town.

"Something wrong?" the young man asked. "You look very . . . business-like."

"Several things," Chet said, dead serious. "Let's find someplace and talk while the women visit."

They slid in an empty booth and the girl working brought them cups of steaming coffee. Chet shed his wool-lined jacket and loosened his collar.

"So what's going on, boss?" Cole asked, his face neutral.

"I got a shock when we made it back from Mexico. Turns out I have a son back in Texas I was never told about. He's four now. His mother and I were deeply engaged in a romance and I would have married her, but she couldn't move out here because of her father's ailing heart. Now she's dead. Obviously, she must have been with child when I kissed her good-bye, but she kept it all a secret. She had a teenage daughter who wrote to tell me about him. Offered me the option to come get him or she would raise him."

"What are you going to do?"

"I'd like you and Valerie to go to Texas and get him,"

Chet said flatly. "Liz is concerned that the Reynolds, that crazy gang that was the cause of us moving here, might make an attempt on my life if I go back. I'm not afraid, obviously, except for the idea of that young boy getting hurt. No one back there knows you as my man, so you should be able to get in and bring him out here with no one the wiser."

"Valerie's back in the kitchen," Cole said, standing up. "Let me get her. I'm certain she'll go, but you need to be the one to explain all this to her. What's his name?"

Chet spread his hands wide. "I don't know. She never told me in the letter. Like she expected me to know or something."

The younger man shook his head. "I'll be right back."

Pretty as ever, Valerie slid in across from him a moment later, with a dollop of pastry icing for him to taste off her finger. "Cole says you've got a job for us."

He took a deep breath and repeated the story for her. By the end of his description, her eyebrows had come together in confusion. "Why didn't she ever tell you?"

"All I can think was she wanted a piece of our affair to keep with her after I left."

Valerie nodded slowly, like she agreed. "I think you knew her better than any of us and probably have the right idea. If Cole left me, I might do the same thing."

"Darling," Cole said. "I'm not ever leaving you."

"You better not," she said threateningly. Then she laughed. "When should we go get him?"

"Can Jenn spare you?"

"I'm sure she can. And she'll want to see this little guy as badly as we do."

"Will Rhea raise him, too?" Cole asked.

Chet looked hard at them. "I know you two are having your own soon, but I wondered if—"

She turned pale. "Oh, Cole we want him."

"Oh, hell yes. We'd be honored to raise him."

"Okay," Chet continued, holding back tears at the depth of the love he felt for these two lovely people. "Part two. A man wants to start a stage line across the northern end of the territory from Gallup to the Grant Ferry on the Colorado River on the Marcy Road. He says he wants it set up in nine months. That's near impossible, and you and I both know there are no towns hardly at all on that route. I'm guessing he'll need twenty stations, at least. I've not talked to him yet, but I would headquarter it at the head of the military road up at the base of the San Francisco Peaks. You know I have land up there, right?"

"Sounds like a good prospect as slow as the railroad's coming," Cole observed. "You'd have it right on their tracks."

"Exactly."

"Where do I fit?"

"If I can see how to make money at it," Chet said, "I want you to superintend it."

"Oh, my"—she clamped her hand over her mouth—"Cole, did you hear him?"

"I heard him, darling. Oh, I heard him good. Hell, Chet I really appreciate you even considering me for the job."

"I'm not just considering you. If I buy in, will you run it?"

Cole looked hard at his wife. She nodded frantically with her fists clenched tight.

"Damn straight, boss man."

Valerie jumped across the table and kissed Chet on the mouth, spilling coffee all over. "Chet Byrnes, I love you. You saved my life, and you've been so generous to the both of us. We're going to go get your boy—what's his name?"

He was laughing too hard to talk for a moment. "I love you, too, Val. But we'll just have to call him Junior until we find out. She never said it in her letter."

"What a mess I made," she said, scooting out of the booth. "I'll be right back."

"What's happened?" Liz asked, coming over with Jenn. She looked concerned.

"My wife just had a fit." Cole laughed, red faced.

"About the boy or the job?"

"Both."

Jenn shook her head. "And me losing my best help I suppose?"

"Tradition." Chet held up his hands in surrender. "I've been hiring your friends and help since I came to this place."

"Chet Byrnes, this place wouldn't be here if not for you. Liz also mentioned your new addition to the family. What are you getting into next?"

"Big secret. A stage line, if it will work."

"Can I buy stock in it?"

"Ask me later."

Valerie returned with a towel to clean up the mess, and Jenn poured fresh coffee for everyone. Val sat on her husband's lap; Liz moved in with Chet with Jenn on the other side.

Jenn covered Chet's hand on the table with her own. "I bet you must be all torn up about this."

A shrug. "It's been a long time. But if I'd even suspected she was pregnant—I'd have done something besides leave her to have him by herself."

"Oh, she knew good and well you had to leave Texas," Liz said. "She had one piece of you left inside her, and she wasn't going to blackmail you with it. That was her memory of what you two had together. I would've done the same thing."

Chet agreed. "Well, these two are going after him."

With the matter of going after his son settled, he went by Bo's office and they discussed the stage line and the stations they'd need if it came to be.

"When you're ready, we can make the trips," Bo told him. "Choose the sites and make the land deals."

"How's your life at home now?" Chet asked.

"Oh, a damn sight better, Chet. We should have done that a year ago, thanks. Good luck on arranging this deal. It sounds like a moneymaker to me."

Chet put his hat back on. "We'll see."

"So now you need to meet this Hannagen, right?" Liz asked when he came out to get on the buckboard.

"I'm having Tanner at the bank check him out first. I don't want an under-the-table card shuffle deal pulled on me."

"I always wonder about how you think. Two letters came in the mail. One about a boy you didn't know about, the other a big business proposal. Twenty-four hours later, it's all sorted out and you're ready for the next event. That's decisive. Isn't that the English word?"

"Yep. In Spanish I think you say, *decisivo*?"

"Yes, that's the word." She hugged his arm. They were headed home between the snow piled on both sides of the road. The ground under the horses' hooves and iron rims of the buckboard was melted and a little muddy.

"And you are the definition of that word." She paused. "Can I ask you a question?"

"About her?" It was obvious from her voice.

"Yes."

"We went to school together, but I never caught her eye. I was pretty wild in those days, so I know why not. She married a man much older than her. They had one child—that girl, Cady. One day he left her, and along with some of the Reynolds, stole my *remuda*. Reg and JD were boys then. We needed those horses for our cattle drive. The three of us went after them. We caught them this side of the Red River, hung them all, and brought our horses home. It was hard on those boys to lynch them. They went to school with some of them. Their mothers said it was just a joke, that they weren't really stealing them. But you don't drive horses hard for over a hundred fifty miles for a joke."

"No. They meant to steal them."

"I told the boys not to say a word. They didn't. But somehow the Reynolds found out and had their bodies brought back for burial. That probably really put fire under the feud. Kathren's husband's still buried up there, though.

"When she and I got together later, she told me he left her with the ranch and his daughter. He told her, that day, that he wasn't coming back. She never said why. Perhaps she didn't know. I think he had a problem and he couldn't make love to her—but why else leave a beautiful woman and your own daughter with a working ranch?"

"I see," Liz said thoughtfully. "And she was the one you originally wanted and did not get with her until then."

"Exactly. But things in Texas were going from bad to worse. A bushwhacker even shot me at her house."

"Your time in Texas was growing shorter."

"Yes. I came out here. I brought Heck along, my nephew. He was one of May's stepsons and those young boys had her treed. I told the younger ones to get along better with her, or else. Then I packed him up to bring along out here."

"Those two boys play piano with her now."

"Yeah, things have changed. One's going to college for her, too, in a few years." He shifted his grip on the reins. "The stage was robbed south of here. They took Heck as a hostage. I took a rifle and a coach horse and chased them down up in the Bradshaw Mountains. When I finally caught them, the boy wasn't with them. I made them tell me what they did with him. They'd cut his throat and threw him off in a canyon. I—I lost control. I killed them," he whispered. "Every one. Then I went back to look for him. Found his bloody body deep in a canyon, and carried him up to the road in my arms."

"Oh, my God."

"Marge arrived in a buggy to help. She saved my life, Liz. I was so unstable mentally . . . she really did save me in the days afterward. But we never did anything. I was still obligated to Kathren. I came back to Texas in shock over my loss of that boy and then she couldn't come with us to Arizona. I left and came back here, to Marge's delight. Poor woman had a bad case on me, I guess."

"You do that to women in your life."

"Liz, you aren't upset, are you?" he asked suddenly. "About all this business happening?"

"Not at all. I have you. Our life is definitely not what I thought it would be. But it's always interesting—more so than my ballroom dancing with stiff shirts."

He stopped the team and kissed her. "We don't have to do much of that, thank God." With her still in his arms he kissed her some more.

And holding his treasure tight, he told himself, *You are the luckiest man in the world to even be alive.*

CHAPTER 16

On a cold night under the stars, with most of the snow gone, Chet sent Cole and Valerie off on the stage to find his little man and bring him home. Those two were still mad lovers. They'd make a honeymoon out of their trip. And he didn't begrudge them any of it.

"You'd think they'd just got married," Jesus said, laughing.

"Worse than Chet and I?" Liz asked him.

"Maybe not *that* bad," Chet teased as they mounted the buckboards to head back home. "Maybe we'll learn his name before they get back."

"Have you tried to guess it?" She hugged his arm as he drove home under the stars.

"Not really. There are so many things I've wondered about since I learned there was another son, but not that. Kathren and I could have been married, but her strong loyalty to her parents kept her from doing that. The tables had been turned on me and I flat could not have stayed."

"It really was a tragedy."

"It was. But the real tragedy in my family was back when the Comanche took my brothers and sister. They took a boy one summer and a year later a pair of twins, a boy and girl. My father went out to find him. He stayed out too long with no water and food, and some rangers found and brought him back, but he was never right mentally after that. That loss about killed my mother. It was a bad deal, but really nothing he or she could have done about it. At fifteen I was running the ranch on my own. We never heard a word about those kids. Lots of children were taken by the Comanche in those days. They said their women rode horses and lost babies and they needed replacements. There were some boys that escaped, and came home, then went back to the Comanche."

"Why would they do that?" she asked.

"The tribal men were warriors. The women did all the work. Back home, they had to work cotton and crops and hay. It was a damn site easier being an Indian male than all that work they found back at home."

"I'd never even dreamed of anything likc that," she said. "I guess this new boy is really your first son, then?"

"I guess he is. If he was a prince, he'd be in line for the king's job."

"Firstborns they say are the leaders. Look at you."

"Well, my poor younger brother never wanted to lead," Chet said with a shake of his head. "Bless his heart, it was hard to get him to do anything when it required him to make a decision. But he could sure bitch all day about how I did it."

She laughed. "That stage line is in your thoughts right now, isn't it?"

"I think since the railroad is coming so slow, it could make some money for us. Lot depends on Hannagen. He may not be all he says he is. Some guys talk a good game, but when it comes to putting up, they don't have anything."

"They have them in Mexico, too. But I like that you never hesitated offering Cole the job."

"Cole's not some common cowboy. What he does, he does well. He's not a braggart or a drunk. He can handle himself in tight places. He expects things of people and has a good way about him. And he can figure someone out in just a short conversation with them."

"I noticed all that, riding with you guys. You said on the first cattle drive he shot two Indians."

"One was attacking us, the other I took prisoner, gave him to Cole. He came back alone. The Apache drew a knife on him. I knew right there I had a good hand."

"Those two are like your sons after all this law and ranch business, aren't they?"

"Yes, they are."

"You have a replacement for him?"

"Not yet. But this deal hasn't gone through—yet."

She nuzzled against his shoulder when they drove in the yard. "Oh, it will. I know how you are."

"You know we need to work on Christmas. It won't be long away."

"I'll start tomorrow."

"Good. I'll work on the books some more."

"Any problems?"

"No, except it sure takes lots of damn money to run these places."

"Are we in a bind anywhere?" She stood as they pulled up in front of the ranch house.

"Not at all." He helped her down. "But it always pays to know what's going on."

Jesus pulled up behind and told Chet that he and the stable boy would put up the horses and he'd be at breakfast if he were needed.

"Better come eat with us."

"I'll be there. 'Night, you two."

Later in bed, she told him, "What a different turn your life would have taken if she had come here and married you. I've been thinking about it."

"I was sad about it, but she had to stay with her family, and I had to leave Texas to save mine."

"Oh, I know. But how different the fork in the road makes things."

"I am very pleased where it led me." He kissed and hugged her.

CHAPTER 17

A few telegrams later, Albert Jefferson Hannagen and three of his staff agreed to meet Chet at the Windmill Ranch in two weeks to discuss the stage line plan. Chet's principal business advisor, Bo Evans, was invited to join them. With the meeting set, Chet, Liz, and Jesus drove up there to talk to Susie about the meeting.

They stopped at the Verde Ranch on the way, partly to play with Adam, and partly to fill Rhea and Victor in about the boy in Texas. Tom and Millie ended up joining them, too.

Millie shook her head and said with a teasing smile, "They call that sowing wild oats, Chet."

He hugged her close. "I had high intentions of marrying her."

"Oh, I am only giving you guff. I was glad you came to Arizona in the first place. Tom'd lost his job and things were slim at our house. I can't believe she didn't use him for bait to get you back, though."

He shook his head. "Kathren wasn't like that. She was a very nice lady. I think she kept the secret to hold on to something of our affair. It was not an easy thing for us to part."

Millie hugged him back. "I am just so glad you came. Will Rhea raise him, too?"

"Cole and Valerie will do that. I sent them to collect him because nobody there knows he works for me. Rhea has her hands full, and I am sure she and Vic will have children of their own, too."

"More than anything," she said, "I want you and Elizabeth happy."

"We are," Chet assured her. "I am very lucky to have her."

And he meant it.

Later, he and Tom talked about Victor taking over the farming of the Verde Ranch.

"He's using my cowboys to reinforce all his fences while things are slack," Tom reported. "He has his own men rebuilding every mower and piece of farm machinery we own. We've talked about fencing some more ground that we can water. He also wants a new hay field up at the Hereford herd area. There's water enough up there for it. It would be a damn sight easier to feed them up there than haul hay, so I guess we'll build more fence."

"I'd say he was taking a hold."

"Oh, he's a new broom but I agree with what he wants to do. I didn't have the time for much more farming." He wiped his brow. "Say, what's this meeting up at Windmill all about?"

"A man named Hannagen wants to run a stage line from Gallup to the Colorado River on the Marcy Road where the train will run someday."

"That's a big deal, isn't it?"

"It could take as many as two dozen way stations,"

Chet replied. "Hay, grain, horses, people to staff them. An upkeep station and blacksmiths to rebuild coaches, wheels, and repair harness. Several horse handlers, drivers, and cooks. It'll be a big operation."

"Didn't a man named Butterfield do that before the war?"

"Yes. Made a run from Saint Louis to San Francisco."

"You going to be in his boots?" Tom asked.

"First, they have to prove to me they're authentic. But if we go into it, all of us may have to put some effort in to make it work. I think there's a mail contract involved."

"Whew. You think too big for me sometimes, boss."

"No, Tom." Chet shook his head. "Arizona needs lots of things to become a state—jobs, industry, and more people. And if a new stage line starts it, so much the better."

"Well good luck there, chief."

"Thanks. I may need lots of it."

"Millie said she teased you about this son?"

He laughed and waved it away. "She's a lovely woman and a good friend. I wasn't offended. I've gone over that whole case a hundred times out loud and in my mind. Kathren couldn't come with me, simple as that. She had him and wasn't going to share. I might have done the same thing. But I had no choice. I had to get my family out of Texas for them to survive."

Tom agreed. "Well, we're damn glad you came here."

"So am I. And we'll see about the stage business in just a few days."

They drove on to the Windmill the next day. With a big smile on her face, Susie ran out and hugged them all, coatless despite the freezing north wind.

"I want to hear more about the story behind this boy

without a name. I can't imagine she never wrote you anything. I knew you leaving tore her up. It did you, too. But not to ever say anything—" She shook her head.

"Sis, I don't know. But Cole and Valerie have gone to get him."

"I can't wait to see him. I want to write her daughter and tell her thank you, as well." She frowned for a moment, thinking. "But that's not why you're here."

"No. We've got another deal in the works."

"A stage line." She nodded. "You told me in your letter. Now who all is coming to this meeting here?"

"Three men, and probably some others will come with them. I'll be here with Bo and Jesus, and Cole, if he's back by then. We can bring some help if we need to. Lea can come over from the big house at Verde to help you with the cooking. You all can make a list of supplies you'll need while we're here. We may need the big tent set up down here, too."

"Must be serious," his sister said. "That's only a few weeks before Christmas."

"I think," he said, heading for the house and out of the wind, "there's a large mail contract in this plan that has to be completed by a certain date."

"Can we do that?"

"If we have to use a buckboard to haul the mail until we get the line running, we will."

Susie grinned at him slyly. "You've been thinking about this a lot."

"Maybe."

"And," Liz added, "his family is getting bigger."

"Oh, my, Liz. That was a shock. But I bet she knew she had his baby in her before we ever left. She had a rough life with her first husband. We all knew that, and I think she told Chet some about him. She did me, too. I loved her like a sister. Like I love you. My brother had finally found a woman. Then it all blew up."

"Well, we won't have much time to think about it," Liz said. "This conference is coming up fast, and so is Christmas."

"This was the closest place I could get them to come," Chet explained. "You and that boy of yours need some excitement up here once in a while. My banker says it all checks out, and they do have the money and credit they say they do. So we'll see if our operation can make money doing it. If we can't, he can do it himself. But since he contacted me, he must need some help."

"Where's Sarge?" Jesus asked.

"Gone to Gallup with the December herd delivery," Susie replied. "He should be on his way home shortly, though. Sure glad you built me a big house for this shindig of yours."

He hugged his sister. "So am I."

They got things all planned out and headed back to the Verde Ranch the next day. There was a cable from Cole waiting on him when he got home. He and Valerie were in San Antonio after taking the train from El Paso, and were planning on taking a mail wagon west from there to get the boy.

The next morning, Raphael had four men ready to take the tent to the Windmill, plus two wagons filled with cots, tables, benches, and cooking gear for a large crowd. Three of the *vaqueros* wives were planning to go along and do the cooking for the meeting. Chet had to smile when Liz took the trio to Preskitt and bought them clothing to wear—heavy coats, scarfs, and gloves.

She returned that afternoon to tell him and Monica

how proud they were. "None of them had enough clothes to wear against the cold. They will now."

Chet hugged her. "You did the right thing again."

"She always does the right thing," Monica agreed.

He saw her hands were empty, though. "No more wires from Cole?" he asked.

"None. He may just need to get back to where there are telegraph offices."

Chet nodded, but kept his own counsel. He distracted himself by tracing the proposed stage route and trying to recall where they might situate stops. Some might be operating ranches that could handle one. That would be convenient, but they would still need to be outfitted with stage stops, outhouse facilities, and places to stable the horses. The big thing up there was water. That would make a difference, too.

The days seemed to drag endlessly with no further word from Cole. Finally, Jesus came galloping into the yard one afternoon waving a yellow telegraph sheet. The boy's name was Rock Chet Byrnes—his father's name— and they were bringing him home. Cady sent her best. Liz was beside herself with joy, and Chet felt a weight lift from his heart.

The day they expected them to arrive, Cole rode in on a tired horse. He had a clear tintype of the boy, and looked weary. Chet thought he'd bust his buttons to be there on time.

"Did Cady tell you why her mother didn't tell me about him?" Chet asked when he'd managed to pull Cole away from the well-wishers.

"Best thing she said to us about it was 'My mother wanted that boy and intended to raise him herself.' She loved him, too, though, boss. It was hard for her to give him up, but she loved you, too," Cole said, the beginnings of a smile playing on his face. "She told Valerie if her mother had tossed you out back then, she'd planned to run away with you. Valerie told her that she'd have to get in line."

Chet laughed so hard he couldn't breathe for a while. "She was a sweet kid."

"Sweet on you, apparently." Cole's eyes sparkled with mischief. "Have I missed anything here?"

"Not really," he replied, still trying to catch his breath. "Got some mail outlining what they need for the stage line. They've got some ambitious plans, I'll tell you that. They look satisfactory about their banking and having money. We just need a deal good enough for us to get involved. Bo should get here today, and we'll head on up tomorrow. I figure we'll need a total of twenty stops on the route. Make our headquarters at the base of the San Francisco Peaks and the head of the military road off the rim. That's close to midway. What do you think?"

"We need a simple plan to build these stops, so that we know every board and nail we need to build them at each site. We'll need poles for corrals for the horses and a water supply." It was obvious the boy had been thinking on the problem while he'd been gone.

"Some won't be easy to have that," Chet told him.

"There's water somewhere. We'll drill some dry holes. And some we may have to haul water to. Horses need water, good hay, and grain to hurry along." Cole stretched. "That was a long way to go. It's good to be back."

"Nice to have you. Get ready to sit in and listen."

Cole looked shocked. "Do I need to wear a suit?"

"No, no. You don't need one. But I do want you to

make a note when you don't like anything said. You and I will have to live with what we accept."

Cole nodded. "I can do that."

"I'm counting on you."

They set off the next morning in their caravan to the Windmill three days before the planned meeting. Sarge, now back, and his crew teamed up with Raphael's outfit to set up the tents. Things shaped up fast after that.

Mid-afternoon, in the warmth of the day, the entourage arrived in three buggies and four outriders. Jesus had ridden out to meet them on the road and lead them to the ranch. When everybody had parked, a portly man in an expensive suit and top hat with glasses on his nose descended from the coach. He turned and stared around at the vast open country, surveying it.

"By damn, it looks like Kansas up here." He turned and strode across the yard toward them. "You must be Chet Byrnes, Deputy U.S. Marshal and a rancher worth his salt in this windswept wilderness. Your reputation precedes you."

Chet held out a hand and Hannagen took it. "Nice to meet you, sir. This is my man, Cole Emerson, and my real estate man, Bo Evans. Also, may I introduce my wife, Elizabeth, and my sister, Susie Polanski, who lives here."

"Glad to meet you all." Hannagen gave a little bow as he shook hands with each. "Allow me to introduce Gladstone Meyers, my attorney; Rodney Carpenter, my expert on stage lines; and Wade Nelson, my secretary."

"There's a meal set up in the tent and drinks if you would like something."

"I don't drink," the tycoon said flatly.

"Nor do I, sir," Chet replied. "I haven't drank anything

in years. But there is plenty of other drinks to have, inside."

"Mormon?"

"Oh, no. Methodist/Catholic."

"That's a strange mix, Mr. Byrnes." Hannagen laughed. He looked around again. "Is this a typical Arizona ranch?"

"No, sir. We gather cattle from our buyers and ranches and hold them here to drive them on up to Gallup and deliver them at four places where the Navajo meet to get their food supplies each month."

"So you have contracts with the federal government?"

He nodded. "And I wait on the script they pay me to be redeemed like any other federal contractor."

Hannagen considered this. "You came here from Texas." It was not a question.

"Almost five years ago," Chet agreed.

"I thought Texas was becoming a prosperous place to live. Why'd you leave?"

"I had an opportunity and Arizona was a good place to come to," he said carefully. "But you aren't planning any stage lines in Texas."

"By damn, you are right. I am not looking at building any stage lines in Texas." His followers laughed, too.

The occasion was festive. There was music, drink, and good food. Chet and his wife turned in early and let them drink and laugh. But the ranch woke at six a.m., and the party folks looked exhausted at the breakfast table. Hannagen didn't act too friendly, but on Chet's part, he didn't care. The man had come for his help, and no doubt wanted some investment, too.

After breakfast, the butcher paper map was spread out across two hastily built boards under the tent. It looked impressive. Chet, Sarge, and Cole looked it over and pointed out things they recognized. The marked points where they thought they'd need a station were marked out by distance, and had not been examined on foot, at least on the eastern third, according to Sarge. That was the area he knew best.

"Does it work?" Hannagen asked, strolling over.

"Well, it's a plan and we need to start somewhere," he replied. "It'll be a large job to get coordinated and completed."

"That's why we are here," the big man said. "And why we asked you to meet with us. You have a reputation for getting things done. Plus, they tell us you have a good handle on the territory."

"They may have told you more than I can do. We have a few ranch operations in the territory. We also have a timber-hauling contract in northern Arizona, and I am in charge of a Marshals' Force on the border to control the bandits."

"Let's all gather 'round now that the dishes are off the table. Your help is much needed in such a remote location. My attorney, Mr. Meyers, can open with our offer to you."

"Can he highlight it? I have attorneys that will analyze it after the meeting."

Hannagen considered the notion and nodded. "Alright. We have a contract to haul mail across Arizona from Gallup to the Colorado River. It must be completed in nine—really eight months now—or we face the loss of it. So this must be completed by then."

Chet thought about it for a second. "Unless you're richer than I think you are, a completed stage line is impossible in that short a time span. I'm a realist, Mr. Hannagen. The acquisition of the needed horses alone will take weeks. An anchor, coaches, construction of the stops, and acquiring responsible employees all will take more time. You can't just snap your fingers and find water in this land, either. This isn't Iowa or the Midwest, where there is water at less than forty feet."

"Alright, do you have a solution?"

"If you have to haul the mail before the way stations are ready, then I suggest you use buckboards to do that with contract people until the line is ready."

Hannagen nodded. "Are there people out here to do that?"

He shrugged. "They can be found."

"Obviously, you have studied this situation." Hannagen looked over at his road man Carpenter. "Will that work?"

"It was never considered, sir."

"Well, we should take it under advisement." The tycoon turned back to Chet. "What would you charge us to set that operation up?"

"I would need to have the details. How many runs a week? What are the time constraints on delivery?"

Hannagen turned to his secretary. "We can get them set up for him today?"

"It will be rough, of course," the young man said. "But yes, sir."

"I'm sure Mr. Byrnes understands that, but if we ask him to do the job, he has to have the requirements he must meet. He has, by the way, quite a system here to deliver cattle to the Navajos every month, run by Mr. Polanski. They must move six hundred head to four delivery points on given days in both territories on that date. Officials say they have never been over a day off, and that was in deep snow."

"Sarge does a great job." The businessman had obviously run some checks on Chet's operation, as well.

Hannagen asked next who would head such an operation, if they decided to hire him for the job.

"The young man to my left is Cole Emerson. He's been with me for well over three years. He understands how we do business, he's worked law enforcement, and he knows how to handle good folks and outlaws alike. He's fought Apache attacks on our cattle drive operation. Cole can get anything done that needs handled, plus he knows the people that we'll hire to haul the mail."

"How much education do you have, sir?" Hannagen asked.

Cole smiled and met his gaze. "I can read and write, if that worries you."

The big man laughed. "I believe you can. I appreciate your offer to start the delivery, and I hope we can afford your plan, Chet."

"You'll have it shortly."

"Now, you see the map, what do you think of our plan?" The big man sat back in the Morris chair brought from Susie's house especially for him.

"I would first try to find a landowner with property on the road who wanted to operate a station. It might lengthen or shorten the length of the individual run, but some of these people could easily provide the station, even handling the operation there. Or your company can make a long-term agreement to have one there. Each stop has to be assessed. Even if you decided a stop must be there, the availability of water will decide that on this road," Chet said.

"I would suggest you have the main maintenance shop at the San Francisco Peaks where the military road forks south to Preskitt," he continued. "You will need one at Gallup, and one at the end over on the Colorado River, but that would center it on your road."

"Carpenter, you thought Gallup would be the place for that?"

"I thought we could manage it better from Gallup, yes, sir."

Chet nodded, then said, "That puts you four hundred miles from the Colorado. Stage coaches have wrecks all the time, and that is a long way to go solve one."

"Is land available there?" Hannagen asked.

"Bo, tell him what to expect. Bo is my real estate man," he explained.

"Land in that area costs about twenty-five to fifty dollars an acre. I think investors think that will be the prime spot the railroad will use for its round houses and such."

"And we would need about how many acres?" Hannagen's attorney wanted to know.

"Chet and I talked about one hundred sixty acres, with plans to sell it when the rails get there for a huge profit."

"Chet, do you own land there?"

"I do, and I agree with Bo. You must have a projected lifetime for how long this stage business can exist?"

"Ten to fifteen years is the longest we can hold on to it by our calculations. So our investments need to gain some value when we close them down."

The man knew his business, at least.

Finally came the question Chet had been waiting for.

"What investment would you like to make in this operation?"

"That will depend on many things," he replied. "And how much you're asking for."

"Well then, what would you charge to acquire these sites?" Hannagen pressed. "You and Bo obviously have more connections here than we have. I like the landowner providing us a station and even operating it. That's a good angle."

"There won't be a lot of them work out, but I think we can find as many as twenty-five percent to do that."

"That impresses me. We never considered it as possible." He took a moment to light a large black cigar. "They also say you're connected to a large lumber mill in the area below the peaks?"

"We haul their logs to the mill. But, yes, I know them and we've done business." He pointed to the map. "They're the closest supplier to your operation. I think you need to write a plan for your buildings down to the last board and shingle, and then ask for a bid."

Hannagen nodded. His secretary scribbled down the information.

"In the meantime, I'll get you the cost of the buck-board delivery operation when I get the schedule that you'll be required to meet. You will need to remember, though, that the route can be snowbound where nothing moves for a week or more. But they seem to understand those things across the U.S."

Without his monocle, Hannagen rubbed his eyes. "Holidays and winter weather will hamper any quick movement. I'll have a price for you and Bo, too. So much for a rancher-built one. A plan for us to build it on his land, and then one where we do it all. Carpenter will have the final say on the location for the company."

"If we take this job, he or his men will need to be available and swift," Cole put in.

"Right," the tycoon agreed. "We can't afford any holdups. Are you satisfied with twenty stops?"

"Give or take. That should work," Chet said. "I had three hundred eighty-seven miles, you have four hundred."

"Should we leave this map for you?"

"If you have another, yes. We can use it."

"We have another. I think you've cut to the facts. If you have a bill for today, forward it to me."

"No bill for this meeting, Mr. Hannagen. I feel a plan for you to haul the mail by buckboards is necessary if you must start hauling it in eight months. Then the location of stations will be the second priority. Locating the horses and coaches will take time, as well as construction of those stops, but that can be done over several months as we run the buckboards."

"Nice of you, but we owe you something. I like the idea of a common design and a material list."

"It is the only way to get it up, or we'll have a White House in one place and an outhouse in another."

Hannagen laughed. "I agree. All your help is much appreciated. This tent setup and the amenities have been very good. You have some great people in your organization, your lovely wife included. Is she Hispanic?"

"Yes. Elizabeth and her brother-in-law have a large *hacienda* in Mexico."

"How did you two get together?"

Chet shrugged. "She found me to buy a horse. I bought her instead."

The man laughed. "You made a good buy."

"I'm pleased," he said with a chuckle of his own. "We'll work hard on a plan after we get the schedule."

"I am very pleased with that idea. I think it's saved us. You'll have that information by wire."

"That will hurry us along."

In the cold morning, Chet kissed Susie good-bye and mounted up. He felt ready to go back home and dig in. The Hannagen party had left before them. The crew was getting ready to take down the tent and head for home. He told them to stop and spend the night at the Verde Ranch since it would be later in the day they got on the road.

They were at the Verde River Ranch by afternoon. Cole went on to be with his wife and promised to be at the upper place by noon the next day to continue discussions.

Chet played with Adam while the women talked and made supper. He told the boy he had a brother named Rocky, which didn't seem to impress the toddler at all. So they rolled the ball, instead, bounced on Dad's knee for a horse ride, and rocked.

Victor arrived, anxious to hear all about the meeting. Chet asked him if he and John the blacksmith could go over several buckboards he might buy and rebuild them for tough service.

"We have Hampt's farm machinery to go over and rebuild this winter, but we can fix any buckboards you have."

"Hampt didn't miss a chance to get his machinery all fixed, did he?"

"When he got word I was going over the ranch's equipment, he got in line. He don't miss much. He also showed me some things I could do better down here."

Victor shook his head in respect. "For a cowboy, he knows lots about farming."

"I appreciate him. Good, if you see a buckboard for sale, tie it up. Even parts from a wrecked one we can use."

"I have seen some around."

"How do you like farming?"

"I like it. We're fencing up at the Hereford setup. Tom needs hay cut up there instead of hauling it from down here. We'll probably need a few more mowing machines."

"How many?"

"Four?"

"Rakes, beaver boards? The same?"

"Yes, sir," the young man replied. "We could use them all."

"I'll see my man in town when I get home. It takes a while to get them here."

"I hope I am not spending too much money."

"If we need these things, we need them," Chet said simply.

"Thank you. Rhea and I appreciate this great house and getting to care for Adam."

"I know you do, and boy, he sure is growing up. I should have made Cole show you his brother's tintype, but he had to get back to his wife. They both look like Byrneses to me."

When he and Liz went to bed that evening, they talked about the stage deal for a long while.

"This looks like a massive job."

"We'll need some way stations for fresh horses, no matter how primitive. Several horses and buckboards, which depends on the schedule he must keep and the employees necessary to support them."

"How many stops?"

"I think ten. About every forty miles. We'd need help from Reg and Lucy on the west, and the Windmill on the east. They'll be crude to start with, and I hope to make some of those with the scattered ranchers across the road."

She rolled over and hugged him. "He came to talk to a farmer and met my husband."

"I thought so, too."

"He had no plans to meet that deadline. You gave him the idea and he has no organization to even set it up." She shook her head in the dark. "Carpenter is not a man I'd have, except maybe in the office. They were going to build stations without water even, just because they fit the distance."

"Exactly. I got a little mad when he asked Cole how much education he had. Cole Emerson could make circles around his man and get it done."

"Oh, he'll learn," she said in a woman's knowing tone. "He didn't intimidate Cole."

"I thought they were kind of aloof when they got there. Is that the right word?"

"Oh, yes, that's the word. They were aloof, but they left talking different."

"What's next?" he asked.

"You."

"Oh, yes. There are times I could shout over our life it is so exciting. And I thank my God we found each other."

CHAPTER 18

Back home the next day by noon, Valerie and Cole had brought his son for his inspection. When he saw the boy, Chet dropped on his knees. "How are you?"

The boy looked at him and smiled.

"What's your name?"

"Rocky."

"Rocky, I am so glad to meet you."

"There is a pony?" he asked Chet.

"I will have to see."

Valerie spoke up. "I'm sorry, Chet, I promised him a pony. They told us he liked to ride, but we've been on the go. I had no idea if you have one. Cole thought there was one here."

"I think the *vaqueros'* sons have some we could use. Raphael will be here soon now we're back. I'll ask him."

"He really must like them. He rode one real good being led around in Texas."

"We'll find you a pony, cowboy."

"Did you have one as a boy?" Liz asked him, taking the boy in her arms.

"No pony. I had a small mustang I rode to first grade

at the schoolhouse about two miles away. First day, they gave me a lunch in a lard bucket, some hobbles, and sent me off to grade one.

"Oh, I had to. My father was out of it when they brought him back. I was eighteen when I first went north to Kansas with cattle. I had lots to do."

"Neither you nor your brother served in the war, though," she said.

"No, we were on the western frontier fighting Comanche. I think if the war had lasted much longer they'd have come after us."

"I wondered. So many Texans were drafted."

"Hey, we'll find you a pony today," he promised the boy. He got a smile in return.

"Cole said we're getting in the stage business," Jesus said as they entered the house.

"Well, everyone sit down for lunch and we'll talk about it."

"Thank you," Monica said as everyone headed to the big kitchen table.

"Oh, you're welcome. Jesus, we're planning to help them keep the contract by setting up a buckboard delivery to handle it until they get the stage line set up. Cole and I talked to them about doing that since there's no way to get the stage stops built in six months."

"That would take some doing, too."

"I agree. But we'll help them if they want us."

"Were they agreeing?" the young man asked.

"I think so. They're businessmen, not doers. Kind of stiff shirt, but realists."

Monica was standing at the kitchen window. "Someone just rode up. He looks upset."

Chet rose and went to answer the door. Looking out

the window, he said over his shoulder, "It's the man runs the Black Canyon Stage Line up here."

"Clark Ryan," Cole said.

He opened the door. "Good afternoon, sir. I'm Chet Byrnes. What can we do for you?"

"Mr. Byrnes, I've been intending to meet you," Ryan began without preamble. "There was a holdup last night on the stage for Hayden's Ferry. Four men held it up and escaped with a large shipment of gold and money. I talked myself blue this morning asking Sheriff Simms to form a posse and go after them, but all he says is his men will investigate and he doesn't believe a posse will do any good. I've talked to his stonewall all morning. Can you help me?"

"A posse of town men won't help," Chet told him. He turned back to the table. "Jesus, get some packhorses and supplies loaded up. Tell Raphael we need two of his men to go along with the four of us."

"Thank you," Liz said, realizing she was counted in that number of posse members going.

"Better get some riding clothes," he said. "It will be cold."

She nodded. "I can do that. Mr. Ryan, please sit down and eat. Monica has plenty of food."

The stage manager bowed his head. "Thank you, ma'am. I sure am hungry."

"Go ahead." Chet showed him a chair. "Now I need some details. How many men were involved in the robbery again?"

"Four. But it was dark and there may have been more. Beside the gold, there was a large sum of money, as well, being sent to Tucson. Ten thousand dollars."

"They must have had a pack train," Cole said.

"Big mules," Ryan confirmed. "It was well planned and they had help and information."

Chet frowned. "Did the sheriff say why he opposed a posse going after them?"

"He said it would do no good."

"Do you think they rode into Bloody Basin?"

"They went that way. The stage line will pay you for doing this. So will Wells Fargo."

"We won't worry about that now. When we get them, you can pay a reward to my people."

Chet excused himself to get ready and met Liz in the living room. Touching his arm, she stopped him. "Should I stay here? Christmas is coming fast."

"If you can stand it," he said quietly. "You might do the Christmas setup while we're on these outlaws' trail."

"I can stand all but not having you. I'll stay and get us ready for the holiday."

He kissed her. "Thanks, partner."

"You be careful, *hombre*. I fear these men are very smart criminals."

"I hadn't thought much about that yet, but they sure sound that way."

"Just be careful." She pulled him down enough to kiss him again.

"I will. Those two little boys sure look like brothers, don't they?"

"Yes, they do. I can pack you a bag. I know you need more information from Mr. Ryan."

"Thanks." He went back to the kitchen. "Liz is staying here to get ready for Christmas, Monica."

"Well, thank God for that."

"I hate to mess up your life," Ryan said.

"It won't, Mr. Ryan. This is our job." He sat back down. "Back to the holdup. No one was shot or hurt?"

"No, they had a fire and the road blocked. One of the men ran back to the coach and told them there was a rockslide ahead and someone was pinned beneath it. The driver and guard rushed down to see if they could help. Perfect plan. The woman and two men left in the coach were unarmed."

"Who were they?" Chet asked.

"I have their names. Why ask about them?"

"Just curious. You said it was carefully planned."

Ryan still looked confused.

"If they were not armed, they could have been there to make sure the plan worked," Cole explained. "They could be suspects."

"Oh, hell. I never thought of that." Clark looked distressed by his words. "I didn't know them, and they went on. But they had been staying in town on business, they said. I have their names and addresses in my office in town."

"We can investigate them later. They probably had nothing to do with the robbery, but one has to look at all aspects. There had to be an insider in this somewhere. The shipment of such things is secret?"

"Of course. And we send lots of stages south every day that haven't got a dime on them. Someone tipped them off, didn't they?"

"Sounds that way. In time, I bet you discover the culprit. But keep your investigation very quiet or they will spook and run."

"I'm learning, Mr. Byrnes. I really am. I was so upset Simms wouldn't chase them down. He acted like they would give up to some other law enforcement agency and he'd just go get them."

"That's just Sheriff Simms's style," Chet said with a laugh. "But we will pursue them, have no concern about that."

"I knew you would. Thank you, sir."

"Did you get a description of the men?"

"Only the man who told them about the rockslide," Ryan said. "The rest wore masks."

"Tell me about him."

"He was fortyish. Looked like a cowboy, but had a belly and a mustache. Wore a dirty gray hat, the usual vest, and a red kerchief. Green eyes and a scar under his left eye."

"That helps. A lot."

"The driver said the one leading the robbery was six foot tall, powerfully built, and had a deep voice. And he was a Texan by his dialect, they said. You could hear his voice from way off."

"Good leads," Chet said, writing them down. "We get their tracks we'll find them."

"I sure hope you do that. Being wintertime, I hate for you and your men to be out there."

"We take the good and the bad."

Raphael showed up then. He met Ryan and told Chet who he would send with him. "Ramon Torres and Bennie Cottrell."

"Are they dressed warm enough?"

"*Sí.* They are young and tough enough to stay up with you. They can shoot, too."

Chet was amused by his words, 'tough enough to stay with you.' "They may outdo me." He laughed.

"No one can do that, señor. But they can stay for it all."

"Glad you have such faith in my staying power,"

Chet said teasingly. "Liz will need help setting up for Christmas here."

"Oh, the whole outfit will help her. They always enjoy your Christmas parties."

An hour later, Cole reported they were ready to ride. Chet kissed Liz good-bye and mounted one of his solid red roans for the trip. He'd be the one to cross the mountains on. There were faster ones, but none near as tough for this trip and the rough country they must go over.

By mid-afternoon, they found the site of the fire where the stage was robbed. Jesus picked up their trail to the east off the Black Canyon Road. The shod mule tracks were a dead giveaway. Headed into the vast Bloody Basin, Chet had memories of chasing other outlaws through this tough country of junipers, prickly cholla, century plants, and pancake cactus beds with cottonwoods long turned yellow in the draws.

The sun was almost down when they made camp in a spring-fed draw. The two *vaqueros* were excited to be along and thanked him for the opportunity.

"No need in thanking me for you being away from your wife, Bennie. And Ramon being away from a warm bed."

"Señor Chet, we both are honored," Bennie replied. "It beats hauling firewood to a big pile."

"Well, the boys and me are glad to have you both along with us today. We'll track down these *hombres* and recover the loot, but we may be on the trail for days. Jesus says they also must have a pack train, judging by the tracks. So they'll avoid people if they can, so their getaway won't be noticed. The last rustlers and killers I chased through here had to stop and rob people for their supplies."

"And the deputy made Raphael come back with him and not go help you," Ramon said. "Raphael has never forgotten that."

"That wasn't his fault. But those *hombres* are no more."

"What will we do when we catch them?"

"Arrest them. We do things by the law today."

"Those horse rustlers you sought chose to fight. I have talked to Lupe about them. She said she took him medicine and he shot himself. That still bothers her."

"None of us expected that. She's a good woman."

Ramon nodded. "I asked Raphael about a *casa* if she would marry me."

"What did he say?"

"He said he would ask you one day when you were in a good mood." They all laughed at his words.

"Ramon, if you want to marry her you will have a *casa*."

"*Bueno, gracias.* When we get back, I will ask her."

"*Sí, mi amigo*," Bennie said. "How lucky you are. Not only getting to ride after outlaws but now you can get married."

"Ramon, don't hold her past against her," Chet warned. "She really worked and helped us. It was not by her choice she was there as much as she was taken there and had no way to escape it."

"She said you liberated her from hell," the boy said.

"We thought that, too, didn't we, guys?"

"Ramon, have you ever been in the mercantile in town?" Cole asked.

"*Sí.*"

"You know the owner Ben's wife, Kathren?"

"I have seen her."

"She was caught like that in an outlaw camp up in Utah and couldn't escape. Chet brought her home and she found Ben. His wife had left him."

"She's a very nice lady."

"We better eat. This won't stay hot long."

At least it wasn't *that* cold so far, Chet mused. But he dreaded the nights ahead. In the daytime they had sunshine. And while it was not the warmest sun, it would keep the exposed side of his body heated. They would have to push hard to catch this bunch of criminals, with a long day's head start on them. Maybe he and two of the others could rush ahead and try to catch them. Have the others bring the pack train on from the rear.

They had the tracks to follow, anyway. They were three days from reaching the Oxbow Road. That was his name for the north-south road from the rim to Fort McDowell. When they reached that route, they'd either go north or south.

When they finished supper, he told them his plan. "Before dawn I want four of us in the saddle in an attempt to ride them down. The last man will bring the pack-horses and catch us. Bennie, you have a wife, Ramon don't. Well, not yet anyway. You bring the packhorses. Don't kill them. You can catch us tomorrow night or the next day. Maybe we can catch this group, but it also may be a desperate run for nothing. We'll go ahead at first light."

"One thing, boss?" Cole asked.

"What is it, Cole?"

"Jesus and I have rode with you for years. We never did this before. And we always got our men."

Chet sighed. "I fear these men are smarter than any

we've ever tracked before. I don't want them to escape. I don't—think we're doing enough."

"We're with you, of course. And this may work. I just liked the old way better."

"We'll see."

Cole shrugged. "You're the boss."

Before dawn cracked the sky, they were loaded and the four men rode on. The trail they took was not as easy as the road that the other outlaws had taken to reach the Verde.

Chet saw the obvious hack marks on trees to locate the way while they pushed the horses anywhere they could, even going so far as to hold their horses' tails when they scrambled up the steep places that the desperate men used. After two hours of this kind of hard riding, several buzzards circled ahead.

Everyone saw them.

"Probably a horse they had to shoot," Chet said aloud.

Cole agreed. "We'll be lucky we don't have to shoot one of our own. These guys are crazy taking all these risks."

"They mapped this escape route. You can see the traces." Jesus pointed to a nearby tree trunk. "Those are not new hack marks."

Chet reined the roan up another hard climb to the top of the mountainside. The gelding made it in six cat hops, and what he saw at the top shocked him.

It was not a horse lying on the ground among the hopping buzzards.

"Get the hell out of here!" He spurred the roan and charged the squawking black birds as they lifted their wings in flapping panic. The man sprawled on his back without eyeballs left in his sockets had a scar on his dirty face and two bullet holes in his heart. The double wounds in his shirt were mere inches apart and had not bled long. This outlaw had died quickly.

Why had they killed their own cohort? Had they argued about splitting the loot? Had he dissatisfied the leader somehow?

"Why'd they shoot him?" Cole asked, swinging down to squat beside him.

"Same thing I asked myself. He answers Ryan's description of the unmasked one at the robbery."

"You thinking what I am thinking, Marshal Byrnes?"

"What's that, Mr. Emerson?"

"Hell I ain't—I got you. Did they kill him because he was the only face they saw at the crime?"

"I'm beginning to believe my theory that these aren't ordinary crooks we're trying to run down."

"Did you get those passengers' names?"

"No. Ryan has them at his office. Three common people, he said. A woman and two men in business suits who lived in Tucson. What if they were to meet these robbers with a wagon to haul away the loot? Fresh horses for them to ride?" Chet shook his head. "We have to push harder."

"What about him?" Cole asked, nudging the body with his boot.

Chet already had his foot in the stirrup to get on his horse. "We ain't got time, boys. God protect him. They're getting away."

He checked the roan and then reset the six-gun in his holster to be sure it was in place. It was a habit he had always used to be certain it was there. Reassured, he set the roan out again for the silver reflection of the Verde far below. A short while later he thought of his field glasses in the saddlebags and took them out. His lens scoured the far side of the river and he saw nothing. Too far away, the dusty junipers choked the far-off mountain, too, so there was nothing to see there, either.

The fugitives needed to ride into an open area way over there. Have something reflect the high sun in a flash. Damn.

He felt edgy pushing the roan in the lead. These were not some ranch hands busy escaping like the horse thieves who killed Marge's ranch foreman and his close-by *segundo*. These men were stone-cold outlaws who killed the most traceable one of their number.

The outlaws' horse apples on the trail were fresh enough for them to be only hours ahead. Chet and his men headed downhill again for the gleaming Verde. They could see it from afar under the giant cottonwoods, their dull leaves rattling in the cool wind sweeping across the land. There were plenty of tracks of saddle horses and large mules when they arrived at the stream. No doubt they were pushing them hard.

Did they know there was pursuit? Or did they simply expect it? Most sheriffs would have rounded up all the angry townsmen they could and raced after them. Men not used to sitting in the saddle all day or popping the brush. Men who wore out after bare hours on the trail, and usually simply gave up when the going got tough. Chet didn't trust them like his posse. The men with him were tempered steel—hard as rock. Ramon was as hard as Cole, Jesus, or himself.

Where the outlaws had crossed the stream was wide and shallow. But the water that had splashed off the horses' legs, fetlocks, and hooves on the smooth rocks and sand had not dried yet.

"They aren't far." Chet reined in the roan and twisted in the saddle. "Their drippings aren't dry here."

"They crossed in the last hour," Jesus said.

"We may be riding into a trap. Get your wits about you, boys. Keep your heads up."

All three agreed. Cole and Ramon limbered their rifles out of their scabbards while their horses drank the brown-stained river water. Chet reined his roan back to do the same. No telling when he'd get him another drink.

The horses were hot and fidgety. They'd drink a little, and then one would snort and raise its head up to look around. All of them acted upset. Chet wondered if they saw the danger or were simply worked up from the long, tough, fast descent off the mountain.

Another tough mountain loomed over them, choked with junipers. Another obstacle they'd need to scale to run down the robbers. Way up there, the Oxbow Road must be their goal. It was the only route out of here. Were there wagons waiting up there?

No way to know.

But these outlaws had made a path to escape cross-country. Marked it and made sure they could use it in their plans.

Who informed them about the shipments? When this was over, he would need to ferret out that individual, too. Were those three passengers Ryan spoke about involved in the crime? Strange how they were there when it happened. He'd need to know more about them.

He swung the roan out of the shallows and loped him across the sandy ground that ages of floods had deposited there. He looked up at the first rise from the river, and the roan cat-hopped up the sedimentary loam to the next level. There was a small piece of cloth marking the way on a juniper for him. Had they left it there for him to follow, or in their haste failed to strip it down?

No way to tell. He was asking himself too many questions. They went that way in a damn hurry, though, breaking off dead weeds brought up by some stray rain shower. A mule even went down there; his imprint was in the soft ground.

They lost no time climbing the mountainside and dodging the juniper on the run. With Chet on one side, Cole came around on the other side of a bushy evergreen. Horses sweaty and breathing hard, they reined them up at the edge of a long, open, grassy bench of a meadow. They needed to be certain they weren't riding into a trap.

The tracks were still there, headed northeast. Chet and his men took a hard look at what lay ahead in the grassy sweep. Jesus dismounted and got on his knee to examine the hoofprints.

"I don't see anything," Cole said, scanning down the open space.

Jesus agreed and stood up. "They're still running."

"They either know we're coming or have a time schedule to meet," Chet thought out loud.

"They also may know they have replacements waiting for them, or they'd use their animals easier," Cole suggested, swinging back on his horse.

"Tough either way. If they'd timed their exit, then they might be following a time schedule."

They had just started off when a puff of gun smoke in the edge of the meadow made them scatter.

Chet went left, expecting more shots as he slid the roan to a stop in the cover of the evergreen boughs. Cole went the other way, and he watched him disappear in the junipers. Jesus and Ramon were still in the saddle when they joined him. Chet was off the saddle and on his soles, jerking the Winchester out of the boot under his left stirrup.

"You see him?" Jesus asked.

Chet shook his head, trying to see where the shot came from. Then he heard more shots and Cole rode out, waving for them to come on. His rifle was still smoking.

"Looks like he got one."

"Boy, that was quick," Jesus said.

"I was afraid we'd never see him alive again," Ramon said, shaking his head.

They remounted their horses and charged down to where he had showed himself. Ramon took the reins as they dismounted. Their horses were so hot they needed to be walked some, and Jesus caught Cole's horse, too, to lead around out in the meadow.

The shooter was on the ground. Cole squatted nearby with the rifle over his knees.

"Who is he?" Chet asked, looking at a man in his thirties, unshaven and in need of a haircut. Hatless, he'd been shot in the right shoulder. He held the wounded arm and grimaced, blood flowing freely through his fingers.

"He won't talk," Cole reported.

"Where is his mount?"

Jesus jerked his head off toward the trees. "I'll find it."

Chet squatted down in the grass beside the man. "Mister, you don't talk and talk fast, I am going to tie you belly down over your horse as we're going after your cohorts. You'll bleed to death and no one at all will cry about your passing."

"Burn in hell."

"Fine. Load him up and he can die when Jesus comes

back with his horse." Chet went off to relieve his bladder, seething with anger.

"You ever seen him before?" Cole asked, working on the same task close by.

"Not in my life. You?"

"May have been his brother. But he looked real familiar to me from Tombstone somehow. I wish I could place him back then. I wasn't down there much but—oh, hell, I don't know. He wasn't a good shot, I can tell you that."

"Thank God for that."

"If he'd waited until we were closer, he might have taken some of us out."

Chet agreed and cast a look back at the outlaw. "I have no sympathy for him. We'll load him and go on."

"Or leave him here to die, for my money," the younger man growled darkly.

"I considered that, too. Bennie is coming. We'll leave Ramon here to guard him and they can load him up and bring him on with the packhorses."

"And we ride on?"

Chet nodded.

"They were desperate to leave him behind," Cole pointed out. "He was not a sharpshooter. Disposable, you guess?"

"No telling how their leadership thinks." Chet shrugged. "They've got a small window of time out of him."

Cole agreed and they marched back out into the meadow together.

"Ramon, you guard him until Bennie comes. Then I don't care how you load him and bring him. He gives you any mouth, you bust him over the head. You have some jerky and water?"

"*Sí.* I will be fine. I wish I could ride on with you, but

I understand. I will pray for you to catch the rest, and I am grateful I rode with you. Someday when I have sons, I will tell them about this trip and how their father rode with you *hombres*."

"God bless you. Let's go, boys."

"Wait. You ain't leaving me with that man are you?" the outlaw demanded.

"That's the plan. Who are you?"

"Lane Johnson. I seed you guys in Tombstone a year or so ago. Listen, if you catch him, you won't do anything to him. He's got too many friends in high places."

"Oh, yeah? What's his name?"

"Take me with you and I'll—tell yah."

"Just tell me," Chet ordered.

"I—I can't unless you take me."

"Tell me."

"Brad—Craw—Crawford. I swear don't tell him I said it."

Chet looked at Cole. "You ever hear of him?"

"No."

"Jesus?"

"I never heard of him, but maybe the men on our border bunch know him."

"Daylight's burning. Let's go."

"Hey! Hey, don't leave me with this gawdamn Mexican."

Chet swung in the saddle and checked the roan. "Hell, Johnson, he may kill you but he won't eat you."

"Don't leave me—"

The other two shook their heads as they left in a thunder of hooves. Who in the hell was Crawford? The lying bastard might not have told him anything. But it made one more thing he needed to mull over, too. Was it truly the leader's name? Maybe not.

He pushed the roan horse harder. There were only a

few hours of precious daylight left to reach the Oxbow Road. His heart thudded under his breastbone. They must finish this run with a capture before the sunset.

The impossible needed to happen.

At dark, they reached the road and still hadn't caught sight of the caravan. According to Jesus, they'd turned north. Chet was shocked. He'd thought they would turn south.

"Rein up, boys." He exhaled slowly and scratched his head under his hat. "We're a few miles from Rye. There's food, water, and horse feed there. Leave the others a sign we went south here. Tomorrow we can pick up their tracks again."

Jesus rode over and pruned some branches off a juniper with a hand ax so they would see it was to the right of the outlet, then they trotted for Rye.

In the empty saloon, the bartender recognized him and said, "You're that U.S. Marshal. Chet Byrnes. What are you doing back here?"

"We need to eat. Can you get us some food?"

"My name's Cy Green. You want something to drink?"

"My boys want some beer. You got a root beer?"

"Hey, Lolinda. These guys want food," he shouted.

A hard-looking Mexican woman in her thirties came out drying a plate. She looked pregnant, but like many such women who had so many babies by that age, they always looked like that. She asked, "What you want?"

Jesus told her beef and *frijoles*. Chet and Cole asked for the same.

She shook her head wearily like it was too much work, and went back in the kitchen. "*Gracias*."

"She's been busy. Some guy I'd never seen before

rode in about two hours ago and ordered food for three people."

Chet's head snapped around. "You see where he went?"

"I don't know," the bartender said. "I think he rode north."

"What did he look like?" Since there was no one else in the place, he continued. "We've been tracking stage robbers from over Bloody Basin way for a few days. He might be one of them."

"I'd say, thirties, five-eight—dark hair. Looked part Injun. Like he might have a little Cherokee blood some-wheres. Dressed like a ranch hand, run-over boots, bull hide chaps, and a droopy hat that used to be fancy. Blue silk kerchief. Wore a gun in a cross draw holster and a big knife, talked like a Texas drawl. Pretty nervous acting—he never was in here before and acted like he needed to hurry."

"Good description. Thanks."

"You say they held up a stage and you all rode clear over here?"

"Yes, we want to catch them."

"They tell me that's tough country you came over on."

"Real tough. Our horses have cooled down. Can we put them in the livery?"

"Yeah, wake up Ira. He'll help you." The barkeep went back to polishing glasses.

"Stay here. Jesus and I can handle it," Cole said.

"My leg isn't broke."

"We can handle it."

"Thanks."

The bartender spoke up again. "Hey guys, Ira has some

bunks you can sleep in over there, too. Tell him what you need, he can handle it."

"Thanks," Cole said, heading outside. "We'll do that."

"You have us breakfast here before dawn?" Chet asked.

"No problem."

"If two *vaqueros* show up, tell them we went north. They'll have a wounded prisoner and may ask where we're at. They have our packhorses."

"I can do that. You came prepared, didn't you? I recall you from four, five years ago. You arrested a pair of killers who raped a woman. Hung them down in the dry wash."

"That was me," Chet affirmed. "Made the *Globe* paper, too."

"I don't know a soul who would have written that—but they did anyway."

"I don't hang them anymore. We have judges to do that."

"I savvy that, but we needed more rope justice back then. You arrested some others over here, too."

"A few."

"You have some big ranches. How do you have time to chase these worthless bastards around?"

"First, someone needs to do it. Second, we need Arizona tamed to become a state. Someday we'll do that, have her tamed and become another state."

"But you have a wife and those ranches—why you?"

"Because, like this deal, the law never formed a posse to go after them. Said when they'd show up they'd arrest them. If they'd formed a posse and gone after them, they'd all fall out of the saddle the first day way over in Bloody Basin. Cronies and businessmen don't make good chasers."

"Yeah, I know about those deals." Green put another polished glass on the stack.

Cole and Jesus were back. "They're all okay. There are some beds. He's got some bug-free blankets. I said we'd be over there after we ate."

"Thanks. Breakfast before dawn here."

"Good. Jesus, you don't have to cook," Cole teased.

"Thank God for that woman."

They laughed and the food soon came. She had plates for them and even some fresh flour tortillas she must have made. They didn't care, they were hungry. Chet gave her a silver-dollar tip. "That's for you. Thanks."

She looked impressed and dropped it in her cleavage. "You *hombres* are alright. *Gracias, mia amigos.*"

Jesus told her something in Spanish about how they appreciated her. His *gringo* partners nodded at his words.

"See you before dawn," she said. "Leave the dishes on the table. I am going to my *casa*." With a shawl over her shoulders, she hurried out the door. When she was gone, the bartender told them her husband had abandoned her and four kids here.

"She's hardworking. Thank you for tipping her."

"Good women like that are hard to find."

He paid him after the meal and they walked under the thousand stars in the sky for the livery.

"You suspect they have a hideout close by?" Cole asked.

"No idea. But we're closer to them than we were."

Jesus spoke up. "No. They would not have sent the guy for food if they did."

"Jesus may have a point," Cole agreed. "Or they had no supplies."

"Or anyone to fix it for them," Jesus finished.

"Tomorrow we'll know," Chet promised them. "Or the next day."

They checked on their horses, standing asleep in their tie stalls. Then they found the bug-free blankets Cole had talked about and went to sleep. Chet was glad that Liz was not with him. The ride had been tough and there appeared to be no letup in sight. He missed having her to sleep with, though.

She and Monica could handle Christmas. No telling what the bill would be, but he could afford it. One good thing with all the mess in D.C. and New York over finances he read about, they were real lucky to be away from all that madhouse.

He bet Hannagen was wondering where his answer was from him. They had the buckboard deal to fall back on. The rest would come along. It had to.

CHAPTER 19

Chet and the boys dressed, then saddled their horses in the lamplight. Leading them down the dark street, they found the light on in the saloon. They hitched the mounts at the rack and climbed on the porch, where Chet stuck his head in the double door.

"This where breakfast is at?"

Her hair all combed and a better dress on her, she smiled from the lighted kitchen doorway. "It's about ready. I have hot coffee. You aren't Mormons, are you?"

"No, ma'am, we are not. We all drink coffee, and we thank you for getting up and cooking for us."

"You bet," Cole added, seeing in the light from the kitchen that the table was set. "Why, this is damn near as good as home."

She laughed and brought out dishes of food. Chet decided she was not holding back on them. Scrambled eggs with hot pepper flecks and cheese melted on them. Homemade fried sausages, German-fried potatoes and biscuits with gravy.

"Great coffee," Chet told her.

"You ever need work again, come to Preskitt; we will find you a real job," Cole said.

"I have four children. How will I get there?" She stood with her hands on her hips. "My name is Lolinda Renaldo. I am no longer married, and while Cy is good to me I need a better income and job. Not much happens here."

"If I pay you twenty dollars," Chet asked, "can you hire someone with a wagon to take you and your kids over there?"

"Oh, *si*." She had a pretty smile, he decided.

"Come to my ranch in Preskitt Valley. People can show you the way. My wife's name is Elizabeth, and Monica is her housekeeper."

"Your name, señor, is Chet Byrnes?"

"That's right. And there are people I know who need a fine housekeeper."

"Oh, *gracias, señor*." She took his paper money and bowed. "I was worried we would freeze if I stayed here. The hut we live in is not very much."

"If we ever get home, we'll see you there."

After breakfast they rode north, stopping to tack a note on a tree for Bennie and Ramon just short of the road. This way, they would be able to see it coming out, but no one on the road would notice.

Leave the prisoner here for care and arrest.
Then come north. We will leave notes or you will
find us—Chet.

With the pink light of dawn coming over the Four Peaks, a pack of startled javelins broke out and, grunting like hogs, ran across the road. Cole's horse had a small fit but he held him in laughing. "We woke them up, huh?"

Mid-morning they came across the mules, set loose and scattered and throwing their heads up to bray at them. All had signs of once bearing a packsaddle, and Chet knew in an instant that the stage robbers had made their connection and they were too late. Six stout mules without a brand on any of them were turned loose and grazing. They did not belong there, but where was the rest of the outfit?

Jesus studied tracks and had no answer. "They must have wrapped the horses' hooves in blankets. I can't find a thing about where they went next."

They sat down to consider their next move. How could three or so bandits simply vanish?

After going over the issue of the disappeared outlaws several times, Chet told the men to catch the mules. They would offer them as stray property at home and then sell them. They were probably worth eighty dollars apiece.

"We'll share them with the *vaqueros*," Chet said. "Let's go back and tell Lolinda she can cook for Jesus and the men going back with their prisoner. Cole, you and I need to get back home and work on the stage business. We'll get our bedrolls and go back cross-country by the way we came. I see no reason to stay around here and look in blind box canyons for them."

"Where do you think they went?" Cole asked.

"No idea. Someone will tell on them, though. We'll get them eventually. They aren't that smart."

"Starting out, you said we may have found some smart outlaws," Cole said, shaking loose a lariat to rope his first mule. "How did they do it?"

"Put wraps on their horses' hooves like you boys

said. I don't know much more, but I feel they're still in the territory and will show up soon, be it in Tucson or Tombstone."

"Do you think they split up?"

"They may have done that, too. They did something and they did it overnight."

Jesus shook his head. "One minute they were here and now they're gone. Last night they needed food. I hear the others coming."

"Good, they can help us catch the mules."

"Wonder if their prisoner died?" Cole asked, looking hard at their line of pack animals.

"He looks to be over a horse. Or what's left of him, at least."

"So we are taking the mules back?" Jesus asked.

"We should."

"It will take almost a week."

Chet agreed. "Those men don't know the way. You do."

"I'll do it. Don't you two get your neck broke going home without me."

They laughed and then welcomed the other two.

"He die?" Chet asked about the prisoner.

"*Sí.* Yesterday. We couldn't do much for him."

"Well, we aren't missionaries. We will have to bury him, though. They left their mules here and the trail ends."

"How did they do that?" Ramon asked, looking around the area.

Cole shook his head. "If we knew that, we would know where they went. Help us catch the rest of these mules. Part of them belong to you."

After rounding up the mules, they rode back to Rye. The bartender told Chet they could bury him in the local cemetery right by the two Chet had hung years before.

Lolinda came out of the kitchen and Chet told her that since they were taking a wagon to Preskitt and the mules there to be sold that they could take her and her kids with them. The bartender didn't know anyone up there had a claim on the mules. Then he cleared his throat and asked Chet, "If I would marry her, could she stay here?"

"You better ask her. That ain't up to me."

"Lolinda, would you marry me?"

She stopped and turned. "You want to marry me? You never mentioned it before."

He got tangled up stripping off his apron and hurrying to get out from behind the bar. "I don't want you to leave. I can build another room on my house for your children. I really want you to stay and help me."

He had her in his arms and they kissed.

"Well, looks like we bury him and go back across country," Chet said with a smile.

"Mrs.—uh, Green, the five of us will be back shortly for lunch."

"Oh, *sí*. You can have your money back, señor."

"No. That is our wedding present to you. Lunch, supper, and in the morning breakfast. Don't go on a honeymoon until you do that. Then we'll be gone."

"Oh, señor, I can do that."

"Good luck to both of you." He turned back to his men. "Okay, let's go buy us two shovels at the store and get this outlaw buried."

"I can do that," Cole said. "Jesus and the men can put up our stock for the day."

Left with nothing to do, Chet settled himself on a chair and rubbed his shoulder. He hadn't had time to notice it aching until then.

"You need something like a root beer?" Cy asked, still holding Lolinda in his arms.

"That'll be fine. No rush."

"I can get it. I will have her for all my life."

Chet winked at her. "Sometimes men wake up and realize what they really have on their hands."

"Oh, yes," he said, and went for the root beer. She shook her head happily and went to start lunch.

The crew came back for their mid-day meal. Afterward, they finished the grave and buried the man. Several people came by for a drink and asked about what was happening. Chet quizzed them all, but no one knew anything about the outlaws.

The dead one buried, they went over their horses and tack. Jesus reshod two horses that had loose shoes and they declared them ready to return home in the morning. Lolinda promised at supper to once again feed them before dawn. She had bought a new beef roast from the local butcher and cooked it all afternoon for them.

For the free meal, many customers came in to meet them and feast. Cy Green announced he was marrying Lolinda and everyone applauded. There was even music, but Chet was busy talking to a cowboy who told him he thought the outlaws had crossed over Four Peaks at night.

"Why do you think that? I understand that's one helluva trail. Especially at night."

"If they had a good guide, it wouldn't be so bad."

"You have a name of that person?"

"I might learn it for a price," the man offered.

Chet sagged. "What's the price?"

"Fifteen dollars. I want a cartridge .44/.40 Colt pistol."

"You can mail me that name and I'll pay for a gun for you at the store."

"That would be good."

Chet shook his hand. "Better yet I will mail you the money when you give me the name."

"Not a word who told you?"

"Not a word."

"I'll find out. May take some time. They're pretty close-mouthed."

"Let me know."

"Oh, I will," the man assured him. "I want that pistol."

Later, he told Cole and Jesus what he had learned.

"That is a terrible way to go over from all we've heard about it," Jesus said.

"Right, but he thinks an expert guide took them over it."

"You said a snitch would know something."

"I'm waiting for his letter with a name."

"He say who?"

"They must use the trail. Sounded like a family deal," Chet said. "We may get a name to come and question them."

Cole and Jesus both nodded.

The whole thing sounded strange, but until he knew more that was all they could do. He paid Cy and Lolinda for the large meal and thanked him for inviting the others. "See you for breakfast."

The next morning before dawn, Lolinda was there, ready, and looking totally relaxed. When she poured him more coffee, she bent over and kissed Chet's cheek. "Tell your wife I love you, too."

"Lolinda, I'll sure tell her."

"Man, boss, what *is* it with you, anyway?" Cole demanded.

They all laughed.

Still dark outside with the mules braying, Chet and Cole mounted with one packhorse and left by the cross-country course for the return trip. The other three were taking the mules back and going home by the south route through Fort McDowell—the very route of the robbed stagecoach, in fact.

In three days, Chet and Cole came up the ranch driveway under a cloud cover he expected to let loose more snow any moment.

Raphael came out to meet them and they explained to him what happened. He asked, in some confusion, "All you got were some mules?"

Chet shrugged. "All we got. They escaped us."

His wife came out on the porch. "I'm coming, get back in the house. It's too cold outside. Raphael, Cole can tell you, too, but those two *vaqueros* are mighty good *hombres*."

Liz didn't listen to his caution for her and shivered under his arm. "I'm so glad you're back."

He kissed her. "Let's get inside. We're empty-handed. They lost us."

"Oh? That's never happened before."

He shook his head. "No."

Inside the house, he shed his heavy jacket and turned to her. "All we have to show are those damn noisy mules the boys will bring back in a few days."

"That's almost funny."

"No, it's not. We have a new set of very smart criminals."

"So what will you do now?"

"I have feelers out. They may not be that smart."

"Oh, Chet, I'm simply glad you're back in one piece."

"Darling, I am glad to be home, *period*."

"We are so glad you did come home," Monica said. "Are you ready to eat lunch?"

"Yes." He turned to his wife. "You two have Christmas under control?"

"I think we do."

"Good." He kissed her again and they sat down to eat.

It was good to be back in his own house, but the escaped outlaws weighed heavily on his mind. There had to be some way to draw these criminals out. He would just have to figure out the proper bait.

The next day he took Liz and went into town. She had more things to get for Christmas, and he wanted the names of the passengers on the stage the evening of the holdup from Ryan. They might have been involved in the deal. There was no telling. Plus, he needed to talk to Bo about the stage deal.

Ryan was disappointed about them losing the trail, but said he understood, and appreciated all their effort.

"I want your list of the passengers. Also do you know a Brad Crawford?"

"I have them right here, sir. You want to copy them?"

Chet read the list. *Harvey Armstrong—Tucson businessman. George Nelson—Tucson businessman—Ruth Carlson—a friend.*

A friend? Was she a mistress, maybe? "Tell me about the lady," he ordered.

Ryan turned up his hands. "I never saw her before. She wasn't some dumb canary, though. Very well dressed and reserved."

"Figure she was a concubine for one of them?"

"If she was, she was a damned expensive one is all I have to say."

Chet laughed. "Where did they stay?"

"Brown Hotel I think. Are you tying them to the robbery?"

"I'd tie anyone to it if they were involved in finding out about the delivery the stage carried."

"I swear no one in my office knew about it until it went on the stage. It came from the bank, and two armed men delivered the strongboxes to the stage office a half hour before the stage left."

"No rumors. So they had to know beforehand it would be on that particular stage and when to rob it."

"Well, they didn't ever rob an empty stage run," Ryan said.

He thanked Ryan for all his work and told him they weren't through finding the culprits.

Next, he went by the bank and talked to Tanner about the operation.

"I'm not accusing anyone, but someone told the outlaws that the money and the gold was going to be on that stage."

Tanner looked perplexed. "You think they knew about the shipment?"

"Those men never stopped an empty stage. They only held up that one, which just happens to be the one carrying a fortune?" Chet shook his head. "That's no coincidence, and it points to some inside information. No one at the stage office knew if there was a shipment or not, according to Ryan. Then they took a trail they made beforehand to throw off a posse and still escaped by taking a perilous shortcut over Four Peaks at night. Someone gave them information about the shipment schedule to set up the robbery."

"From this bank?"

"Tanner, I can't see anyone else who gave them the information at least two days ahead to be ready for the holdup."

"Who do you think might have been involved?" Tanner asked.

"Two people called businessmen, and an attractive woman listed as a friend were passengers on that stage. I'm thinking they're part of the brains."

"Let me check. Who do you think got the information?"

"Number one, the appraisal for that female was she might have been an expensive concubine."

Tanner frowned. "What was her name?"

"Ruth Carlson."

Tanner wrote it down. "Wait here. I'll be right back."

In a short while, he returned with two young bank workers.

"This is Earl Hudson and Rupert Norman." Chet rose and shook their hands.

Tanner had them sit down before his desk. "Now, there was a woman in town a week ago. Either of you meet her? Her name was Ruth Carlson."

"I met her, sir. I am not very proud of that meeting," Norman said, looking at his feet.

"You have an affair with her?" Chet asked.

"I guess I got very drunk and we had sex. I think I was doped."

"Did you tell her when the money and gold was being shipped?"

Norman shook his head. "I can't recall doing it, but I

was not in control of my wits. I don't know what I might have told her."

"How did you get in that trap?"

"I met her when she needed a hundred-dollar bill broken here at the bank. She mentioned a small get-together at the hotel that evening. She was very good looking and I was tempted. But when I got there, it was not a party but a meeting between her and me."

Tanner shook his head. "Marshal, obviously your suspicions have been confirmed. How does that work?"

"We know one thing now. I have more things to check. What they were doing up here besides this robbery?"

"They never spoke to me," Tanner said. "Either of you speak to—what were the names again, Chet?"

"George Nelson or Harvey Armstrong," Chet said.

"No, I never heard of them," Hudson said.

"She told me sometime they were mine investors, those two men she worked for," Norman said. "They were dealing on some property down in the Bradshaws. That she could get me their large deposits for this bank." He shook his head. "I guess I can believe that was a lie, too."

"Obviously."

"She live in Tucson?"

"As if you could believe anything she said," the young man said sullenly.

"I understand," Chet said.

"You may go," Tanner told them.

"Yes, sir." They left the office.

"I don't know what to tell you, Chet."

"I figured she was a black widow spider."

"How can I trust him?"

"I think he was very open. A powerful, good-looking

older woman took him in, in my book. They hired her for her sharp skills at seduction and doped him. I think he learned a sad lesson. He's not the first, nor the last she'll deceive.

"Did that help you?"

"It confirmed my suspicions. And I'd give him a chance, if it were me."

"I will take that under advisement."

"Good. I need more information on those men. I never asked Bo Evans. Maybe he knows something more about them."

"You want me to inquire in Tucson about their business down there?" Tanner asked. "I have some friends who work down there."

"Excellent. Add Brad Crawford to that list. Not a word, but he led the holdup according to his dying man."

"I never saw her, but that must have been a wild party." Tanner laughed.

"I thought the same thing."

They shook hands and he went back to Bo's. "You have an affair with a Ruth Carlson?" he asked Bo quietly.

"Hell, no," Bo shot back. "I wouldn't have done that behind Shelly's back or in front of her. Why did you ask me that?"

"Were the men she was with serious buyers of anything?"

"I showed them some mine property. I had the feeling they were using me to see the district."

"Stalling for time?"

"Yeah. But I knew nothing else."

"You know why they had her along?"

"I'm not a green boy, Chet. But I had no idea how they'd use her."

"She was how they learned about the shipment on the stagecoach."

"I heard that you went after them."

"They got away, but I am tracking all this down. I know lots more now about how they did it than I did then. And this adds to the list."

"If I learn anything else I'll tell you."

"Married life alright?" Chet asked.

He dropped his gaze to the desk and nodded his head. "I think it is a miracle—she does, too. I am lucky, and yes we're very happy."

"Good. I have a good one, too. See you."

"Thanks, Chet."

He gathered his wife, who had several things to load in the buckboard at different businesses. They picked them up while he explained all he learned that day.

"My, my, you tracked down a lot," Liz said. "What comes next?"

"My Force can do some detective work down there on these suspects. Perhaps we can tie them together."

She squeezed his leg. "You can go so deep when you get after someone. I can't hardly believe all you did today."

"I'll get them. I want to stop at the stage office and tell Ryan what I learned today."

"Of course. It isn't that cold today."

"I'll only be a few minutes." He tied off the team and went in the stage office.

Ryan stood as he entered. "What did you learn?"

"Not a word on what you hear from me. Ruth doped a

man who knew about the money and no doubt got the schedule out of him in a sex-dope deal."

The manager shook his head. "That ties them in, huh?"

"Makes a connection between them and the holdup men."

"We knew there was a slip, and this proves it."

"I want my men down in Tucson to find out all they can about them. We may solve the whole thing."

"Wow, that's great. I see your wife out there. Don't keep her waiting. Please keep me informed."

"What did he think?" she asked when he came back to her.

"We knew a lot more. He's excited."

"Next plan?"

"My Force can investigate all of them."

"Good, you'll be here for Christmas, then?"

"Yes."

"That's very good."

He thought so, too.

CHAPTER 20

He began the letter to his crew.

Dear Roamer and Shawn
Two weeks ago, the Black Canyon Stage south
of Prescott was robbed of money and a Wells
Fargo insured gold shipment by road agents.
There were two businessmen and one woman in
the coach—unarmed.
George Nelson, businessman—Tucson
Harvey Armstrong, businessman—Tucson
Ruth Carlson—a friend
They claimed they were unarmed, only going
home after a visit to the area.
No one shot. They were reported as just
passengers.
The stage line manager was suspicious. There
had not been a stage line robbery when the stage
did not have loot. I will describe our case and
how they slipped away from us.
Ruth Carlson is a black widow. I learned she
had a sex-dope deal with a man who told her the

schedule. She obviously is attractive and we need to know what else she did for those two others while here.

The outlaws made a marked trail from the Oxbow Road over to Bloody Basin. They had six large pack mules and made a fast exit on this tough trail.

We found the only man that the stage passengers and driver could identify shot dead on the trail. Farther on, another member of the gang tried to bushwhack us. His name was Lane Johnson, shot by Cole and none of us were hurt.

Johnson told us the leader was Brad Crawford, a man he said we could not arrest. I don't know him except they gave us the slip at Rye by going over the Four Peaks narrow pass at night. He is no doubt in the Tombstone or Tucson area.

I want you to find out all you can about the four of them and let me know all about it. I want them in prison. I will continue to investigate from up here.

> *Merry Christmas,*
> *Chet Byrnes*

He sealed the envelope.

On the calendar on the wall, he saw there were five days until Christmas.

He sent the letter via a messenger so it got on the stage that evening.

"All you can do is wait for their answer?" Liz asked, standing at the back door when the youth swung in the saddle to head for town and the post office to deliver the letter.

"This crime is going to take tough work to solve it and arrest the criminals."

"You have names, don't you?"

"But you have to have evidence to go with the name. That means gold bars, witnesses, and proof to convince a jury."

She hugged him. "They can't say you didn't try your best."

He kissed her. "And I'm not through hounding them."

"I'm glad I didn't break the law. I'd hate to have you after me."

"That's what makes the law work. It makes people reconsider committing crimes in the first place."

"Let's steal away?"

"I thought you'd never ask."

"Silly man."

CHAPTER 21

Everyone came to the Preskitt Valley headquarters for the ranch's Christmas Eve party. There were sidewall tents set up like an army camp all over in a large, orderly plan. The weather was winter warm in the daytime, dropping below freezing at night. But no one would freeze. The big tents had wood stoves and tables.

The ranch women fed everyone. There were toys, blocks, and rag dolls made from men's heavy socks. Every man got some riveted pants, a new long-sleeve shirt, and underwear. How she got all their sizes, Chet realized he would never know. All ranch foremen got new *Boss of the Plains* Stetson hats, while under-foremen got clothes and a silk scarf. The ranch women got dress material, thread, and buttons, plus one cast iron skillet apiece. They did the gift giving before the party folk arrived.

There was candy, fruit, and fruitcake for everyone, plus a large meal. Draft beer and sarsaparilla were served, while Victor and the "ranch band" made music.

Cowboys danced with the *vaqueros'* wives and all had a fine time.

"I don't know how you did it, but it was wonderful," he told his wife.

"I watched you last year. I asked the women what they wanted the most. An iron skillet came up most often. Your friend Ben asked if I'd need more later he'd sure have to order more. You know, his wife Kathrin speaks highly of you for bringing her down here. Her place up there must have been bad?"

"It was and she had no way to escape. You know she always comes here to help. When Adam was born or when we had a problem, she was out here to help us."

"She laughs about it, but she told me her first husband went off and married two sisters because she could not get with child. But her and Ben have no problem doing that now. It must have been number one's fault."

"Yes, but she needed help up there in Utah, and I am glad we saved her."

"I'm grateful, too. You saved me from becoming an old maid."

They laughed.

"I've spoken to the foremen who left men at home to watch the ranches. They're going to take their presents to them. Rhea will take some to her housekeeper and her man. Don't your foremen look good all in matching hats?"

"Like army officers, huh?"

Her hand in the crook of his arm and her skirt in the other, she traipsed along beside him. "A neat world you've built out here. JD and Bonnie are doing something similar down there tonight. And Reg is walking better. Will he always limp?"

"I hope not. I need to talk to him."

"Boy, he has a fun wife, doesn't he?"

"I love her. She was just an enthusiastic ranch girl when she guided us all over that country up there."

"That was your honeymoon with Margaret?"

"Yes. Reg was still in Texas, married to a beautiful girl we knew when she worked on the ranch. She'd worked there at the house, and they got married. He stayed behind and was running a ranch for an older couple that was going to become his eventually. But his wife was killed in a buggy accident and that about killed him—I never knew the details—he never told me. But he came out here, and next thing I knew those two were getting married."

"She is quite a businesswoman."

"Yes, she turned that way after their wedding, but she can out-rope any man living."

"I heard that," she said. "And the maverick business that turned the ranch into a paying place."

"I'll sit down and talk to them before they go home."

"Good. They have a cute baby girl."

"No lack of them, is there?"

"Yes, but I doubt I will be granted one."

He swept her around in his arms. "Quit that. What we can't control we must accept—it doesn't bother me. Stop letting it weight you down."

"Chet, the Bible says marry and multiply."

"But it does not say depress yourself because you can't."

"I will try to be braver."

"For me, anyway."

"For you."

Before bed, he spoke to Reg at length and Lucy joined him.

"That leg still hurt you?" he asked.

Reg nodded grimly enough.

"Can we find a good doctor to look at it?"

"I think we set it wrong. Everyone tried. I'm no baby, though. I can live with pain."

"He won't stay off of it, either," Lucy piped up.

"Aw, don't go into that—I had things needed to be done."

She shook her head. "Stubbornness runs in your family."

"Hey, you're getting fifteen purebred bulls this coming spring," Chet told him.

"Well it's about damn time—"

Lucy cut him off. "Mind your mouth. He does all he can do for us, Reg Byrnes."

"We're the last ranch to get them," he objected.

"You are so hard to please anymore—I'm going to find better company. Excuse me, Chet, and thanks for the bulls." She kissed his forehead and left.

"You ever pull a cow out of a mud hole she's been stuck in?" Chet asked.

"And she got so mad she fights you when she got out?"

"You know what they do. Reg, you need to count your blessings and I am ordering you to go see the doctor in town before you go back to the upper ranch."

"Ordering me?"

"Hell yes, I'm ordering you. Someone needs to look at your leg and see what they can do."

He sunk down in the folding chair and shook his head.

"That is an order, and I want a report on what he tells you."

"Damn Lucy's hide—"

"No, damn your hide. You can listen some to her. You're worse than that cow you hauled out."

Chet had enough. He repeated his order and left him to think about it.

When he joined his wife, she asked, "You have a fight?"

"No. I told him I wanted a doctor to examine his leg before he went back home, and he had a fit."

"Will he do as you say?"

"He will or she won't drive him home."

"*Hombre*, when you get upset, who would stand in your way?"

He hugged her shoulder. "Sometimes, things need to be done right."

"Any answer to your letter you sent to Tubac?"

"Nothing yet."

"You still thinking about that deal?"

"I can't forget it. I want them in jail."

"Hey, I have a Christmas present for you. All you have to do is unwrap it up in our bedroom."

He smiled at her. "All you have to do is wait until I thank Raphael for all his work."

"He's a good man. I can wait."

His chores completed, he herded her to the house while the party went on. Reg better come to his senses. Life was too short to be depressed and feel bad, too.

Once in the closed-in porch he shed his jacket and put it on the post, his new hat beside it. It had been a great Christmas for his people.

He stopped in the living room and spoke to Sarge and Susie, who were putting their son to sleep.

"Did you know the *vaqueros* found your other son a small horse?" Susie said.

"No."

"He is very well broke and they showed him to Valerie and Cole. The boy acted excited."

"Lots happened here tonight. I bet the boy is pleased. I held and talked to him, I guess before they did that."

Susie said, "Did you know about Lucy and Reg?"

"I ordered him to see a doctor about that leg before he went back home and told him he better count his blessings. No need in him being the wounded bear."

Susie and Sarge agreed.

"He no doubt is in pain, but a doctor might ease that. Biting everyone's head off won't solve his problem."

"I hope he finds an answer."

"He's going to have to. Good night. Shame to waste time on such things when it is the season of Christianity."

In their bedroom, she hugged him. "I hope you settled it."

"I better have."

The next morning Chet learned Reg had ridden off and not gone to bed. Lucy was crestfallen, and could hardly talk about it while holding their daughter, Carla.

"Where would he go?"

"Home?" she asked.

"I'll ask Jesus to go look for him. Do the stable boys know anything?" Chet asked.

Christmas morning, a day to relax and celebrate the birth of Christ, and a new family problem surfaced. He told everyone in the kitchen to stay there. He put on his coat and went to the horse barn.

Raphael met him.

"They say Reg rode off last night. Does anyone know anything about where he went?"

A groom said, "No, he wouldn't let us help him, señor. He saddled his horse and rode away."

"Which way did he go at the gate?"

The stable boy shrugged. "We couldn't see him in the dark."

"Where is Jesus? Tell him I need him to check the way he went."

Raphael said, "I will have some of my men help find him."

"Don't get in a war with him. I only want to be sure he's okay."

"We can find him."

"I'm going back to the house. Let me know when you learn something."

The matter was in their hands. He walked back a little defeated. Reg was someone he highly counted on. Obviously, his pain and some internal pressure had sent him to escape to God-knew-where.

He told the others at the house what he'd done. Then he turned to Lucy and asked if her two men at home could handle it until Reg showed up.

"If he's not found, send Fern's boyfriend, Drew, to help us. The four of us can make it, and Fern will help me besides. Did I do this to make him run away?"

Chet shook his head. "His pain may have set this off. Also his desire to be an achiever may be pushing him too hard."

"I have tried everything I know. He's not been himself since the horse wreck he had."

"You will never know about what men have in their

minds. I had problems like this with my first husband, but he finally recovered and apologized," Liz told her.

With a worried look, Lucy shook her head. "He don't need to apologize. Simply come back."

The clock ticked loudly. Chet had little heart to play with Adam who was there with Rhea and Victor. Lunch was silent.

Monica looked out the window. "Jesus is coming back. Chet, you might check on him."

Rising, he put his napkin on his plate and excused himself. Chet knew coming out in the cold air—something was wrong with his man. He could read it.

"Jesus, did you find him?"

He made a grim nod, hitching his horse at the rack.

His steely look at Chet telegraphed the seriousness of the answer on his lips. "He's dead, Chet. I am sorry. He shot himself. The men are taking his body to the funeral home." Wearily, Jesus shook his head and tears ran down his cheeks. "Why?"

Chet hugged him. "I don't know. I really don't know."

"He's dead?" Lucy cried out from the porch. She'd followed him out and heard what Jesus had said. "You found him dead?"

Liz and Monica ran outside. Lucy was screaming uncontrollably, rocking her daughter.

"He's dead, Chet?"

"Lucy—"

"Is he dead?"

Chet held his hands out to her. "There is nothing we can do, Lucy. He shot himself. The *vaqueros* took his body to the funeral home in town. I need to go tell his mother. JD needs to hear about it as soon as possible."

She collapsed, nearly dropping the baby. Chet folded her in his arms. "I am so sorry."

"Oh, Chet! Oh, God! His son will never see him." Lucy sobbed. "I told him a week ago we would have another child next summer. He said he was so pleased—we both hoped for a boy."

"Let's go back inside," he said. "Thank you, Jesus. Sorry you had to be the bearer of such hard news."

Jesus turned his hands up and shook his head in disappointment.

"No, you did the right thing. I'll write a letter to take to Drew and tell him he is your foreman. We'll hold back about the funeral until as many as possible can come."

"You're going to write a letter for them to take?" Jesus asked. "I can go down there."

"No, you've been through enough. Raphael has a boy can do that. I have to ride down and tell his mother—"

About then Cole, Valerie, and Rocky arrived in a fast buckboard. Cole reined up, his face pale and drawn. "Tell me it isn't so?"

Chet held up his hand. "No, Cole. You heard the truth."

"Oh, Lucy." Valerie handed the boy to her husband, jumped off the buckboard, and ran to Lucy. Both women were in tears as they held one another. The scene knifed him. Had he been the final one to drive the suicide knife into Reg? *Go see a doctor before you go home*.

No, it was deeper than that and he would probably never understand what happened. Somewhere in Reg's mind, bad things in his life had shifted against him. His limited ability to walk, ride, or move through life may have sentenced him to such a terrible act. But he had always been a leader—a shadow of his uncle.

Chet closed his dry eyes from the bite of the north wind. This was the worst damn Christmas day he'd ever had in his life. Even worse than the day when they realized the Comanche had swept away with the twins. Maybe he wasn't old enough then to know how serious that loss was—but this day struck him harder than losing a wife or finding a woman he loved murdered in her bloody bed.

Lord, find me the strength . . . to face the dark days ahead.

CHAPTER 22

Louise and Harold Parker had not attended the Christmas party. Usually, they came together, but Louise approached him while they were in town the week before Christmas and apologized to him for their absence in advance. They were taking that evening for Harold's family and ranch crew. Chet understood and told her not to worry about it. Then she said, jokingly, "I know JD can't come. Lord he's like you busy running that big place. I'm lucky his wife Bonnie writes me. I'm certain Reg and Lucy will bring the baby by while they are down here."

"Oh, yes."

After years of his aunt barking at him about everything, when she'd met Harold and married him, all that had settled down. Now he was going to have to steel himself to tell her about Reg.

Liz accompanied him and they drove to their fine ranch headquarters. The wind was still sharp, but the sun radiated some heat on their front side driving south. The stock dogs started barking up a storm as they came up the drive, and

Harold came out, dressed to the tees. Even at home he wore the smart clothes of a successful businessman.

"Merry Christmas, to the both of you," the older man said pleasantly as they dismounted.

"Harold," Chet said in a low voice, keeping a tight rein on his emotions. "I come on a mission with sad news. Reg shot himself last night."

"He did?" Pale now, Harold turned and caught his wife coming down the porch steps to greet them. "Louise, let's go back inside. We—well, they're here with some bad news."

"On Christmas?" Louise asked, confused.

Chet took off his hat when he entered and held it before him, his grip so tight on the brim his knuckles were white. "Louise, I am so sorry to tell you this, but—well, last night, Reg took his own life. None of us know why. He left no note."

Her mouth dropped open. "Are . . . are Lucy and the baby alright?" She looked very pale. He and Harold showed her to the couch, where she shivered and tried to catch her breath. "You have no idea why?"

"No. Lucy doesn't know, except since he had the bad horse wreck a few weeks back and was laid up. He was still in pain but I asked him to see a doctor about it while he was down here."

Tears spilled down her cheeks. "My God! Harold, my oldest did that. He was twice as strong as the others. Oh, I just want to go cry by myself."

"You aren't by yourself, my dear," her husband soothed her. "You and I can do many things. We have, and this, too, will pass. Cry now but realize that life counts on the living to carry forth."

Chet felt he could not have said it better himself,

and with Harold to comfort her in their very perfect, decorated house, he and Liz would slip off and leave them. It was the respectful thing to do.

Harold saw them out and thanked them kindly. Chet shook his hand and promised him they would be told when and where the funeral would take place.

"My first visit to her house," Liz said after a few moments of silence. "Would you like your house to look like hers?"

Chet shook his head violently. "Not no, but hell no. And I am *not* wearing a buttoned vest and suit coat to relax in, either, my darling."

"She was dressed just as well, too. It's not Sunday, either. I suspect they dress like that every day."

He flicked the team into a trot. "That woman was pure hell to live with under the same roof in Texas. I could have killed her more than once. I offered to sponsor her to go back to New Orleans, where my uncle found her. No, she *had* to come to Arizona to supervise me. Then Harold came along and they suited one another. Thank *God*."

"I know you're taking this hard, Chet. But Reg's decision to take his own life was his and his alone. None of us did anything but support him in every way. He had a working ranch, a loving wife, a beautiful baby girl, and another one on the way. We don't know what pain and misery he'd had since the wreck, but it shouldn't have driven him to what he did. So stop blaming yourself, like I know you are. Reg made his decision, and you would never have been able to stop him if he had his mind made up."

"I'll try. Liz, I'm sorry I brought you into this."

"I came for you, darling. I didn't expect it to be a walk

in the rose garden. Life always has one more kick in the belly for us to show us how bad things can really be. You lost that boy, Heck. Back in Texas you lost a woman to a killer, you left a woman behind who bore you a son. Then Marge. Buck up, my cowboy," she said with authority. "You and I are the survivors. From that bloody pool on the tile floor my husband died in to Reg in a casket today, they left us here for us to continue on. I'm proud to be here, and to help you through this bitter tragedy. I want to light some candles while we are in town."

"So it shall be."

She hugged his arm. "Later today, we will find a corner to hide in and make love. We need to get back on track."

"Thank you, sweetheart. You are a great part of my life. And we do need to renew our own good fortune."

"Remember when I told you I had a Christmas present for you and then never gave it to you? Well, I have a pocket watch." She stopped. "It was his. My husband's. But I think you should wear it. I know you tell sun time very well, but a man with a stage line to run needs a gold watch."

He chuckled darkly. "Hannagen may think I died, speaking of."

"Oh, no," Liz said knowingly. "You're his only hope for his stage line. All our lives hinge on you."

Her hand slipped into his own, and something heavy rested in his palm. He looked down at the shiny golden disc and the rich engraving around the casing. "Take it and tuck it in my vest," he said. "One more thing to remember, I'll need to keep it wound up."

She kissed his cold cheek and stuffed it in the vest side pocket under his open coat.

He held his cheek to hers. "That was a sweet Christmas present. Thank you, darling."

"A sweet gift for the sweetest man."

They rode together in silence for a few minutes, just enjoying being together.

Finally, she asked, "You think Drew can run the ranch up there?"

Chet frowned. "He's a serious young man, and with Lucy to guide him, I think it'll be fine. Plus, now he and Fern can get married."

"Matchmaker." She laughed. He had to smile. Leave it to her to bring him out of the darkness. What else was he? Just a man pleased to have her seated beside him.

In their discussion at the funeral home, they left the actual date open. They went by the church for her to pray and light candles, then they drove back to the ranch in the golden light of the late afternoon.

Monica had supper already set up in the dining room. Cole and Valerie were there with Rocky. Jesus and Anita were in attendance, as were Lucy and her girl. Susie, Sarge, and their boy; Victor, Rhea, and Adam were also waiting. About the time they were ready to eat, Tom and Millie arrived, too.

Chet looked around at all the solemn faces at the table. He saw sadness, despair, shock, confusion, anger. Reg's suicide had left a hole in every one of them. How could Chet help them all in their grief? How could he make it better?

"Let us bow our heads before we eat, and I will try to pray for all of us." They joined hands and closed their eyes. Chet took a deep breath and prayed for the strength not to falter now. "Most Heavenly Father, on the day of your son's birth, let us thank you. Lord, one of our family has gone to be with you. Hold him in the palm of your hand. He was a good young man with a very troubled mind. Help him find his way in your Kingdom. I am sure he will be healed and found well in the light of Your love.

"Lord on this day, bless our food and be in all our hearts when we part and go down the trail of life. Thank you for the strength you share with all of us, for we are weak but thou art strong. In his name we pray. Amen."

"Amen," they all agreed.

"Thank you all for being here. Today, our family had to part with a loved one. A father, a nephew, a husband. A great man. But let us look forward, at the dawn of a new day. We must go on, for life is for the living, no matter how hard it is. We must take a step down a new road. This day will be over our shoulder and a brighter one will lighten the sky. Let us live our lives better, count our blessings, and be grateful for the good life we have as a family—"

"Hampt and May are here," Liz whispered from his side. "I'll go greet them." She got up, and heads turned. She waved them back down. "I'm coming back. Everyone eat."

Liz met the couple at the front door. Tears streamed down Hampt's face and May looked ashen. Liz gathered them both into a hug.

"Why?" Hampt sobbed.

"It's a question we've all asked ourselves a thousand times since it happened," Liz told him. "He left no note."

"Is Lucy alright?" May asked.

"She's trying to be strong. She'd just learned they'll be having another child next summer. Come in and join us for dinner, now, though. Everybody's here."

May nodded, wiping her eyes.

Hampt shook his head. "He's the last one I'd expected to do that," he said as they walked into the dining room.

Chet agreed. "I thought the same thing." He sighed. "Come eat. Monica carried plates in for you two. Life must go on."

"But this is such terrible news," May said.

"Nothing we could have done, though. It was his decision."

Hampt nodded, shrugging out of his heavy coat. Liz had taken May's to hang up on the porch.

Everyone settled. Chet had no appetite and picked at his food.

Down the table, Tom cleared his throat. "Chet?"

"Yes, Tom?"

"I, um, I misunderstood something you told me last night. I went ahead and sent Bennie on up to the rim ranch to get a jump on taking over. I forgot to have him come talk to you first."

Chet waved a hand dismissively. "No problem. It's been a rough day. I can talk to him anytime. That young man has his head on straight."

Lucy nodded. "Drew can handle things until I get back. He's a good worker."

Tom said, "He sure is. I will miss him."

Chet nodded and thanked the Lord for his work. This had been the longest day of his life, but things were already coming back to some kind of normal.

CHAPTER 23

The funeral crowd overflowed the Methodist church, and many had to stand out in the cold sunshine at the end-of-the-week ceremony to show their respect. Reg was laid to rest in a gravesite near Marge's. Afterward there was a meal ready for all back at the ranch.

Tanner approached and asked him how the stage business was progressing.

"Slow, with all this business," Chet replied. "But Cole and I plan to attack it tomorrow at our house. We've solved one problem for them. We'll handle the mail with buckboards until we get stations built. They had no idea what they were doing, I can tell you that."

"If they're smart, they will listen to you."

"And if they don't, they can have it for themselves."

Tanner agreed. "You still working the stage robbery?"

"My Force down south is. I found a few leads for them to look at."

"I hope you get them."

"We will," Chet assured him. "Takes time now."

He shook the banker's hand and went on to talk to others.

Frey, the liveryman, said he could sell the mules from the stage heist getaway for ninety dollars apiece if they wanted to sell them.

"Try your buyer at a hundred and twenty," Cole said, listening at Chet's shoulder. "They're good mules, and we have to pay for their feed."

"I'll let you know." Frey nodded his head at the answer. "Horse traders, you know."

"They all drive hard bargains."

"Coming and going," Frey agreed. "I better find Gloria. We need to get back to town. Great meal. I didn't know Reg myself, but folks from around here and up there talked highly about him."

"We'll never know why," Chet said sadly.

"I feel sorry for his wife."

"Lucy's a survivor," Cole told him. "She'll make it."

"That's good. I better get going."

That evening in bed, Liz told him she spoke to Lucy at great lengths about her own experiences and why she must keep her eyes open. How she had refused to accept the gold diggers and at last woke up and found him.

"I told her to leave her options open."

"I love you for it."

"Oh, you're too easy to please."

He tickled her for that.

Life went on. He and Cole went over the stage line details they needed to work out. The telegram from Hanna-gen mandated a mail run every three days to meet the contractual agreement. That was much better than a daily schedule. But they'd still need temporary stopovers for fresh horses and drivers. Their figures pointed to a minimum of at least fifteen buckboards and twice as many teams. A dozen drivers and the support teams would be needed to staff this system as a whole. The supply stops would need to be stocked with food and palatable water for the drivers on the road.

The requirements grew larger and larger.

"We have some time," Chet said finally. "I think you and I need to divide up and go locate folks willing to meet these buckboards at appropriate places with food and water, fresh horses and fresh drivers at regular intervals. Maybe even a place for our drivers to sleep for a few hours. We'll have traffic coming and going from east and west."

"We might also find us some ranches or farmers who can host and operate a stage stop later on," Cole added.

"They're a little wide apart for these runs compared to what we'll need for a stage line. But yes, we'll do that. Folks see someone making a little money, it might be easier to sign them up."

"We sure picked a great time to find them," the younger man agreed. "Bound to be lots of snow up there from here on."

"That won't matter," Chet said. "By June or July this service has to roll. No snow then."

"I guess no one else is going to do it but us, huh?"

"Pretty much. You go west and I'll go east. We can use the big map for about where we need the services to be set up. If we can't find anyone near that point, then we'll need to scout out a place close by to put it."

"You taking Jesus?"

He nodded. "Yes."

"Can I take Bennie and Ramon, then? It worked them

riding with us the last time. Those two guys are sharp and no one will give the three of us any trouble."

"You sure can. We'll talk to Raphael."

"Who else you taking?" Cole asked.

"Maybe that orphan boy from the Verde Ranch, Spud. He hustles."

"He'll bust his buttons to join you. Tom may complain, though. Drew was his best hand, and now you're taking off with Spud."

"Yeah he might at that. But Drew and Fern have some plans. I am sure he's grateful to be near her."

"Tom spoke highly about him to me. I know Lucy is a real rancher, but having another baby and all—"

"Cole, I can tell you running that ranch is all she wants to do. I know she was cut off below the knees by his death, but she can run it forever for my money."

"Oh, I think she can run it just fine, and with good help, do it well. But not many men would let a woman do that. That's loyalty right there, boss."

"You guys are my family," Chet said. "Families stick together. She's gutsy enough. And if she can't, she's honest enough to turn it back to me."

"That's why you're the boss." The young man turned back to the map. "Let's finish plotting out where we need these stops, though."

"When do you plan to leave on your part?"

Cole stopped. "You mean—"

Chet smiled. "You're going to lead this deal, I'm making it your decision."

No hesitation. "Monday. New Year's Day."

"Fine by me, partner. Line up your men. Now, the map."

They agreed they'd each locate four stations on each side from the base planned on their land at the base of the peaks. He nor Cole needed to worry about the first or last stations. That would be on Hannagen and the company.

"That isn't half as bad," Cole said, sounding relieved.

"No, but it would be much neater in the summertime."

"You two stage coach planners want lunch today?" Liz asked from the doorway. "Monica has it ready."

"We'll come to eat." Chet rose from the chair. "We're planning the stations we'll need for the buckboard delivery. He's taking the west. I'm going east."

"Who goes with him?" She indicated Cole.

"Ramon and Bennie."

"You?"

"Jesus and that orphan boy Spud who works for Tom."

"You think I'd freeze if I went along?"

He caught her up in his arms. "You tell me."

Cole rolled his eyes in mock disgust. "C'mon, you two lovebirds, break it up. I need my appetite."

Liz laughed so hard her face turned red. "I'd better stay home and split my time between Val and Rhea and their boys."

"It won't be an easy trip."

She hugged his waist and they went on to eat lunch.

Someone had gone for the mail and brought it by with a letter from Shawn at Tubac. Chet put his lunch aside to read it.

Chet,

We have located Nelson and Armstrong in Tucson. They run an import company. It may be a front, though. Not much comes or goes at their warehouse under our observation. Fred Dodge is helping us cover them. The woman, Ruth Carlson, can't be found. No one seems to know where she

*is at. Brad Crawford is another no-show. Roamer
thinks he's over near the action at Tombstone.
Lots of private big stake games over there, and
our information says he is a gambler. Sorry I
have no more information. I will write you again
next week about what we find.*

Shawn

Nothing there. He handed the letter over to Cole for him
to read.

"Shawn and the boys down south haven't learned much."
Cole put down his fork to read the letter. "Wonder
where the loot's at?"

"Probably wherever Crawford is at," Chet mused. "That
gold was in bars. They may have to send it to Mexico and
melt it down to sell it."

"Think they'll slip up?"

"Yes, and we need to be ready."

"I can't see how you two will do that while you're out
finding stage stops." Monica shook her head.

"Oh, Monica, don't forget we have ranch business, too,
to deal with on the way."

"Chet Byrnes, you get any more to do, they'll have to
make a second one of you. And them boys of yours are
too small right now."

Everyone laughed.

Chet sent a note off for Spud to prepare to head out
New Year's Day, and that they'd pick him up as they
passed by the lower ranch. Cole went home to get Valerie
and Rocky. They would spend a little time on the ranch
before he and his men left the same time.

* * *

The weather held off. A bunch of the outfit showed up at the ranch to ring in the New Year. Chet told them all about his plans at ten o'clock and went to bed. Liz thanked them all for coming and joined him.

Up before daylight, Monica had breakfast ready for Chet, Liz, the two *vaqueros*, Jesus, Cole, Valerie, Liz, and the oldest boy, Rocky. Liz gave Chet a hard time about leaving in the cold, and he told her things had to be lined up for the stage business to get going.

They rode out in the pre-dawn and reached the canyon road as the sun crept over the horizon. Dark shadows stretched out all around them, but thankfully, there was not much ice, and they were soon out on the flats and at the lower ranch house.

Rhea and her housekeeper, Lea, expected them and had coffee and pastry laid on. Spud was there waiting for them, pleased they'd invited him to join the expedition.

Chet explained they were going to try to set up stage stations for a buckboard mail run from Gallup to the Colorado River. Victor and Tom came in from the cold and joined them. Chet repeated his plans to them, then was soon off once again.

They rode north for Robert's place up at the sawmill. His wife met them in the afternoon and Robert came in early. There was snow on the ground, but he said the skidding was going good enough and the mill was running six days a week to fill orders. Part of them slept in the workers' bunkhouse, the rest in the house and left again before dawn.

They got ready to split up a few hours later at the base of the mountains.

He and Cole had gone over the plans and what they could pay for the stops, and what to do if there was no ranch or farm available at or near the location. When they'd return to the ranch, they'd combine their report for Hannagen.

"Sure appreciate this chance, boss," Cole said as they shook hands.

"Nobody deserves it more, Cole," Chet replied. "Take as long as you need. *You're* the boss on this one. Be careful. And check on Lucy for me, would you?"

"You know it."

Chet knew Lucy could handle things, but he wanted to be sure she didn't have problems. It wouldn't have been such a worry except that she was facing having another baby. That would be bad enough without a husband, let alone running a ranch. He hoped that Fern's man could run the place. Tom thought Drew could, and knew him better as a worker than Chet did. That counted for a lot.

He, Jesus, and Spud were out of the snow when they camped near the first stop east that night. They set up a sidewall tent on the open prairie just below the junipers, where they could pick up enough firewood for a day or so. But so far, they had seen no farms or ranches in the area.

"Tomorrow we split up," Chet told them. "And look for someone to be a station agent or find a place to build a stop."

They slept fully clothed in the tent, and in the morning crowded to the heat side of Jesus's cooking fire. This station hunting would be a challenge. They rode off into the morning three separate ways, with the understanding to return to camp to compare notes by an hour before sundown.

Chet returned late afternoon to a surprise—a man seated at their campfire waiting for him.

"Good afternoon, sir," Chet said warily, keeping his hand close to his six-shooter. "This is our campsite. Is there something we can help you with?"

The stranger stood and introduced himself as one Herman Rothschild. And in a friendly way, he asked what they were doing up there in the cold.

"Chet Byrnes. You ranch up here?" Chet asked, shaking his hand and putting his glove back on.

"Oh, a short way north of here. A young man came by and said you needed a station or something, so I rode out to say hello. What's this all about?"

"You must have spoken to my man, Spud. We need a way station near here for our buckboard mail run. Eventually, it will be a full-fledged stage stop."

"He was very honest with me," Rothschild said. "I think I've got what you need."

"Well, let's discuss the operation before you make a commitment. You would need to keep fresh horses, feed the driver or the replacement stationed there. He may from time to time have a passenger or two. That's in the near term. In the future, we will need an actual stage stop. There are many plans available for that. You provide it and we rent it, or we build it on a leased deal, or we buy the land and build it."

The other rancher considered this. "Can you use a place a mile or so north of here?"

"I imagine so, if you have water and want to operate it."

"What would you pay?"

"Fifty dollars a month. And we'd buy your hay for seven dollars a ton. Do you have corrals and water enough for the horses?"

"I do. But I also have a Navajo wife. Would that bother you?"

Chet chuckled. "If she won't scalp them, I'd say no problem."

"Oh, hell, she speaks English. But some folks are prejudice. You just never know."

"My men should be coming in anytime soon. I'm glad Spud found you. Let's hear what else they found, and we can make a deal if they haven't promised someone else."

"Fine by me. I have nothing pressing this evening."

Chet dismounted and stretched. "You find your wife out here?"

"Oh, yeah. Mine died in west Texas coming out here from Arkansas. When I met her, I was taking care of my two young boys while trying to get my wagon and mules out here. I was camped, fixing a harness, and she came along. Never expected her to stay, but she was good at fixing leather. I wondered if she'd become my wife—the boys loved her. She said yes."

"What's her name?"

"I can't pronounce it," Rothschild said, red-faced. "I just call her Darling."

"Good deal. Tomorrow we'll stop at your place."

"You can't miss it. I'll tie a red hanky on a stake so you find it."

"Thanks. We will be there in the morning."

"Mr. Byrnes, I ain't begging, but I could sure use that fifty dollars a month."

"Herman, I understand."

His two scouts came in empty-handed. Spud said he had spoken to a big man named Ruth-child, and that he was the only one acted interested.

"He came to see me a while ago, Spud. You did a fine job. I think we can use him. How does his place look?"

Spud scowled. "It ain't the Verde Ranch."

"Well, what is?" He and Jesus laughed. "We just need a place for the horses and driver; it don't need to be real fancy out here."

"Oh, that place isn't near fancy," Spud said. "But he acted like a man understood what you need."

"Good. If we think he can do the job, we can spend some money on improvements. These places are crucial for the buckboards. No one else you saw today interested?"

"I saw two women who said their husbands were away working and they would not talk about anything without them being there," Jesus reported. "But they didn't have what we needed, from what I saw. So I thanked them and left."

"Alright." Chet slapped his hands together. "Unless this one falls through. He needs the income and acted excited to help. Let's eat and get some shut-eye, and we'll go see him in the morning. I suspect our days ahead will not be so rewarding as today."

They were at the low-walled cabin an hour or so after dawn. On initial inspection, the corrals, Chet agreed, would need to be expanded. He could see the well house and wondered how good it was.

Rothschild's wife came out to greet them.

"You must be the stagecoach men. I saw this young man yesterday," she said, pointing to Spud. "Please, my husband calls me Darling."

"Is he here?" Chet asked.

"I can ring the bell and he will come. He is clearing some land for a garden next year. He is a hard worker."

She pulled the rope and a schoolhouse bell on the tall post peeled away.

With a hoe and ax on his shoulder, Rothschild came up hill and smiled.

"You met my wife?" he asked, dropping the tools.

"Yes, sir. And my men and I think you should get the job, if you want it."

"That's the best news I've heard all day," the rancher exclaimed.

Chet jerked his head toward the wellhead. "How good is that well?"

"Twenty-eight feet deep and it has a real vein of water coming in it," Rothschild replied, leading them that way. "When I broke through the rock bottom, the water rushed in so fast, Darling had to reel me up in the bucket. There's sixteen feet of water in it and that's enough to shut it down and flow underground. I was amazed. I'd dug several wells in the Ozarks, but never expected to find one like that out here. I witched it and there's a spring course under here."

Chet dropped a small rock in the well and heard the splash. Satisfied, he said, "We think we'll need to build some larger corrals for the horses and bring in some hay. Depends on how many horses we have to keep here. If I had the poles delivered, could you build the corrals if we are short-handed?"

"I'd be glad to build them."

"When the poles get here, we would start the payments at fifty dollars a month."

"That would help."

"I also can stake you to two hundred pounds of *frijoles* when the men bring the poles and posts."

"Oh, I will repay you."

"I am not that concerned about that. I want you and your family to have food enough to get by until this works. It's wintertime, and my team will have to fight the good and bad days to cut the poles and then get them here."

"Digging post holes is hard in this cement. I'll need a plan and measurements so I can start digging them."

"We can do that right now," Chet said. "Jesus, you have a tape in our packs. We can set that corral out with stakes. Spud, get an ax and use some of his firewood to make the stakes."

"Good. I'll get some twine and cut me some lengths to measure the spaces, too." The man rubbed his hands together excitedly.

"Jesus, can we get enough lodge pole–like pines for twelve-foot spans?" he asked.

"That shouldn't be a problem," his tracker replied.

"Now, Herman, don't kill yourself," he said. "I trust you. Do what you can and rest in between. We're going to make you our man up here. I need for this buckboard deal to work. Worst comes, we can use your pens until we find the help."

He swallowed hard. "I can do it. I won't let you be disappointed."

"Jesus, you and Spud make us some lunch. Herman and I are going to walk this off. We need a good space here from the house so the dust doesn't bury the cabin."

Herman shook his head. "I never thought about that."

"We'll plan this to work. I want it to work for you, too."

They walked off the space Chet felt they needed for the big corral, some smaller ones to keep crippled horses in, to separate horses with bad dispositions from the others. Darling came and helped the boys cook lunch, and they were soon laughing up a storm. He felt good about this deal. A quarter of his needs for stops would work at this ranch.

He made notes of the pole and post needs, as well as gate hinges, latches, and nails to hold them up. Then they'd need some forage brought in. Rothschild's supply would winter his stock, but not the company horses as well. In his notes, Chet added a sled and some barrels to bring the water to the pens, plus some boards for water tanks, and caulking to seal them.

The sun had warmed things. They ate lunch on a makeshift table with the two young boys and Darling. She spoke good English and it was clear how much the boys loved her. Herman sat down to eat and asked to say a prayer. His flowery words thanked the Lord at their having found him, and asked for the strength to be ready for the buckboards' arrival. He blessed the food and their business. Amen.

After lunch, they staked out the rough plan for the pens. Spud rode out to hunt and shot an antelope. They dressed him properly and Darling cooked them some ribs for supper. With their camp and tent set up, Chet made out a written agreement with Rothschild and they both signed it.

Chet felt good. One down. Three more, and they would have the east half sewed up. He wished Liz was there to share in this first success. After all, it could be a while before they had another one. The next station needed was forty miles east. He'd bet that one would not be so easy, but he was ready to move on and find out what awaited.

The sun rose on another warm morning, typical of winter up on top of the rim. All they needed was another day or two of good weather, and they'd be settled in the next area. Hopefully before another blue northern blew in.

They set up camp in the new map grid in the afternoon, and Chet decided to do a little scouting before sundown. A couple of miles down the trail, they came across a store/saloon. Chet nearly couldn't believe his luck. If a deal could be struck, this would be another perfect site. Hitching his horse outside, he adjusted his gun belt on his hip and marched on in, Spud trailing along behind. Jesus stayed with the horses.

A grizzly old man owned it. Rue Kline had two teenage wives that were filthy, dirty, and lazy. Chet formed a quick opinion that they worked as prostitutes, as well as waitresses for Kline's clientele.

With one watery eye shut in a mask of white whiskers, Kline sized him up from behind the dirty counter, wearing a filthy apron soiled by blotches of blood and cow shit.

"What'cha business, mister?"

"I'm looking for a stage station and a place to change horses."

"You found it."

"I am talking about a place where travelers will need to change coaches, eat, and rest while horses are changed. This pig pen wouldn't be used by my company."

Kline showed his yellow, broken teeth in a smile. "They can like it or lump it, because I don't care. I've got the only water and only place for twenty miles. And I can tell you I ain't doin' it fur nothing. So get ready to shell out five hundred dollars a month to use it." His high-pitch laughing sounded near maniacal.

"Well, we won't use it I can guarantee you that," Chet spat, anger building. "Good day."

"Hey, you fancy gawdamn sumbitch," the old man crowed at his back. "I'll charge you a thousand dollars to use it when you come back begging me for it."

"One more outburst like that and you won't have any teeth to chew on your tobacco."

Chet waved Spud on outside, almost expecting a bullet in his back. But the uppity old fart was all mouth like he figured.

Two days later, they met a man on horseback named Clyde Covington, just outside Covington's ranch. Chet told him about the operation and what he needed, now and in the future.

"Oh, you ain't using ole man Kline?" A smug look crossed the man's face.

"No, thank you. I stopped and saw right off the company would never use him."

"How's it work?"

"This first thing we plan is a buckboard delivery of U.S. mail over this road. We need stations every forty miles to change teams. Care for our horses, make the changes, put up our drivers, and feed them and an occasional passenger or two."

"What's it pay?"

"Fifty dollars a month to operate it. I'll provide the hay or buy yours."

"That's six hundred a year, ain't it?"

"Yes, sir."

Covington frowned, considering. "Would you maybe

buy two hundred steers for your Navajo drives from me next year if I set you up on my place?"

"They need to be at least three years old and fleshy," Chet replied, sensing a kindred spirit. "Since you're here and those will be unfamiliar cattle with ours, you'll need to provide four hands to help us get them to Gallup."

"No problem." He leaned back in the saddle. "Come to my house and camp there. I'll build the corrals, drill a well to water them, and build a house to hold them."

"You know my terms for the cattle sales?"

"Hell, yes. No problem at all. You just ensured me that I could keep on ranching. I'll put the stop two miles east of him on the road. Is that close enough?"

"Oh, yes. I may have plans coming for the house."

"Hell, I don't know how you made that Navajo beef deal work. I am amazed. But, Chet Byrnes, I'm about to cry over our cattle deal. Come on to the house, I need to tell my wife. Thank God you came by and saw me."

He rode ahead to get supper set up for them. Jesus spoke first as the dust settled. "How much will he get for his cattle?"

"Sixteen hundred dollars."

"He was about to cry," Spud said. "Why?"

"He has no market for that many steers around here. His sale is a fortune to him. It'll cover his expenses for several years."

"Chet, after you guys told me about that old goat in the sinkhole," Jesus said, "I thought we'd never find a place for a stop out here. I hope they appreciate you back at the headquarters of this outfit. No one else could have made that deal but you."

"Hey, we may be halfway done tomorrow," Spud added.

"Good thing, too," Chet said, seeing the high clouds in

the north fixing to sweep down on them. "More winter's coming."

Spud took his hat off and slapped his horse with it. "Damn it! I was just thawing out."

They laughed. Chet was proud of his choice of the young man to ride with them. It wasn't like having Cole riding alongside, but Spud would make a real hand in time.

It snowed that night. Clyde's wife, Iris, baked some raisin-dry apple pies and fussed a lot over the three of them continually. Chet found her to be a straight-backed woman with a good sense of humor. She and her husband had come to this land from Texas and established a ranch with a few Navajo boys as their ranch hands. They had lost two children over the past three years since the move. While he knew many people lost their offspring short of three years of age, the idea bothered him now more than ever before. Maybe because he had two boys of his own now growing that way.

"What's your wife doing while you're up here?" Iris asked.

"Elizabeth's probably playing with my boys."

"They aren't hers?"

"No, they're from my past. My first wife was lost in a horse accident shortly after we had a son. Another woman I intended to marry had to stay in Texas to care for her family, had a child after I left, and never told me. She died of pneumonia not long ago, and her grown daughter informed me about the boy."

Iris smiled. "Tell me about your current wife. I would love to meet her."

"She was a widow, owned a large *hacienda* in Mexico.

She wanted to buy a special horse from me and so we met down on the border. I feared I would never see her again, but we corresponded and she came back to marry me."

"Oh, that sounds so romantic to me. You have plans for a family?"

"We do. But no results yet."

She nodded. "I understand that. We have the same problems."

"Maybe some day."

"I pray a lot."

"So do we. When she's with me next time, we'll stop by and you can meet her."

"Wonderful."

"It's a deal."

They both looked up when the men came in floured with snow from caring for the stock and storing their pack items.

Covington shook his head. "Looks like you need to sleep in here tonight where it's warm."

"Thanks, Clyde. I meant to ask if you know anyone forty miles east of here who would serve as a station."

"Your best man is Simon. He owns the trading post 'round those parts. He likes money and has the facilities to handle the job."

"You know him?"

"Met him. He drives hard deals, but in the end I imagine you and him can come to an understanding."

"I had no idea what this trip would bring; things are going well. I've got another team working out west. I plan to set up our main station where the military road goes south below the San Francisco Peaks. There's a small settlement there now."

"I was there once. It should work. Your ranch isn't there? Isn't it on the east leg of the road going down to Preskitt?"

"You mean the Windmill? Where we gather the cattle to drive to Gallup?"

"Yes."

"I decided we needed a point east to start from. So we gather them up there, settle them down, then drive them to the Navajo. The grass is good and the cattle stay fat. We put up lots of prairie hay when we can and so we have a supply in case of drought or snow."

"You figured out a lot since you came here."

"I feel I came here at the right time. The Indian troubles were holding many folks out. Cole and I were attacked on the first cattle drive to Gallup. I wondered if we could survive, but we did."

"I met the man runs that for you, Sarge. He's a real military man."

"Sarge is a strong boss, but he keeps help. They know what he wants and they do it."

"He told me he had no say about where they buy cattle."

"He didn't lie to you. The plan was made to sell our cattle first. That's what makes my operation work. We do buy cattle outside, of course, and Tom, my Verde Ranch foreman, heads that. It isn't we don't buy cattle, what we need is quality cattle to fill our contract. We take that very serious. Ranchers supplying cattle know we will turn down anything less than top-quality beef. We try to keep at least a month's supply on hand to meet our needs at the Windmill."

"I saw that. Mine will be what you need next year."

"Fine. I'll tell Tom what to expect."

"Iris and I are looking forward to being a small portion of your supply chain."

At that point, she served some of her piping hot apple pie. "I don't have any champagne to serve you. This will just have to do."

"This suits us better anyhow," Jesus said.

"Yeah, you can always get something to drink," Spud said. "Great pies is lots harder to find."

Later that night, Chet and Clyde signed the agreement to set up the stopover.

The cold stayed, but the snow only gave them a dusting. They rode east the next day, blasted by a cold north wind every step of the way. That evening they reached the trading post Covington had talked about, and Chet met Simon. He was a tall man, in his forties, with an untrimmed beard sprinkled with gray. He stayed solemn and thoughtful while Chet explained his proposition.

"Fifty dollars is all you pay each month?"

"That's my deal. As a stage station we will, of course, increase our payment. For the buckboard portion—which will last perhaps nine months—that fifty dollars is our payment."

"How many horse changes will we have to do?"

"I suspect one per day," Chet told him. "Maybe less."

"Feed drivers?"

"About the same."

"I don't think you're being fair to the station owner." He poured himself some whiskey in a tin cup that he had offered Chet and he had declined.

"We'll buy the hay from you or supply it."

"Yes, but I have to worry about them arriving, feeding them, and even put them up to sleep."

"Well it's fifty dollars more than you make now."

Simon sipped on his liquor and wiped his mouth with the back of his hand. "What will I have to do to have a stage stop?"

"We have several plans. We build it. You build it. We will have a standard plan for it."

"I don't think I am interested."

"I will have a stopover in this area." Chet sighed. "I came to you first as the leader in business here."

"Where will you put it? This is tribal land. You can't get any permit to build on it."

"You don't understand, this project supercedes that authority in order to get the mail through."

He shook his head at Chet. "That will take years to get through the red tape."

"You have a federal permit to have this store here. What if they don't renew it?"

"You threatening me?" Simon demanded.

"Oh, no. Just asking a question?"

"I want two hundred fifty a month for messing with you."

"I'll be here for a few days. Consider it?"

Simon shook his head and tossed down more whiskey. "I won't even think about it."

Chet left the man, disgusted with even wasting his time on talking to him. There had to be someone else to talk to. He went off and slept full-dressed under a pile of blankets.

"I wished we'd stayed back at Clyde's," Spud grumbled, moving about to get ready to make breakfast.

"Good comes with the bad in this deal," Jesus told him. "It's cold here but it was colder in Utah a few years ago." His breath was steaming out of his mouth.

"Glad I wasn't there. Hey, here comes an Injun woman to see us."

Chet went out the flap. "Good morning, can I help you?"

The thin young woman wrapped in a blanket turned her face from the wind. "He says you come eat breakfast. He wants to talk some more."

Both of his men stared at him, waiting for his reply.

Chet almost chuckled out loud. "Tell him we accept and are coming."

"Amen," Spud said under his breath.

She nodded, satisfied, and lifted her hood back up from the blanket. Then she went back for the post.

They followed. Chet was not sure if his veiled threat about the federal permit had changed Simon's mind, or the fear of more competition in the area. They settled the deal by noon. He offered them a warm room to stay in, and Chet accepted it.

The weather settled down and he wrote Hannagen a long letter detailing the deals he'd made for all the needed eastern stops, and that Cole was working the western side. He finished by saying before they headed home they needed one more place forty miles east of him.

"Johnny White Feather is a full blood been to school for Injuns in Pennsylvania. He maybe a mile or two differences, but he'll work with you. He's the money-makingest guy I ever met."

Two days later they signed up the six-foot-tall Indian with his four wives. Chet liked the friendly, tall Navajo and he acted excited about becoming a stage stop owner. The man had three Navajo wives and one from a different tribe. But Chet considered her as more educated and maybe the boss; her name was Rose.

"You know she's a Comanche?" Spud said, riding beside him.

"Rose?" Chet turned in the saddle.

Spud nodded. "He met her at school back east."

"How did he get her? Did you learn how he did that?"

"Yeah. She wrote him to come get her and she would help him manage his business."

"Where was she?"

"In the Oklahoma Territory, Fort Sill."

"We heard them talking about her," Jesus said.

"Well I hope Cole's done this well. We swept this deal in my opinion."

Chet felt confident they would make their end work, but the fourth wife being an outsider was sure different. He went to making plans.

They would need a team to cut poles for the corrals and then deliver them to Rothschild. He hoped the plans for the buildings at the stage stops were already drawn. Lots to do and he didn't have a clue how well Cole was doing. When they'd first parted, he told Cole and the men to come back to the Preskitt Valley house. They'd meet them there—whenever.

They stopped at the Windmill Ranch, taking a short-cut home. Susie greeted them. That evening he explained his plans with her and Sarge.

"I know that trader Simon. He's an old grump," Sarge said. "I avoid him."

"I would, too, but I needed a stop there and he has the facilities. He wanted lots more money than I wanted to spend at first. But when I told him his federal trader license might be in jeopardy, he must have taken notice."

"Could you have done that?" Sarge asked with a small smile.

"Maybe. We'll never know, though. He signed on the dotted line."

"Oh, Chet, it sure gets complicated, doesn't it?" Susie asked.

"Susie, it has for years."

"I guess so. Lucy wrote me and said she was fine, by the way."

"That's good. I haven't shaken that. It stabs at me a lot."

"Oh, it was so sad. I wish we had an answer why he did that."

"Something provoked him is all I can say."

She shook her head. "You have lots on your mind."

"Part of my job. We as a family continue, which is as I want it to be." Chet sighed, and changed the subject. "We made very good progress with the stage deal and I hope that Cole is doing likewise out west."

"He's a serious part of your team," Susie said. "And Valerie is tickled to death to have that boy."

Chet agreed. They turned in early to ride on to the Verde Ranch the next day. They made it there by late afternoon and Rhea was excited when they rode in.

"You weren't gone long."

"We work fast." Chet hugged her. "How are you guys doing?"

"Liz was here a few days ago; we had a good visit. I love my big house and being married. And I will get a big supper ready for you three."

"Sounds good. I sent Jesus to find Tom. What's Victor doing today?"

"He and his men are fencing land up at the Hereford unit for a hay meadow."

"You know how they're coming along?"

"You know Victor." She laughed. "He said they'd complete it by Friday."

"Well, that's married life, huh?"

"Oh, I am a happy woman and Adam keeps growing and talking. I'm going to get the boy for you and then I'll work on supper."

Jesus returned. "Tom is coming. He was doing bookwork and will be here shortly. He couldn't believe we did all that already."

"He didn't send kids to do it," Spud said. "Well he did send one—me."

They laughed.

CHAPTER 24

The next morning, Chet and his men rode on to the Preskitt Valley house. Tom was going to assemble some wagons and teams for the pole crew, and put together a list of the tools they'd need. They discussed a leader for the team but made no decision on the man to do it.

It was noontime when they rode up to the upper ranch. When Chet dismounted he heard his wife shout, "You're home!"

She raced out to hug and kiss him. Out of breath, she held him tight. "I worried you might have frozen."

"No way. We found all four places and came back to make them happen."

"Were you frostbit?"

"We were fine. It was cold and snowed up there, but no problems. We have the four stop sites east of the peaks. We'll see what Cole's done when he gets back."

"Good. Have you had lunch? Of course not. You guys come, too. Monica and I will feed you."

"Thanks, ma'am," Jesus said.

"Anything wrong here?" Chet asked, putting away his hat.

"Not a thing. You have some letters I didn't open. Hannagen sent a telegram for you. It was real short, just said, 'Thanks. Job well done.'"

"Good. There's lots of work to do and until Cole returns, we won't know about the other half. Good to be home, though. I was glad you weren't out in that deep cold."

"Oh, I behaved and stayed home. I visited both boys. They're healthy and growing. Monica and I played cards. She won."

"The stagecoach men have returned and aren't in bandages."

"Monica, we are careful men."

She looked hard at the ceiling for help and then shook her head. "I'm glad you are home safe."

"And I'm glad to be home." Chet went into the living room to read his mail.

Shawn wrote again to tell him they were watching the two parties from the stagecoach robbery, and that there was no sign of the Black Widow or Brad Crawford. In other words, Chet thought, they hadn't learned a single thing more.

A second letter postmarked St. David interested him more.

Dear Mr. Burns,

My name is Norma Shields. I am a widow in St. David. I understand that you are looking for the outlaw Brad Crawford. If I could have the reward, I would be pleased since my assets are small. He and a woman named Ruth are living on

*a ranch next to mine. My small ranch is a mile
east of the St. David Mormon Ward.*

*I can point out the ranch from mine. They
openly ride around the ranch, but never come
to town.*

Norma

Chet slapped his palm down on the table in excitement. He would write Norma immediately and thank her for the information, then wire Shawn as to where they might be at. That was a bonus.

Feeling better, he went back to the kitchen. "I think we just got word where Crawford is hiding with Ruth Carlson."

Jesus looked up. "Where's that?"

"A ranch east of Saint David." Chet waved the letter from Norma Shields. "We just got a tip."

"We going down there to arrest them?" the younger man asked.

"Shawn and Roamer can do that. Where's Anita?"

"She's babysitting Rocky so Val can help Jenn for the day at the café," Liz explained. "She didn't know you guys were coming back today."

"I simply wondered."

Monica served them her quickly prepared lunch.

Chet weighed whether he should ride out to help round up Crawford. He'd wait a day before he sent the wire to Shawn. Maybe he'd decide one way or the other by then. That cruel killer should be behind bars or hung from the neck. He must be pretty damn sure of himself to be riding openly around that ranch.

There was one more part to it, though. He would need real evidence to prove that Crawford was involved in the evildoings. Something that would hold up in court. There were no living witnesses to the murder on the trail. Only the stolen gold bars and cash could tie him to the crime. If they didn't have that, a good lawyer could get him off.

Would Crawford keep the gold bars on the ranch? Hidden? That was a risk.

Could he maybe trick him into showing someone the bars? He sighed. How in the hell could he do that? There had to be some way. It would be tragic to arrest the man and not be able to convict him of the crimes. Damned if he did and damned if he didn't. But evidence was what he needed.

After supper, he spoke to Jesus about Crawford and his concern that they still had no evidence clearly tying him to the crime.

Jesus was thoughtful. "I don't know a way but to testify as to what the dead man told us when we quizzed him."

"If the gold bars are there we have him, but a good lawyer will get him off otherwise."

"That don't sound right, boss. But he will."

"I'm going to think on it before I send the Force in to get them."

"As if you don't have enough on your mind already."

"Hell, Jesus, it's just part of the job."

"Well, I am going to bed." Jesus stood up and stretched. "Anita will come home tomorrow or your wife said I can go get her if I want to."

"Do that. I won't leave without you. Tell her I said hello."

"I will. Spud's down at the bunkhouse if you need him."

Chet went upstairs. His wife sat at her mirror brushing her hair. "Are you ready to sleep?"

"I don't know about sleep, but I'm sure ready to hold you. I've missed you, Liz."

"Still upset about Reg's death, aren't you?"

Chet shook his head. "I just can't figure it out. What a damn waste."

"I think he had too much on his mind," Liz said, rising from the vanity. "It began with his first wife's death. They said he wandered around for a long time before he came here. Then he met Lucy and started turning things around. But the horse wreck shattered his ability to shake off his loss of being invincible—that is the word, yes?"

"Yes."

"He was not himself, in pain all the time, but he couldn't do what he wanted to do and couldn't see himself ever doing it again."

"You mean he felt hopeless that he'd never be the same again?"

"That's right." She hugged him tightly. "And don't you ever consider such a thing."

"I won't." Chet shook his head wearily. "A thought like that never entered my mind."

"I think Reg was a person who was very critical of himself."

"Yes, he was." He sighed. "Let's go to bed. We won't ever solve it, but thank you. You've really thought about all the aspects, and what you said seems to settle me a little."

"I was bored without you here to entertain me," she said. "Might I have gone too far?"

"No. I count on your wisdom. I don't ever question your judgment; you're about the smartest person I know. On top of that, I love you."

"Good."

Thank you, Lord.

CHAPTER 25

He had breakfast with Jesus early the next morning before the young tracker rode out to get Anita. After he was gone, Chet settled down to read the latest issue of the *Miner* when his wife joined him.

"You make any decisions?" she asked.

"Not one different than last night. I wonder about Cole, but have to realize he couldn't make decisions like I did over east."

"Will you build another house up there at the Peaks before you get it done?"

"Cole and Valerie will need one if they're up there for a while."

"A house like you built Susie?"

"Yes, ma'am. Same plan as when we built Tom's."

"And Millie's and Lucy's." She nodded. "We should go up there and plan it."

"Good idea, darling. But first I'm considering going down there and arresting that outlaw Crawford as soon as Cole gets back here." Then he explained his concern to her about the lack of evidence.

Liz listened intently, but had no fresh outlook on how to trap Crawford into showing them the gold bars.

To take his mind off the problem, Chet suggested they work on bringing the ranch books up to date. A few hours later, he sat back in his chair, satisfied that their financial situation looked as good as ever.

He asked Liz, "Do you think Bo Evans could convince him he wanted to buy the gold bars? Few people know him. But he sure looks the part of a businessman."

"He might look even better with Ramon and Bennie along to make him look like the *gringo* out of Mexico seeking to buy cheap stolen gold bars."

"What will his new wife think about it?" Chet asked. "You'll be close by."

"I don't want Bo shot." He tossed down his pencil. "No, I need to trick Crawford into believing he can buy his way out and show me the gold."

"When?"

"When Cole gets back. He and Jesus are the only ones I trust to walk into that kind of fight with."

"Meanwhile you walk the floor." She jumped up and kissed him. "I love you so much."

"I love you." But he'd damn sure be walking that floor some more.

Three days later, Cole finally showed up, grinning from ear to ear.

He'd found the four stops they needed. Chet could tell by the smile alone.

Chet came off the porch and wrapped him in a bear hug. "You found yours?"

"Hell, yes, I did." Cole laughed. "Was there ever any doubt? You must have beat me, Old Man!"

"Old Man nothing! We've won this war, partner. I'm

going to have Jesus drive you home. In thirty hours we're headed down south to arrest Brad Crawford. The buckboard will come get you tomorrow night and we'll talk about it all on the way."

Cole was still grinning. "We really did something, huh?"

"Damn right, we did," Chet said, slapping him on the shoulder. "We got lots to do, but I want that killer Crawford in jail first. That whore he's with can rot with him, too, far as I'm concerned."

"You know where they're at?"

"Unless they rode off, yes, I've got a good idea."

"I'm ready. I'd like to have closure on that deal, too. Tomorrow night?"

"Tomorrow night," he affirmed. "We take the stage."

Jesus drove up with the buckboard and Cole climbed on. "My bedroll?"

Chet waved him off. "We'll pack it for you, saddle and all. Go and rest. Give Val and my boy my love."

"You got it, boss."

Jesus drove off.

"You need a horse holder?" someone asked from behind him.

He turned to find Elizabeth looking down at him from the porch. He pulled her down and hugged her tight. "Hell, yes."

He wired his crew at Tubac, setting everything in motion. One of the group was to secretly talk to his witness in St. David, Norma. The other was to have five horses ready to ride when they got there on Wednesday to arrest Crawford.

Lord, let him be there . . .

God, how he hated unfinished business.

CHAPTER 26

Wrapped in blankets once again, he and his four partners piled into the coach. Cole was fresh from his short reunion with Valerie, Jesus from his with Anita. Then there was Spud, who was about to bust his buttons getting to go along with the big men again. Elizabeth was tucked comfortably in the crook of Chet's arm.

The Black Canyon Stage rolled south, and with every mile it traveled, Chet felt more at peace. For the first time since they'd met the dead end at Rye, he felt like they were on their way to wrapping up this business with the stage robbery. It had been like a thorn in his brain since the moment they'd come home empty-handed.

Well they wouldn't be empty-handed much longer.

The cool, dark night enveloped them, rocking them gently into slumber. As the coach swept off the juniper-pinion slopes into the *saguaro*-clad mountains, the dawn arrived pink and cheery, and the aroma of creosote filled the warmer air. They soon arrived at Hayden's Ferry, where they unloaded to wait for the next southbound stage.

"I've sure had better places to sleep, haven't you, Spud?"

Liz asked their newest companion as they sat down to breakfast.

"Oh, Mrs. Byrnes," the young man gushed. "I am just so glad to be with y'all, I can't complain about one little thing."

"You're too easy pleased," Chet said, and sipped his coffee.

"I am that, sir," Spud said with a smile. "I sure am."

Back on the stage, they rocked out for Papago Wells and Tucson. Reaching there by nightfall, they stored their saddles and gear at the stage office, went for supper, and checked into a hotel. Exhausted already, they were told the stage for Benson left at six a.m. Sticky-eyed and travel-weary, they were there nonetheless and climbed on board. The coach reached the small village on the San Pedro River at noon. Shawn, Roamer, and the horses were there waiting for them, just like Chet had ordered.

"Howdy, boss," Shawn greeted them. "Two visits in a month. Feels like things are heating up."

"Gotta keep my eye on you young bucks," Chet replied, shaking his deputy's hand. "Make sure you're not making me look bad."

Hugs were exchanged all around before they mounted up and rode south for the Mormon community of St. David. He asked Shawn if their man was still there.

"I spoke to the nice lady you sent me to see yesterday. She told me both of them were still there."

"She expects some of the reward money," Chet explained. "And we'll sure take care of her if she's right."

"Too right," Roamer said disgustedly. "We damn sure couldn't have found him without her. His cronies in Tombstone told us they hadn't seen him in six months. And those guys who were on the stage during the robbery?

They've been close to their import business the whole time, never once went anywhere out of the ordinary. We have a man keeping an eye on them, too. As for the woman, well, I guess she's been hiding down here with Crawford the whole time."

"Well, keep your fingers crossed. It ain't over yet. We still need some of that loot to hang the crime on them."

They rode quietly through the community of small irrigated farms, not even looking at her place when they passed it. On the dusty road, they left town headed east. Shawn pointed to the cottonwoods.

"That house is in the middle of them."

"Get your guns out and keep sharp," Chet ordered. "This man will kill you, make no mistake. I'd like him alive, but it isn't necessary. Don't anyone get shot up." He jerked his Winchester out of the scabbard. "Liz, stay out here until we get them."

With a pained look, she reined her horse up and dismounted. With everyone else armed, they charged up the lane to the stucco house. A woman inside screamed. Cole dismounted in a spray of dust and took the open front door in a rush. Chet's horse carried him around behind the house, where he saw a man clear the wooden rail fence, running for his life. He reined the horse down and fired his rifle in the air.

"Stop or die, Crawford," he yelled.

The fleeing man came to a shaky halt and raised his hands over his head in surrender. While Chet covered him with his rifle, Jesus put the cuffs on him. He frisked the man, then shoved him around toward the front of the house.

"Brad Crawford?"

The man shook his head. "I'm not him."

"Yeah? Well you'll do for him." Chet dismounted and handed Spud his rifle. "We finally meet."

Cole had the woman of the house by the neck, forcing her outside through the front door. She wasn't coming easy, either. She looked mad as a badger, her face was red as her hair. But even in her roughed-up condition, Chet saw why the guy at the bank told her everything about the shipment.

Liz arrived and reined up her horse. "That was it?"

He about laughed. "These are the ones involved in the stage robbery."

"Lady," Cole told the woman, "if you sit down and be quiet, we won't put you in irons. You make a break, though, all bets are off."

Dismounted, Chet marched up to Crawford and got in his face. "Where are the gold bars?" he demanded.

"I don't know about any gold bars," Crawford said.

"Oh, you know alright. And your memory will get better."

"Liz," Cole said. "Will you make certain this lady doesn't get up and run?"

"She won't. She won't like those irons on her."

"She better not. But we need to find that gold."

Crawford chuckled. "You won't find any here."

They looked; they searched. They pulled up boards and tore down sheds. The crew finally came out and shook their heads.

Chet'd had enough. "Take him down to the stock tank and hold him under the water until his mind clears up."

Ten minutes later, Spud came back to Chet, clothes dripping. "It's buried in the yard."

"Get him a shovel and have him dig it up."

"He may have a hard time with that. He's gasping for breath and puking."

Chet shrugged. "We can wait. He planted it, he can dig it up."

Jesus and Cole drug Crawford back up to the yard. He was struggling, and when they set him on his knees he fell flat on his face.

"Take the cuffs off him and give him the shovel." Chet bent over and collared him up. "You said the gold is here. Dig it up, or you'll be taken back and drowned this time."

Crawford nodded his understanding and began pecking at the ground with the shovel. His efforts were worthless. Chet kicked him in the ass, knocking him flat again. "You better stand up and go to digging, you son of a bitch. I think you just might want to drown in that tank."

Dirt began to fly. Then the shovel finally struck metal.

Chet called for a halt. "Drag his sorry hide out of there. Spud, take the shovel and get the gold out of that hole."

He about laughed as Crawford sprawled on the ground still coughing and choking. On his knees, Jesus began stacking the gleaming bricks Spud handed up to him.

Exactly half of the ones that were stolen, by Chet's count.

He fixed the woman with a stern gaze. "Where's your part of the money?" he demanded.

Crawford shook his head. "Go get it." He sighed.

She glared at her partner in crime. "You dumb bastard."

"Cole, Liz, go with her."

Liz followed them inside. Shortly, Ruth came back out, covered in flour. Cole and Liz emerged behind her with four floury sacks.

"They were in the bottom of that barrel," Cole said in disgust, brushing off his clothes. "We didn't look hard enough during the search."

"Half of it?" Chet asked.

The younger man shook his head. "This isn't all of it."

Chet agreed and turned back to Crawford. "Why kill the men who helped you rob the stage?"

"I didn't need—" He had a coughing spell. "Them bastards."

"I figured that," Chet said. "Do your partners have their share at the business?"

"How should I know?"

"You can tell me or else."

Crawford said, "We delivered it to them."

"Where'd they store it?"

"In the warehouse, I guess. I'm not their mama."

"Brad Crawford, you are under arrest for the Black Canyon stage robbery. And so are you, lady. You'll be housed in the Benson jail to await federal charges in Tucson. There was mail on that stage you robbed, and that makes it a federal offense." He turned to his men. "Let's go, boys. We have some more work to do at dawn."

The gold and money was loaded on a buckboard. Roamer was to drive it into town and deposit it in the local bank for Wells Fargo to count and record. They put the two captured fugitives on horses, each handcuffed to their saddle, and hauled them into the Benson jailhouse. The town marshal who greeted them asked why they didn't take them to Tombstone.

"They can't lock the doors down there," Chet said, and stuffed a ten-dollar bill in the man's shirt pocket. "They'll be here when the marshals come for them, I trust."

"Oh, yes, sir."

"Thanks."

They grabbed some burritos from a street vendor and rode all night long for Tucson, eating in the saddle. They arrived road-weary and tired. When the first one of the perpetrators came to unlock the warehouse door after daylight, Shawn stuck a gun in his back and told him to get inside.

The others with Chet came out of the shadows and joined him, careful not to make a scene.

"What's your name?" Chet asked the thief in the back office.

"Who are you?"

"Give us your name and then shut up."

"George Nelson."

"U.S. marshals. We arrested your partners in Saint David yesterday. We want you to get us the gold and money you have."

"What partners? What gold and money?"

"You know what I mean. Or I can take you out back and put your head underwater until your memory recovers. I don't want to do that, and have you choking and strangling like Brad Crawford did before he dug his part of it up. You aren't as tough as he was, are you?"

No answer.

"Take him out and—"

Nelson stopped them. "No, wait. I can show you where the gold and money is."

"That's what I thought," Chet said smugly.

The door opened behind them. "Put your hands in the air and go through that door," they heard Jesus order.

Another man was shoved into the room.

"Well, glad you could make the party," Chet said. "Your partner was just about to show us where your share of the gold bars and money are hid."

"Don't do anything, George."

"You want to go swimming in the horse tank, too?" Chet asked.

"Huh?"

"Here's the plan. It's a fun one, too. We hold your head underwater until your memory improves, or you drown. Brad Crawford spent so much time in the tank, we thought he was part fish. He liked to have drowned."

The older man slumped in a chair. "Who are you?"

"Deputy U.S. Marshal Chet Byrnes. Go show them the loot." Chet indicated for Nelson to go do it with Jesus and Cole.

The three were gone only a short while before Jesus returned with Nelson. Jesus said, "The money's back here, at least."

"Ruth Carlson and Brad Crawford are in the Benson jail awaiting federal marshals to bring them here. Since there was mail on that coach, the charges are federal."

"You can't prove that."

"No, but with your being at the scene of the crime, and the recovery of the gold and money in your possession, we sure will prove you two were involved. I expect with the murder charges, you may even hang."

"I am not saying another word. You can speak to my lawyer."

Spud stuck his head through the door. "The gold bars are here, too."

"I will be out of jail in an hour," Armstrong bragged.

"Not on a murder charge, you won't be." He turned to Spud. "Tell Cole to come up here."

"Yes, sir."

Chet picked up the cuffs. "Put your hands behind your back."

"You can't do this."

"Mister, I can and I am. You're under arrest." He handcuffed them both, then removed a derringer pistol from Nelson's vest pocket.

He walked over and hugged his wife. "You asked me a while back if there was something that would settle me down. Well, this is it. When this case is closed and they're in jail or swinging from a rope, and the money's all back at the bank and counted, I'll be ready to sit back and relax."

"I could sleep for two days myself," she said, and nodded that she approved.

"We'll do that. Check into a hotel and sleep."

Liz shook her head. "These men of yours amaze me how tough they are. They never complain. They're tough as any men I've ever seen."

"Good team. This wasn't their first rodeo, either."

Tight-lipped she nodded. "I was there. I remember arresting the rustlers."

"I think all of the gold and money not accounted for yet is back there," Cole said, and put his back to the wall.

Chet could see he was as weary as the rest. They still needed to lock up the prisoners and count the loot, though. He wished he had a big shot of wakeup to clear his head and mind. These things needed to be handled.

"We need these men in the jail. The combined city-county jail is over on Congress Street and we'll need a wagon to take them over there. Then another wagon to deliver this gold and money to the National Bank. As far as I know, Wells Fargo is the owner." Chet shook his head tiredly, trying to clear the buzzing in his ears. "I know you're all just as tired as I am, so let's split up. Jesus, you get us some wagons off the street. Liz and I will take the prisoners to the jail. Spud, you take the horses to the livery and put them up. Cole, when you and Jesus get that money and gold loaded and in the bank, we'll all meet at the hotel. Jesus, here's ten dollars for the money wagon. I'll pay for the prisoner wagon. Spud, you have money for food?"

"Yes, sir." He was off to help them load the loot.

Jesus was right back from the street. "A wagon for the prisoners is outside for you. Another is going around back to haul the loot."

"Good. Now go find a vendor and eat something, Jesus. You look like you're about to fall over."

Chet herded the prisoners outside, boosted them on the wagon, and put Liz on the seat. Then he handed her the rifle and climbed on it. "Take us to the jail," he told the driver.

The Hispanic man nodded. "Are they killers?" he asked Liz.

"*Sí*. Bad, bad ones," she replied in Spanish. "Evil men."

Chet laughed and shook his head. He was too damn tired to hardly think, but they were jail-bound, and he had the evidence he'd need to convict them. Unloading at the jail, he paid the driver and marched the grumbling pair inside, Elizabeth trailing along behind.

"Marshal Byrnes?" the deskman asked, recalling him.

"That's me. I got two federal prisoners here. No bail. They'll be charged with robbery and murder."

"I will lock them up, but you'll need to fill out the paperwork."

"I'm short on sleep, partner," Chet told him. "Tell the acting Chief Marshal I'll be back to file charges after a few hours of sleep. No bail."

"I savvy that, Marshal."

"Damn, forgot." He shook his head to try to clear it. The cuffs off them, Armstrong went to complaining some more. "Shut up," Chet told him. "Where you're headed, they won't hesitate to gag your mouth."

Two prison guards took them back to frisk them and issue them stripes.

Chet thanked the deskman. He took Liz's hand and they went outside together in the bright warm sunshine that about blinded him. The hotel was two blocks away and he shook his head. "Sorry, it's been a long spell. I'm so tired, every step is hard. Look for a food vendor. We need to eat something."

"I could sleep without it."

He hugged her close. "It's a wonder one of us didn't fall off our horses coming over here. But I couldn't let those two get warned that we had arrested Crawford."

"I understand. I'm as proud as you are about getting them in jail."

They paused for some flour tortillas and beans from an old Mexican lady. He ate about half of his and fed the rest to a yellow cur dog. She did the same.

"So much for our feast."

Even weary and dead tired she had humor. He was damn lucky to have her.

He paid for three rooms, left the deskman the names of his men, and headed upstairs. The stair climb made him dizzy and once in the room they fell across the double bed and slept.

CHAPTER 27

Pounding on the hotel room door.

Chet rose up on the bed, unsure of the time or for how long he'd slept. The light coming through the window was weak and pink. Sundown?

The knocking continued.

"Yeah, yeah," he muttered. "I'm coming."

He opened the door to find a bleary-eyed Cole sweeping the hair back from his face. "Sorry, boss. Fred Dodge sent word just now that those two killed the Benson town marshal and escaped the jail."

"Crawford and the whore?"

"That's right."

"Damn it!" Chet pounded the door frame with his open palm. "I bet they're headed for Mexico."

Cole nodded. "That's where my money would be. But you have Liz along. We can go track them down."

"Hell, no. Spud can take her—" He stopped as he saw her shaking her head out of the corner of his eye.

"I am going, too," she said firmly.

He sighed. "Get everyone up," he told his partner. "We'll eat and get the horses. I'll bet Shawn and Roamer are headed back to Tubac already. We'll wire them there. By the time they get the news, Crawford and her will be south of the border already. Wire Dodge that we're on our way. The U.S. Marshal's office here will need some details on those prisoners. Damn, looks like another long night in the saddle."

Cole agreed. "It was too easy catching him."

"I thought that man could keep them in jail until I got someone out there to bring them in here. That's what I get for thinking, huh?"

Jesus and Spud were there by then.

"Ragged-looking bunch. Liz is coming. We'll go eat."

"They kill that old man?" Spud asked.

Chet nodded. "Desperate men do desperate things. He must have felt he had nothing to lose."

Everyone agreed. Liz joined them, finally, looking amazingly fresh. "Where to next?"

"Food."

"Oh, do we get to eat?" she asked.

"This time, yes," he said. They went downstairs to the restaurant. He picked up a tablet and two pencils in a general store on the way to eat. While they waited on supper, he wrote out the entire story about the crime, from the involvement of the two businessmen, and the prostitute—Ruth—helping them learn the shipment schedules, to the killing of the outlaws to cover their tracks. He also listed the name of the witness in Preskitt who pointed them out. He ended the letter telling them about the money and gold bars that had been recovered and now resided in the vaults of the Benson and Tucson National Banks.

Then he detailed what he knew about the Benson jailbreak, the murder of the jailer, and where he was going next. He signed his name, folded the paper up, and addressed it to the acting Chief Marshal.

"I hope they can read it."

"They will," she said. She'd read it as he wrote. "This'll do the job."

"I'm going down to the courthouse and giving it to the desk man. You guys get the horses. We'll ride all night and get over there in the morning—sleep a few hours and then find out what direction they went. I also have to wire Fred Dodge and Tubac for the Force."

"You figure they're chasing them with a posse?" Cole asked, finishing his coffee.

"By now whatever posse they had has faded. Crawford's not your average dumb outlaw. He completely lost us at Rye. If he could do that, he'll have no trouble losing a posse of useless townsfolk. We have one advantage, though. I don't think he had any more money left at Saint David. He'll have to rob for what he needs."

"He'll leave tracks somewhere," Jesus said. "I don't care how smart he is. He's a *gringo* in Mexico with a redheaded woman. People will notice him."

"And there's your answer. Let's move out."

After shooting off the wires to Dodge and the Force at Tubac, Chet dropped the letter for the U.S. Marshal off at the jail desk and he paid the man five dollars to be certain who got it. The jailer tried to give him his money back.

"No. You deliver it in person in the morning. I want to be certain he gets it."

"I will handle this very carefully, sir."

He and Liz hurried out of the jail. His men and the horses awaited them at the hitch rail. It was pitch-dark already when they wound their way out of the walled city and headed east on the Butterfield Road toward Benson. A half moon shone on the tall cactus forest as they rode.

He was glad to be away from the city. Tucson was a pretty stinky place. Chet wouldn't miss its atmosphere. No one there collected the dead animal carcasses, and it wasn't unusual to find turkey buzzards and stray dogs arguing over the corpses in the street. Smelly toilets and uncollected garbage piled high all made the town a less-than-enjoyable place to visit, let alone live. Chet always wondered why they kept moving the capital back and forth from there to Preskitt, but he knew there was lots of power in Tucson and the money to go with it.

With the city smells out of his nose and the creosote aroma replacing it, they rode hard for Benson and what he feared would be a long search for Crawford and his partner. A very long search that may very well lead them south of the border.

CHAPTER 28

The sun was about up over the Chiricahua Range when they topped the mountain west of town. Far beneath them, the village was sprawled along the San Pedro River. Fred Dodge must have been on the lookout for them. He was the first person Chet saw upon entering the town, jumping out of a chair on a store porch to come meet them.

"You have the others in jail?" he asked without preamble. Then he saw Liz and removed his hat. "Beg pardon, ma'am."

Liz bowed in the saddle. "Mr. Dodge."

Dodge looked back to Chet. "Well?"

"Yes, they're there. And all the loot we could find is safely in the bank." He dismounted and nearly fell as his sea legs about folded under him. He looked back up at his wife. "Get off slow, Liz."

"I will."

"Has anyone found how he got out of the jail?" Cole asked the marshal.

Dodge shook his head. "Not much to tell. He cut the

jailer's throat from behind and got the keys off the body. Damn bloody mess, let me tell you."

"Ah, hell." Cole spat. "He must have had a knife concealed somewhere we didn't find."

"Seems to be a theme with this *hombre*," Jesus agreed.

"He must have held him up after he cut his throat, managed to get the keys off him," Dodge continued. "The poor man sprawled forward when he was let go, else he never could have got them keys from inside the cell."

"He's a tough one," Chet admitted. "He outsmarted us at Rye and shot his own men to silence them."

"Well, they stole some good horses and headed for the border. A posse rode out after them two hours later, but we haven't heard anything from them."

"We need a few hours' sleep. We only had a few winks in Tucson. Nelson and Armstrong are in the jail on robbery/murder charges. It may be hard to make that one stick, but they were in on the crime. They can't be bailed out. For now. Their share of the money and gold is at the Tucson National Bank being counted."

"Good. I'll have my associates handle that end and the loot, too."

"We need to put up these horses and catch a meal. If you can find out anything about the posse and where they are at, leave us word, please."

"Where are Roamer and Shawn?"

"On their way back to Tubac. They took the loot to the bank here when we rode for Tucson so we could head off those two before they could run."

"My God, man," Dodge exclaimed. "You guys are super. And, ma'am? You have my sympathy."

Liz shook her head tiredly. "I would not miss a minute of any of it, Mr. Dodge."

"Well, your husband has done things a great many other men simply gave up on. And my company sure appreciates all he's done about crime down here."

"Come see us in Preskitt," she said. "We have lots of beds."

"Someday. Someday I'm definitely coming. Thank you very much. All of you get something to eat and then rest."

She and Chet headed for a nearby café, the boys dragging along behind like tired children. When they were given a table, they all remained standing until she was seated.

"Be seated, gentlemen," she said, blushing. "Very cavalier, but I am one of you. Please treat me like that. I love each one of you, but I am Liz the horse handler, remember that."

"Liz, we were all raised this way," Cole explained, motioning for the waitress. "Wait for the ladies to be seated. My momma would've slapped my head for not doing that. You go ahead and hold the horses, but you're still the ranch's boss lady."

"Thank you, Cole. Rest easy on the out trips, though, please?"

"I'll try."

They ate the meal of eggs, pancakes, and fried bacon. Dodge sent word the horses were being cared for and would be rested when they got up.

"How long should that be?" Cole asked. "Five hours?"

"Sounds good to me," Jesus agreed.

Chet nodded. "We'll assemble at the livery and ride from here to Tombstone, or wherever the posse went to pick up their trail." He wiped his mouth on a napkin and stood to help his wife to her feet. "I'll pay for our rooms at the hotel. They'll have your keys. Three thirty at the livery."

Everyone agreed and they marched out in a group, spurs jingling as they crossed the street for the hotel. Chet ordered the rooms and they each went their own way. He and Liz went to their own, half undressed, and fell on the bed to sleep.

They met at the livery, as arranged, at three thirty that afternoon. Chet arranged for two packhorses and gear. When they had panniers on them, Jesus and Spud went to the store for supplies. Chet and Cole checked on where the posse went, but the only word on that was southward.

Southward it was. They departed immediately, a bare hour before winter sundown threw them into darkness.

Chet's mind worked as he rode in silence. There was no way to catch up to the posse in less than a day's hard riding, and even then, they'd probably disbanded when they'd reached the border. It didn't matter, though. No matter the risks involved or the problems to solve, Crawford needed to be brought back.

Dead or alive.

Off in the hills, a few coyotes barked in the night, some even howling for a reunion of the pack. The top-knot Gambel's quails were silent, roosted on the ground in the spiny chaparral. Some white tail deer moved out of hiding to graze in the open areas. A few grumpy *javelinas* hustled around to find some pad cactus and pear fruit to eat—spines were no problem to them. The desert owls brushed by in silent flight, searching for kangaroo rats and small rodents. Down on the sluggish San Pedro, Chet imagined a mountain lion stopping for a drink of water.

They made camp around midnight at the base of a small hill. Off in the distance, some cow bawled for her errant calf. Their horses snorted hard in the dust. They wanting to roll on their itchy backs, but they were hitched so as to not run off or spook. Rolling on their backs in this spiny land held too many dangers for them, anyway.

He smelled the sweet mesquite smoke of the fire. Liz, Spud, and Jesus were hard at work fixing the food. They had a large hunk of prime beef they'd found at the store and bought for supper. Laid on a grill over the red-hot coals, the smell of the cooking meat made his mouth water. There were baked potatoes, as well as fresh-picked green beans grown in some patch nearby. Liz's peach upside down cobbler was bubbling in a large Dutch oven standing on its short iron legs over more hot coals, a shovelful of glowing ashes on the lid.

Chet found a spot to sit on a rug of canvas and waited patiently. This region's ground was covered in sharp goat-head burrs, a low growing plant brought to Arizona by Mexican cattle, planted by their hooves. The canvas sheet would protect their backsides since they had none of their usual folding chairs.

Eating the great meal by the firelight settled his bunch down.

"How far ahead is the posse, do you think?" Spud asked.

"Thirty miles, give or take." Chet shook his head. "And by now, they're probably down to about half the number of riders they had to start with."

"Spud," Cole explained. "The boss man hates posses. They are usually made up of storeowners and clerks trying to chase down criminals. They're not real horsemen, don't do much riding, and aren't outdoors men."

The youth chuckled. "I was camp helper up on the rim a while back. Worked for an outfitter who took two fat businessmen in bush helmets hunting for bears. They each shot a yearling black bear apiece that my boss called a grizzly. He told them they'd tan the hides and ship 'em to them. When those dudes went back east, we ran all over hell for six weeks finding two small real grizzlies 'cause he said some college professor would tell them they'd been lied to, seeing black bear hides. So I asked him, 'Why didn't you just take them shooting grizzlies?' 'Oh, hell,' he said, 'those dudes might have gotten ate up by a momma grizzly and my outfit business would be ruined!'"

Busy cutting up his steak, Chet asked, "Spud, do you know what he charged them for the hunt?"

"Yes, sir. He got five thousand dollars apiece from them. I got paid ten dollars for my part."

Holding up his tin coffee cup for Liz to refill, Cole couldn't help but laugh. "Jesus, you, me, and Spud need two hunts a year like that, don't we?"

"Maybe just one," Chet said.

Jesus said, "If it's like hunting that old stinking cow grizzly Chet and I burned out of that cave up north on the Verde Ranch, that ain't enough money."

Still laughing, Chet said, "I agree, it's not enough money."

"I want to hear that story," Liz said.

"Sometime when I have all night, Jesus and I will tell you the whole thing."

"But, Liz?" Jesus said.

"Yes."

"That bear smelled so bad they could smell her clear up at your house."

"Oh, Jesus, you've been here so long you tell stories taller than Chet." She was laughing so hard tears spilled down her cheeks.

"It's a good thing you didn't smell her." Jesus shook his head and went back for cobbler.

They slept till just before dawn, then saddled up the horses while their mounts ate cracked corn from feedbags. They'd water them at the river and ride on after a cold breakfast of the leftovers and hot coffee.

"First night we've had enough sleep." Cole yawned and stretched his arms over his head.

"Speak for yourself, *amigo*," Jesus said. "I could've slept all day."

They rode through St. David again, where only the farm wives were awake, busy milking their Jersey cows. They passed their informer's house, after which the posse's tracks went on toward Tombstone. An hour later they met two businessmen in suits, haggard looking as their horses. After a quick introduction, they told Chet they had left the posse the night before in order to get back to their stores.

He asked how many men were left. The older man shook his head. "Probably not even a dozen. I think some broke off and went to Tombstone last night for libations."

When they'd ridden on, Spud leaned in close to Chet. "What the hell was that he said they went for, sir?"

"Libations, son," Chet told him. "Whiskey, and such."

"Oh, you mean to get drunk, huh?"

"That's the idea. "

"Oh. I understand that. I never heard it called that before."

"You aren't alone," Liz said. "I just learned what that word meant, too."

"That's what you call it when you can afford it," Cole added.

This set the whole bunch to laughing.

Short of Tombstone, the posse tracks turned south instead of off toward the border. Chet picked up the pace, heading for the army fort at the base of the mountains. Noon came and went, and they ate dry jerky in the saddle, washed down with water out of their canteens.

Chet thought about stopping at the fort but decided to cross over into Mexico, instead, in the same place Coronado had crossed decades before. He told Liz of the explorer and how he'd come to this land looking for the fabled cities of gold. Poor man. Instead of riches, he'd fell into disgrace for his troubles.

"I hope we don't do likewise," Cole muttered.

"Me, neither."

"Wonder what they're eating?" Jesus mused thoughtfully.

"Who?"

"Crawford and the girl," he said. "No one knew much more than that they stole horses in Benson and rode away."

Chet considered it. "I figure Crawford knows this land better than most. He knew better than to show up in Tombstone and thought he was untouchable back at that farm they were at."

Jesus agreed. "I agree. He may have a larger plan than we can imagine."

That afternoon, they caught up with what remained of the posse down below the border. They were stopped at a small *cantina* eating, drinking, and looking haggard.

One of them, a big man who Chet sized up immediately as a fellow rancher, came over and introduced himself.

"Hiram Adams. I know you. You're Chet Byrnes. How did you get down here?"

"We rode hard," Chet told him. "Do you know when Crawford went through here?"

"The man who owns the place says about twenty-four hours."

"You sure it's him?"

Adams nodded. "Big man traveling light with a pretty, redheaded woman."

"That's him, alright," Cole confirmed.

"I'm afraid these men are all worn out. We expected to overtake them long before now." He took off his hat and shook his head. "He's smarter and tougher than I thought he would be."

Chet snorted. "We know. He lost us in our own backyard, just as smooth as you could believe. Any idea where he may land?"

"A Mexican man back in Arizona told us he's headed for Rio Deloris."

"Why there?"

"He thought Crawford had some mining interests there."

"That's a day's ride south of here," Liz said.

Chet nodded. "Any of your men want to ride on?"

Adams shook his head. "I don't think so. We've about eaten all the dust we want. Nice to meet you though, Mr. Byrnes. I want to thank you and your men for making the territory a better place to live. Men like Crawford should have been drowned when they were born. Is there anything I can do for you?"

"Do you know the dead marshal's family?"

"Yes. He had a wife and two married daughters."

"Would you see that his widow has what she needs? Liz and I live at Preskitt, but we'd do anything to help. You can't handle something, just write me. I didn't leave those two there to get him killed. But the cell doors have been left unlocked before—I made sure he wouldn't do that this time."

They shook hands, then went to meet Señor O'Leary the *cantina*/storeowner whose women had waited on them.

"So good to meet you, señor! And you too, señora," O'Leary said. Then in Spanish, he told them how his Irish father years ago started the *cantina*, and how glad he was they had stopped there.

The man was a good storyteller and they enjoyed his family yarn. The food and wine were good and the man repeated that Crawford had mine interests in Rio Deloris. He told them there was no river there, only a dry riverbed.

No doubt Crawford must have friends or something there. But why didn't he go there after the robbery instead of staying in the Mormon settlement? It didn't make sense.

"Señor, if you go down there, I know he will run. I know some tough men who can go and locate him for you if he is there. If you ride in there he will only run some more. Say for five *pesos* a day, I send some of them down there and you may stay here. When they find where he stays, you can go arrest him, no?"

He looked at his men for their opinion.

"Sounds good to me," Cole said.

"Worth a try," Jesus added.

"I go with you whatever," Spud said.

"Let's try it," Liz said.

When Chet told him to go ahead, O'Leary sent some of his working girls off to find the men he listed. He offered them hammocks to sleep in and a bath for Liz, who gladly accepted the offer.

O'Leary's teenage sons fed and watered the horses. Then they let them roll in the dust of the corrals, after assuring Chet it was quite free of goat heads.

In a small adobe *casa,* they set up the bathwater for Liz and told him he could bathe, too. He accepted the woman's generosity. It would all be on his bill, but who cared? Roamer and Shawn arrived in the night to join them. They had a real team now. If this man O'Leary's spies found the outlaw as he promised—they'd be able to take both of them. Time was on their hands.

His men caught up on their sleep and even took baths and relaxed. Chet had a leather-bound book to write in, and he put down some more notes about his plans for the buckboard mail run.

O'Leary's men returned that evening. Seated at a scarred table, the lead man, Alfredo, told them where Crawford was—staying with a *gringo* businessman named Coats. Coats was well known in the area. His house was a walled fortress, and he had armed guards and big mean dogs.

Alfredo said they must poison the dogs and take out the guards. There was only one way in or out and that was through the two thick wooden gates.

"You're certain he's in there?" Chet asked.

"*Sí, señor.* We saw him come out with a woman in a buggy. They went to shop and then drove back in."

"How often do they do that?" Chet asked.

"They did it today very open-like."

Does he have money here? Chet wondered, but had no answer.

One of the other men in the group piped up. "I saw him go into the bank and come out smiling."

"Good," Chet said. "That answers my next question. Can we move in close unobserved? I'd like to take him outside of the rich man's *casa* if at all possible."

"There will be less to tell the authorities, heh?" O'Leary asked.

The man was fast. "Exactly."

"We have a place we can conceal your horses and wait until he rides out," Alfredo said.

"Good."

"Tonight, we will move you there."

"You don't think someone will warn him, do you?"

"No, but we don't know for sure. They might. We will try to get you in place late at night."

Chet agreed. "We really need to arrest him and get back to the U.S."

O'Leary smiled. "I am helping you?"

"Yes, what do I owe you right now?"

"Is a hundred *pesos* too much?"

Chet smiled. "Not at all. If we get him in the next two days, I'll double it."

"Will we?" he asked his man.

"Sí."

That evening Chet, Cole, and Jesus rode out with Alfredo under a million stars to Rio Deloris. Once there, they put their horses in a small corral hidden behind a tall adobe wall that surrounded a deserted house. One of Alfredo's men who met them there left on foot about dawn to keep an eye on Crawford's activity.

Chet did lots of pacing as the sun grew higher and warmer. He looked up and his guide was smiling. "Good news. Your *gringo* drove out to shop a short while ago. Get your horses."

Cole and Jesus were already moving. Chet followed. They swung up in their saddles and followed the man who led them on foot. He entered an alley, dodging piles of brown bottles and garbage, and scattered some half-wild cats. He raised a hand for them to halt. Chet dismounted and saw the redheaded woman sitting with a man at a table in an outside café.

He signaled to the others. On foot they came up the alley, guns drawn. Crawford saw them at once. He started for his gun, but Chet's pistol in his face stopped him in his tracks, despite the desperation clearly written there.

Jesus disarmed him.

"You can't arrest me in Mexico," Crawford said as Jesus handcuffed him.

"You keep telling us what we can't do," Jesus whispered in his ear. "Yet here we are."

Still seated, the woman reached for her large purse. Chet caught her arm. "I'll take that."

"Gawdamn you!"

"Lady, he may damn me, but you won't shoot me with this peashooter." He chuckled and put the Ladysmith .22 revolver in his belt and the purse on his shoulder. He raised her out of the chair and shoved her forward. "Head for the alley."

She snarled but obeyed. Alfredo set off to procure a wagon to haul the pair. Chet and Cole walked to the east end of the alley, while Jesus brought their horses.

A wagon and team arrived. Jesus brought a pair of ankle irons for her.

"I don't need those," she said.

"You ran away," Cole told her. "I told you what would happen if you ran away, didn't I? Put them on her, Jesus."

She broke into a stream of cussing as they loaded her into the wagon, leg irons and all.

Alfredo was telling the anxious-looking driver not to worry he would be paid well.

Seated in the wagon they left in a hard run out of town, led by shouting riders to clear the way. In three blocks they cleared the town and were crossing through the strange organ cactus desert, headed for O'Leary's *cantina*.

Spud had everything loaded when they arrived. Liz looked pleased helping him finish up.

"Will you take them to the United States for forty dollars?" Chet asked the driver.

The man smiled and nodded, though he looked pale.

O'Leary and his crew came out to see them off. Chet gave each of the women ten dollars, and O'Leary himself two hundred for his efforts. Alfredo got another twenty. They all thanked him and waved good-bye.

Before they headed out, Chet looked back south for any sign of pursuit. No dust. Then he spoke to his friend. "*Amigo*, I hope you are safe from any revenge."

O'Leary shook his head to dismiss the concern. "We will watch our backsides."

Finally they headed back north, the driver jogging the wagon team. Chet could only hope they weren't pursued by Crawford's friends or partners. Once they reached the border, Jesus and Shawn set out to find two more saddle horses and saddles for the prisoners to ride. Chet gave them money and told them to be careful.

"We'll be back," Shawn promised him.

The short man who drove the wagon said after them, "May God help you both."

Liz shook her head. "What a mess we're in."

Chet shook his head. "We've been in lots worse, Liz. Arizona is only miles away."

Roamer laughed. "One time, Liz, we found some bandits in a bar over in Mexico. We arrested them and forced them across the border, all while they were screaming for the border guards to come help them."

"We've had some real tough deals," Chet said with a shake of his head. "We'll take turns standing guard tonight, though."

She shook her head in the firelight. "Well, you guys certainly know this business. It still amazes me at times."

The boys returned with the extra horses and saddles after midnight.

The next day, they reached Fort Huachuca and the Army welcomed them. Their prisoners were placed in the fort jail, and after a big meal, Chet and company slept in the officers' quarters. Using the fort's telegraph station, Shawn arranged for a buckboard with guards to deliver the pair to the Tucson jail. Chet wired the acting Chief Marshal that the pair was on their way. Meantime, he, Liz, and Cole would head to Tombstone and from there catch a stage. They would be in Tucson in twenty-four hours to straighten out the charges. That left Jesus and Spud to bring the horses and gear back home.

Another buckboard was hired to take them to Tombstone, where they met the stage. Cole sat with the driver on the top seat, with Chet and Liz in the second row as they made the sweeping ride across the desert and over the hills to the silver city.

They arrived at the stage depot and bought tickets for the ride to Tucson. Fred Dodge met them and thanked them for catching and returning the pair. They ate lunch with him and visited about the new stage line being developed. He promised that the rewards on the capture would speedily be sent to Chet to divide with his men— with Norma Shields receiving part of reward too.

They shook hands and climbed into the coach for the next leg of the trip. Chet was pleased that after this next stop, they would be going home to work on the buckboard delivery plan. They sent a wire to Monica and Valerie giving their expected arrival.

Arriving in Tucson late the next night, they ate and took hotel rooms. After breakfast they met Chief Deputy Marshal Rick Sewell. He and two clerks went over the charges with two prosecutors. Chet told him about the Preskitt stage office man who interviewed Ruth Carlson and the two men after the stage robbery, as well as about the bank employee who testified he told Ruth Carlson the shipment schedule. Chet also reported the murders of Crawford's gang members to silence them.

The loot they recovered from Crawford and his partners was secured. The trials should be cut and dry, the prosecutor said. However, the court in Cochise County would also want to try the pair for murder of the marshal when they were in the jail.

Sewell shook Chet's hand and thanked him and his men for all their hard work.

They climbed on the stage that evening and headed home.

Liz wrapped, again, in a blanket against the night's growing cold, hugged him. "We are going home at last, *hombre*. I am so pleased you allowed me to go with you. I never regretted it. And things went so smoothly. Those two thought they were so safe down there. They had no idea you were coming for them."

"Those kinds of people believe they live above the law without regard. And I always enjoy your company. But let's push our brains into this stage line business now. We need to get it rolling."

"I will do all I can."

"I know that. We just have to get our sights on that project next."

Talk became difficult over the drum of the horses and the creaking suspension of the coach as they headed north under the stars. The sharp creosote smell of the desert was in Chet's nose as they headed for Picacho Pass and the stage stop there. They drifted in and out of sleep on the run. Hours later, he felt stiff dismounting at the Papago Wells stopover.

Cole spoke up as they waited. "If I end up living at the base of those peaks on the Marcy Road, I might ask Raphael if I can have those two men ride with me securing the buckboard stops. Bennie and Ramon. They're smart and can handle things if aroused. They could substitute-drive if needed, recover stolen horses, fix harnesses, and manage things if I was gone."

"No reason not to use them. Would the married one move?"

"They told me if they had a chance at it, they'd both move up there. Ramon said he'd marry Lupe and she'd go up there with him, too."

"Let's make it happen, then. You'll need some good backup, and I agree those two are quite versatile."

When they reached Hayden's Ferry, the northbound Black Canyon Coach was about ready to leave. After using the facilities and grabbing a bite to eat from a street vendor, they climbed aboard. They'd be home by midnight—or at least at Preskitt by then. Chet looked forward to the big house and regular meals from Monica.

"I want to tell you both something," Cole said, breaking the silence for the first time in an hour. "I want to thank you—both of you—for letting Valerie and I raise Rock. She really needed that boy. We enjoy him so much."

"I know how bad she wanted one," Liz said. "He's in good hands, just like Adam. And this way, Chet's spoiled wife gets to go with him on his adventures."

"No more spoiled than I am," Chet said.

Cole went on, "I know my traveling days are about to end with you two. It makes me sad. Jesus is like a brother to me. You two are like—well, almost like my folks. And while I enjoy every minute at home with Valerie, I still love running down criminals and settling things with you."

"You'll have a plate full up there, I imagine."

"And I won't have you to figure them out, either," the young man said.

"I have no fears. You can take those reins."

"Went by and saw Lucy when I was up there. I told you it was okay. Despite all her losses, it looks like she and Drew are doing a great job working together. There's a big gap without Reg and I know he won't ever be back, but she still misses him a lot."

"We all do. I don't know what I'd changed otherwise. He was like a son to me. Something slipped, maybe, and I didn't foresee the depth of his internal problems. We'll miss him for a long time."

The two buckboards were there waiting under the stars for them. Cole shook his hand and hugged Liz good-bye. "Day after tomorrow I'll be at the ranch. You go somewhere, boss, you take at least one of my future men along with you."

Chet chuckled. "I promise to do that."

"Good enough. See you then. And thanks for everything."

Their things loaded, Chet helped Liz into the second seat. Looking at the outline of the hills around them against the brighter sky—it was good to be home.

He'd even be happier in his own bed with her to hug. He thanked God for all his blessings.

CHAPTER 29

At dawn, he found Monica in the kitchen. She shook her head at the sight of him. "I see you are back in one piece. I take it that your lovely wife is unharmed as well?"

He smiled at her sassy ways. "She's fine. I let her sleep in. Everything alright here?"

"I know of no great problems that will draw you away. I have your mail laid out from when you were gone. Not a soul has been by to ask for your help, which I consider as very unusual. I guess Cole came back, too?"

"Yes, he joined us. Spud and Jesus are bringing the horses back from the border."

"Then everything is alright?"

He nodded. "The criminals are in jail in Tucson. We recovered most of the loot."

She poured him some fresh-smelling coffee. "The many times you have left here and I wondered how you can do this impossible thing—and you always do it."

"Someone has to do those things if we ever intend to become a state."

She shook her head. "Maybe someday you will be elected governor."

"I don't want the job."

"I thought you'd say that." She backed up to the sink as if considering something. "You would make a damn good one, though."

He shook his head. "I have enough ranches to look after, not the entire territory."

"Oh, we will see."

He spent the day going over his books with Liz. He read a letter from Bonnie about how hard JD took his brother's death, and how sorry he was about being unable to help bury him because he was so far away. Chet took the time to answer it and apologized for the time elapsed since they were busy after the stage robbers.

"The water is hot for you. I laid some fresh clothes out, too," his wife said.

"You must not like my beard."

"Oh, you won't ever be a Mormon elder. Better shave it off. I can do that, if you like."

Chet shook his head. "No, I can handle it. I know you have letters to write, as well. I answered Bonnie's so far. JD took the loss hard. Our accounts look good, but we'll need money for our development at the peaks. Someday, that will be the rail headquarters for northern Arizona."

She kissed him and he went off to bathe and shave. After he finished, he came downstairs and heard Liz talking with Raphael.

"There he is now."

"Stay seated. I'm coming."

"It's good you and her are back and safe," his foreman gushed. "Everything at the ranch is fine. She tells me you finally got them in Mexico and brought them back. I wondered if you needed anything from me."

"Cole would like for Ramon and Bennie to be his employees on the buckboard business."

"Where will they live?"

"Eventually, up at the junction of the Marcy Road and where the military road comes down from the mountains. We have to build the headquarters there."

"If he needs them, I am sure they will want to go. They have had a big time going with you and Cole both. They are good men. I hate to lose them, but there are more good *vaqueros* that I can find."

"Thanks. They'll get a raise and a nice house for Bennie and his family. And when Ramon is ready, a nice house for him, too. Lots of work."

Raphael nodded. "I have no problems. If you see something I need to do, please tell me."

"I am proud of your job and what you do for us. Why, we'd all freeze if we didn't have your wood delivery services."

His man smiled. "I will leave you two. It is an honor to be the foreman here."

"We are honored you are in charge."

"Yes," Liz said. "Very proud."

After Raphael left, she asked him, "Is he worried about losing his job?"

"I don't think so, but two *gringos* used to be over him. When they were killed I finally put him in charge and never regretted it. He has limited education and I think he feels like he has to compete with Tom, Hampt, and JD. I don't worry about that, though. His men are good workers and they run a smooth outfit."

"What did Hannagen have to say in his letter?"

"He wants my plans for stations and how long it will take to get them up and in operation. He sounds impressed with what Cole and I did. So we're plunging right ahead."

"What comes first?"

"Get a few teams to cut rails and build corrals. Some water development."

"Sounds peaceful enough."

"I hope so. But we'll have problems and need to be prepared."

She laughed. "I need to go to town tomorrow. I know you and Cole plan to work on the buckboard business."

"I can get you a driver."

"That would be fine."

"I'll handle it after lunch."

"Good. What can I do today?"

"Check that list of cattle sales at Gallup and how we were paid when the money became available. I want to make sure we didn't miss any payments."

"I can do that." They spent the day tracing bills and income.

His eyes were tired by evening when they quit book-keeping. Things were going smoothly enough until a man arrived and came to the back door.

Monica called for Chet to talk to the visitor.

The man in his thirties introduced himself as Harold Faulk and said he lived near the Marcy Road. He came to see if Chet needed help building corrals.

"You rode all this way down here to ask for work?"

"Yes. Jobs up there are like sand. There is lots of that, but not many paying jobs. I have some boys and neighbors need jobs to feed their family. We aren't afraid of work. Can we help you?"

"Why don't you wash up and come in and eat with us. Monica always has plenty of food. We can discuss our needs over dinner."

"I know you are a busy man; I didn't come to complicate your time."

Chet shook his head. "Not a problem. I do need some construction crews."

"If I am no problem?"

"No problem. I will stick my head outside and have them put up your horse. You can stay the night."

"Sounds like too much."

"No problem at all."

Chet directed the boy to put the man's horse up for the night. Harold acted a little overpowered at Monica's kitchen table.

"How many men could you muster?" Chet asked him.

He finally smiled and chuckled. "I haven't heard that word since I was discharged. Big boys and men that will work? Say twelve."

"I'm on a busy schedule. Would they work six days a week?"

"How much would you pay them?"

"Two dollars a long day they work."

"I could get men that would give their all for that kind of pay."

"Would you have a woman or man who would clean and cook for them for that?"

Harold nodded. "My wife and daughter for that much."

"I will have teams and wagons, saws, axes, and digging

tools. Tents to live in on the site, cooking equipment, a chuckwagon for the cook."

"When can we start?"

"When the snow lets up and you can fall the lodge poles for corral construction. There'll be teams and wagons to haul them to my stops. Cut enough and haul them, then switch to building the pens. You know men that have wagons to haul them for me?"

"Surely. What can you pay?"

"Five dollars a day when they haul only and they feed themselves, or pay us for meals."

"How many?"

"I'll let you order them when you get the poles cut."

"I can do that. If I find pines we can cut, can I start?"

"Absolutely. You will need to see Tom Flowers at my Verde Ranch for the chuckwagon. He should have all the things you need—shovels, axes, saws, everything."

"How will you pay it?"

"You or someone must keep a log of who works and what we must pay him."

"My daughter could do that. Will you have a form?"

"We can make a notebook," Liz said. "Or buy one for her. Can she come here? I can teach her how to do it."

"I think that would be best. She is smart."

The next morning, Harold breakfasted with them, thanked them, and prepared to leave. Chet paid him thirty dollars for his expenses and told him he wanted his crew to start by the first of March. Monica sent food along for him to eat on his way home.

When he left, Chet shook his head. "I hope that man's plan pans out. Or every one of my cowboys will be building corrals up there."

Liz laughed and shook her head. "I hope that doesn't come to be."

"We'll see."

That night he went to sleep wondering how his buckboard runs would ever make the trip. Things had to thaw out for him.

CHAPTER 30

During a break in the weather, Chet, Jesus, and Cole decided to check on one of their proposed stops west of the junction. One of the men who Cole had signed up, Dwight McCrown, had not answered a letter Cole sent him regarding his progress.

Snow depth at the Junction was still too deep for them to do anything about the headquarters Chet had planned. They rode west and camped that evening at a road ranch/store/saloon. A very busy stopover for freighters and travelers on the road, Cole checked and they had elk roast on the menu for the evening meal. He put reservations in for three meals and the girl wrote it down. Satisfied, they set up camp, put up a picket line, fed the horses, and walked back to eat their evening meal.

There were several freighter rigs parked there and numerous shaggy-saddled horses at the racks. When they entered the smoke-filled, sour-smelling interior, a bar girl waved Cole over to a side table. She took their order for two beers and one root beer.

"Turn in your food order now or later?"

"We already turned the orders in."

"Okay then, it'll be coming out shortly," she said, smiling. "We're pretty busy for a weeknight. You guys live around here?"

"Preskitt," Cole offered.

"Nice to have you up here." She was gone in a wiggle.

A bearded man on a stool was playing a banjo on the stage. Chet noted the gamblers were unusually loud in the poker game across the room. Most card gambling was quieter than this. One loud guy especially was jumping up and down when he won a hand. "Is he drunk?" Cole asked.

"Or crazy," Chet said. "That game over there's about to explode. Be aware if it threatens to break out into a fight or shoot-out."

The girl brought them each a big, thick elk steak, baked potatoes, and green beans on a platter.

"Need anything else?"

"Do you have some bread and butter?" Chet asked.

"Sure."

"I'd like some butter for my potato, too."

"Sure. The bread's coming. We're kinda busy right now."

A shot erupted, and everyone hit the deck. Marked confusion filled the gun smoke–filled room. Cole took the barmaid down to the floor. Chet had his gun out, on his knees behind the table. It had gotten noticeably darker in the room. The percussion of the first shot put out many of the candle lamps on the wagon wheels hung overhead.

Two more shots rang out across the room, and the screams and protesting grew louder. Chet spotted the hatless gunman parting the crowd and moving toward the door, threatening everyone in his path. But there were too many people in the room for him to try to take a shot.

Where was Jesus?

Chet stayed low, looking around.

"Where's Jesus?" he hissed.

His man could only shake his head.

The gunman backed to the door. About the time he opened it, he shot his pistol in the floor and fell forward. A few women screamed.

"Don't anyone shoot," a familiar voice shouted. "He's out cold."

The crowd gave a sigh of relief. A hatless Jesus, gun in hand, came through the door. He kicked the gun away from the prone man's hand, skidding it across the floor. "Any more shooters?"

Some guy hollered, "Hell, no. You got him."

Several men rushed over to meet him.

"What's your name, mister?"

"Where did you come from?"

"My name is Jesus Martinez. I'm a deputy U.S. marshal. Watch him. I need some rope to tie him up."

"I got some," the bartender said. "What do you drink, mister?"

"Probably another beer."

Everyone wanted to thank him. He holstered his six-gun and smiled. "I'm alright. Excuse me, but my damn supper is getting cold."

His words drew some laughter. The girl who'd served them was brushing sawdust off her front and thanking Cole for protecting her.

"Isn't he part of you all?" she asked about Jesus.

"He damn sure is," Chet said as his man returned to their table.

"Your plate got broken," she said to Jesus. "But I'm getting you a fresh one. How did you do that?"

Jesus shook his head like it was nothing. "I sure will appreciate some more food."

"Well, don't you worry one bit about that." Then she turned to Cole. "And thanks for taking me down. I was about frozen when that shot went off."

"Marshal Martinez, what should we do with him? He's tied up."

"Lock him in a shed to sober up if he didn't kill anyone," Chet said to save his man, who was taken aback by his title being said out loud.

"Hang the sumbitch!" went up the cry.

"No hanging tonight. Let him set there. How bad is the man he shot?"

"He never shot anyone," the bartender said. "Just shot a hole or two in the ceiling. It will live. May leak a bit, but he never killed anyone." Everyone laughed.

"Where's the local JP?" Chet asked.

"Over the hill."

"Send for him, and he can hold court right here."

The crowd agreed, though they sounded reluctant. The help was busy letting down wagon wheels and relighting the lamps.

The barmaid called Jill was back with bread, butter, and a new heaping plate for Jesus. She asked him, "That enough?"

He shook his head. "Probably more than I can eat."

She kissed him on the cheek. "You guys were the greatest. What do you do?"

"We ranch, do some law work, and we're going to build a stage line from Gallup to California."

"Well I am sure glad you three were in here tonight."

"Thanks for my meal," Jesus said, and started back to eating.

The head bartender came over. "Your meals are on us. We stuck the troublemaker in the back room till the judge gets here. You need anything you holler—I never realized we had U.S. Marshals in here. Glad to have you and stop by any time. Did I hear someone say you're building a stage line across Arizona?"

"That's right," Chet confirmed. "That young man is Cole Emerson. He'll be the superintendent of operations."

"I'm sorry, I forgot to introduce myself. My name is Harry Jensen. You are?"

"Chet Byrnes. I own the Quarter Circle Z." They shook hands.

"I've read all kinds of things about you. Nice to finally meet you. My boss would sure like to have a stage stop here."

"Cole, we can look into that?"

"Certainly. I'm not certain about the final stage stops yet. We're going to use buckboards at first to meet the requirement of our mail contract."

"Well, let me know what we can do. We're a main stop now and would like to stay that way."

Things settled down and they went back to eating.

Chet, busy cutting up the elk steak, said, "Jesus, you got out of here quick enough."

"I damn near was on all fours to get there, but I knew he'd come outside and I could stop him there."

"Very professional. You two are great companions."

"After all we have done, we should be good at this business."

"Yeah, Cole saved the lady," Jesus teased.

"Hell, I had to. You broke your plate getting out of here and I wanted you to eat when it was over."

"Well, thanks."

"Not that it did me much good. She kissed you, not me."

Chet was shaking his head. "We will miss him when he gets his next job, won't we, Jesus?"

"You might."

They laughed some more.

Jill came by to check on them. "Is there any work in Preskitt?"

"You want to be a waitress?"

She looked around. "I simply want a better job. My ex-husband dumped me off here. No money, no clothes, nothing."

"We—my wife helps a lady who has a busy café down there. She'd probably hire you. Her name is Jenny Allen."

"Would one of you write that down and give me a recommendation?"

They looked at each other and agreed. Chet tore a page out of his notebook and wrote on it. "We recommend Jill— Last name?"

"Oh, Corpsman."

"I have it. You two sign it."

They did.

She tucked it in her apron. "I thank you. Maybe I'll see you three again."

When she was gone, Jesus made a face. "He sure must have been a sorry bastard. She's a nice, clean young woman."

Chet agreed. "There're lots of folks who don't know when they're well off."

"She will make a lot more money down there, I bet," Cole said.

Chet and Jesus both agreed.

The JP had not arrived when they were ready to leave for their camp. Chet told Harry thanks when he refused to take his money. Chet gave Jill a five-dollar tip and her eyes about bugged out. "I hope to see you again."

"You will, Mr. Byrnes. You sure will. Good night, fellows."

Out under the stars, Cole said, "I think we got Jenn a winner again."

"I bet we have," Chet said.

"There must be a helluva story about her husband dumping her here."

"Jesus, when she gets to Preskitt, she can tell you the entire story," Cole promised him.

"I'm not certain I need it."

"You two are a mess. Will we reach this person we are checking on tomorrow?"

"McCrown's not far west of here. We should be there by noon."

"If the weather holds. I also want to go on after that to see Lucy and Drew and be sure they don't need anything."

"I'm just curious why that guy never answered my letter. He may have problems or something may be wrong."

"Good idea. I bet the guy who owns that store/bar back there might move to have his place be a stage stop."

"He might. Everyone on this road is looking for more business or better work."

"Just like Jill," Jesus said.

They both clapped him on the shoulder.

"You still thinking about her?" Cole asked.

"Well someone needs to. Her dumb husband dumped her off out here."

Chet agreed.

They made it to their camp and crawled into their bedrolls. Chet slept till just before dawn. The trio saddled their horses and packhorses, drank some fresh coffee, complained they were all still full from the last night's meal, and hit the road headed west.

CHAPTER 31

A woman came out when they rode up to the low-walled log ranch house. She had to hold her prematurely graying hair back from her face with her hand to talk to them. Right off Chet felt something was wrong here.

"Ma'am, is your husband here?" Cole asked.

She shook her head. "He was shot and killed three weeks ago."

"I wondered why he didn't write me. I am so sorry." Cole dismounted to go to her.

"No more than I am, Mr. Emerson. I got your letters, but I can't read or write." She began to cry. "He did all that."

"Who shot him and why?" Chet asked, dismounting his horse.

"Come inside, please. It's warmer in there." She sniffed some more.

Cole showed her to a chair at the table, and she looked up with wet eyes and told them to sit down.

"Two men rode up here one day. Crown was off getting wood and I spoke to them and told them he was off cutting wood. But I could see that would not satisfy them. They dismounted their horses and roughly shoved me inside.

"There was nothing I could do to stop them. They both mistreated me on that bed." She stopped and bit her lower lip. "When he came back, he discovered what they'd done. He didn't wear a gun, but he went for the rifle over the fireplace. They gunned him down right there. Then they left. I had no clothes on and with his blood all over me, I told him I never caused them to do that to me.

"Before he died he said, 'Kary, I know you never did.' Then he died. I wanted him to know I never done wrong on him, with him dying and me not going to get another chance to ever tell him the truth. He forgave me."

"I realize how sincere that was. Who were they?"

"Gilbert was one. I don't know his last name. Got a scar on his right cheek. A bad one. His right eye don't work. Maybe blind in it. He's got hair all over him like a bear." Her whole body shook in revulsion as she told them about him.

"And the other attacker?"

"His name was Lum. He was crazy, out of his mind. He'd say things made no sense to me at all. Had long blond hair that came to his shoulders. He never washed, either. He smelled bad enough I threw up when he was attacking me. Never stopped him any, but I about gagged to death. By then I wanted to die—just die. And then McCrown came in. I didn't want him to come in—I knew they'd kill him. Then what would I do?

"They killed him like I said, then they rode off. Stole the paint mare and tried for the mule, too, but he kicked so hard they left him. Guess he thought they smelled bad, too."

"Anyone come help you?"

"Old man Ivy lives north of here did. Took both of us to bury him. I didn't care—I planned to hang myself. But I couldn't. Then I was going to shoot myself. I couldn't—"

"Did you report his death?"

"To who? I had only a mule to ride. Where would I go? Folks brought me food. Said they cared. What for? My man was dead and buried. And I could not kill myself and join him."

"You know, Kary, maybe God didn't want you to do that," Chet said.

"There ain't no God in this land. God would never have let those men rape me. He'd never let them kill my dear husband. Never done—" She slipped out of the chair onto her knees and went to crying hard on the seat of it. "Just leave me here to die. I have no will to live another day."

"Kary, we all get dealt some tough hands in this life. We don't ask for them or want them. But they happen. You obviously couldn't kill yourself. So you must face the days ahead and you need to find your God. Somewhere, he's the rock you need."

"No. He abandoned me. No loving God would do that. Not have me go through that horrible day with those two raging mad animals and then let them kill him."

"Kary, we are going to try and help you. Do you own this homestead?"

"I guess I do."

"Did he file papers on it?"

She climbed up with both him and Cole's help. Then, blowing her nose in a rag from her apron, she went to a steamer trunk and came back with a paper.

"Here."

"You own three hundred and twenty acres. This is the patent."

She shook her head. "That means nothing to me. I can't farm it or do nothing but cut some firewood and pack it in here."

"Did he have any money?"

"No."

"How much food do you have?"

"I got some in the cellar. I can shoot a deer."

"Cole needs a stopover for his buckboard mail operation. Your husband promised him a stop here."

She nodded. "But he's dead. I don't have—I mean—I can't build it."

"Is this where you need it?" he asked Cole.

"Yes. He dug a well and it works. The mileage is right. Her husband was a hustler."

"But he's dead," she cried.

"Yes, we know, and we hate that for you and our purposes. Kary, would you sell this place if we resettled you?"

"Where?"

"Say Preskitt. We could find you a house and a job."

"Doing what?"

"Cleaning people's houses or working in a restaurant."

"How could I hold my head up living among people?"

"How will they know unless you tell them?"

She shook her head. "I won't tell a soul after today."

"Now you decide. We could try to sell it for you?"

"I guess sell it. I can't live here and be reminded of him."

"Cole, you go speak to Harry's boss and see if he wants this place and can afford it. It will assure him of being a stopover when the stage line comes and have

success with his business for the next decade until the
tracks come here.

"Jesus, you and I are going to look for the men who
shot him."

"Why do that for me?"

"Besides being stagecoach investors, we're also U.S.
Marshals. If they're in this country, we will find them
and make them stand trial for his murder."

"Oh, you've said so many things my brain is about to
explode."

"There is no worry about that happening. Now, do you
think they live in this region?"

"They never told me where they live, but they did
mention Peach Springs."

"That's on the Indian reservation," Jesus recalled.

"Yes. We may get some help on that one. Cole is going
to talk to a man who might buy this place. Jesus and I are
riding west. I own a ranch near that place and they may
be able to help us find those killers."

She frowned at him. "You really think you can find
them?"

"We've found lots of criminals like them before. You
keep the door locked and your gun handy. We'll be back
in a few days with some answers."

"Oh, I'd give anything to have them hung."

"Well, we are going to look into finding them."

And so they split up. Chet and Jesus rode west. Cole
headed east to find a new man for his project.

The next day, Lucy's stock dogs barked at them as they
rode up the land. She came out on the porch holding her
daughter. Drew came from the horse barn and waved.
Fern took the baby from Lucy so she could greet them.

Lucy came down the stairs and hugged the two of them. Chet noted she had begun to look pregnant.

"Why are you here?"

"One, to be sure you and Drew are getting along. We've been helping Cole with his stage stops." She herded them up the stairs and into her house. "And we're looking for two men. One's called Gilbert. Big facial scar, blind in one eye, big hairy man. Number two is Lum, no last name, either. But he is daft."

She made a face. "They live over near Peach Springs, don't they, Drew?"

"Yeah, if they still are there. I can show you where they live."

"Good. They killed this woman's husband and assaulted her."

"That sounds terrible," Lucy said.

"It is worse than that. No one investigated his death or her deal. These men need to be arrested and tried."

"We will do all we can to help you. Fern will make some coffee. Let's sit at the large table."

Chet talked to the new foreman. "Drew, you have enough help up here?"

"I told Lucy, we could use some more. Feeding hay take lots of hands to pitch it on the sleds and then off to the cattle. I could hire, say, three more boys to help us and use them on the hay crew next summer."

"If they'll work, hire them."

"I also want to talk about how Victor is getting his mowers and his hay equipment rebuilt this winter. How do we get in that line?"

"Probably get a freighter to bring the mowers to the Verde Ranch and get them repaired."

"They're going into their third summer and the men

say we need two more. We only have two, and if I can hire those boys we can put up more hay."

"I'll order them and hope they get here."

"Thanks. I know my men will be glad. We should have a good-size number of cattle to ship next year. We've rounded up over a hundred head of mavericks since I came up here. Hay feeding, we should get another hundred and fifty that come in to eat. Those cattle could pay for most all the things we need."

"You've done an amazing job. You and Lucy are doing well."

"Reg had been laid up for some time before . . . otherwise he'd have done that," Lucy said.

"I am certain he would have. Thanks for the job you two are doing."

"If it's okay, Fern and I are going to get married. Living in the same house is not the right thing to do."

"You want to marry up here, or at the ranch?"

"Oh I think—Fern, where should we get married?"

"We can wait till March and do it at the ranch."

"Is that what you want to do?" Drew asked her.

Looking embarrassed and a little red-faced, she tried to smile. "I'd marry you anywhere you want, Drew."

"Me too. We'll talk and tell you, Chet, before you leave."

"Fine, you can get married anytime. I'm pleased you two are together again."

"Hey, we talked about me going down to the Verde. My time with Tom Flowers was worth us being apart. Tom is a great foreman. He shared his secrets and experience on men and ranches. I learned more than a book full about ranching with him."

"Drew, he speaks very highly of you. I felt you'd served the ranch well. Do what you want. I know my wife will put Fern in a beautiful dress, have a super ceremony, and a big deal afterward." Chet felt that was settled. "Now, tomorrow I want to go try to find those two killers."

"We can go up there," Drew volunteered.

"Don't you need to stay and feed cattle?"

"No, the men I have will be so happy that I'm hiring more help, they won't notice I'm gone."

Jesus and Chet laughed with him.

Later in the evening, when her daughter was asleep, Lucy had time to visit with Chet by himself.

"I should have talked to you last summer. I don't know what I did wrong or if it was him or me, but Reg started taking off by himself for, say, a day. He wouldn't tell us anything about what he did or where he went. I don't think he had another love interest. Or at least, I never found anything, but I finally figured he was just avoiding life. Oh, the ranch operated. The men did the work. But they didn't hunt mavericks, and the last time he did, that was when he had the wreck that hurt him so badly. I suspected he did that on purpose to destroy himself. I should have told you. But I couldn't believe he wouldn't return to what I thought were his senses. Do you see?"

"I see your part, and I am sorry I wasn't informed, but I doubt I could have changed his decision."

"The last nine months, he was not the man I married, Chet. It was hard."

"Lucy, you know you're like a daughter to me and he was like a son. I don't know what came over him. Perhaps I didn't pay enough attention to him."

She shook her head. "Something in him changed. He withdrew from all of us. Fern asked me what was wrong with him. If you asked him anything, he'd bite your head off and you'd done nothing."

"I guess his recovery was hard on you all?"

"Bad. After Drew came, even with this weather, he's brought in a hundred and some mavericks. And he's not lying, he'll bait in a lot more. Nothing I could do. But I don't think if I had not had the baby it would have gone any better."

"Did he resent her?"

"It was like it wasn't his."

"Oh, Lucy. I am so sorry. You didn't deserve that."

"I'll be fine. I appreciate getting to stay here and help run the ranch. Drew was a good choice, for Fern and him and this ranch. He and I get along. I cherish your friendship and your wife's. She really helped me that first week. I love her and I see why you do. When I heard you'd found her I first felt guilty for Marge and her memory. But I didn't know her. Liz is what you said. An honest angel. But you knew that."

"I am so fortunate to have her. If I had not given those horses for Bonnie's return, I would never have found her. She saw them in Mexico, on that ranch, and came to find the man who had them. She thought he had bought them from me."

"How are JD and Bonnie?"

"Best I can tell you, they pray together on their knees every night before going to bed."

"Really?"

"I about cried when she told me that. Those two started out so wild and crazy, I hardly had any hope for them."

"She wrote me such a nice letter after the funeral. I'm pleased they found each other. About makes me jealous." Lucy bit her lip.

"No need for that. Life has twists and turns, but you will find a way and a life for yourself."

"Thanks. I will look for that path."

"Any way I can help, call on me."

"I will. Thanks."

He trudged upstairs, wondering why he wasn't home with his wife—but they still had those two outlaws to arrest and the stage stop problem for Cole to solve. Things became more tangled all the time in his life.

CHAPTER 32

Drew rode with Chet and Jesus. The wind out of the north was in their faces as they crossed the juniper-covered rolling country, headed for where Drew thought they could find the pair of assailants. It wasn't bitter cold, but Chet had seen better days to ride across high country.

They had ridden several miles and Drew had talked to several people on the road about the pair. Some knew a little about them, and one rancher told him where they lived up in a canyon. Most just said they were worthless and not worth going over there for anything.

Chet silently agreed, but kept his opinion to himself. After a few hours, they reached the turnoff. Drew halted his horse and checked his six-gun.

He shook his head. "I don't use this Colt much. I figured I'd better be sure it was loaded. I'm bad enough that I shoot at a coyote or wolf and then not reload it. Nope. It's full to the empty under the hammer."

Jesus smiled. "You ever go after outlaws, you'd know your gun was loaded."

"I bet that's so. You have much trouble capturing them?"

"We went to arrest some horse thieves and we shot four of them. The last one shot himself."

"Why did he do that?"

"He couldn't face jail time," Chet said.

"Takes all kinds to make up the world."

"We've seen them, too," Jesus said.

They rode up the canyon they had been told about until the pole corrals came into sight. A shack and a pile of trash were beyond that. Jesus slid his Winchester out of his scabbard and levered in a round. Chet did the same and moved his horse in front of Drew's.

"There's lots of junk around that shack, Jesus. I don't think you can charge around on that horse."

"I'll get off and go around."

"Be careful."

Jesus nodded and took off on foot. Drew spurred his mount to catch Jesus's loose horse.

"Don't worry, he won't leave my mount. We better get down and walk up there. They go to shooting, get some cover. I got shot riding up to the front door down by Tombstone a while back."

"I recall hearing about that. You think they're here?"

"We'll see." Chet stopped, set the rifle against the corral, and drew his pistol. He fired it in the air. "U.S. Marshals, come out or else."

Nothing happened. Jesus must be in the back. No one shot at him. Were they even in there? They kept closing in on the house. On the porch, they both stood opposite beside the door. No sound.

Chet pulled the latchstring and the old door creaked open. No sounds. Gun ready, he stepped inside. The house stunk—but he expected that from Kary's words about them.

No one was in the beds. Spoiled food was on the table. They must not have come back after they attacked her. Where could they be? He opened the back door and waved Jesus over. "This place is empty. They haven't been here for a while."

Chet reloaded his revolver with a new cartridge and holstered it. "Drew, where can we look next?"

"Tomorrow we can go to Hackberry. Someone might have seen them over there. We can also put up reward posters. I'd bet they are within fifty miles of here."

"Well, we need to find them before they rape someone else."

"That's for sure."

"Drew, I wondered if you knew anything about my nephew's problems before he committed suicide."

"No, but you might talk with Lefty about it. He was closer to him than anyone but Lucy. He's never said much."

"Thanks, I'll talk to him. May not be a thing there. I'm simply looking for answers."

"It beat me. He was living my dream, Chet."

"You never know. I sure wouldn't have believed it could happen if someone had told me."

"They must've headed out?" Jesus said, remounting.

"Drew thinks we should try Hackberry tomorrow."

"Those guys aren't smart. They may still be in the area," Drew said.

They went back to the ranch. After supper, Chet caught

Lefty on the porch smoking a corncob pipe. The sun was down, and the light from the living room window shone on the porch.

"How did your day go?"

"Aw, Chet, went like most of my days on this outfit, pretty damn nice. I had three square meals, wore clean clothes, got a warm bed ahead of me, and the weather ain't too bad. This job gets tough when the snow comes, but we'll sure appreciate those boys he's going to hire."

"No problem." Chat sat down in another chair. "I'm looking for some answers about Reg. I know something was eating him up and I haven't found that cause yet. You were close to him. Could you tell me anything?"

He took the pipe out of his mouth and leaned forward. "I only saw her once." Lefty paused. "Now I don't want you telling a soul. I ain't absolute sure, but her name might have been Jeanie Downey. How he was hooked up with her, I don't know. But they must have had an affair and broke up, but then I think they got back together. Don't ever tell Lucy, though. It would kill her. Then they split and he had that bad wreck."

"Lefty, thanks. I don't need to know any more."

"You and me knowed that boy and we loved him. He just lost his mind over that gal. He told me some things I didn't need to know. But it ate him up. Told me it was doing that. I'd done anything he'd asked of me. But I sure couldn't help him there."

"Our secret, Lefty. You're a true friend."

"I hated that she thought it was her what was wrong. But I won't ever tell her. She don't need to know."

"Amen. Amen."

Chet left Lefty on the porch and walked a long ways

under the stars and then back. Lots on his mind, and he, as usual, missed Liz. Maybe they'd do more the next day. He sure hoped so. This one had ended on a sour note for him. But at least now he knew—*Lord, Lord let me sleep tonight.*

CHAPTER 33

They rode into Hackberry the next day under steady cloud cover and a cool breeze. They dismounted at the store and went inside to leave a list of things Lucy wanted. The storeowner recognized Chet and came out of his office to talk to him. He spoke to Drew and Jesus, as well, and shook their hands.

"Mr. Byrnes, what brings you to our small town?"

"Supplies."

"Oh, does Mrs. Byrnes need anything special?"

"I can't imagine Lucy Byrnes needing anything special."

The man laughed. "Well, if she did I'd find it for her if I had to go through hell and high water to find it. She pays her bills monthly and never misses a day on them. Extraordinary lady. You, sir, are very busy I suspect, running your many ranches."

"They keep me busy. But I have some other business I have to deal with right now. Maybe you can help me. You know two characters named Gilbert and Lum? They killed a man over east a few weeks back."

"Gilbert Tillman?"

"Scar on his face."

"He was in here early this morning when I first opened."

Chet narrowed his eyes. "Where did he go?"

"I don't know, but he didn't have a horse. He left on foot."

"Where do you think he went?"

"There are a few people have a camp south of town."

"Drew, you know about that camp?"

"Sure do."

"Good."

"Here is Lucy's list. We'll be back later." Chet handed the storeowner the paper.

Mounted on their horses they charged out of town. Drew led them down a side road. Before they even reached the place, Chet saw the ragged tents and campfires and they halted short of them. They dismounted, hitched their horses, and began searching for the two men they were after.

Jesus pointed. "There goes the guy with long blond hair."

Chet put on a burst of speed. The man saw him coming and began to run hard out, but he was no match for Chet's long legs. Chet reached out and jerked him back by his collar, which proved rotten and came off in his hand.

But it threw the man off balance, and that was enough. Lum stumbled and plowed his face in the dirt with Chet riding him into the ground.

"Where is that other sumbitch Gilbert?"

"I don't know any Gilbert. Why you want him?"

"We got him," Jesus shouted.

Drew and Jesus had the other guy in cuffs. Chet saw the scar on his face and nodded—they had their killers.

Chet climbed to his own feet and Jesus handcuffed his

prisoner. Lum was babbling about something that made no sense, as Drew dragged him to his feet.

"You two are under arrest for the murder of a man named McCrown." He looked over the scowling crowd.

"Damn, let's get out of here," Jesus said softly.

"How?" Drew asked.

"Double them on my horse, you can lead him. Jesus and I can ride his horse double," Chet said.

Chet tried to ignore all the filthy, rag-wearing people armed with hoes and rakes, complaining about the arrests. The prisoners were tossed on his horse and Drew caught the reins. Jesus was mounted on his own horse and Chet caught the horn and swung up behind him—that goosed the bay up a few feet, but he never bucked and they were headed in a good lope for Hackberry.

Chet looked back—no pursuit. But he noticed those two did smell bad even in the wind.

At town, Cole rejoined Chet, Jesus, and Drew, and Chet hired two wagons. One rig to carry Kary McCrown, her belongings, and her furniture. She looked very settled in the new long, wool coat he had bought for her. She was seated beside the driver, her head wrapped in a colorful blue silk scarf.

The second wagon carried the two grumbling prisoners in leg and hand irons under some blankets headed for the Yavapai County jail. Cole, Jesus, Drew, and Chet rode guard on them.

"We've been through lots of things to get here," Chet said. "Cole is about to start building this stage line. We have things started. It looks to me like we are in for a big effort to get this job done."

"Will it make money?" Jesus asked.

"You never know about that. Some things do, others

don't. But I think we have to make our money on this project before the railroad gets here. This territory is growing, and we'll grow with it if we can get in. Cole got Kary's farmstead sold and his new man is moving west to set up. That means in time Cole will have an individual that will build a stage stop and also have a business there."

Cole agreed. "He says he will."

"That's good."

Four days later, they were at their house on the mountain. Liz came out and hugged him.

"What do we have?"

"That's Kary McCrown. Her husband was murdered. Those men in the second wagon did it. Here, Kary, let me help you down. This is my wife Elizabeth."

"Oh, I must thank you. Your husband and his men have saved my life." Her face beamed with her excitement.

Liz hugged her.

The two women left him for the house, talking up a storm. His men would care for her furniture and haul the prisoners in to be jailed. Cole and Jesus could handle that matter. It was a beautiful, sunny day, and Chet went and sat on the front porch to simply think about things.

He'd made a full circle one more time. This emerging stage business looked like a viable way to make money. Time would tell, but it wasn't like if it didn't work he'd end up penniless. Far from it. But it was no time to spend a fortune on a dead horse if this turned out to be one.

Raphael joined him, *sombrero* in hand.

"Have a seat, my friend." Chet patted the end of the bench.

"So you return from the rim. They told me those prisoners murdered that woman's husband."

"They did and will pay for their crimes."

"They have a saying in Mexico about seeing it all. You have seen it all, haven't you?"

Chet made a grim face before he said, "No, *mi amigo*, but sometimes I see or learn something. This trip was no exception."

"Could I ask what you learned on this journey, my friend?"

"How some men can lose their mind over a woman that turns his head. He can be big and tough enough to whip several men. But a bad woman can spoil his brain and turn him to do things he's been taught to avoid. Then in the end, she would spurn him and break his will to even live anymore."

"That was a powerful lesson you just told me. I have known such real stories about some powerful men who fell madly in love with some wrong women and when they could not have them—they went mad."

"Yes, well, I guess I better go find supper. Everything alright here on the ranch?"

"Oh, fine. We have a new baby. A big boy. We still have lots of hay to feed and spring is coming. Things are good here. Soon the new calves will come. Many of them will be twice from the shorthorn bulls, *mi amigo*."

"They should be great ones."

"They will be."

Chet pounded his shoulder. "I appreciate all you do. All you do."

"*Gracias.*" Raphael rose and left the porch. He put on his *sombrero* and went to check and see what chore someone forgot to do.

"You alright?" Liz asked, opening the front door to check on him.

"My love, I am fine now that I am back with you." He kissed and hugged her.

"Come have supper. Mrs. McCrown is a very nice lady. Your other woman arrived two days ago—Jill. I took her to Jenn's today to work there."

"And?"

"Chet Byrnes, you find these poor women like they were popcorn. Everyone has a big problem—"

"Yeah." He stopped her. "If I hadn't gone down in Mexico to recover Bonnie Allen, you'd never stopped in at my office in Tubac."

She shook her head. "I know, big man. I know they don't bother you. I just don't know what I'd do if they did."

"Rest easy, girl. I've got the best deal in this territory or Mexico."

"*Hombre,* I knew that about you in Tubac."

"You can keep on believing it. I'm not going anywhere without you or you in my heart."

They went in the kitchen to eat supper with Mrs. Mc-Crown.

Just another stray . . .

Dear Fans New and Old—

Hard for me to believe that this book is #8 in this series. In the past year or so my publisher reissued book #1, *Texas Blood Feud*, so you should be able to get the entire set now from your book supplier. Plans are for another book in the series that will be available down the road. Check my web site dustyrichards.com for more information.

Since starting this series, I have heard from many of you at my online personal address. I try to answer all of them and struck up some fine conversations with many of you with questions and comments. Like I have told you before in these letters, I must have read a thousand paperback westerns before I ever started thinking about writing my own.

Along about 1985, I met Jory Sherman in Branson, Missouri—God rest his soul—and he handed me a form to join Western Writers of America. I had sold a few short stories to some small publications. I didn't believe I could qualify for membership. But they accepted me. Best outfit I ever joined. Of course I am still a member and their past president.

That June in San Antonio I went to my first WWA convention and walked through what I considered a Hall of Gods—people whose books I had read. They took me into the fold—I almost received a speeding ticket driving home, with me so high from meeting my idols. If bits of hay had not flown out of my wallet getting my driver's license out and made that Texas Highway patrolman laugh—he gave me a warning instead.

Top of that list was Elmer Kelton, no greater individual ever lived. We became friends. Not only Elmer, but also a host of names that were on my marquee as superstars at writing sagebrush-scented pages. Sad but many of them have gone on. But new ones ride in and I try to answer their questions and help them down this trail. I have so enjoyed spinning yarns about an era I have loved since I was a boy.

Early on in my life I once sat on Zane Grey's original cabin porch on Mrs. Winter's ranch atop that Mogollon Rim and spoke to his ghost. I told him that someday I'd be on the shelf with his books. He never answered me, but they are there. And I thank all of you for the honor of being a tale spinner you support.

God bless you, your family, and America. Western literature rides on.

Dusty Richards
dustyrichards@cox.net
saddlebagdispatch.com